Fried Green Zombies

By
JOHN A. ALLEN

for Lahni

Chapter 1   Somewhere Else.

The voice came out of the darkness, thin and wiry. "I can't see a single thing. Where are the lights? I mean, really. Damn this piece of junk."

Another voice came out of the darkness amid the sound of someone randomly pushing buttons. "We took a pretty big hit. The radar's out again." A few random lights flickered on a console, not really bright enough to illuminate anything.

The first voice had moved. "Okay. I'll work on the lights, you fix the radar. But those aren't our biggest problems. We're up a creek if we don't make it. How fast can we go?"

"Can't go over eight."

"Well, you're screwed."

"You're screwed too."

"I'm not the one who got this hunk of scrap metal you call a ship all shot up."

"Well, neither did I. Now quit your bellyaching and help me figure out what we're gonna do."

Roscoe, the owner of the first voice, paused, blinking in the darkness. "We've gotta dump."

Earl turned his head in Roscoe's direction. "No way."

Roscoe continued. "We're in the ass-end of nowhere, we dump, get away clean, get repaired, come back to pick it up and finish the run. We'll be a little late, there'll be hell to pay, but we get done."

"Ain't doing it."

Roscoe fumbled around in the darkness and hit a button. "Don't have a choice. Just did it."

"Ass. It'll spoil."

Roscoe pointed out the massive window to the patch of white in front of them. "Not in that big ice patch, it won't."

Chapter 2   A Little Town Called Bovina

Nine Mile Cutoff is an aptly named stretch of dusty gravel road winding through a town so small it lacks both a post office and a dot on the map. What it cuts off no one has ever really figured out, though it does connect to two more rural blacktop roads. Four or five little churches used to call the Cutoff home, but they and their small cemeteries – having remained unused for the last half century – became hidden and forgotten as the weeds and brush took back over.

The road was usually empty, so the rattlesnakes and cottonmouths calling it home didn't normally have to worry about hurrying across it while they were making their way from pond to pond chasing mates or eating rats or whatever it is that snakes do in their free time.

Some people say snakes and animals know about earthquakes and natural disasters before they happen. The rattlesnake making his way across the road that day would probably say it's true; lying in the ground all day makes one sensitive to all sorts of things – changes in air pressure, tremors in the ground. What he couldn't predict was the sudden presence of flaming objects falling from the sky and cutting his tail off.

Flaming falling things would ruin anyone's day, even a snake. For years he had been working on one hell of a good set of rattles, and now it was laying somewhere else having a good time without him, wiggling and dancing around. Of course, he couldn't look at it too long with all the other stuff on fire hitting the ground all around him.

Normally he'd have curled up and put the death in anything that tried to mess with him, but he knew it was time to haul half-tail out of there. Into the ditch. Into cover. Back to the woods.

Chapter 3 A Little Town Called Bovina

Nine Mile Cutoff was still an aptly named stretch of dusty gravel road. Perfect for winding up one's big-block 440 jacked-up Scottsdale four-by-four. Chett and Harry had just been forcibly removed from their job at Alco Construction. They were pissed too. Accidents happen. That's why places like that had insurance. And they weren't drinking on the job. For the most part. Well, they weren't drunk. For the most part. And the resulting accident from their little tipsy revelry wasn't *that* bad.

It was a little joke, that's all. Chett was normally pretty good with a nail gun. And had his aim been any truer, no one would have gotten hurt. Okay, so maybe they were a little tipsy.

But what's so bad about sitting down to pee anyway? That guy's got it made for the next six months. Worker's Comp, sexy rehab nurses. He'd recover. They should be so lucky. He gets the royal treatment and they got fired.

No, no, Chett and Harry had just *quit* their job at Alco. They couldn't be happier. It's all a matter of perspective. They had a cooler of beverages in the back and a date with a musty rusted RV at the hunting camp. The only thing between them and Rocky Bayou was seven more miles of Nine Mile Cutoff.

The snake, having made his way to the woods only to realize that suddenly it was too damned hot thanks to the bits of burning brush scattered throughout, turned around, confused, to make his way to somewhere quieter and cooler. The air was much hotter and steamier than he remembered.

Back on the road, halfway across, and he began to grow more confused. It's not enough that stuff was falling out of the sky. Now there was a distinct tremor he felt in his belly. Earthquakes? This too? What a strange day.

But maybe if he recognized Hank Williams Jr. he'd have known that it wasn't an earthquake after all, and he'd have gotten out of the way of the big-assed tire that was about to make his day much worse. But snakes are dumb like that; the tire flattened what was left of his already shortened back end.

Now, like its disconnected cousin in the road, it too was wiggling and dancing and hurting like hell. Because unlike its disconnected cousin, it was still attached to his front end.

The snake was certainly having the worst day of its life. After the flaming things and the big tire, he was doing everything he could in light of his uncontrollably twitching tail to get across the street. Except now his progress was impeded by something else clobbering him. Though, unlike the fiery objects from the sky, whatever was hitting him now was freezing cold. And round. Cold, hard, short and round – not a snake, not any sort of animal – but he decided to put the death in one, no matter what it was, just in case. Which turned out to be a bad idea. Snakes don't have the instinct not to bite a beer can that has just been thrown from the back of a truck.

He struck and was rewarded with a mouth full of bitter liquid. Try as hard as he could, one fang was stuck. He was definitely raging mad. He had a deep, biological need to kill something even if it killed him in the process.

What luck! An actual animal of some sort approached. His eyes were clouded over with beer, but he could see that it was very tall and very black. He pulled loose from the beer can and struck at the shape that was now reaching for him.

He was rather surprised when he missed, but not as surprised as getting jerked up from behind his head. Try as hard as he could, he couldn't bite anything. The other animal had grabbed him and had too good of a hold on him. He tried again to make out what kind of creature was attacking him. It had the general shape of a human, but not the smell.

He heard another quick loud hiss and saw that the other animal was attacking the cold round objects too, sucking the guts out of them. He was happy – served it right for spraying that nasty crap all in his mouth. Then the last thing he saw was darkness, and the last thing he heard was a really painful crunch.

Chapter 4   Still on Nine Mile Cutoff

"Hey, man, pull over! You lost the cooler."

Chett tapped the brakes, yanked the emergency brake, and turned the steering wheel a quarter turn – performing a perfect bootlegger's turn on the gravel road. "Did we kill it?"

"Better have or I'd get a refund on those tires."

"What was that other stuff?" Chett asked, looking up through the windshield into the sky.

"Dunno. Looks like someone blew something up."

"I think it dented my hood!"

"How could you tell?" Harry looked at the pock-marked truck through the cracked windshield.

"Funny." Chett took his eyes off the hood and looked ahead at the cooler. "What the hell? Who is she? What is she wearing?"

Harry saw the six-foot-tall woman in a black burqa, holding a beer in one hand and a dead snake in the other.

Chett asked again, "Do we know her? Who is she?" Then, in another thought, "Why is there stuff on fire still falling out of the sky?"

Harry said nothing, himself wondering why a woman would be out by herself traipsing through the woods in black bedsheets. "Is she a Muslim? Do we even have those around here?"

Chett looked at Harry. "Should we go see if she needs a ride?"

"Are you crazy? I think we need to be getting out of here fast. Forget the beer. We don't even know if it's a woman under there."

"I think that's pretty obvious," Chett replied.

It was. Both of them could make out the curves under her garment.

"Could be bombs," Harry said.

"What is there to blow up out here?"

"Seems something's just been blown up. And if not, any woman who goes around wearing that stuff and holding dead snakes crosses the weird line as far as I'm concerned. Isn't she hot?"

Chett looked her over. "Can't tell with all the sheets on."

"Ass. You know what I mean."

"Well, I'm going to ask her if she wants a ride."

"Not with me in here."

"You gonna walk?"

"Seriously, man. Something's not right."

"You've got the Saturday Night Special in the glove compartment, right? Just tuck it under your shirt. And ease up. Nothing's going to happen." Chett eased the truck into first and drove up to the burqa-wearing woman.

Their windows were already down, so all he had to do was stick his head out the window to talk to her.

Dust flew by as the gravel crunched slowly under the tires.

Chett waved the dust away from his face. "You like snake?" he asked, pointing to the six-foot brown and black headless and tailless body dangling from her right hand.

No response.

"Tastes like chicken?" he asked again, jovially.

She looked down at the snake and offered it to him.

"No thanks. Just had some."

Harry whispered to Chett, "Come on, let's get out of here. Leave her with our beer."

Chett ignored him. "Do you need a ride?"

She kept looking through her veil.

"Do you even speak English?"

Again, no response.

"Do...you...need...a....ride?"

"What, she doesn't understand English but she understands slow?"

"Shut up, Harry." He turned to the woman and made a takeoff motion with his hands, followed by bouncing his body and faux-turning the steering wheel.

She copied the motion.

"She rides in the back," said Harry.

"She does no such thing," Chett answered. He got out to let her in the middle. "But the snake stays." He motioned to the snake and shook his head for no. She threw it to the side and climbed in the truck while Harry climbed out to collect the beer.

"We won't be able to drink this for a month as shook up as it all is."

"It'll be fine by the time we get to the camp."

Harry finished loading the beer and climbed back in the cab of the truck. Burqa woman sat in the middle.

Chett looked at Harry. "Think she likes riding stick?"

"Who knows."

"I bet you there's a stick-riding maniac under that bedsheet."

"Dude, she's right there."

"And she doesn't speaka tha engrish." Chett looked at her. "Besides, I was just kidding, right?" He started the engine.

"Just one problem," said Harry.

"What?"

"Where you going to take her?"

"Oh."

She took her veil off and smiled at them. Sexy, straight, raven-black hair spilled over her shoulders. Chett thought he had just seen the most beautiful set of blue eyes in the universe.

Chapter 5   Rocky Bayou

Rocky Bayou is an aptly named Hunting Camp. Two thousand acres of deep ravines, bayou, brush, ponds, thick forest, and open fields sliced neatly in half by a rocky spring which ultimately feeds the Big Black River, which itself ultimately feeds the Mississippi River. The camp is bounded by the Interstate on the north, Highway 80 to the south, a cattle pasture to the west and more private land to the east.

Somewhere deep inside the camp another pond was missing, and all the critters calling it home were either flash-boiled or atomized. At the center of the empty pond was a little metal ball, no bigger than a large marble. It was cracked, though. And leaking.

A drop of something oozed out slowly. Something so black that light seemed to fall into it and get lost. It fell out of the little metal ball and sank into the mud.

Somewhere a few feet below the former bottom of the pond, something stirred.

Chapter 6   Harvard on the Hill

"That is absolutely the most dumbest thing I've ever heard."

"How so? You got a better way of explaining it?"

"Yeah. You need to get a life."

Carried by the strengthening breeze, the two voices echoed down the open-air brick corridor between the two low, squat buildings that housed what counted for classrooms in the local community college.

Clayton Hensworth scratched a painful pimple (one of an unfortunately recent bloom) on his cheek. Sitting down on the hard wooden bench, he tried to make his point. "Not all of them are stupid," he argued, "just the ones from earlier movies. I think it's because they're kinda like ghosts, in a way."

His opponent was walking away.

Clayton talked louder. "You know how ghosts are souls that have unfinished business? Well, maybe the ones that come back stupid don't have any souls, and the ones that come back different do."

"No," said the preppy-looking future frat president as he stopped briefly to turn around. "I think you misunderstood me. When I said 'zombies are stupid,' I wasn't referring to some sub-genre of whatever freak shows you like to watch, I meant that whole thing - the whole idea of zombies - is stupid. It wasn't an invitation into a conversation." He flipped his blond mop of a haircut out of his eyes and turned back around.

"I just heard you and your friends talking about going to see the newest *Terms of the Killing* movie, and I thought..." Clayton trailed off.

"That was your problem," came the voice as it grew more distant. He kept talking without even turning around. "The last two words you said. 'You thought'."

Clayton was hurt. Well, that guy wouldn't get to copy his science homework again. It didn't matter that he didn't copy it directly; he actually copied it off a friend who copied it from Clayton.

Easy enough to fix. Clayton just wouldn't let anyone copy at all. That'll show him.

Of course, that came with its own set of problems. Mainly, that his friend wouldn't tease him if he let him copy. But if he stopped, then the teasing would certainly come back with a vengeance. But then he wouldn't be teaching preppy guy a lesson.

Oh, the conundrums of geekdom.

He just hoped he wouldn't run into either of them at the bar tonight. Not that the bar he was headed to would ever be frequented by the likes of the preppy guy. It was probably going to be filled with drunken rednecks, which were almost as bad, although rednecks tended to hold people in a less condescending light.

Clayton rubbed his now oozing pimple and hoped it would dry up enough not to draw attention to itself. He'd heard of beer goggles before and hoped to score some hotty that might be sporting a rather large pair of them.

Now all he had to do was wait for his ride. And if anyone could show him how to have fun, these guys would.

True, they were a little older, but it was pretty universally known: If someone wanted to have the wildest time available in such a small town, there were only two people to turn to.

They'd be too busy having fun to worry about the ins and outs of why some zombies were smart and quick and others were dumb and slow. They wouldn't tease him about talking zombies.

Talking zombies, Clay thought. *Now* that's *stupid.*

Chapter 7 The Gas Station

"Well, hell, Harry, what are we supposed to do? We can't just leave her."

They shopped for Slim Jims and more beer while they were inside the store. Burqa-woman was still standing outside by the pay phone, where they had left her with a quarter in hopes that she would call someone to come get her. Instead, she just stood there drawing attention from people filling up their tanks.

"She with you?" a voice behind the counter asked.

"Um, well, sort of. Yeah. I guess."

Just a cocked eyebrow for a response.

"Maybe we should call someone, like the sheriff's department."

Chett didn't bother to respond verbally. Instead, he offered Harry the same cocked eyebrow the cashier had just given him.

"Okay. Maybe not the cops. But we have to do something with her."

"Fine. Go pay up. I have a plan."

Harry shook his head. "Oh, God. No more plans. That's what got us fired."

Outside, Chett walked over to burqa woman. "Do you have a name?"

No answer.

He pointed to himself. "Chett." Then he pointed to her.

She made a sound.

"What? What was that?" Harry looked at Chett. "Maub? Mob? Mbob?"

"I think she said Bob."

"Bob," the woman said.

"Great, a Muslim woman named Bob. Could this get any weirder?"

"Maybe it's short for something," Chett answered. "Like Roberta. And you don't know she's a Muslim."

"You got another reason she's wearing that getup and not speaking English?"

"Good point. Hey! Idea! Don't they go to a mosque?"

"I think so."

"Then let's drop her off at one! There can't be too many around here."

"Was that your grand idea?" asked Harry.

"Actually, no. It involved calling the cops."

"Then I like this idea much better. But I don't know of any mosques within a fifty-mile radius."

Chett picked up the tattered phone book hanging by a cable from the phone and flipped through it. "Nope. Nothing under mosque. Worship says 'see church' and there's nothing that looks like a mosque under the church heading." He turned to look at the woman.

"Mosque?" He made a sign of praying with his hands.

She mimicked the sign. "Bob," she said.

People were still staring, but at least it was a new fleet of refuelers.

Chett looked around. "All right, Bob. You're not going to be any help."

"Bob," she replied.

"Bob. Good. Can I have my quarter back?" He made a circle with his thumb and index finger. She looked at him through her veil for a few seconds and then handed him back his quarter.

"What? What is this? What did you do to it?"

"Dude, she bent it in two!" exclaimed Harry.

In Chett's hand was a quarter bent viciously in half. "She must have dropped it and it got run over. Look where the rocks made little indentions."

Harry looked at it and said nothing.

"Well, this does us no good. Go pilfer a quarter from someone so we can make a call."

"To who?" asked Harry.

"The cops. Get me a quarter."

"Nope."

"Dude, get me a quarter, unless you have a better idea."

"Nope and I don't."

"Fine." Chett walked to the truck and dug around in the fold of the seat, fishing out not one quarter but three, two nickels, a dime and a penny, as well as an old french fry and his favorite pocket comb and miniature Swiss Army Knife. "Aha!"

Chett walked back over to Harry and the woman. "Relax. We're calling from a pay phone, so it's untraceable. I'll just ask them if they've had any missing person reports filed and tell them that we saw a woman wearing what she's wearing who was wandering around the roads and that she's at the gas station. Then we leave. The cops will take care of her."

"I'm sure they will. You know how dirty they all are. Corrupt, I mean. Not that they're not perverted too. I'm sure they are."

Chett placed the phone call and reported back to Harry. "Nothing. No missing persons report, and a deputy is on the way. Let's head." He turned to Bob and offered his hand. She took it. "Bob, nice meeting you. An officer will be along to help you. Have a nice day." Then to Harry, "Now, back to the camp."

"It's about time. Bye, Bob!"

"Bob," she replied, looking at them as they walked away.

Chett and Harry climbed back in the Scottsdale and fired it up, pissing off everyone within earshot. Not having a muffler will do that.

Chapter 8   Back on Nine Mile Cutoff

The truck bounced down the road a few miles from Rocky Bayou.

"Where did all this smoke come from?" asked Harry. A definite haze had developed and was hanging low to the ground.

"Probably someone out burning brush, the idiots. Put Hank back on. Let's get this party started right." The next few miles were uneventful. Until Chett saw something big and black in his rear-view mirror and slammed on the brakes.

"Shit!"

"What the...?" is all Harry got out before he saw the black thing fly over the roof and tumble onto the road in front of them. Then he took another stab at completing his thought. "What the hell?"

"It's the lady again," Chett said.

"How did she get back there?" asked Harry.

"She must have snuck in at the station."

"Dude, I say this is where you found her, so this is where you leave her. Put the truck in reverse and let's get out of here."

Chett looked at Harry. "Who's gonna be reverse this time, me or you?"

"Oh, yeah." Reverse was broken and entailed either pulling a bootlegger's turn if they were going fast enough or one of them getting out and pushing the thing backwards if they were stopped. It was a big truck.

"But shouldn't we, you know, check on her? Make sure she's okay?"

Chett and Harry looked at the woman who was now standing up, dusting herself off and walking toward the truck.

Harry answered, "Doesn't look like we need to. She's doing fine. Come on, she was out here for a reason, she knows what she's doing. Or she's batshit crazy. Either way, we can serve her no more."

"I'm with you on that one," Chett said.

They looked at her as she approached the truck.

"There's not enough room to go around her," Chett said, "so get out and push."

"Look, I know there's not enough time for me to remind you of every reason that this situation is not just weird, but creepy to boot."

She walked up to the window and made a praying sign with her hands. "Bob?" She questioned.

Chett answered, "Yes, you're still Bob. But Bob, we don't know what you want. We don't know where to take you. And frankly, we've had a tough day already without getting you involved. Not to mention that you're just giving us a nasty case of the creeping willies. You want to ride, but you don't know where."

"Bob. Ride?"

"Yes. We've covered that. Look, if you'd tell us, or even motion..."

"We'd be happy to play a game of charades," interjected Harry.

To Harry, "like she knows what that is." To her again, "You know, motion," making his hands dance, "then we could probably take you there."

She did a dancing motion with her hands.

"Very nice," said Chett, "but we're going to our hunting camp. Just us."

"You know, hunting?" Harry asked, pointing his hands like a gun at the trees in front of the truck. "Boom. Boom."

"Bob. Ride?" she said.

Chett looked at Harry.

Harry said, "Look, we've done all we can. If she wants to go to the hunting camp with us, fine."

"Really? You're okay with it now? I mean, after she flew over the truck and all?"

"Which was your fault. Yes, I'm okay with it. But I'm patting her down for bombs."

"Dude, just because she's a Muslim doesn't mean she has bombs."

"Could have guns. Or knives. I'm patting her down. Cover me." Harry hopped out of the truck.

"Cover you? Good grief." Still, Chett grabbed the .38 that Harry had dropped on the seat, just in case.

Harry walked around the front of the truck. "Listen, Bob? I'm going to pat you down to make sure you're safe." He took her arms and spread them out.

Chett laughed. "Funny how the tables are turned. How many times you been in her shoes?"

"Shut up." Then back to Bob, who had dropped her arms. "No, leave your arms here." He picked them back up. "Good." He made the patting motion over his body, then over hers without touching her so she would understand what was about to happen. "I'm going to pat you down."

She made the pat-down motion on her stomach with her hands.

"Yes. I'll be quick, I promise."

"And how many times have you said that to a girl?" Chett laughed harder.

"This isn't funny. Shut up." He patted her stomach gingerly to make sure she was okay with it. She watched him through her veil. He continued around her back and under her breasts. He turned his head to talk to Harry.

"Dude, I'm sorry. But I've got to see this body. If you were feeling what I'm feeling..."

"You need to get laid," Chett said.

"Seriously." Harry moved to pat down her legs, careful not to touch anything sensitive. "Oh, my God."

"What? Is she packing?"

"No, just... just... nothing. Jeez. I haven't even seen her and I think she's the sexiest woman I've ever met."

He stood up and looked at her. "Okay, you're clean."

She looked at him for a few seconds and placed her hand on his shoulder. In one quick motion she spun him around, kicked his feet apart, and pushed him on the truck.

"Oh, Jeez. Ouch. Be careful."

She repeated the process, though not skipping the sensitive parts. Chett was laughing his ass off.

"That's not cool," Harry said while the pat-down continued. "Ooh."

"What?" Chett asked.

"She just grabbed my package. Ooph! Hey now. Mmmm. Okay, okay, stop," he said. "That's enough. And weird." He jerked away.

"Come on, you two. Let's go. Get in the truck."

Bob followed Harry to the passenger side of the truck.

He offered her his arm. "After you." She took it and climbed in the truck. They drove off to Rocky Bayou.

It was Thursday. The end of the world was still a few days away.

Chapter 9 Rocky Bayou

Rocky Bayou was devoid of other people. The only things in season were raccoons and frogs, so everyone else with better things to do was probably out doing them.

Six P.M in the summer means there are still two good hours of light left. Chett and Harry had planned to show up, down a few cold ones, shoot some stuff, maybe ride their four-wheelers and generally fart around until they passed out.

They exited the truck and looked around. In front of them was the little musty brown and yellow 70's era RV. To the left was a tattered picnic table, and to the right a little lean-to aluminum shed that sheltered their generator and a few muddy tools.

"I got us a surprise," Chett said after unloading the cooler.

"What?"

"You'll have to wait. But it fixes a little problem we've had in the past. Kinda."

"Oh?"

"You'll see. That and it's just damned cool. Got a good deal."

"Mmkay. What about her?" Harry pointed at Bob.

"Well, I guess she's staying with us."

Chett and Harry opened the door and stepped in. Bob waited at the picnic table out front.

"Where's she sleeping?" asked Harry. The RV had what amounted to a queen bed in a room the exact size of a queen bed at the back (still a marvel and constant source of conversation between them – did they build the RV around it as Chett thought, or did they bring it in a piece at a time and assemble it in the room, as Harry thought), a small bathroom, an even smaller sitting area with a couch, a fold-out table, a sink and a microwave, and place in the wall for a TV. The front of the RV housed two mustard-brown ripped Naugahyde bucket seats and a host of wires and dangling electronic gadgets protruding from the dashboard and a place where the radio used to reside.

"Good question," answered Chett. "Normally I'd say she could sleep with me, but I don't think I'll get the picture of her and the snake out of my head. I thought I'd never say this, but I'd rather sleep next to you and let her take the couch."

"And I'd normally say you're gay and make fun of you, but I agree with you."

Chett maneuvered around Harry and stuck his head out the door. "Okay, Bob. This is where we're staying. Come on in and I'll get the generator hooked up."

"What are you telling her that for?"

"Oh." Chett motioned for her to enter the RV. "Careful on those steps. They're cheap." He stepped down and helped her up, then walked over to the rusty brown shed. The shed door was one of those kinds that slides open horizontally, much to the chagrin of anyone that's ever had one. One little spot of rust and the things put up a serious fight to get them open and in the process sound like you're killing a whole herd of buffalo.

The generator slid out easily enough, and Chett unstrapped the gas can in the bed of the truck to fill it. He primed it and gave it a few pulls, and it fired up. He killed it to save gas.

"Generator works," he said as he climbed the steps to the RV. "We'll turn the lights on when it gets dark..." he trailed off. Sitting on the couch, smiling, was a half-nekkid, large-chested, raven-haired beauty. The only thing that took Chett's eyes off her chest were here deep blue eyes – so blue they almost seemed to glow.

"What the hell?" asked Chett, flustered.

"Don't ask me," answered Harry without looking away. "You walked out, she walked in and promptly stripped."

"I don't know what to say."

"Makes three of us."

"Huh."

"Huh."

"Bob, ride?" she added, smiling.

"Oh, Lord," wheezed Chett.

"Oh, Jeez," answered Harry.

"I, um, I don't think she means it that way, but damned if half of me don't want to find out right now."

"Makes two of us."

"I thought Muslims were, you know, supposed to be more... I don't know... modest?" Chett couldn't stop staring.

"Yet again, makes two of us." Neither could Harry.

She looked at Harry and made a C with her the thumb and index fingers on her left hand and an inverted-C with her same fingers on her right. She turned them perpendicular to each other and pulled her right index finger in and made a sound. "Cch."

They looked at her and she did it again. "Bob. Cch."

"Beer?" asked Chett. "You want a beer."

"Cch. Beer," she answered.

"Not a problem. Harry, get her a beer." Harry walked to the front of the RV and opened the cooler sitting on the passenger seat. He turned around. She was standing right behind him.

"Oh. Crap. Oh, here." He opened it and handed it to her.

She took it and smiled. It was gone in one chug. "Beer. Cch."

"More?" Harry was shocked.

"Beer."

"More beer? Okay." He got another out and opened it. He looked at Chett. "You realize that she's cutting into our beer supply."

"So? We'll make another run."

The second beer was gone. She just stood there.

"Another? I can't turn down a nekkid woman wanting beer."

She looked at him perplexed and smiled. She didn't motion for another beer, though.

"Okay. No? No more beer?" Harry shook his head exaggeratedly for no. "No?"

She kept smiling, standing in the narrow passage between the cabin and the back.

Harry looked over her shoulder. "Chett, she's kinda in my personal space and she won't move."

"Ask her to move."

"Bob, will you move?"

"Ride?" she asked.

"Um, Chett?"

"Yeah?"

"How do I answer that?"

"Say no."

"Okay. No." Harry looked back at Chett. "Why not?"

"Because it's not fair."

"Haha. Funny." Harry looked at Bob. "Excuse me, Bob, but I'm going back to the back now." He bent over and stepped in front of the passenger seat. He hoped to do one of those puzzles he used to love when he was a kid and would keep himself busy when he'd take long trips with his parents – the kind of puzzle where you'd slide one piece around and then slide the other until you made a picture. He was good at those – and so he put his hands on her shoulders, while attempting to look firmly in her eyes. Those breasts were like magnets! He pulled her up in front of the driver's seat and walked out of the driver's compartment. He could have just turned her and slid by her, but damned if he wasn't just a little scared shitless. Turned on, for sure, but even his penis was watching out for its safety. He didn't want to get that close to her. Yet.

She sat down in the driver's seat and fiddled with the knobs and switches. She mashed her feet on the pedals and jerked the steering wheel from side to side.

"Oh, no, honey," said Chett. "This thing ain't run in years. Have fun, though."

Harry walked back to where Chett was sitting on the bed. "I changed my mind. She can sleep with me."

"No, I think she still needs the couch."

"Now you're gay."

"No, seriously. This ain't right." Chett looked at Bob, still sitting at the steering wheel messing with things. "Don't care how you slice it, this is just plain up screwy." He looked back at Harry. "Harry, you've seen the movies. We're going to wake up dead."

Harry thought about it. "I'm with you on that one. This is a little odd."

Bob walked back to the couch. "No ride?" she asked.

Chett and Harry looked at each other. Harry answered. "Not right now, sweetheart. We have a headache."

"We have headaches, Harry. We're not sharing a collective headache."

"I beg to differ."

"Oh."

"Well?"

"Well what?"

"What now?"

"Don't have a clue," said Chett. "You go open the windows so it doesn't get stuffy in here. I'll check the sheets for critters."

Harry did so and returned. Chett confirmed the critter-free state of the mattress. Bob laid down on the sofa and yawned.

Chett saw her and said, "Guess that's our cue to let her get some rest. Come on. Let's go frog gigging. I've got that surprise to show you anyway." He turned to Bob. "Listen, I don't know if you understand me or not, but don't use the bathroom, okay?" He pointed to the small dark room with the toilet and shower. "There's no tank, okay? Anything you do in there is going to foul up our little piece of paradise here." He shook his head in what he hoped was the universal sign for 'no' as he kept pointing. "So no use the bathroom here, okay? If you have to, go outside." He made a big show of walking to the door and down the stairs.

"Okay!" she beamed.

Harry followed him outside.

Chett climbed half into the truck to lean the seat forward. "This here's part one." He handed Harry a new bottle of Southern Comfort. "And these here are part two." He handed down two sets of goggles attached to headstraps.

"No you didn't. Are these what I think they are? How'd you get them?"

"Military surplus."

Harry waited for Chett to climb down and handed him back one set so he could scrutinize his new hands-free night-vision goggles. "These are nice! Must have cost you an arm and a leg."

"Must have."

"But, uh, what for?"

"Night hunting. Spotlighting. Frog gigging. Whatever. Gives us an edge."

"Cool with me."

Chett put his on, turned them on, and looked around. "Everything's green. Huh. We'll put 'em on tonight and see how well we can target with 'em."

"Cool. One question, though."

"What's that?"

"Are we planning on staying here all weekend?" Harry asked. "Because technically, we've got class tomorrow afternoon." Harry and Chett, after taking a break from high school for a few years, had returned to Harvard on the Hill Community College to take general courses. "I just want to know so I don't get too funky if we can't get home to change."

"You can take a shower up at the main cabin," said Chett.

"And go to class buck nekkid?"

"Oh." Chett paused. "Get dirty. We'll figure it out later. Let's go get us some more beer. It's your turn to be reverse."

Harry forced the truck backwards. He climbed into the truck and they roared off.

Chapter 10   Harvard on the Hill

Harvard on the Hill was an ironically-nicknamed community college branch located closer to town. Halmond Community College was the place where people of all different backgrounds and creeds sought refuge – recent unsure high school graduates, retirees, middle-aged recent GED graduates, and all those in between.

Clayton Hensworth sat outside watching the sun set and picking idly at a pimple. He grimaced. "Assholes."

Neither Chett nor Harry were answering their cell phones. They were supposed to have picked him up an hour ago to go to the Brick Company bar. After all, they said they owed him drinks. If it weren't for him, they wouldn't have passed the last chemistry exam. And he went to a lot of trouble to let them cheat off him.

He wouldn't have done it had he known they'd be like this. Sure, they'd been assholes like everyone else and made fun of him. Didn't he leave that behind in high school? It wasn't his fault he was actually really interested in this stuff. If he wouldn't have spent so much time playing with fire and/or various household cleaners and/or electronics (there was that infamous combination of all three that forever branded him as "Hey, aren't you the guy who blew up your dad's shed?"), then he probably would have actually completed a homework assignment and received a GPA suitable enough for a scholarship to a real university.

As it stood, though, here he was – hoping to show enough dedication in two years to make up for the twelve he wasted previously. And helping those two assholes pass. Well, not again. Sure, they picked on him endlessly, but he always seemed to be in on it. They gave him a hard time like they gave each other. Their kind of picking was different; good natured.

Like the time he wore his Star Trek shirt to class. The professor had just finished handing out the exams and had praised him for having the highest grade after not only answering all the exam questions correctly, but for getting all ten bonus questions right. Chett and Harry had said, "All right! Space Geek gets an A!" and actually high-fived him in the middle of class. They seemed genuinely happy for him. Could they have been picking? No, they were good guys.

But that was before they stood him up, leaving him stuck with no ride. He had gotten his mother to drop him off because he thought they were going to actually take him somewhere. Now he couldn't reach her because she was at the Elks Lodge or wherever it was that old people with nothing better to do go to play Bingo.

And everyone else had left campus. He could call the city's only cab, but he was saving all he could from his job at RadioWorld to both get the newest Deities of Destruction video game and build the fastest, baddest, pimped-out and tricked out computer that could ever be built.

He had been holding out hope for Chett and Harry, but slowly it began to wane and he had given up. He picked up his phone to dial, but before he started dialing he heard the sound that everyone in town knew signaled benign trouble. At first it was a low bleating of a missing muffler and the quick wah-wah-wah-wah-wah's of oversized tires on pavement, then it was the Hank Williams Jr.

They had remembered after all!

Chapter 11   Highway 27

"Damn that wench. She drank all our beer." Harry was cussing her as he dug through his wallet. "All I've got is a ten."

They cruised down Highway 27, windows open, music blaring.

Chett spoke over the radio, "I've got you covered. I got a twenty. And we can pick up our checks tomorrow."

Harry happened to look up as they passed Halmond Community College. He squinted to see better. "Some poor sap's still out there."

"I'm not giving anyone a ride." Chett was going to do his best not to get tangled up in anything else for a long, long while.

"No, dude. It's Clay!"

"Damn." Chett slammed on the brakes.

Harry bumped his head into the window. "You've got to stop doing that."

"We forgot Clay. That poor guy. We told him we'd buy him a beer for helping us out."

Harry hopped out and helped Chett wheel the truck around in an exaggerated three-point turn in the highway. "Tomorrow, Chett," he grunted, "we fix your transmission."

Harry, breathless, hopped back in and looked confused. "What are we going to do with him?"

"I reckon we're going to pick him up, tell him that we had truck trouble, take him home and hope he'll accept a rain check."

"We already owe him a hundred rain checks," said Harry.

"Well, now we'll owe him a hundred and one."

They sped up the drive and pulled in front of Clayton.

Chett hollered out the window, "Dude, we are so sorry."

Harry leaned forward to be seen. "Still want a ride?"

"I had almost given up on you," Clayton said. "I'm ready for ladies night!"

Chett and Harry looked at each other. Chett spoke first. "Um, well, something's kinda come up. Turns out we're not going there tonight."

"Like what?" asked Clayton.

"Truck trouble," said Harry.

"Sounds like it's running fine to me. Come on, let's go."

"Sorry man, no can do. We have some things to take care of. I'm sorry we're late, but hop in and we'll give you a ride home."

"There's no way I'm not going out tonight."

Harry leaned over to Chett and whispered, "He's sure as hell not coming back to the camp with us."

"Wasn't even a question," said Chett. Then, to Clayton, "Look, man, I know we said we'd take you out. And we will. But you know us, right? I mean, you know who we are and that, well, trouble kinda follows us around? We're kinda taking care of some stuff tonight that you probably don't want to be involved in."

"Do you know how boring my life is?" asked Clayton. "I sit around playing video games."

"And blowing sheds up," snickered Harry.

"That was years ago. Anyway, I'd welcome the excitement."

"Look, Clayton, we like you. We really do. But you're not coming with us. If you want a ride, we'll take you home. But that's it for tonight."

"What about tomorrow night, after class?" asked Clayton.

"We might be able to do something tomorrow night," said Chett.

"What about *her*?" Harry whispered.

Chett whispered back. "Hopefully *she* won't be around tomorrow night. I'm not planning on having her hanging around, are you?"

"Tomorrow night works great," said Chett, talking loudly over the roar of the truck. "Hop in and we'll give you a ride home."

Chapter 12   Back at Rocky Bayou

"Where is she?" Harry was already in the RV and had noticed immediately the lack of a large-chested Raven-haired woman named Bob.

"Did you check the whole RV?" yelled Chett from outside.

"You're kidding, right?"

"Well, what about the main cabin? Maybe she needed to use the restroom."

Harry considered it. "Okay. Maybe she did. How can she see? It's dark out there."

"I know you're not thinking about going to look for her. I mean, after all the time we spent trying to get rid of her."

"Yeah, but there's something wrong in letting someone like that with a body like hers wander around in the woods. We were trying to leave her somewhere safe."

"How do you know someone didn't come get her?" asked Chett. "Look, she's gone. We can get on with our night. Grab the goggles and a flashlight. Let's go gigging. We'll sleep tomorrow before class."

"Shouldn't we leave her a note or something if she comes back?" asked Harry.

"You think, what, that she can't speak a lick of English but she can read it? Come on. Let's go. We're wasting moonlight."

They put their hip waders on and walked into the woods. Harry noticed a switch on the top of the goggles and flipped it. Instantly the green surroundings went dark and Chett, who walked in front of him, started glowing. Flipping the switch back, Chett was his normal green and Harry could see the trees again. Hit the switch again and Harry glowed, no trees. Turn it off and he could see everything again.

A few hours later, the night-vision goggles were giving both of them headaches so they took the goggles off and turned on their Maglights right before they got to their favorite pond. Except when they got to the shore, well, the pond was missing. The flashlight beams got lost in the darkness.

Chett looked at Harry. "Are we in the right place?"

Harry knelt down and felt the mud. "Hmm."

Chett kept shining his flashlight into the darkness and onto the empty mud in front of them. "Where did the pond go?"

Harry put his goggles back on and surveyed the empty stretch of green before him before taking them off, bumping them on his hand, and putting them back on. "You might want to see this," he said to Chett, who in turn put his set on.

The two goggled men stood on the banks of what had recently been either a big pond or small lake.

Harry turned to speak to Chett, "You thinking what I'm thinking?"

"Yeah. Excellent mud riding spot."

"Bingo."

"No way to get in here, though."

Harry answered quickly, "Sure there is. Remember the old trail? On the other side of the pond. It's grown up a little – but it's all brush and weeds. Nothing we couldn't handle."

"Done deal. We'll get to it Saturday."

Harry looked back over the new mud-riding grounds and flipped the switch on top of his goggles.

"Will you quit that?" Chett asked. "You're going to wear them out."

Harry didn't answer. Instead, he flicked it off and on again and turned to look at Chett. He repeated the flicking process at Chett and then looked back out at the lake, still flicking the switch on and off.

"Seriously, man. Give it a rest."

Harry kept his attention on something. "That's weird. Chett, you see anything weird in your goggles?"

Chett squinted and scrutinized the landscape as well as he could through grainy green vision. "No. Why?"

"Flip your switch."

As soon as Chett did it, he saw the glow coming from the middle of the pond. He flicked it off and went to normal night vision mode. Nothing. He flicked them on and off several times seeing the glow before he looked at Harry and flicked them on and off.

"Will you quit that? You're going to ruin them," Harry said mockingly.

"What is that? I guess it's got some sort of heat mode, like Predator."

"It's called Infrared."

"Look who's been paying attention in class," said Chett. "I thought these were always infrared."

"They are," said Harry, "but there's two kinds of infrared. There's the kind you see when you flick off the switch – the kind that's everywhere. Then there's the kind that gives off heat. That's what you're seeing when I'm glowing."

"How do you know those things?"

"Discovery Channel."

"Oh." Chett thought for a minute. "So what's so danged hot out there in the middle of the lake?"

"Dunno," said Harry. "Let's go find out.

That idea turned out not to be so good. Harry was the first to hear something. "Is that an airplane?" It was the only thing he could think of that would make such a deep rumbling sound from far away. But then it went away and the rumbling stopped.

Both of them had stopped to listen. Once everything was silent again, they continued forward. Until it happened again.

It almost sounded like someone starting an engine that didn't want to be started. But it sounded really muffled.

"What is that?" Chett asked Harry.

"Like I would know?"

"You know all about infrared."

"Doesn't make me an expert on weird sounds," said Harry.

"You know, I've about had enough weird crap for one day."

Harry agreed. "I say we call it a night and pack it in."

Chett kept talking, "I mean, who else is out here? It sounds like they're stalled."

As they crept closer to the source of the infrared glow, the sound started again. But this time, the ground shook a little more as well.

"Do you feel that?" asked Harry.

"It feels like it's right under our feet," said Chett. He put his head to the ground to listen. "Harry, you gotta hear this."

Harry put his ear to the ground. About forty feet in front of them, as if on cue, the ground exploded in a volcano of mud and dirt clumps. The noise was deafening as the Hemi-Powered Dodge Ram Four-by-Four of Death shot out of the ground. It landed and swung around in a perfect semicircle and revved the engine.

In a voice that sounded unnaturally "gravelly" - as in "having a lot of gravel in it," - the driver yelled "Hooo-yeah!"

"Sumbitch" moaned the passenger. If Chett or Harry could describe a voice as "Holey," as in "having holes in it," then that's exactly how they'd describe it.

But they wouldn't describe it like that at all. Because they were both too busy breathing hard as they hauled ass into the woods. They only thing that either one of them had said had been, "Shit. Run!" And Chett thought that was a wonderful way to describe the situation.

The Four-by-Four of Death did donuts in the mud, looking for a way out. Chett and Harry had tripped several times over roots and fallen branches, each one of them clawing through the woods and dragging the other down when he fell.

Running through the forest at midnight wearing infrared goggles means one thing: someone's going to get lost. Maybe an hour later, maybe fifteen minutes, Chett and Harry slowed down to a jog. Then they came to a complete stop, panting with their hands on their knees, hacking up phlegm from the back of their throats. They looked around and knew instantly that they were lost.

Still catching his breath and looking at the ground, Chett asked the question he knew neither one of them had the answer to. "What... the...hell...was...that?"

"Don't...have...a...friggin'...clue... Don't...want...to...either."

Chett took a minute to breathe and slid down a tree, sitting on a protruding root. "I think we should be close to camp."

Harry took his goggles off and grabbed for the flashlight in his cargo pants pocket. Chett barked at him, "Dude! No way. No light. Leave it off."

Harry said nothing and put his goggles back on. All he could see were trees – trees in differing shades of green. He flicked the switch and looked at the glowing fog Chett exhaled with every breath. He took them back off and focused back on the patches of bright moonlight.

"We're not that lost," said Chett. "All we have to do is walk straight. We'll either hit the highway or a fence we can follow. Or the creek."

"If it still exists," said Harry. "Where the hell did the pond go?"

Chett looked at Harry. "Dunno." He paused. "But this day is just too friggin' weird. I say we call it and head."

"Enough said."

They stood up with their goggles on and walked. And walked.

An hour or so later Harry spoke up. "Um, I've got this nasty little blinking light that keeps coming on."

"Me too. Batteries are almost dead. This is going nowhere," Chett said.

They sat down.

"I have an idea," said Harry. "Toss me your phone."

Chett fished around in his cargo pants and found his cell. Harry caught it and flipped open the screen. "Good, we've got a signal. We can't be too far from a tower." He dialed a number.

"Who are you calling?"

Harry motioned for Chett to wait. "Clayton, hey! How you doing?" Pause. "Oh, is it three already? Sorry, we kinda lost track of time." Pause. "You don't want to know. But we need help and you're the guy for the job. We're lost. We need you to find us." Pause. "I don't know – isn't that what you're good at? Can't you track our cell phone or something?"

"Good idea," said Chett.

Harry kept talking into the phone, "That's never stopped you before. Look, I don't want to beg, but I will if it'll help. We're in a jam." Pause. "Can't explain now. I promise I will, though. Just tell us how to get out of the woods." Pause. "Okay, we'll be waiting."

Chapter 13   At Clayton's Mom's House.

"Sons-a-bitches." Clayton muttered to himself as he rolled out of bed. "Go out and have a wild time and don't call me. Assholes. I shouldn't be doing this."

But he still stumbled over to his computer. He turned on the monitor and blinked a few times, letting his eyes adjust. He yawned and grabbed a Mountain Dew from his mini fridge and started the process of hacking the cell phone company.

"Assholes."

A few minutes and proxy servers later, he had the information and picked up his phone.

Chett answered after the first ring.

"You owe me." Pause. "This is the last time I help you guys out. I've got what you need. What are you going to do for me?" Pause. "Really? I mean, really? You mean it?" Pause. "No bullshit. Okay, then. But you promised." Pause. "You're about a mile away from the highway. You're about two away from the camp."

Pause.

"Look, I'm tired and I don't really feel like getting involved in whatever you're doing." Pause. "Yes, I know I said my life was pretty boring, but I'd like to keep my criminal record nonexistent." Pause. "Fine, I'll be there in about thirty minutes."

He hung up and threw on some shorts and a t-shirt. The door creaked open as he was zipping up. He looked up to see an old, thin, wiry woman wearing an oversized mumu.

"Who were you talking to?" asked Clayton's mom.

"Chett and Harry," said Clayton.

"And where do you think you're going?"

"To go get them."

"At three in the morning? I don't think so."

"I didn't mean to wake you up, but they had some car trouble."

"No, you're not getting mixed up with those boys."

"Well, too late. I already am. I told them I'd come get them."

"Call 'em back. Tell 'em you're not. Go back to bed."

"Do we need to have this whole 'you can't tell me what to do' fight right now?"

"As long as you live here, I can."

"Okay, fine. We'll handle this in the morning. Right now, I'm picking them up. You go back to sleep. I'll be back in a few."

"They're not coming back here," she said.

"Fine. Wasn't considering it. Just going to go pick them up, drop them off, and come back to bed. Simple and easy. I'm tired."

She turned and walked away.

"Assholes," he murmured again.

Chapter 14   Somewhere in the Woods.

"Dude, why did you tell him that?" asked Chett.

"Only thing I could think of," replied Harry. "You got a better idea? Come on, let's get moving."

They made good time, all the while their battery lights blinking more and more fervently. They lost power right before they made it to the highway, but they could see the occasional yard light through the trees.

A few minutes later, Clayton pulled up in his early nineties' model rusted Honda Civic. Chett and Harry walked up to the car as Clayton began speaking. "Remember your promise?"

And before either could answer, they heard something that they could only describe as death on wheels rumbling in the distance.

"Shit," said Chett. "Get in, get in, get in!" Harry dove in the back seat as Chett took the passenger seat. "Go, go, go, go, go!"

"What?" said Clayton. "What's going on? I'm not going anywhere until you tell me what's going on."

Chett looked and saw that the Civic was still in drive. In one quick motion he picked Clayton's leg off the brake and pressed it on the gas. "Less talking, more driving. You need to go. We need to go."

The car gained speed as Clayton looked at the dim lights in his rear view mirror.

Harry listened to the sound of the accelerating Civic. "Nice pipes," said Harry. "Shitty paint job, though."

"Thanks. Flomasters. Now who are they?" Clayton looked behind him.

Harry answered. "We don't know, we don't want to know, and what we do know is just plain fucking weird."

Chett jumped in the conversation. "Can't you go any faster?"

"It's a ninety-one Civic. What do you think?" he yelled. "You guys need to fill me in, and quick. Because I'm not in a mind to get arrested. Tell me now, or I'm going straight to the police station."

Harry was still looking over his shoulder. "That's not such a bad idea."

Clayton was stunned. "Oh, shit. You guys *are* in deep."

Chett spoke to both of them. "We need to go back to camp. That's the closest place we have some guns."

"Oh, hell no," said Clayton. "I'm not getting into anything involving guns."

"You already are," said Harry.

"Assholes," said Clayton.

"But, Chett, I don't think going back to camp is such a good idea."

"They're behind us, we've probably only got one stop to make, and as far as I'm concerned, that stop needs to be where guns are. Any argument?"

Neither one spoke up.

"Thought so. To the camp, Clayton. And make haste. Speed limits be damned. A ticket's the least of your worries."

Behind them, the headlights of the muddy four-wheel-drive drew closer.

"Are we really in trouble?" asked Clayton. "Or does someone just want to kick your asses? Because if that's all it is, I'd really rather not get my ass kicked or get my car torn up in the process."

"Look, Clayton, have we ever run from getting our asses kicked?"

"Well, yeah," said Clayton.

"Oh, come on. Just that one time. But to answer your question, no. We're not running from getting our asses kicked. And I'm scared that you'll find out all too soon what we're afraid of that's behind us."

"It's some jerk in a truck," said Clayton.

"No. Not at all. Look, I know we're both full of shit," said Chett, "but I mean it when I say we need to be as far away as possible from whatever's in that truck."

"Whatever? You mean whoever."

Chett and Harry remained silent.

"You mean whoever."

Again, silence.

"What do you mean, whatever's in the truck? They got some sort of animal after you?"

"As much as I'd like to say yes just to satisfy you, I can't, because I don't think you'd quite understand exactly how dead we might be if they catch us."

Harry chimed in, "And we don't mean dead as in 'oh, we're in a lot of trouble this time and we've gotta pay for it with jail/money/hard labor' – we mean it as in 'our families will be making arrangements with the funeral home."

"Oh, you guys don't mean that," said Clayton.

Chett stared at him. "Actually, we do. And we've gotta figure something out, quick, because they're less than a hundred yards away. Clayton, listen to me. Whatever's behind us – whoever's in that truck – means to harm us, we're pretty damned sure of it. It probably wants to kill us. Literally. Take our lives away."

"And now, by extension, mine," Clayton said out loud, to himself.

"More than likely," said Harry.

"You two are assholes." Clayton wanted to cry.

"We didn't know this was going to happen," said Chett. "We just thought you'd pick us up and drop us off somewhere."

Behind them, the truck gained distance as the Civic topped eighty.

"We're really in trouble?" asked Clayton.

"Really, really in trouble," answered Harry from the back.

"Fine." Clayton hit a little red button on his steering wheel that neither Chett nor Harry had noticed. The car shot forward and by the time Chett glanced at the speedometer they were approaching one-twenty.

Chett let out a whelp and asked, "What the hell do you need nitrous for? You don't race."

"Don't have to race to like going fast," said Clayton.

"You just got a hell of a lot cooler in our books," said Harry.

Chapter 15   At the Waffle House

"Should we call Sheriff Barrack?"

"For a noise call? Rookie, you better be kidding."

"Oh. I just thought, you know, that it's out in his neck of the woods."

Detective Moses was a very heavy-set black man with a thick black mustache, now sporting crumbs from the fine dining establishment they were about to leave. He looked at the new kid as they stood up to pay. The rookie looked pure military. Crew cut, stocky, very proper and mannerly. That'll last a few months before apathy sets in. "Wally, you got a lot to learn. Let's go."

Outside, the night was still and muggy. Yellow sulfur lights shined down on the empty street. Wally yawned and tried to rub the fatigue from his stinging eyes.

"You'll get used to it in a few months. Drink some coffee. Your body'll adjust."

They climbed into the idling cruiser and Moses backed out of the parking lot to speed down to the highway where the calls were coming from. The residents had called 911 and complained of someone possibly having illegal mufflers speeding down the road and waking everyone up. Repeatedly.

"Aren't we going to turn the lights and sirens on?"

"On a call like this? No, you want to catch them in the act. Gotta sneak up on 'em," said Moses.

They sped down the highway as the dispatcher radioed them again.

"They're turning. We're never going to catch them this way," said Moses. "We're getting more calls down on Warrior's Trail. They're headed out into the country. We gotta cut them off."

He swung his cruiser around and headed down a back road – paved for the time being. The gravel would come in a few miles.

"Are we going to call for backup?" Wally asked.

"For what?"

"To help cut them off?"

"We're the closest ones. And we'll just pull them over, give them a field sobriety test, and go from there. No need for backup, unless they get rowdy. Even then, I'd like to see them try." Moses smiled and patted the standard issue nine millimeter on his hip.

Minutes later, they pulled up to where the blacktop road met the gravel Nine Mile Cutoff. Moses killed the lights and the engine and turned to Wally.

"They should be here in less than two minutes."

And on cue, in the distance, Moses and Wally heard the thunderous grumbling of the vehicles they sought. Moses cranked the cruiser, put his hand on the light switch and spoke to Wally. "Get ready, boy. This here's the fun part." He had his left foot on the brake and his right on the gas to give chase when the vehicles sped by.

And they indeed sped by. Moses turned on this lights right before the cars came around the curve. Wally caught a glimpse of the Civic as it flew by, then he saw a muddy jacked-up Dodge Ram with flame stenciling on the side and felt the ground shake with its unholy exhaust.

For a second, Moses didn't move. Then he hit the gas and jumped out in the middle of the street. He cussed and slammed the car in reverse.

"Shit. Ah, shit."

"What's wrong?" asked Wally. "Why are we backing up?"

"Ah, shit. We got problems," Moses said – mainly to himself. "This is not good."

"What's not good? Are we calling for backup now?"

"You could say that."

Wally picked up the radio to key in. Moses snatched it from him.

"No. No, oh no. No radio."

Wally was stunned. "How do we call for backup?"

"Sit tight and you'll find out."

"Are those bad guys or something?" Wally wanted to know what was happening.

"Yeah. You could say that."

"Who are they?"

"That I don't know," said Moses. "But we sure as hell shouldn't be seeing that truck."

With that, he turned around and raced the car into the darkness.

Chapter 16   Close to Camp

Harry peered out the back window of the Civic worriedly. "Um, Chett?"

"Yeah?"

"We really aren't gaining any distance from the truck. Is camp such a good idea?"

"Don't know. Why?" Chett asked.

"Because we're basically headed into a dead-end situation, pun intended. But there's a turn-off that'll let us get back on the blacktop about a mile away, and, well, I'm thinking that outrunning them might be our only shot. They're too close for us to hop out at the camp and arm ourselves. They'll be on top of us as soon as we stop."

Chett looked back at the glaring lights of the truck. "Clayton, turn." Then to Harry, "But we gotta make it back. We need our guns. We need our truck."

"We'll make it back," said Harry. "But tonight, I really think our number one priority should be putting distance between us and that truck." Then to Clayton, "How are you on fuel?"

"Fuel's good. Got enough Nitrous to put a few miles between us on the interstate."

"To the interstate, then," said Harry.

Chapter 17 At a Nice House off the Highway

Sheriff Barrack opened the heavy wooden front door and squinted into the night, grumbling sourly. "Jesus Christ. You're gonna wake the neighborhood."

Wally looked around the vast sprawling country estate for any sign of neighbors as Detective Moses talked to a groggy, pissed-off sheriff.

"You couldn't have called? What the fuck's going on?"

"Well, sir, there's a problem. And I just thought I'd play it safe and not use the radio or cell phones."

Wally watched as the sheriff immediately changed from pissed off to worried.

"Oh? Come on in, then. What's going on?"

Detective Moses and Wally walked into the spacious living room, decorated in the deep reds and browns and African wood carvings and masks that upper-middle class white people use to appear worldly and eccentric.

"Pier One?" asked Wally.

Sheriff Barrack flashed a look at Chief Moses, who turned to Wally.

"That look said two things. One, we don't have time to bullshit. And two, he actually got them on Safari, in Africa, where he killed all the animals you see up there."

Wally followed his gaze to the vaulted ceiling and saw at least fifteen exotic animals staring down at him from the walls. It weirded him out.

"Now what the fuck is going on that you need to wake me at four in the morning?" the sheriff asked.

"Well, um, I don't know really how to say this, so I'll just tell you what I saw."

"Please do, so I can go back to sleep."

Chief Moses stared at the sheriff. "The truck."

The sheriff paused. "What truck?"

"The truck."

"What about it?"

"Just saw it."

"Bullshit."

"Nope."

"We're not talking about the same truck then."

"We are," said Moses. "Tell him what you saw, Wally."

"What? The dodge truck?" asked Wally.

Both Sheriff Barrack and Detective Moses continued waiting.

"What? It appeared to be a large, very muddy, gray-black Dodge Ram with a four- or five-foot lift kit. Roll bar with KC lights. Illegal pipes."

They were still waiting for more.

"And flame decals. Not just at the front. All along the body."

Sheriff Barrack quickly shifted his attention to Moses. "Did you see the driver?"

"No, sir. But that's the truck," answered Moses.

"What truck? Whose truck?" asked Wally.

"Can't be," said the sheriff.

"Then it's its twin," said Moses.

"Grab the crew," said the sheriff as he shifted his heavy frame to stand up. "Let's head down to the camp and see what the fuck is going on."

Chapter 18   Almost to the Interstate

The roads were deserted at four-thirty in the morning. The Honda Civic sped toward the interstate exits with the Death Truck in tow.

"Which way? Which way?" asked Clay.

"East," said Chett. "We'll get stuck if we head west towards Louisiana. Not enough room to run before we hit the bridge. Going east will give us more room to run and hide, and more back roads to make our way back."

Clayton took the east exit to the interstate at about eighty. "Can you be a little more specific? I mean, I have a little boost left, sure, but I'd like to use it as wisely as I can."

"He's right," said Harry. "How far do we want to go straight before we turn?"

"I say at least twenty miles," answered Chett. "Keep the gas pedal pegged and use your happy go-fast gas as you see fit to put as much distance between us and them as you can."

"Will do," said Clayton. "I really think we'll lose them. We really couldn't go too fast on those short, curvy roads. There's no way it'll keep up with us on the interstate."

They were mostly right, because as they topped eighty-five, Clayton noticed the little blue pin-pricks of light in the rear-view mirror that meant they'd soon be joined by another chaser, this one sporting a badge and possibly a gun.

"Crap," whined Clayton.

"Dude, whatever do you, do not stop," said Harry. "If anything, go faster."

"No, not right now," said Chett.

"What?" yelled Harry.

"Wait," said Chett, and turned on the radio. "We need some ridin' music." He found a hard rock station and left it there.

They continued the chase down the interstate as the blue lights grew brighter in the mirrors.

"Hang on," said Chett. "Wait until he gets closer."

After a few minutes, the cruiser caught up with them, pulling in behind the Death Truck. The truck refused to cooperate, and the officer driving the cruiser turned his bright car-mounted beam light on the back of the truck

The light gave the effect of silhouetting the occupants of the truck against the hazy back window. "Damn," said Harry, "those are some creepy looking sons-a-bitches."

And they were. Chett looked back and could see the sheer mass of the lumpy pair that was chasing them.

The cruiser tried to maneuver into the left lane, but the truck cut him off.

"Dude, this is it. Hit it!" said Harry.

"No! No! Do not hit it!" yelled Chett. "Wait. Wait until the cruiser gets around the truck and gets behind us."

"How do you suppose he does that?" asked Harry. "He can't get around the truck."

Behind them, the cruiser continued switching lanes as the truck held the center of the road.

"Look, Chett," said Harry, "We need a better plan. Because I've got a feeling we're going to be heading into some stop strips very soon. He's going to call ahead and have someone blow our tires."

"Good point. I was going to wait until he got behind us, but screw it. Hit it. Let's go."

"Consider it done," said Clayton as the car shot forward. Behind them both the fierce glow of the truck's KC lights and sharp strobe of the cruiser's faded into the night.

"Keep going until it's all gone," said Harry.

"Can't," said Clayton.

"Don't really have a choice," said Chett.

"Tough," said Clayton. "Because this car ain't going to take me emptying the bottles. It's good for a little boost, but she's kinda like your mom," said Clayton.

"What?" said Chett, stunned.

"You know, good enough to roll, but too old to take everything I can give her."

"Ohh!" laughed Harry. "You just got burned! By Clay!"

"Dude," said Chett, "Have you even seen my mom?"

"That's true," laughed Harry. "She could kick the shit out of a marine drill sergeant."

"Whatever. Clay, if what you're saying is true, then I have a better idea. Find a spot to cross over the median and double back. There's probably someone already up ahead waiting for us. We won't make it to the exit."

"Good idea," said Harry.

"And by the sound of the car here, I don't think she's going to take much more. We need to take it easy."

Chapter 19   Nine Mile Cutoff Again

Wally and Chief Detective Moses followed Sheriff Barrack's cruiser down the bumpy gravel road. Wally was the first to speak.

"Why can we only communicate over our cells? What's wrong with the radio?"

"Look, rookie – I hate that you got caught up in all this. But you gotta get something straight. Sometimes you got to bend the rules a little to make things run the way you want them to, understand?"

"Not really." He could see the frustration growing in Moses' face.

"Well, you're caught up in it now, so I don't see any reason not to fill you in. But I'm gonna warn you once, so pay good attention. What you see tonight? You don't ever talk about it with anyone. Not the sheriff, not me, no one. You do, and you're dead." Moses made a cutting motion across his neck. "And that's all I'm going to say. Think I'm kidding? Then try it and find out. The sheriff had a little business to take care of. Well, he had someone take care of something for him. And apparently, that business, which we were all good and damn sure was taken care of, has just untaken care of itself. Get it?"

"Uh...the truck? What? It's some jackass racing around. What's the big deal? Have they been banned from the county or something?"

"Something like that." Moses reached for a new pack of cigarettes and began packing them.

"And so, uh, this is some 'unofficial' business the sheriff has. On the side."

"Yep." Moses held the cigarette between his lips and reached for the car lighter.

"Should I be concerned?"

"Yep." He replaced the lighter and rolled the window down. "Hold on."

They followed the sheriff as he turned off the road onto a path so overgrown that Wally doubted there was a path at all. The only thing that gave it away was that the grass and brush had already been mashed down.

"This is the trail to the pond. See the grass? That's not a good sign," said Moses. "Looks like someone's been here recently. Like tonight." His phone rang and he answered. "Yes, sir. I see it." Pause. "I don't know, sir." Pause. "Yes, sir. They should be on their way." He hung up and turned to Wally. "If what we're thinking has happened, then we're in for some deep-dish shit."

"Look, you might need my help. So do me a favor and tell me what in the hell is going on."

Moses thought for a moment. "Okay. That truck? Well, the only way I can put it is that it's supposed to be at the bottom of a pond. Good and buried."

"What? The truck? Buried? Why?"

"The sheriff had a little problem with its owners, and saw to it that the problem was neutralized."

Wally thought about the implications for a minute. "So they found their truck and dug it up. Okay. I understand."

"Not really. Shut up and ride. You'll see what's going on."

A few bumpy minutes later, they arrived on a small levy. The sheriff turned his car to face the open area in front of it, and then turned his searchlight on. Chief Moses followed suit, then jumped out of his car, extinguishing his cigarette.

Wally could hear the sheriff yelling before he even exited the cruiser.

"What...the...holy...fuck?" he turned to Moses. "Where is the goddamned water? Where is the goddamned pond?"

The sheriff grabbed another search light from his car and barked orders to Wally and Moses. "Grab your brightest lights and get your asses down there."

After negotiating the muddy twenty-foot drop into what was apparently until recently a pond, they gathered around a deeper hole in the center.

Chief Moses broke the prolonged silence as they all stood around the small crater in the middle. "Shit. Oh, shit shit shit. Oh, shit. Shit shit shit."

Moses and the sheriff traded a long, worried look. Finally, Moses turned to Wally. "Get my cigarettes from the car."

Wally hesitated.

"Now."

Upon returning, Wally could detect the abject fear and worry in the sheriff's voice. "Get that truck," he said, softly. "But only our guys, understand? Every one of them. If they're on duty, pull them off whatever they're on and get them to spread out. Then you find out who's behind this. Truck first, asses second."

"Where do we start?" asked Moses. "It could be anywhere."

"Fan out, do whatever you need to. Find it and stop it."

"Um, sir?" asked Wally as he walked back up to them. "You might not need to fan out. The dispatchers are on the radio right now. There's a highway patrolman that radioed in and said he was giving chase to two vehicles racing down the interstate, headed east. One was a large pickup.

They're trying to raise the patrolman again, but he's not responding. They're requesting backup."

Chief Moses cussed again, but this time he was joined by the sheriff.

"Get our guys there first. Phones only. Find out what's going on. Clean up the scene. Now! Go!"

Wally took off running but slowed down to match the pace of the heavyset pair behind him. He helped them climb up the bank and jumped into the running cruiser.

Chapter 20   Back on Nine Mile Cutoff

The Civic and its three occupants crept down the road as the first hint of purple began tinting the sky. The road was still too dark to see without headlights, and everyone was quiet now – their windows cracked open to listen for the truck should it come around.

Clay was the first to notice the faint glow of other headlights in the distance and immediately switched off his own. "Hey," he whispered loudly. "Lights. What do we do? I don't hear the truck."

Chett answered. "Neither do I. There's an old church maybe a hundred feet up here to our left. The driveway and parking lot's really overgrown. It's a good place to hide. Get close and we should be able to see our way to it."

They turned onto the overgrown driveway and pulled into the church parking lot.

"The stories we could tell you about this place," Harry said as he looked out the back window.

"What, about a church? What kind of stories would you have about a church?" Clayton thought they were bullshitting.

"Oh, no," said Chett, "It's been closed for what, like ten years?"

"Sounds about right," said Harry. "And during that time, we've had some wild get-together's out here."

"Still, though. At a church? You guys are going to hell."

"Shut up, Clay," said Harry.

"No offense, but if you're having wild parties in church parking lots..."

"No, I meant, shut up. As in 'be quiet' or 'listen'."

They all concentrated on the silence. The cars whose headlights they had seen drove by.

"Police cruisers? Are they looking for us?" Chett craned his neck to watch their tail lights pass by.

"Probably," said Clay. "You guys have really screwed me."

Harry shushed him.

"What? Seriously, I'm up shit creek."

"Hush," said Harry. "Listen."

"What?" Chett rolled his window down again. "They're already gone."

"No, I could have sworn I heard something. Before they drove by."

"What?" asked Chett.

"Well, it sounded like a deer."

"Mmmm hmmm..." Chett peered out into the early morning darkness. Each minute brought a little more sunlight into the church parking lot. He had heard the sound of something stepping on a dead branch too, but had originally chalked it up to over-imagination fueled by the weirdest day he'd ever had. "We need to go. Now. Deer or no deer, I don't want to find out. You heard something. I heard something. It's dark and creepy. Let's get going. Now."

"Don't need to tell me twice." Clayton started the car and pulled back on to the road.

Chett cleared his throat. "Um, Harry?"

"Yeah?"

"Were they looking for us?"

"We can only assume."

"You think going back to camp is a good idea?" asked Chett.

"Well, they're heading away from camp, so I'd say it's okay," Harry answered.

Clay spoke up, "And guys, we might need to swap cars. I'm having all sorts of problems."

"I can tell," said Harry. "Rattling, jerking. Not sounding very good. Riding like a piece of shit."

The night's events and lack of sleep had left all of them jittery. Shadows danced in the thick brush on the roadside. Chett and Harry had been awake for nearly twenty-four hours without caffeine or any other stimulant. They wanted to pick their guns up, go home, and go to sleep.

That wasn't going to happen. Back at the camp, Chett was the first to notice something missing. "Where the hell is our RV?"

"Aw, man. What the hell? That thing didn't even run. Did someone tow it?" Harry hopped out after Chett and started looking for tracks in the early morning light.

"Why would someone want to tow it? It would cost more in the gas to move it than it was worth," Chett added.

"And they took our generator."

"Sumbitch." Chett spat. "Sumbitch. That means our guns are gone too."

"I don't see any tracks. It's just gone," Harry noted.

"That's impossible," Chett said.

"Damn. How are we supposed to find it? We sure can't call the cops," Harry said. "But I don't even know where to start or what to do."

"Let's just go home. Clay, we'll call you."

"Oh, no," Clay answered. "You're not leaving me to take the rap if I get pulled over. I'm sticking with you guys."

"No, you're not." Harry said. "You're going to go home and stay there until we call you. You're in enough trouble without us getting you deeper."

"Forget it," Clay said. "I'm going with you."

"No, you're not," Chett replied as he and Harry climbed in his truck.

Clay walked away, dejectedly. He heard Chett as he opened his car door.

"Oh, what now?" Chett cursed.

"This is bullshit!" yelled Harry.

"I don't believe it. Go see what's wrong," Chett said as Harry jumped out of the truck to look under the hood.

"Well, for one, your plugs are missing." Harry kept looking around.

"Who took my plugs? Well, that ain't so bad."

"No. Not too bad," Harry answered, "Except you're missing a few belts, wires, hoses and other essential parts."

"Screw this. You're kidding." Chett jumped to the ground and walked to the front of his truck. "No, you're not. Damn." He looked around. "Clay!"

"What?"

"We're riding with you."

"The hell you are."

"Seriously. We need a ride."

"No. You guys always do that. Forget it. You're on your own. Besides, you guys promised me something, remember?"

"Don't be that way," said Harry. "We were only trying to save you trouble. We actually need your help. Don't we, Chett?"

"Yeah – I mean, we couldn't have made it out without you. We were only trying to make sure that you didn't get hurt."

"So if you really want to help us, then you're with us. Right, Chett?"

"Yeah. But it's obvious we're in some kinda trouble. And if you don't mind being involved..."

"Are you kidding? This is the most excitement I've ever seen!"

"Okay then," Chett said. He and Harry climbed into the Civic to discuss the situation.

"I've got a pistol and a shotgun at the trailer," said Harry. "I do have a bit of ammo – but only the two guns. The others were all in the RV."

"All my guns were in the RV too," added Chett. "Sons-a-bitches. Took my RV." He turned to look at Clay. "What about you?"

"My mom would kill me if I had anything like that."

"Figures," Harry said.

Chett kept talking. "Okay. Home first to sleep. Clay, you'll crash with us."

"Awesome!"

"Then, we need help," he continued. "We can't go to the cops. But we need to get my truck fixed and figure out a few things – like where the hell's my RV, who the hell is trying to kill us, and what the hell else is going on with all this weird shit."

"There's more?" asked Clay.

"Oh, yeah," replied Harry. "Missing lakes, crap falling out of the sky. And of course, that truck..."

"The one that was chasing us?" Clay asked.

"Kinda just popped out of the ground at us," Harry finished.

"What?" Clay looked from Harry to Chett and back again for clarification. "Huh?"

"Let's go to our place. We'll explain on the way."

"Then," added Chett, "We'll go see Uncle Crank."

Harry sighed. "Aw, hell."

Chapter 21   Somewhere Else

"How much longer?" Earl paced nervously in the dark, listening to his voice echo. "We've got a deadline. So to speak."

"I dunno. He said it was fixed, actually." Roscoe fumbled for his remote entry keys. "Dang. I can't see a thing."

"Why did we have to sneak in here?" Earl asked.

"I just wanted to make sure he was working on it."

A large collection of extremely bright lights flashed twice, leaving both of them temporarily blinded. "Found them!"

Earl rubbed his eyes. "Gaah. Couldn't you have warned me?"

Roscoe waited until the ramp lowered. "Come on. Quit bitching. Get in. Let's go."

"Mister King of Two-Word Statements speaks to the masses!"

"Very funny."

"That's five!"

"Shut up."

"Six!"

"You wanna live to make it out of here?"

"Yeah," Earl said.

"Then get a move on and quit the crap."

"Roscoe?" Earl asked as he surveyed the scene.

"Yeah?"

"How are we going to get out of here? There's not an exit, so to speak."

"Yeah, I had figured on that. There will be."

"Oh. Okay. Hmmm. Yeah. It's going to be kind of noisy – this exit – isn't it?"

"Yep."

"Shoulda known."

"Yep."

"Okay. That's all."

They climbed up the ramp and prepared to make a nasty exit. In a minute, there would be a series of quick, loud explosions. Alarms would sound and all hell would break loose. For now, though – for just a few minutes – they were still undetected.

Roscoe looked over to Earl as they strapped themselves in. "You ready?"

"No. Am I ever?"

"Here we go!" The cockpit lit up with the brilliant flash that used to be the hangar wall.

Chapter 22   On the Way to Uncle Crank's

Harry yawned as Clay's Civic bounced down Nine Mile Cutoff. "Okay. So what's the plan?"

"I say we see if Uncle Crank's got any spare parts lying around in his junkyard. We're decently armed, but we'll see if he can't get us some more guns. Then we go fix the truck."

"Then what?" asked Clay.

Chett looked at him disdainfully. "You think with the way the last few days have gone we'll even make it that far?"

Clay looked worried. "What do you mean?"

"Relax, man," Harry assured. "He didn't mean we'd get killed. Just that chances are something else'll come up and we'll have to deal with that."

"Oh." Clay turned down the bumpy, overgrown driveway that led to Uncle Crank's house. "Wow, he really lives out in the boonies, doesn't he? I don't think anyone can live farther out."

And he was right. He saw a small blue 1950's-era singlewide trailer leaning precariously in a direction that looked as if a gentle breeze should catch it, it would just calmly tip on over with no fuss and lay there pleasantly.

A large, rickety, two-story wooden barn with heavily chained and boarded up doors also leaned precariously in the breeze, fighting to stay upright. As if to add to the effect, several large pieces of timber had been placed haphazardly on the leaning side to prop it up.

Next to it slept at least a few hundred cars, vans, and trucks. Some were newer additions, some almost completely hidden by kudzu. Most of the ground was bare and dusty. A few chickens pecked around as an elderly bloodhound looked up from where he lay chained in the shade under the trailer.

All three of them could see the trailer shaking violently as they drove up. And when Clay killed the engine, they could hear muffled cursing.

Chett muttered, "What the hell?" as he and Harry checked to make sure their firearms were loaded.

"Should we be leaving?" Clay asked. But it was too late. Chett had already exited the passenger side of the car with Harry in close tow. "Guys? Hey, guys? What about me? Do I get a gun?"

Chett had taken about three steps toward the trailer when the extremely torn screen door flew open to allow the commotion inside to spill outside. He pulled his twelve-gauge to his shoulder and pointed it down, prepared to shoot, as what looked to be a small, naked dog – or pig – no, chicken! - as a small, naked chicken jumped out of the trailer and ran into the dusty yard, followed immediately by a wiry, extremely tanned, shirtless man with camo shorts and crazy hair sprouting from under a trucker's cap. The man grumbled incoherently as he stumbled out of the trailer, running after the chicken with a frying pan.

This had the dual effect of scaring the other chickens away and exciting the dog to a barking and baying frenzy. Chett and Harry laughed and lowered their weapons as Uncle Crank stumbled through the yard chasing the chicken, occasionally throwing the pan and missing. Every time he would lunge one way, the chicken would go the other.

At least, until the chicken drew too close to the trailer and the bloodhound got it.

But by this time, Clay, Harry and Chett had noticed something odd.

"Damn thing. Leggo! Let go!" Uncle Crank wrestled with the dog to get the chicken free. He turned to the trio, finally acknowledging them. "S'okay. He ain't hardly got no teef. Now gimme! Mine!" He finally succeeded in freeing the flapping chicken. "Bad dog! Bad dog! 'At's my chicken!" He turned back to them. "Stupid dog."

Harry couldn't take his eyes off the chicken. "Um, Uncle Crank?"

"Yeahwazzat?" he responded.

To Clay it looked like Uncle Crank had forgotten anyone else was in the yard.

Harry continued. "That chicken ain't got no head."

"Yeah. That's right. That's right," he replied softly as he gazed away.

"But it's still flapping around," Harry said.

Chett looked over to Harry. "You ever heard of 'running around like a chicken with its head cut off?'"

"Yeah, but this is different. There's no blood. And he looks a little crispy."

"Hmm. Yeah. Okay. That's a little strange," Chett conceded.

Uncle Crank had already walked up the steps of his trailer, fighting the chicken. He turned back to the group. "Y'all want some? This bad boy's going in the microwave." He didn't wait for an answer.

"What?" Clay looked at Harry, then Chett. "Did he say microwave? He can't do that! That thing's still alive."

"Clay, meet Uncle Crank," Chett said as he motioned to the trailer in Uncle Crank's absence.

"Oh," said Clay.

He followed Chett and Harry inside and was immediately struck by how damned hot it was. If it was in the eighties or nineties outside, it must have been over a hundred inside. Throw in extra humidity, the smell of stale cigarettes and body odor, and a shirtless, snaggle-toothed man beating the everlasting shit out of a headless chicken with a frying pan, and it made for a nauseating experience. Clay tried to find a place to sit down, but the only area not covered by newspapers, car parts, or other unidentifiable crap was an old armchair which obviously belonged to the crazy man. And Clay didn't want to take the crazy man's chair, even if he was losing a battle with a headless chicken.

"Uncle Crank," Chett yelled over the banging and cursing, "Need some help?"

"Damn chicken wings." Finally, Uncle Crank won the battle and shoved the chicken, still banging around, into a microwave that looked like it was about to fall in under the weight of the stack of papers on top of it.

Clay felt another wave of nausea as he watched him turn the knob to nuke the flapping chicken.

Uncle Crank watched the microwave for a few seconds, then turned his head away and covered his ears. Chett and Harry were quick enough to do the same. But by the time Clay had figured it out, it was too late. He got to witness the chicken explode inside the microwave, which is all it took to send him back outside, throwing up into the dirt.

"Heh heh. Pansy," said Uncle Crank as he pulled the mess out of the microwave and shoved it on a rack in the oven. Satisfied, he looked back up at Chett and Harry, who were staring on in horror. "It'll be a few 'fore it's ready, but y'all can have some. I ain't gonna eat it all, anyway. I'd just end up giving the scraps to Buddy."

"No, that's okay," said Harry.

"We just ate," echoed Chett.

"Suit yerself. More for me and Buddy."

"Um, Uncle Crank?" asked Chett.

"Yeahwazzat?"

"What was wrong with that chicken?"

"Huh? What? I guess he didn't think it was his time, you know?"

"Yeah, but, well..." Chett stuttered.

Harry picked up. "But he looked a little, well, already cooked."

"Yeah. That's right. That's right," Uncle Crank said as he gazed away.

"Uncle Crank?"

"Yeahwazzat?"

"I said he looked a little cooked."

"Oh, right. Right. Yeah, he was a little tough. Damn hot dogs and chickens."

"Hot dogs?" asked Chett.

"Yeah. Hot dogs and chickens. Just bein' hardheaded, is all."

"What?" Harry asked.

"Oh, it ain't nothing but some hardheaded hot dogs. You want one?"

"What? A hardheaded hot dog?" Harry asked.

"Yeah. I got some left over."

"Why don't you give them to Buddy?"

"Aw, he won't go near 'em."

Clay walked back in as Uncle Crank opened the antique refrigerator door. And he turned right back around for round two when he saw the four wieners wriggling on the shelf.

"What's wrong with that boy? He need a hot dog?"

Chett found himself trying not to get sick. "Um, I don't think your hot dogs should be doing that."

"Whazzat? They's hardheaded, is all." He took them out of the refrigerator and set them on the only clean spot on the counter next to the stove and commenced to whacking them with the frying pan. "You just gotta get 'em calm enough to nuke 'em."

Chett, fighting fierce nausea, reached to restrain him. "Stop, stop, stop."

Uncle Crank continued to fight the wieners.

"Seriously. Stop. You can't eat those. Those are not right."

"Naw, they's fine."

Harry maneuvered around the counter to aide Chett. "No, Uncle Crank. You need to forget about them. I'll buy you some more."

"You will?" he asked.

"Yes."

Uncle Crank slowly released the frying pan and picked the muted – but still wiggling – hot dogs off the counter and carried them to throw them out the door.

They landed next to Clay, who mistakenly believed he had just finished completely emptying the contents of his stomach. He peered at them for a few seconds before running to his car to throw up some more.

Uncle Crank laughed. "Heh heh heh. That kid's funny. What's wrong with him?"

Chett answered, "That's Clay. He's a little sheltered."

"Mmm hmm. Need to check the chicken." He turned around and walked back to the oven.

Chett followed him, nearly tripping over something round lying under some old Playboys lying on the floor. He reached down, brushed away the magazines, and came up with an intact harpoon.

"What the hell is this?" he asked, showing it to Uncle Crank.

Uncle Crank looked at him like he was stupid. "I reckon that'd be a hurpoon, there, Chett."

"What do you need a harpoon for? You live in the only ten acre desert for hundreds of miles."

Uncle Crank scratched his stubble. "In case a whale shows up."

"What?"

"And what's going on out in your shop? Why's it all boarded up?"

Uncle Crank looked away.

"What are you working on now? It ain't another one of your dune-buggies, is it? Because I thought you'd been ordered by the law to stop making them things."

Harry chimed in. "Last one you made hit what, a hundred and so, before catching itself – and a few of the cars you were passing on the interstate – on fire. You're lucky to be alive."

"He he. That sure was some fast sumbitch." Uncle Crank looked away wistfully.

Harry rolled his eyes. "They all were. But fiery death traps too. You're not working on another one, are you?"

Uncle Crank was still gazing away.

"Uncle Crank," Chett tried to get him to snap back into reality.

No luck.

He tried a little more loudly. "*Uncle Crank!*"

"Yeahwazzat?" Uncle Crank's head whipped around.

"You're not working on another one, are you?"

Uncle Crank's face twisted into a toothless grin.

"Seriously. Tell us you're not."

Still grinning, he fished around in his shorts for a pack of cigarettes. "Naw, naw. Ain't making no doom buggy."

"Dune buggy," Harry corrected.

"Right. 'S what I said. Doom buggy. Ain't making one."

"Because you remember what the sheriff said," Harry said. "He said if he caught you making another one you'd go straight to jail."

"Huh?" Uncle Crank looked genuinely puzzled. "That's that sheriff for ya'. Too bad it ain't that undersheriff he had. Whashisname? Fred? Fredrick? Huey? Sompin' like that. Cause he was a good fella. He didn't mind. He was a good boy." Uncle Crank walked to the kitchen and got down on all fours to peer under the stove.

"His name was William, Uncle Crank," Chett cut in. "William Rayburn. And he's been long gone. He took a job up north, where they weren't as crooked as down here."

"Ain't none a' that true," said Uncle Crank. "They's crooked everywhere. Ain't gone up north, either." He was laying prone now, his arm all the way under the stove. He pulled out a golf ball, an oven mitt, a mouse trap or two, and an old laser pointer (which he clicked several times, amazed that the batteries still worked), but apparently not having found what he was looking for, he stuck his arm back underneath it again.

Harry looked on. "Then where'd he go?"

"Don't claim ta know."

"Okay, Uncle Crank. Now, about what we're here for. We need some help."

Finally he dug out a cigarette pack and stood up, peeking cautiously into the oven. "Not done yet. Damn that chicken."

Harry leaned over to Chett. "What in the bloody hell is going on? I'm done with weird shit for the week. And we keep walking into it. No matter where we go, something insane is happening. And I also think it's only a matter of time before we stop stumbling into it and it starts coming to us."

Chett whispered back. "I know. But we need our truck. And Uncle Crank's probably got the parts we need out there in the junkyard." He turned back to Uncle Crank. "Listen, how much would you charge for some hoses, wires, and spark plugs?"

"Aw, you boys just take what you need and leave me a few bucks. You boys need any ball bearings?"

Chett looked at Harry quizzically. "No, I think we're okay on bearings."

Uncle Crank held a Virginia Slim cigarette to his lip and lit it. "Mkay." He exhaled a little smoke and continued talking with the cigarette hanging in his mouth. "That's fine. Just got a shipment in earlier today, and damned if I know what to do with 'em. Reckon I can take 'em up to the Mechanic Zone and sell 'em?"

Chett answered, "I've never heard of them buying loose ball bearings, but it wouldn't hurt to try."

"Yeah, that's fine, that's fine." He walked over to check on the chicken again. "'Cause some of 'em's broken anyway."

Harry looked at Chett and spoke in a half-whisper. "What? How the hell can you break ball bearings?"

"It's Uncle Crank."

"Oh." Then to Uncle Crank, "So why don't you send them back?"

"Don't know where they came from."

Chett was wondering how that was possible when they heard a muffled yell from outside. It was Clay.

They thanked Uncle Crank and walked outside to see what was going on with Clay and rummage for parts.

"Chett? Harry? What's going on? I don't feel so good. My mom... Oh, God, I'm going to be sick again. Can you make those things go away?" He pointed to the wieners that were slowly making their way to a very scared dog.

Uncle Crank burst out the door. "Here, give 'em to me. I'll get rid of 'em." He picked them up and headed back indoors, chuckling to himself. "Funny kid."

Clay regained a little color. "Ugh. Disgusting."

"What about your mom?" Harry asked.

"Oh, no. Mom. She called." He looked up at them. "We're in some trouble. She's pissed because the cops showed up and they're looking for me."

"You?"

"Yeah, me. I asked her and she said they didn't say anything about you."

Chett and Harry gave each other a high-five.

Clay was insulted. "It's not funny. I'm in trouble."

"We told you that you would be."

"Yeah, but you're not."

"That you know of," Chett responded.

"Can we just get whatever parts you're looking for and get out of here? I need to take my car to the shop as it is, before it dies."

"Fine, fine. C'mon, Harry, let's go find some plugs and hoses."

Fifteen slow minutes passed for Clay. He reclined in the shade of a dying pecan tree, keeping tabs on the occasional rustling of a breeze or bits of mumbled conversation drifting in from the vast field of cars and trucks and vans where Chett and Harry searched for parts. Occasionally some banging noise made its way out of the trailer over the choppy mid-range voices emanating from the black and white TV that Clay had seen resting on the coffee table. The dog would raise a lazy eyebrow and go back to sleep, reassuring him that no more dead food-things would run his way.

Until a dead cat-thing ran his way. Clay could see the exposed ribs and occasional other bone as the cat made its way menacingly towards him. Four things happened simultaneously: the cat jumped towards him, he screamed like a little girl, the dog started barking, and he kicked the crap out of the creepy cat, which took a second to gather itself before making a low, growling, dead-cat sound and coming back for round two, at which point the process repeated.

Uncle Crank flew out of the house with his trusty frying pan, but stopped short of winging it at whatever was causing the commotion. He froze momentarily and ran back inside, only to return still holding the pan in one hand, but now also holding a revolver in the other. "C'mere, boy. I'll teach that damn cat to stay away. Scat!"

Clay ran towards him as he took aim and fired. A bit of cat something-or-other flew off, which seemed to upset it, but not enough to keep it from advancing.

Uncle Crank kept talking as he took aim again. "You didn't feed it, did you? 'Cause once you feed 'em, they just keeps coming back."

Clay shook his head as Uncle Crank took another shot. By the third shot, Chett and Harry had run up to investigate. Neither said a word as they saw Uncle Crank firing round after round into a very determined gory cat. They ran to Clay's car, retrieved the shotguns, and proceeded to blast the unholy cat from a distance until nothing was left except a few twitching parts.

"That cat was seriously ill," Chett said.

"Oh, Fluffy always was a mean one," said Uncle Crank as he turned to walk back inside.

"You knew that cat?" Harry asked.

"Oh, yeah. He and Buddy didn't get along too well."

"So you got rid of him?"

"Naw. Buddy did, though."

"But you hadn't seen him in a while?"

"Naw." Uncle Crank lit a cigarette and reached inside the trailer to grab a piece of chicken. He took a bite. "Not since I buried him a while back."

"I don't reckon we want to walk to camp?" Clay asked as he leaned against the side of his steaming, open-hooded car.

Harry peered out from under the hood. "Chett, you don't remember seeing any Civics at Uncle Crank's, do you?"

"No. And we can't call Clay's mom for a ride. Come on, we're walking. Harry, you grab the bag of parts and the twelve -gauge. Clay, you grab the pistols and the 30-30. I'll take the 30-ought-6."

As they loaded up, Harry cocked his head to one side. "I hear a car."

Chett listened, then replied, "Crap. Probably cops. Hurry up and get everything. Let's head into the woods."

They made it a few feet behind the tree line and crouched down to hide as the vehicle approached. Clay was shaking so much that Chett had to reassure him.

"Will you relax? We'll be okay," he whispered.

"But what if they stop? We're really close. We won't be able to get away."

Chett was about to respond when he caught site of the passing vehicle, which turned out not to be a cop car, but a musty and rusted RV. Without thinking he ran out into the road and yelled, "Hey!" He fired one of his guns into the road. "Hey! Come back! That's my RV!"

Harry and Clay joined him on the road, only to make a hasty retreat with him when the RV unexpectedly stopped, reversed, and started backing quickly towards them. The three of them dove back behind the tree line again as the RV pulled parallel to them.

Chett sighted his rifle on the driver's compartment as the window rolled down.

The veiled driver spoke first. "Bob, ride?"

"Oh, what the hell?" Chett kept his rifle sighted but looked to Harry and Clay, each of whom shook their heads in confusion.

"Bob. Ride?" she said again.

Chett, still holding his rifle on her, signaled the others to walk with him to the RV in the same manner. Harry and Clay remained on the passenger side as Chett circled behind it to talk to Bob.

She spoke again. "Bob. Ride!"

"That's right. Ride. You took my ride."

Harry yelled from the other side, "Um, yeah, but she gets points for getting it running. Seeing as how it didn't really have most of anything that it needed to run."

"Not now, Harry. She still stole my RV."

"Not to mention that I don't think it's been cranked in twenty years. I'm amazed, actually."

"Do you mind?"

This time, Bob spoke a little more forcefully. "Bob! RIDE!"

Harry yelled from the other side of the RV. "I think she's trying to tell us to get in."

"Oh, I'm getting in, all right," Chett replied. "But I'm getting in the driver's side." Then to Bob, gun still pointed at her. "Come on, honey. Get out."

Bob stared at him.

"You heard me. Out." He motioned with the gun.

Bob looked over at Clay and Harry, then back to Chett.

"Last chance."

She opened the door and stood next to Chett. In one swift motion, she wrenched the gun away with one hand and picked his two-hundred-fifty-pound frame up around his waist with the other. She carried him around to the other side, dropped the rifle, opened the door to the living compartment and flung him in effortlessly.

Clay watched, frozen and wide-eyed, as she made her way to both of them. Harry's fight or flight instinct tilted instantaneously toward the latter. He began running but was quickly caught, disarmed, and dragged back to the RV.

Clay watched again, frozen and wide-eyed, as she came back for him. He dropped his gun and waited until she picked him up, (maybe a little more gently than the rest, he thought – at least she carried him cradled in her arms).

With the crew having been firmly deposited in the back, Bob gathered the weapons, tossed them in the passenger seat, and took off down the road.

The three unwilling passengers huddled in the back room of the RV and tried to make sense of the situation.

Harry spoke first. "Relax, Chett, I know what you're thinking without you saying it. You're not going to get the guns. Forget about it."

Chett shot him a frustrated look.

Harry continued, "And I don't think she wants to hurt us. If she did, we'd be dead."

Chett saw something in a bag on the bed. He opened it. "What the hell?"

"What is it?" asked Harry.

"It's my freakin' wires and hoses, that's what it is!"

"She took them?" asked Harry.

"Apparently so."

"Why?"

Chett didn't answer, still peering into the bag in disbelief.

Clay, visibly shaken, opened the door to peek at the driver. "Who is that?"

"We don't really know," answered Chett. "But what I do know is that she stole my RV and dismantled my truck and I'm really starting to get freaked the hell out!"

Harry ignored him and tried to fill Clay in. "We kinda picked her up yesterday. She was standing in the road about a mile or so back. We tried to get rid of her, and she just kept following us."

"That's a girl?"

Chett and Harry both gave him a wide-eyed stare.

"Boy, is she," said Chett.

"I'll say," added Harry. "Clay, meet Bob, the girl we promised you."

Clay tried his best to stare holes through Harry's head. "Assholes."

"Hey," Harry responded. "At least we kept our promise."

Chett kept on trying to piece the situation together. "Now what was Uncle Crank talking about? He buried that cat? That cat was dead?"

"Oh," said Harry, "It's Uncle Crank. What do you expect?"

"No, that cat was dead."

"It's impossible," said Harry.

"Oh, like the headless cooked chicken and the hot dogs make any sense?"

Clay started to get sick again.

"Can it, Clay," Chett admonished. "Look, in the last day or so, we've seen a four-by-four shoot out of the ground, the chicken and hot dogs, and an undead cat."

"Not to mention Bob," added Harry.

"And not to mention Bob. It's time to admit that something not quite right is going on."

"Admittedly, okay, it's gotten really weird really quick," said Harry. "But what do you propose is going on?"

Harry actually had an idea of his own - however far-fetched - but before he could speak, the conversation was rudely interrupted first by the sudden stop of the RV, throwing all of them against the wall, then by the sound of gunfire.

They tried to right themselves, but were thrown even more violently around the back as the RV pulled a bootlegger. They heard more gunshots. Chett made it out of the back first, in time to see the Burqa-wearing Bob leaning out the driver's window and firing a shotgun at a figure standing in the road.

Bob leaned in and the RV lurched forward again, toward the figure ambling toward them in the road. Chett was focusing so intently on the thing in front of them that he failed to notice Bob thrusting a gun in his direction.

"Boom!" she said and pointed toward what now looked to be a person standing in the road. "Boom! Boom!"

"I think she wants you to shoot it!" Clay yelled.

"Thanks! Kinda figured it out for myself!" Chett jumped into the passenger seat and rolled down the window. The gun was still loaded. The person in the road was less than thirty yards away. He could also see that the person wasn't quite a person like he was a person – it was more like a person like the cat was a cat. It did not look good. He didn't have to think twice. He fired and watched as bits of the creature exploded, knocking it back a few feet. But it was still standing. And Bob was still gunning the engine.

"Slow down!" Harry yelled.

They were ten yards away and Chett was trying desperately to reload.

"Slow down!" Harry yelled again.

Bob kept speeding up.

Harry managed to yelp and cover his eyes as Bob ran over the thing in the road. Its body went under the RV and bounced under the tires, but its head bounced up the hood and smacked into the windshield.

Chett looked up in time to stare the head in the eyes. It was human; at least it used to be. Chett had seen enough of them in movies and video games to know what they were. "Zombies."

Bob turned the windshield wipers on and the head rolled off the window. She slowed down enough to turn around again and inched the RV up to it. Everyone but Bob cringed at the crunchy bump.

Clay passed out.

Chapter 24   Close to Chett and Harry's Trailer

Clay came to as the RV turned onto the road to the overgrown yard and low-end trailer that Chett and Harry called home. He was staring into the dark veil of the woman in whose lap his head was resting.

Chett was driving.

Clay sat up gingerly. "What's going on?"

Harry looked back into the living quarters of the RV. "We decided that after all the drama we would probably be better off not going to camp for a while."

Bob looked out the window and yelled, effectively scaring Clay back into a brief unconsciousness.

He woke back up to a deserted RV. His head hurt. Outside, the black-sheet-wearing woman they had called Bob was inspecting a huge black metal satellite dish. Inside, Chett and Harry were pacing back and forth and arguing about their next course of action.

Every attempt he made at entering the conversation was ignored, so he went back outside to see what the strange woman was doing with the satellite dish.

He spoke tentatively. "Hello?"

The veiled woman looked up briefly and returned to studying the dish. She was tall, but it looked to Clay that she was having trouble trying to reach the horn.

Clay walked around to where the cables entered the ground to make their run to the trailer. "This should be easy." He ran inside, past Chett and Harry (who were locked in a heated conversation), and surfed the ancient K-band dish to point at another satellite closer to the horizon.

Bob jumped as the dish rotated, lowering the horn to chest-level. Chett ran back outside and flashed her a thumbs-up. She cocked her head to the side and raised a covered arm and gloved hand to flash the symbol back at him.

"No problem. Name's Clay." He stuck out his hand.

She waited. He gently thrust it forward again. She took it and whirled him around, awkwardly spreading him out against the dish and patting him down.

"It's okay, I'm okay!"

Once the process was completed, she raised her arms and turned around. Clay stood in place, frozen and unsure what to do. She looked over her shoulder impatiently and seemed to be waiting for something.

"Oh, you want me to pat you down? It's okay. I trust you."

She shrugged, but still stood with outstretched arms.

"Okay..." Clay said hesitatingly. He walked up to her and began to gently pat her down. He could feel her figure under the garments, but was too scared to make it any lower than outer mid-thigh and any higher than mid-back. But he could feel the sides of her breasts and that was enough to make him even more uncomfortable.

She giggled. "Bob."

"Clay. Nice to meet you."

"Nice to meet you," she replied.

"You can talk?"

"Talk?"

"Can you speak English?"

"English?"

"I take that as a no. Parlez-vous Francais? Habla Espinol? Sprechen se Deutche? No? What do you speak?"

She emitted a series of gibberish spattered liberally with consonants and vowels and clicks and whistles.

"Nope. Not doing anything for me. Can you understand what I'm saying?"

"Saying?"

"Yes. Saying."

Bob was silent.

"Well, this is going to be a challenge. Where to start?" He looked around and saw a stick in the ground. "Got it!" He took it and motioned for Bob to follow. He found a dusty patch of ground and drew a line. "One." He drew another line. "Two." He made it to ten and looked at her.

She counted to ten and pointed at the lines.

"Yes! Good!" Then less enthusiastically. "Now for the rest of the English language."

She took the stick from him and drew a circle in the ground.

"Yes. Zero. I forgot about zero."

Then she drew some more circles. "I'm not following."

She shook her head and rubbed the drawings away with her foot. In its place she drew a box. Clay watched as she drew ten more boxes inside it, in the lower half. In the upper half she drew a larger box with zigzagging lines.

"Oh. Is that a phone? Do you need a phone?" He fished in his other pocket. "Here, you can have mine."

She took it and shook her head, handing it back to him.

"No? That's not a cell phone? Sure looks like it."

She pointed at the drawing with the stick, then pointed at herself.

"Oh! That's yours?"

She kept looking at him.

"You're looking for that?"

She kept looking at him.

He pointed from the drawing to her. "You're looking for that? It's yours?"

She nodded her head.

"Yes?" he asked.

"Yes."

"Good."

Once again, she rubbed the drawing away and started fresh. This time, she drew a circle. Clay watched with interest as she made little dots outside the circle, and a smaller circle off to the side. In the circle, she drew squiggly lines just detailed enough to make out the continent of North America.

"Good idea," he said. "Point to where you're from and I'll get us a dictionary!"

She looked at him, placed the stick next to Earth, and ran away – leaving a trail of footprints in the dust next to where she drew the line. She stopped about twenty yards away and symbolically flicked the stick out of the ground, throwing a divot of dust a few feet farther. She turned to look at him again.

"No...Way..." Clay said.

She nodded.

"This... is... marfarkin'... awesome!"

She nodded again.

Clay gave her the thumbs-up sign again and ran inside. Chett and Harry were still inside, arguing.

Chett spoke frantically, waving his hands around and spilling his beverage. "Dude, they're freakin' zombies!"

Harry responded just as frantically. "Normally, I'd say you're batshit and laugh at you. But I'm with you on this one. Where do zombies come from?"

"The ground?"

"I mean, why are they here?"

"To eat brains?"

Clay thought this would be a good point to interject. "She's an alien."

Neither one heard him. Harry continued talking to Chett. "You watch too many movies."

"You got a better idea?"

Clay spoke up again, a little louder. "She's an alien."

Harry was still talking to Chett. "How do we kill 'em? If a twelve-gauge don't knock 'em out, I say we're in some major trouble."

Clay yelled this time. "SHE'S FROM OUTER SPACE!"

Chett and Harry swung around and spoke simultaneously. "What?"

"Bob? The chick? She's not from earth."

They spoke simultaneously again. "What?"

"How much more plainly can I say it? Bob...is...from...outer...space..." Clay looked up and waved his hands around his head to attempt the universal sign for 'up there.'

Both of them stared at him for a moment before Chett finally spoke. "Look, dude, no offense. But we're kinda in the middle of trying to figure out how not to get killed. We've already told you that we've got your back, but save us the crazy and go fantasize somewhere else."

"Suit yourself," Clay said dejectedly. "But do you happen to have a computer?"

"Nope," Chett answered. "Got repossessed."

"Don't lie to the kid," Harry said. "It crashed and Chett kicked the shit out of the thing. Threw the monitor out the window."

"Out the closed window. Speaking of which, you got any duct tape? I gotta patch that thing back up."

"Why? It's been that way for weeks."

"Yeah, but there's zombies out there now."

"And you think a duct-taped window will stop them?" Harry asked.

"Whatever."

"Anyway, the computer's probably in India somewhere right now, but they won't fix it under warranty because it shows obvious signs of physical damage."

"Damn slurpie-selling computer geek won't fix my 'puter."

"So back to the answer," Harry said, "No, we don't have a computer."

"Well, I need one." Clay said. "Toss me the keys; I'm going to borrow the RV."

"You are out of your Star-Trek mind," Chett said.

"Assholes." Clay stormed out of the trailer and did the thing he dreaded most. He called his mom for a ride. "I guess no one's going to class tonight."

Chapter 25   Sheriff Barrack's House

Outside, evening had begun fading into night. Inside, Detective Moses paced and smoked a cigarette, sweating through his shirt. "Well, sir, we found the car abandoned on the side of the road. Traced it to Clayton Hensworth."

The four or five deputies, including Wally, sat in the living room listening to the conversation. Wally kept staring at the animal heads hanging from the vaulted ceiling.

Sheriff Barrack had been rubbing his temples for the last thirty minutes. He squinted to recall the name. "Clayton Hensworth. Isn't he the kid who blew up his daddy's shed?"

"That would be the one, sir."

The sheriff took a sip of a virgin Bloody Mary. "Mmm Hmm. Where is he?"

"Don't know, sir. But I don't think we need to be looking for him."

The sheriff turned red. "Goddamnit, I don't pay you to think. I pay you to do what I say. That boy's the only link to the truck we've got so far. And we're luckier than hell that the Highway Patrol don't have a description of the truck. Last thing we need's a bunch of blue-shirts sticking their noses down around here, and you can bet your ass they're already going to be a few of them buzzin' around here like a bunch of damned wasps." He looked Detective Moses in the eye. "I don't get stung, understand?"

Moses understood exactly what the sheriff meant. He'd do everything in his power to place the blame on everyone else – meaning everyone including Moses.

But Moses didn't have a chance to respond. They were interrupted by what felt to him to be a small earthquake, accompanied by an unholy roaring outside the window.

Then it quit almost as suddenly as it began.

"What the hell?" Detective Moses ambled his heavy frame to peek out the window just as a collection of extremely bright lights started glaring silently through the curtains. He shielded his eyes against the optic onslaught as the roaring started again. He stumbled back, more out of instinct than anything else – which, when he considered it later – saved his life.

Because at that moment, a very large, loud, and muddy truck crashed rather gracefully through the window, knocking the couch on which the sheriff sat squarely into the wall. The truck sat still, its idling exhaust too loud to talk over. The sheriff stumbled to stand and find a safe place to hide. He glanced into the truck. Through the flickering lights, two ghastly, rotting, grinning faces stared back at him.

The next two thoughts to cross the sheriff's mind were 'shit!' and 'shoot!' - Shit, meaning 'This can't be happening,' and shoot, meaning 'grab my gun and start firing.' He moved to grab for his gun and the truck revved its engine, forcing everyone to cover their ears. Sheriff Barrack froze and the truck settled down to its idle roar. He made a motion for his gun again and the truck followed suit with a roar. He tried again slowly, inching his hand down little by little. Little by little, the truck got louder – until the sheriff finally drew his pistol and took aim. The truck shot forward through another wall as he emptied a few rounds into the driver's chest and jumped out of the way.

Through the dust and debris, he and the deputies could make out the large truck-sized hole leading into the kitchen.

"I just bought that damned fridge, you sons-a-bitches," the sheriff yelled as he fired three more rounds into the back of the driver, who turned around and grinned at him again. "Oh, shit. Run."

The truck crunched over the fridge and tried to turn around in the kitchen.

"I mean it, let's go!"

The group ran out through any nearest exit they could find – some chose the front door while others jumped out the newly made exit.

Sheriff Barrack turned back briefly to watch the truck pulverize his beautiful house as everyone dove into squad cars. The truck would be turning around any second now to come after him. He had already started his cruiser and was backing down the driveway when the doors flew open and two bodies clamored over the doors and tried to jump in. Luckily for them, the sheriff identified them as Wally and Detective Moses before he could grab his sidearm and dispatch of them.

"Where the hell's your car?" the sheriff asked angrily, still wheeling out of his driveway.

Detective Moses, breathless, pointed to an interestingly crushed police car fading into the distance.

"Shit," said the sheriff. He picked up his cell phone and dialed. "Parker, tell everyone we're headed to the lake house." Then back to Detective Moses. "Whatever that thing is, we gotta kill it."

Chapter 26   On the Way to Clay's Mom's House

"Mom, you really need to give it a rest."

"You are not getting in this car until you tell me what's going on, young man."

Clay and Bob were standing outside the old brown Buick Regal piloted by a skinny gray-headed woman in a mumu. "Come on, I need to get home."

"Where's your car?"

"I'll tell you on the way."

"Why's she wearing bedsheets?"

Clay said the first thing to come to his mind. "She's allergic to sunlight, mom. She needs some medicine."

"I don't think we've got anything she could use."

"I've got to order it for her."

"Why can't she order it for herself?"

"Because she's also a deaf-mute, mom. Can we go now?"

"You know the cops were looking for you?"

"You told me."

"You are coming home, with me, alone. You are in trouble. And she is staying here."

"Mom, I'm too old for you to tell me what to do." Clay reached through the open driver's side window and unlocked the back door. "After you," he motioned to Bob.

She sighed. "Get in. I told you hooking up with them boys would be trouble."

On the ride back home, Clay told a little truth and lied a little. He left in the stuff about his car and Chett's truck breaking down, but left out the stuff about dancing fried chickens and dead cats.

His mom only spoke once. "If your dad was here, he'd know what to do with you."

Clay thought that was mean.

At home, Clay raced to his room and turned on the computer. The last of the sun was setting outside, and Bob watched it through his venetian blinds.

Clay opened a program he had purchased for his astronomy class. It was, in a nutshell, a map of the universe. He fiddled with the settings to get a good view of earth and turned to call Bob over, and was promptly rendered speechless by a tall, large-chested, fair skinned, very toned topless woman.

She smiled at him, and even if he were counting, he'd have lost track of the number of times his eyes danced over her body. She was the perfect collection of all his favorite Playboy models. The dark hair, the ethereal and twinkling blue eyes, the light freckles – all on a six foot frame.

He could have been staring for seconds or minutes as far as he knew. Until he heard his mom from down the hall.

"Clay? Clay? You want some suppe... Oh. Oh! Oh, my!"

He scrambled to grab a blanket to cover Bob.

"Oh. I'm sorry. I'll just close the door."

Clay didn't know which shocked him more – the hot naked lady, or his mother's absence of freaking out.

He placed the blanket around her shoulders, and without her help, it fell off quickly. He tried again to no avail. The third time afforded a little more luck and it stayed put. Until she walked over to the computer chair and sat down. She pointed at the screen.

Clay explained. "Earth."

"Earth."

"Good!" He pointed out the computer's functions.

She repeated each word he said and seemed to comprehend.

"You're catching on really quick." He was talking to her breasts. "You must be really smart."

She giggled and maneuvered the mouse around the screen. "Earth," she said again, and zoomed out to show the solar system. She spent a few seconds rotating the view and watching the planets zoom around before she zoomed out to a view of the Milky Way.

"That's our galaxy," Clay said. "We're kinda out there on one arm of the spiral. Nothing really interesting in our neck of the woods."

She didn't respond, instead drawing a square around a bright group of stars much closer to the center. The group magnified and gained a little resolution. She repeated the process a few times until the only thing they could see was a really fuzzy ball. She turned and looked at him quizzically.

"That? There? Is that where you're from?"

"Planet?" she asked, circling the mouse around the fuzzy ball.

"There are planets around that star? Really? I mean, wow." He looked from the screen back to her breasts. "I guess there aren't any on the program because..." He tore his eyes away from her breasts and looked her in the face. He immediately realized why he felt better looking her in the chest. The deep blue in her eyes seemed to hold all the secrets of the cosmos. Clay could look in them and see the passing stars, the luminous nebulae, and the strange and exotic shorelines dotting the unknown.

He was brought back to reality by Bob's giggling. "Oh. What? What was I saying? Oh, planets. Yeah. I guess there aren't any on the program because we haven't found them yet. That's really, really, really, really far away. You'd have to be traveling..." his eyes grew wide and he spoke at a whisper "...at *warp*speed!" He shook his head. "What are you doing here?"

Bob continued to look at him and smile, innocent and topless.

"Oh, good lord. This is so cool!" He shook his head again, though a little more violently this time, trying to clear his mind. He picked up a DVD from his bookshelf and slid it into his computer. "This is the Encyclopedia Brittanica. I figure this is a good a place as any to get us on the same page. Have fun. Take your time. I'm just going to sit here and watch. And when you get done, if there's anything you still want to know, we've got the internet."

Clay watched in amazement as she started quickly navigating through the program. She stopped for a moment to pat her waist and look up at him in despair. She flattened one hand and made a squiggly motion with the other. He knew immediately what she wanted and handed her a pen and notebook. She smiled and accepted them, and Clay watched in further amazement as she began scribbling symbols and diagrams and the occasional alpha-numeric character.

Hours later, Clay was growing sleepy. Bob was still at it, but Clay had noticed less and less strange symbols and more and more of the alphabet he was used to. "If it's okay with you, I'm just going to lay here and take a nap. Wake me if you need me."

She looked at him and smiled.

"And Bob? Please don't go anywhere."

Chapter 27   Chett and Harry's Trailer

"Where the hell did twerp go?" Chett was peeking out his window and noticing the absence of both Bob and Clay.

"He said something about calling his mother," Harry responded.

"Dude, I do not feel good about this."

"You've been wanting to get rid of the both of them since yesterday."

"No, that's not it. Let's see. Why don't I feel good? Could it be that we killed a zombie? If there's one, there's bound to be more. Or is it that we really don't have a plan or anywhere to go and we're stuck here in this godforsaken trailer without my truck? I mean, if I had my truck, I'd feel a lot better about getting away from whatever's out there. The RV could handle a couple of zombies here and there, but it'd be no match against that unholy Dodge that's after us."

"Well, then, there's our plan."

"What's that?"

"Go get our truck," Harry said. "We've got the parts. We've got the guns. Let's go."

Chett looked at him disgustedly. "Do I need to remind you of what happened last night? Yes, we need to get the truck. Tomorrow. But tonight, we stay put and definitely do not go chasing trouble."

Chapter 28   Somewhere Else

Somewhere, a few million billion miles away, a patchwork ship piloted by two tall, skinny, big-eyed, bald, goatee-sporting aliens who – save for their slightly greenish-gray skin – looked like humans was tearing silently through the void of space.

"Clutch works!" Roscoe was giddy.

"Bossman's gonna be mad that we're late," Earl replied.

"Eh, he'll understand."

"Um, Roscoe?" Earl checked some lights on the console. "We're the only two people on board."

"So?"

"So, where is she?"

A look of alarm flashed across Roscoe's face. "She's not here?"

"That would be what I meant when I said 'We're the only two people on board.'"

"Maybe she got out in the hangar." Roscoe hoped that was the case. "Check the computer. When did we lose her?"

"Well, Roscoe, we 'lost' her when our sensors went out. Right when, oh, our main computer bank took that blast. Remember that?"

"Oh. Well, was she still on board when the computer came back online?"

"You mean at the Hangar?" Earl asked.

"Precisely."

"Nope."

Roscoe stood up to walk to the back, but floated up instead. "Apparently no one got around to fixing the gravity. Remind me to complain when we get done."

"You stole the ship."

"It's our ship."

"You didn't pay him."

"Why should I? Look at this shoddy work." Roscoe bounced off a console above him, accidentally pushing several buttons. An alarm went off. He spun around to mash the button to stop and in doing so pushed himself squarely into a storage bin, knocking it open. "Ouch. Give me a push, will you? I'm trying to go check on our girl."

Earl turned to look at the lanky floating alien. "Just thought of something."

"Oh? What's that?" Roscoe was executing a series of moves, trying to push off one wall on to another then back again – all in an effort to right himself.

"Think I figured out when we lost her."

"Oh? Did you now? Tell me, oh smart one, how you could do that without the computer. When, sir, did we lose her?"

"When you hit the button to dump the load. You had her tied up in the cargo bay."

"Oh." Then, "That either makes things really easy, or complicates the hell out of them."

Chapter 29   Chett and Harry's Trailer

"Look, I don't know how much longer I can take this. I know we slept not too long ago, but it amounted to little more than a catnap, and I'm about give out." Chett yawned and leaned up from where he had been resting on the couch. His neck and his head were throbbing, and he was too nervous to watch TV. His logic was to turn off most all the lights so as not to attract any attention, and keep the TV off so he could pay attention to any sounds that might come from outside.

The idea had done little more than making them a horrible combination of bored and jittery. Every snap of a twig or rustle of a breeze had the both of them grabbing their guns.

Harry was sitting on an old torn navy-blue recliner. He rolled his head to face Chett. "Let's take turns keeping watch."

A brief successful rock-paper-scissors match later Harry fell asleep on the recliner.

Three hours later, at three o'clock in the morning, they changed shifts.

Another three hours later, Chett woke to hear Harry whispering.

"Chett! Chett! Psst! Chett! Get up!"

Chett mumbled underneath the arm he had draped across his head. "Give me another hour."

"No. I mean get up and come over here. Now!"

Chett peeked out to see Harry staring out a window, rifle in hand. He stood up to walk over to him.

"Get your gun."

"What is it?"

Harry motioned for Chett to look out the window. Chett pulled the shabby curtain away from the shabbier venetian blinds and promptly jumped back, cussing.

"What in the blue hills is that thing? Damn!"

"I think it's a zombie," Harry answered calmly.

"Why's it just standing there?"

"Dunno. Been there all morning. It's moved around a little. Hasn't come any closer though. Just seems kinda lost."

Chett grabbed his gun and headed for the front door. Harry lunged to stop him.

"No!"

"Why not?"

"There could be more. You wanna go throw rocks at a hornet's nest?"

"You see any more out there?" Chett asked.

"No, I checked all the windows. But just because I don't see them doesn't mean there's not more out there."

"Good thinking." Chett thought for a moment. "But what do we do? I don't like waiting here. We still need my truck, and that damned thing's just standing there in the driveway. If there are more out there, then eventually they're going to make their way closer. And frankly, I think our odds are a little better if those things were still kinda scattered around. Don't really want them ganging up on us."

"I was afraid you'd say that." Harry shouldered his thirty-aught-six and pointed the scope at the zombie. "I figure he's a good hundred yards away. Our RV's only thirty feet away. And the way I figure it, we got two options." He paused. "One, I blow its head off from right here and we make a run for it."

"I like it," Chett said. "Let's go." He grabbed his gun again and headed for the door.

"Not so fast. There's no way we can carry all that ammo to the RV in one load." Harry motioned to the large wooden boxes of shotgun shells and other illegal incendiary devices. "So we'd have to make a couple trips, both of us, with our hands full." He paused again. "The second option is just to sneak out there, one of us, with the other covering him. You'll have to make a few more trips, but it'll attract less attention."

"I don't like how you just said that."

"Said what?"

"You said one of us would have to sneak out there. Then you said 'you', as in me," Chett pointed to himself, "would have to make a few trips."

Harry continued staring at the zombie as he spoke. "I figured since I was the better shot, I'd be the one covering you."

"Since you were the better shot? Since when?"

"Since always."

Chett remembered all their summer youth hunting camp days as children, and how Harry had won the marksman awards every time. "Rock, paper, scissors?"

Harry still looked out the window, but motioned to the ammo. "Get moving."

Chett sulked and walked over to the boxes. He grabbed a .45 magnum and strapped it to his belt. "Just in case." He grabbed the top two boxes and propped them on his chest to open the door, trying to see his feet so he could navigate the three metal steps that led to the ground.

Chett had only been outside for three seconds when Harry heard a crash, followed by curse, followed by three or four gunshots, followed by Chett yelling for Harry, followed by three more shots, then by a few empty clicks, another few curses, and a refreshed scream for Harry.

The zombie that Harry had been watching from the window looked up and started ambling toward the sound of the commotion. One bullet later and a headless zombie was now ambling in circles in the driveway. Harry reloaded as he jumped out the trailer door and met head-on the walking corpse that had scared Chett. He spun his rifle around quickly, hitting the thing in the side of the head, knocking it off balance. He ran a short distance, took aim, and took part of its head off. Another quick reload later and the rest of its head was gone, dropping the jerking zombie to the ground.

"Well, that blows that idea," he said.

"It was right there, just sitting against the trailer when I came out," Chett said breathlessly as he reloaded his .45. "Those things are impossible to kill! I put seven slugs in it!"

"Apparently, you gotta go for the head."

"That don't kill 'em all the way," Chett said. "Take a look at our friend in the driveway."

Sure enough, still wandering around in circles, was a headless zombie.

"Well, we need to get going. Grab the big stuff and let's go. I'm going to stay right here and shoot. Toss me a twelve-gauge."

Chett tossed him the gun and ran back inside. He came back out and almost jumped in the way of a very unfriendly blast from a shotgun. "Whoa! Warn me, okay? I'd like to not die today!"

"Sorry," Harry yelled back. "He just came around the trailer. I'll yell next time I see one."

"Don't need to. Look!" Chett pointed behind Harry to another zombie that had come around from the other side.

"Shit." Harry took aim and shot his head off. "Toss me a couple of slugs, will you. And quick."

Chett fished in the box and ran over to load Harry's pockets with shells. The next minute or so was spent with Chett hauling a few more boxes to the RV as Harry alternated between the thirty-aught-six for the few zombies coming out of the woods and the twelve-gauge for the ones that had managed to sneak around the trailer.

Finally, the RV having been sufficiently loaded, Chett jumped in the driver's seat as Harry took the passenger's.

"Who'd have thought this thing would ever run again?" Chett yelled.

"What?" Harry yelled back.

"Let's go get my truck!"

"What?" Harry yelled again. He couldn't hear a thing over all the ringing in his ears.

Chapter 30   At the Sheriff's Lake House

"Sheriff, I know the rest of the department knows to keep their noses out of our business, but if half the workforce doesn't show up for work today, they'll know something's up." Detective Moses lowered his binoculars, took a drag off an exhausted cigarette, and exhaled two streams of smoke through his nostrils as he stood watch at his window.

Wally spoke next. "I don't see anything, and haven't for the last six hours. I think we're safe."

"Shut up boy." The sheriff spoke as he rose from the couch and walked over to the coffee pot. "We're safe for right now because we lost 'em. It. We lost it. Whatever it is." He waved his hand, spilling some coffee. "Come clean that up, boy." He walked back over to the sofa and addressed Detective Moses. "But you're right. We gotta head back. But just as sure as we leave here, you can bet on whoever's in that truck causin' some major trouble for us." He shook his head. "I just don't see us coming out clean."

Detective Moses took another drag and continued looking out the window. "We need a scapegoat."

The sheriff looked up from his coffee. His interest was piqued. He thought for a moment. "Get me the owner of that car. Clayton whatever."

"Hensworth," Wally offered.

"Shut up, boy." Then to the group of Sheriff's Deputies standing watch at the various windows, "Get Clayton Hensworth. Bring him here. As far as I'm concerned, he's driving the truck, understand? He crushed your car, Moses. He crashed my house. You find him, you bring him to this lake house, understand?"

The deputies nodded.

"Unharmed. If I gotta stage something, I don't want no damned coroner going and saying he died of blunt force if I need to be shooting him up, understand?"

They nodded again.

"Let's go to the basement. I want each of you to have enough firepower to stop that truck."

Detective Moses looked away from the window to the sheriff. "Does that mean the heavy stuff?"

"Not the really heavy stuff. Just the shotguns, automatics and the semi-automatics. Fill your trunks with 'em."

The deputies marched down to the basement to stock up.

Chapter 31   At Clay's Mom's House

Clay rolled over as morning broke and snuggled up to the warm soft thing next to him in bed. And then he screamed and jumped out of bed, taking some of the sheets with him.

Bob wiggled deeper under the blankets that were left.

"Jesus. How long have you been there?"

Bob mumbled groggily from under a pillow.

"What?"

The pillow lifted a little bit. Not enough for Clay to see her, but enough to let Clay know she was looking at him. And he suddenly realized he had an embarrassing problem. One that would go away in a few minutes, but for now was making itself obvious. He grabbed the blankets from where he had dropped them on the floor and covered himself.

Bob giggled. "Good morning," she said.

"Good morning." Clay paused, letting it sink in. "Oh! Can you talk now?"

"Little," she said.

"Good." He had a life form from another planet in his room – someone possessing far superior technology, someone who could answer some of life's most puzzling questions. "Are you naked under there?"

"Mmhmm," muffled from under the pillow.

"Can I, can I see you? Naked?"

"Uhn uh."

Clay was confused. She was in bed next to him naked. She had taken her top off last night. Bashful she wasn't. Why now? Still, Clay decided not to push it. He had learned that human women didn't make any sense. Why would alien women be any different?

"Light. Bright."

Clay looked over to his Lite-Brite showcasing his latest rendition of StrongBad from Homestarrunner.com. Then he looked over to his window. The blinds were closed, but the curtains were open. He closed them and she kicked off the blankets.

She yawned and stretched, stood up, smiled, and walked over to her burqa. Clay's embarrassing problem wouldn't be going away any time soon, except that his mom opened the door.

"Clay, honey? I cooked you some, oh, oh dear. I didn't know you still had a guest." She looked down to the floor. "I'm sorry. It's my fault. I really should have knocked. Would your guest like some breakfast?" She didn't wait for a response, flustered. "Okay, I'll go and cook some more."

She backed out the door, accidentally banging it on her foot and flinging open a little.

"Hi!" Bob beamed.

"Oh, hi," Clay's mom mumbled, still backing out the door while looking down. "So nice to meet you. Breakfast will be ready in a few, honey." She closed the door behind her.

Clay was terrified.

"Eat!" Bob beamed again as she pulled the burqa over her head.

Cute, sexy, and an alien. Clay was in love. Terrified, embarrassed, and in love.

"Eat and go," she said from under her veil. "Find balls."

Clay looked down. He was still covering himself. "What?"

Bob laughed a cute laugh. "Eat, go find balls."

"Oh, you're looking for something?"

She nodded in agreement.

"Okay." Clay went to open the door, then hesitated. He definitely did not want to face his mother.

They walked into the kitchen, and his mom was finishing setting an extra place at the table. "Here you go, honey." She looked up and was momentarily taken aback by Bob's black burqa. She pulled Clay aside. "What's she wearing?"

"Oh, uh, it's a costume, mom. It's the only thing she had clean."

"What?" She looked up at him with a mix of incredulity and indignation.

Clay thought quickly. "We were at a convention last night, and she spilled fruit punch all over her clothes."

She bought it, nodding and looking back to the stove. She became a little meeker, something Clay was unused to. She spoke softly, unsurely. "Thought you said she was allergic to sunlight?"

Clay remembered saying that last night. He was right! She must not be used to a bright sun. He tried to cover for himself. "Yeah, she is, but that's why she chose that costume. She's supposed to be a Klingon." He knew she had no clue what a Klingon was supposed to look like.

She continued speaking softly, making small talk to herself. "Oh, okay then. You two have a lot planned today? Good, good. You two have fun."

At the table, Bob was already eating. And much to Clay's happy surprise, she was using utensils. Though sliding the food under her veil was taking a bit of work.

Clay looked around and realized all the windows were open. He thought if it weren't so bright then maybe Bob could take her veil off, so he ran around and quickly shut all the blinds and drew the curtains.

She responded by looking up and freeing her head, letting her hair fall over her shoulders and smiling coquettishly at Clay. But she didn't stop with just her veil. In a few more seconds she had stood up and freed the rest of her.

Clay's mom passed out.

He rushed over to her and made sure she didn't break anything on the way down. At least it was a soft fall, not a plodding thump. Still, she had bumped her head on the counter. Clay bent down to pick her up at the shoulders and was joined quickly by Bob, who picked her up at her ankles.

"To her bedroom," Clay grunted.

Bob nodded.

Clay backed into her bedroom. He always hated going in there – he felt out of place and it smelled funny. The décor was straight out of the nineteen-seventies. It gave him the heebie-jeebies. He navigated the narrow doorway without banging his mother around too much, but when Bob got to the door, she stopped.

"Bright," she said and set his mom's ankles down.

He sat her front end down on the floor and walked over to draw the blinds. Once completed, they picked her up and set her on the bed.

Bob was still leaning over her when she woke up.

She blinked. "Clay? Honey?" She was still getting her bearings. "Where am I?"

"You're in bed, mom. You bonked your head. You need to take it easy for a few."

"Oh, okay." She turned over and found herself staring at Bob's perfectly-shaped breasts. "Oh," she said again and passed out.

Clay grimaced and looked at Bob. "I like 'em," he shrugged. "Oh, well. Let's get out of here. Let me grab my laptop. We'll take her car. I'll leave her a note."

"Okay!" she beamed.

Chapter 32   At the South Pole

The weather in Antarctica was a balmy thirteen below zero. A light blizzard carried the sound of wisping wind around the mountains of snow. The few penguins out braving the weather were busy huddling around each other to stay warm and keep an eye out for the evil leopard seals. One of them happened to be looking up as a shadow the size of a city block came over them.

"Huh," the penguin thought. "Funny time for night to fall. Oh, well. My turn in the center of the pack. Gotta keep warm!"

Had the penguin ever seen a blinking red light before, he might have taken the shadow a little more seriously.

As it were, the spaceship landed right on top of them, crushing the whole lot.

Another penguin standing in a group several yards away rejoiced. "Dibs on the wifey when she gets back from fishing!"

Then a hatch opened and the projecting metal crushed him too.

The remaining penguins milled around and flapped about a bit. "Never liked him anyway," one of them thought. He watched as two figures emerged from the ship carrying little boxy things. "They don't look like leopard seals," he thought. "Maybe they have food!" He took a step forward. "Ah, wait. Could be a seal in disguise. I'll just wait here and see what happens."

Penguins aren't the smartest birds. Not as dumb as owls, but stupid nonetheless.

Chapter 33 - Still at the South Pole

Two tall, slender, greenish-gray aliens stood at the ramp. Roscoe and Earl, in short-sleeved uniforms, made their way out the hatch with scanners in hand. The snow whipped around them and into the ship. Roscoe slid his sunglasses on as he made his way down the ramp. Earl followed suit. Neither one seemed to mind the cold.

"Thought you said it should be around here somewhere," Earl said as he alternated between looking back and forth between his scanner and the gray-white landscape.

"I don't understand. We should be close enough to pick up the signal." He bonked his scanner with his hand, and when nothing came on the screen, he bonked it against the ship. "Batteries must be dead."

"The batteries aren't dead, Roscoe. It's just not here."

Roscoe bonked his scanner again and surveyed the landscape.

"This is where I put the coordinates. I don't understand."

"Well, we're not going to find anything here. I'm going back inside." Earl walked back up the ramp and into the ship.

Roscoe cursed and followed him.

Earl was staring at a wall-sized computer screen in the ship's planning room. The display showed a map of Antarctica. Roscoe walked up as Earl explained the situation to him.

"Basically, our sensors are only sensitive enough to scan an area about one one-hundredth the size of this island at a time."

"That's okay. It's not that big of an island."

"It's gonna take us at least a day, Roscoe."

"So?"

"We're late on delivery already."

"Exactly. One day isn't going to hurt us any more."

"It might."

"It won't. Besides, if you get a better idea, let me know. Put this thing on auto and let's play a game or something."

"But there's one more thing," Earl said.

"What?"

"What if it's not here at all?"

"Of course it is," Roscoe replied. "Why wouldn't it be?"

"It's not anywhere close around here, is it?"

"Apparently not. So?"

Earl took off his sunglasses and shot him a beady-eyed glare. He rubbed his goatee. "Because it could be anywhere, Roscoe." He hit a button and the display zoomed out to show the entire planet.

"So it'll take a few days, what's the big deal?"

"What's the big deal? What's the big deal!? I don't want to die because of some mistake you made! And I hope you realize that we're probably already dead as it sits now!"

"Mkay," Roscoe said coolly. "Can't kill us any deader than dead. So it takes a few days extra." He hit a button and a card-type game with alien dice replaced Earth on the display. "Grab your drink. We got a few days to kill!"

Chapter 34   On Highway 27

Clay and the burqa-wearing Bob were on their way to find Chett and Harry when his cell phone rang. He looked at it and cursed. "Hello?" He looked in the rear-view mirror and glanced at Bob. "Well, no sir. I'm sorry." He grimaced again. "I, uh – I can't come in today." He paused. "I'm sick. I've been throwing up." He paused again. "Why does it sound like I'm in a car? I'm, um, on my way to the hospital."

He covered the mouthpiece and looked at Bob, whispering, "It's my boss. I was supposed to work the floor today at RadioWorld."

Then, back to the phone and sounding sick, "Everything's fine, sir, other than me being sick. Why?" He paused for the reply. "Police? Looking for me? Not that I know of. Yes, sir. Yes, sir. Slip from the doctor? No problem. Okay, bye." He hung up and looked at Bob. "I think I really am going to be sick."

"Sorry," Bob said. She reached out her gloved hand to mime holding something. "Computer." She pointed to her hand. "Me computer."

A very pasty-looking Clay looked over at her, slowly.

"You have a computer? Is that what you're looking for?"

"Uh huh. And balls," she answered.

"And balls, of course." Clay rolled his eyes.

"Where is your computer?"

"Forest. Boom!" She made a gliding motion with one hand and smacked it into the other.

"Where you wrecked?"

"Erect!" She said.

"No, you wrecked."

"Erect!"

"No, you need to say 'I wrecked.'"

"Erect!"

"Oh, good grief."

He made a sharp curve around a bend in the road and ran right into a zombie, who rolled up the hood and landed in the sharp cradle made by the crushed window. Clay screamed and slammed on the brakes, partially dislodging the flailing undead from the windshield.

The car stopped on the shoulder of the road with Clay still screaming. He undid his seatbelt and placed his legs against the zombie's ass, which was sticking through the windshield, and kicked with all his might, further freeing the zombie. It rolled onto the hood and moaned.

Clay, still screaming, flung his legs around, dropped the car into reverse, and gunned it. The zombie rolled off the car and onto the ground at the same time Clay looked in the rear-view mirror to see a large approaching eighteen-wheeler. It blared its horn loud enough to scare him into putting the car back in drive and flooring it again. He whipped quickly to the right to put his car on the shoulder and then whipped quickly to the left to keep from going down a small embankment and into some trees. The quick motion to the left knocked the zombie directly into the path of the eighteen-wheeler, which – even after having slowed down – still made mince meat of the offending thing.

Clay flinched as the body crunched under the squealing tires. The eighteen-wheeler jackknifed in the road. He watched in horror as it slid to a halt. The driver jumped out, yelling.

Clay chose not to wait around for the ensuing drama. He pulled the Buick around, headed back the other way, and took off. Three seconds later he determined that he couldn't see out the ass-sized hole left by the zombie or the resulting spider web of shattered glass that had been his window, so he rolled the driver's side window down and stuck his head out.

He wanted to curse, cry, yell and throw up, but his finely-honed flight instinct was in full force. His sole mission in life was to get as far away from the scene as possible. He had to head back down Highway 27 for almost ten miles to get to the nearest road to Chett and Harry's.

Which meant he needed to take the back road, because it would be just a matter of minutes before the cops were on the scene, and thanks to Chett and Harry they were already after him anyway. He had really hoped to forget about the incident with the RV the other day on Nine Mile Cutoff. He knew when he woke up from being unconscious that it had seemed like a bad dream. But now, every time he blinked against the wind in his face, he saw the head resting on the RV's windshield, blinking and staring at him.

All he wanted was a nice peaceful ride to their trailer with his hot space vixen (the guys at work are *not* going to believe this!) and to find her computer.

Now he had just confirmed that his nightmare yesterday was indeed not a nightmare at all and that he had ruined his mom's car in the learning process.

Nonetheless, he managed to make it to the turnoff and get off the highway before he heard the sirens. Hopefully, he was safe.

Chapter 35   Nine Mile Cutoff

"Holy crap. They're everywhere!" Harry didn't know yet what an understatement that would turn out to be.

It had been a little over half a mile since they had run over the last zombie. They were still talking about it when another one ran out of the woods. Chett reacted on instinct and jerked the RV away, clipping the greasy, ghoulish figure and sending him spinning back into the tree line.

Harry held on to the dashboard with one hand and his rifle with the other. "Why did you jerk away? I thought we were trying to kill them," he said.

"We are. I didn't know what it was. Instinct."

"Where are they coming from?" Harry asked.

"If I had to guess, I'd say it would be from all these little church cemeteries around here."

"There's another one up there," Harry pointed out.

Chett looked ahead and saw the creature a few hundred yards ahead and was already aiming for it when he yelled and swerved suddenly to the left. Harry had been trying to sight the thing and had therefore not seen the nasty, smeared, broken-windowed Buick that lunged out of a small connecting road.

"What? What is it?" Harry asked and looked around.

"A car. Go ahead and shoot the zombie. I'll take care of it." Chett rolled down his window, grabbed a shotgun and climbed out to take aim at the tattered car over the RV's roof.

"Shit! Shit! Don't shoot! Don't shoot! It's me, Clay!" he yelled from inside the car.

"Clay? What the hell are you doing out here?"

"Can I tell you later?"

"Yeah. Sure," he yelled back, "but you might want to turn back. We're having a little problem out here!"

Harry leaned out of his window and aimed at something ahead, fired and reloaded.

"Can't go back. Got problems of my own!"

Chett looked ahead briefly. He looked back to the car. "Fine, follow us. Stay close, and watch out. You got a gun?"

"No!"

Chett slid back into the window. A second later, Harry hopped out the passenger side of the RV with a shotgun and ran over to the car.

"Listen," he said as he handed the gun to a very nervous Clay,

"Don't point that at her!" he screamed. He pushed the gun towards the windshield. "Now listen, like I was saying, this is a big gun, okay? It's only good for close range and it packs a kick. Here's a box of shells. Please, God, try really hard not to shoot us. Stay right behind us, and let us do most of the shooting. If you see something closer to you that we can't get, then and only then do you shoot, understand?"

"Yes, sir?" Clay said meekly. He was trembling.

Harry ran back to the RV and jumped in as Chett started driving. Clay turned in behind them and followed as closely as he could.

Bob took the shotgun from him. "Drive. Me shoot."

"You can handle one of those things?"

"Uh huh," she nodded.

"Great."

The next few miles were eventful for the RV as it stopped every so often to take out a zombie or swerved to run one over. Clay hated the ran-over zombies the most, because he couldn't see when that was going to happen. All he knew is that he'd see the RV bounce and he'd have less than three seconds to react to the body that would shoot out from under it.

Clay glanced out the passenger window and saw something jump out of the woods near them. He screamed as Bob shoved the shotgun out the window and fired. Bits of the zombie flew into the woods behind him. It was still standing as the Buick pulled away from him.

With less than a mile to go, the RV ran over another one. With the limited time he had to react after the RV hit them, Clay had been trying to roll over them with his tires or miss them completely. This one he caught dead-center of the car. It doubled over and grabbed at the hood. He screamed again as he hit the brakes and it slid lower down the hood. He floored it and watched it disappear below the grill and waited for the bump that would signal that the body had been cleared. Instead, he listened with growing unease to the scraping sound that meant he was dragging its body in the gravel.

He slowed to a stop and the scraping stopped with it. He put the car in reverse and tried to free the car that way, but to no avail. He cursed and put the car in drive again, trying to catch up with the RV. As he sped up, the thumping noise under the car grew louder. Even when he tried jerking the steering wheel left and right, the noise remained. His two options were either getting out of the car and dealing with it, or ignoring it for the rest of the trip.

It was the longest half-mile he had ever driven.

Once they reached the camp, Chett and Harry jumped out of the RV and ran towards the truck.

Clay yelled to them. "Wait! Wait! There's one under my car!"

Harry ran over to the Buick with a wrench in one hand and a shotgun in the other as Chett popped the truck's hood. Clay watched from inside the car as Harry leaned down in front of it, cursed, and jumped back. He took a few steps back and called out, "Um, yeah – you got a zombie under your car, all right." He flipped the wrench in the air and caught it. He spoke slowly, with an exaggerated drawl. "I can fix it fer 'ya, but it's gonna cost ya. Yep." He flipped the wrench again.

"Seriously, man, is it under there?"

Harry leaned down again. "Yeah, but he's stuck pretty good. He ain't wiggling, so I reckon he's dead. You can probably just jump out. You'll be fine."

Clay opened the door slowly and looked at the ground for any sign of zombie. "How am I going to explain this to mom?" he whined.

Bob took a cue from Clay and opened her door, jumping clear and walking over to the truck. Clay opened the door as wide as he could and stood on the bottom of the car near the seat, using the door and roof for support. He guessed a jump of three feet would land him far enough away.

As he turned around to jump, something jutted out from under the car and wrapped itself tightly around his ankle. He screamed as it started pulling on him and looked down to see a hand – gray, swollen and flaky – squeezing tighter and tighter. Still screaming, he started alternating between kicking it with his free leg and trying to jerk his trapped leg free.

Finally, with a sickening snap, his leg shot free forcefully, knocking him to the ground beside the car. He wasted no time in clawing the ground with his hands and feet, turning over onto his back to keep kicking at the zombie he feared was still after him, then turning back over to keep putting distance between him and the car.

Chett and Harry ran over and lifted the breathless but still screaming Clay to his feet. "Oh my God," he said between breaths. "We've got to kill it!" He looked down and started screaming and kicking again, strongly enough that he broke free of the hold Chett and Harry had on him.

"Dude! What's wrong? Chill out!" Harry was running after Clay, who was – in his blind terror – running back to the car.

"It's on me! It's got my foot!"

Chett shot past Harry and tackled Clay. He held him to the ground and barked orders at Harry. "For Pete's sake, get that thing off his foot."

Harry fell to the ground and wrapped Clay's hand-laden leg under his arm. The other leg was still kicking wildly. "Clay! Chill! Ow!" Then to Chett, who was still holding Clay's upper half in a bear hug. "Make him stop. He's kicking me in the kidneys! Ow!"

Chett grabbed Clay even tighter, making him gasp for breath. He spoke calmly. "Clay, you're okay. Calm down. I will knock you out if I have to. Harry's gonna pop it right off, okay? But you've got to hold still."

Clay calmed down enough for Harry to start tugging on the hand. It wouldn't budge. He fished his oversized pocketknife out of his pocket and turned to Chett. "I'm going to have to cut it off."

Clay, being able to see only Harry's back as he held his feet, assumed the worst and started screaming and kicking again.

"Ow! Damn, Clay, that's not a smart thing to do when someone's got a big-assed knife in his hands! I'm cutting the hand off, not your damned foot."

Bob walked over to Clay and straddled him, holding him to her chest. He calmed down immediately.

"Thank you," Harry mumbled.

"Welcome!" Bob beamed.

"She can talk?" Chett was surprised.

"Mph hmph," Clay mumbled from between her breasts.

Back at Clay's feet, Harry was trying to pull the hand free. Each time he would grab the hand, he would only succeed in pulling off a layer of rotting flesh. "Aw, man, this isn't cool." He looked over to the truck, then back to Chett. "Hey, toss me your work gloves. This is nasty."

Chett looked down at Clay and relaxed his grip. "You okay?"

"Mph hmph," Clay mumbled.

Chett ran over to the truck and tossed the gloves to Harry, who put them on and started struggling with the hand.

"Man, this thing's got a death grip on you."

Clay listened in continued horror as he heard a loud snap. Harry tossed a finger over his shoulder. "Well, we'll just have to do it this way, then."

Four more sickening snaps and tossed fingers later, Clay was free. Harry and Chett stood around the hand.

"It's still wiggling," Chett noticed.

"Told you. Them things are hard to kill."

"Hey, Clay, wanna come see this?" He turned to look at the pair still laying on the ground. "Clay?"

"Mphm rpheally."

"Did he say 'not really'?" Harry asked.

"Think so."

"Can't really blame him. Better view where he's at."

Chett raised his large work boot and brought it down, quickly and repeatedly, on the wiggling fingers. "Okay, Clay, you're safe."

"Mmph kmph."

"Clay, you can get up now."

"Mmph."

"The hand's dead."

"Mmph."

This time, Harry spoke. "Clay, come on. There might be more headed our way."

"Mmph."

"Oh, fer crying out loud. Chett, let's go fix the truck. I'll keep an eye out for zombies."

They left Clay and burqa-bedecked Bob in the odd embrace and set upon making the truck run again.

"You know," Chett said to Harry as they walked, "I've given up hope of anything making any sense. I'd say that them two like that is just really weird," he motioned to Clay and Bob, "but that's about par for the course lately. Hand me the spark plugs. Let's fix this truck and go home. I'll drive the truck. You drive the RV. We'll split the ammo fifty-fifty between the two of us."

Chapter 36   On Highway 27

Sheriff Barrack, Detective Moses and Wally had just pulled up to the jackknifed eighteen-wheeler that was blocking traffic in the road and stepped out of the car when the smell hit them.

"Ugh!" Wally held a handkerchief up to his nose. "What is that?"

The sheriff grabbed his own handkerchief, but Detective Moses wasn't lucky enough to have one so he buried his nose in his elbow.

"That's rotting meat, boy," answered the sheriff.

They surveyed the scene as they walked up to the driver. Traffic was backed up for a half mile in both directions. Wally peered under the tires and saw what looked to him to be a two-hundred pound chunk of hamburger meat. He tried not to get sick.

The sheriff walked up to the truck driver. "What the hell did you hit?"

"Oh...God..." The driver stuttered. "I don't know. There was this car, and it hit it, I mean it hit him, or it, or whatever it was..."

"Get to the point, boy," the sheriff ordered.

Detective Moses coughed. "Go easy on him, sheriff."

The sheriff turned redder than he already was. "Are you in charge here? Shut the hell up, Moses." Then, back to the shaken driver, "Go on. What happened?"

"This brown car. It was ahead of me and it went around this curve here. By the time I get up here it had stopped and was backing up. I thought I was going to hit it so I laid on the horn and hit the brakes and tried to get in the other lane, and it pulled back off the road but there was this guy standing in the shoulder or whatever, just standing there kinda stupid like he was drunk or something, and this car – this brown car, had its window all smashed in – well it goes back on the shoulder to miss me or whatever and ends up knocking that guy... knocking that guy... right into me."

Wally could see that the guy was trying either not to cry or not to get sick.

Sheriff Barrack and Detective Moses, still covering their noses, looked under the truck. Flies were everywhere.

The sheriff looked back at the driver. "How long ago did this happen? We just got the call."

"Just a few minutes ago."

"You gotta be kidding," he snorted. "That thing's been dead for days."

"No sir," the driver answered. "It was standing when that car hit him."

"Huh," he snorted again. "Where's that car?"

"It left, officer."

"Can you describe it?"

"Yes, sir. I mean, kinda. I was trying not to hit whatever that is so I didn't get too good a look at it. But it was a brown older-model Buick. Like a Regal."

"Get a look at the license plates?"

"No sir, but it shouldn't be hard to find. Its windshield is pretty smashed up. I mean, not just cracked, but seriously smashed in."

"You get a look at who was driving?"

"Looked like there was two people in the car, sir. After I hit that thing, I jumped out. There was a guy driving, and he had his head out the windshield. He was a younger guy, maybe even a teenager – couldn't tell. Had glasses. Black hair. Kinda nerdy."

"Clear the scene," the sheriff said. "Wally, you go and get them turned around and heading back the other way. Get them to a detour. Drive my car up there and block off the road with some cones. When you get done that way, come back up the other side and do the same thing for those cars. Understand? Moses, what kind of car does that kid drive?"

He understood the sheriff was referring to Clayton Hensworth. "He drives a Civic, sir. We found it on the road, remember."

"Right. A Civic, not a Buick. Have we found him yet?"

"No sir, but we're patrolling his mom's house and his job. So far no sign of him."

"What about his mom?"

"Don't think she's home, sir," the detective replied. "No cars in the driveway."

"Well, I don't know why, but I think the kid in the Buick is the kid we're after. Call it a hunch."

Detective Moses knew how accurate the sheriff's hunches were. "We'll keep an eye out."

"Good. Now grab that shovel and bag up that rotting mound of hamburger under there. We'll have the coroner look it over 'off-the-clock', understand?"

Moses understood well. The coroner worked for the sheriff on the side.

The sheriff turned back to the truck driver. "Look, I don't know what you hit, but as far as I'm concerned, you didn't kill it. Damn, the smell from that thing alone tells me it ain't a fresh kill. You say it was a person, but it coulda just been an old deer carcass someone was hauling off."

The truck driver looked under the eighteen-wheeler at the nearly two hundred pounds of meat. "Sir?"

"Maybe it was diseased or something. You gonna argue with me?"

"No, sir."

"Didn't think so. You got a tow truck on the way, so sit tight. We'll clean the mess up, and you're free to go. You say a word about this to anyone and I'll make sure it'll be the last thing you say. Understand?"

The driver nodded a reply.

"Good."

Sheriff Barrack turned around and walked over to Detective Moses. He held his handkerchief even more tightly to his nose as he spoke. "If that was Clayton in that car, he was headed down this road. Where would he be going?"

Detective Moses panted. "Could be leaving the city."

"Headed south? What's south of here? Nothing but a bunch of cow pastures and woods. The next town's twenty miles farther, and it's even smaller than here."

"Reckon he's headed to the hunting camp?" Moses asked.

The sheriff thought it over. "Wouldn't hurt to check it out. If his windshield's as busted as he said it was, then whoever's in that car ain't getting too far. Finish cleaning up. I'll call Sergeant Parker to come pick it up and take it to the coroner. You get someone to go by Missus Hensworth's house and check over there. I'll put out an APB, and then we go to the camp. Understand?"

Moses understood.

Chapter 37   At the South Pole

"Look, you drunk bastard, this'ss goinn nowhere." Earl staggered away from the computer screen, where he had been furiously trying to focus on the criss-crossing lines and squiggles that made up the map of Antarctica.

"Drunk? Drunk?" Roscoe's slurred voice took on a higher pitch. "You're drunk."

"Oh, shuddup. Look, man, we've done combed this entire island. It ain't here. And if it ain't here," Earl paused to push a button causing the computer screen to display a flat map of the earth, "it could be anywhere. Even unnerwater." He sloshed his head around to focus furiously on Roscoe. "We gonna die for sure if we gotta look everywhere. Too much time. Not enough time." He thought he was going to be sick.

"Let's rig us up something," Roscoe said.

Earl was extremely doubtful. "Whatcha got in mind?"

"Well, on our way in, didn't you pick up some energy surges coming from those ancient satellites floating around?"

"Yeah. So?"

"Just because those things would be ancient to us doesn't mean they'd be ancient to the creatures living here. They may be brand new to them."

"You seen the creatures here? Short and stupid. Ugly noses. Don't have the sense to move away from an opening hatch. It's a wonder they could even put anything up in the sky at all."

"Well, they won't miss one. We'll borrow it and see if we can't tune it to scan for our shipment."

Earl closed one eye to keep from seeing two Roscoes. "That may just be the smartest idea you've ever had."

"Do you dare doubt the great Roscoe?" He said as he stretched his arms out and tripped over a chair. "Computer!" he barked. "Computer!"

An agitated female voice filled the room. "Yep?"

"Get us outta here."

"'Kay. Where to?"

"Find us a satellite to borrow."

The computer clicked off to do its job.

Earl was holding his head, still looking at Roscoe. "Why her?" He couldn't stand the personality Roscoe had assigned to the computer.

"She reminds me of our wife. So every time I get homesick, I get reminded why it's better out here. Better sit down."

They didn't have a chance. The centrifugal force of the launching ship anchored them to the floor.

The annoyed voice came back on. "Should've been sitting down."

Chapter 38   At Chett and Harry's Trailer

"Thank you, sir." Harry accepted the cold beverage Chett had just handed him. "Race starts in just a minute."

After the past few busy days, the motley group of four had bunkered themselves in the trailer, wanting nothing more than to take a break from crazy shit. Clay and Bob were in the kitchen, trying to cook grilled cheese sandwiches (Clay having been put off of hot dogs for life). Chett and Harry were sitting on opposite sides of their ratty couch watching Busch league NASCAR.

Harry glanced into the kitchen and watched Bob. "Why does she always have to wear that thing? Is she one of them Moslems?"

Clay was quick to reply from the kitchen. "She's allergic to sunlight."

"Where'd she learn to talk?"

"She taught herself."

Harry remembered how good she looked without the Burqa on. "Bob, is it? You can come sit over here when you get done." He patted the couch.

Bob looked at him. He couldn't see her face to tell if she was smiling or not.

Clay tried to act like it didn't bother him. "She can't. After we eat, we've got some stuff to do."

"*We've* got some stuff to do? What the hell are you two gonna do?" Harry looked around the small trailer. "There ain't nothing to do but take turns watching NASCAR or keeping watch for zombies."

"Well," Chett replied indignantly while flipping their sandwiches, "that's what you think."

"Suit yourself," Harry said.

Chett and Harry settled in, got comfortable, and got lost in the race. They were loudly cheering a rather nasty wreck when the TV went to snow. Chett stopped in mid cheer, his hands still in the air. "What the hell?" He walked over to it and applied the classic broken-television repair maneuver. He hit it squarely on top. It blinked a little, but all he could see was snow.

"The TV works fine," said Harry, "it's the satellite that's out."

Chett checked the cables to the back of the TV. "Everything seems fine."

"Outside, Chett."

"Damn." He looked around. "Where did they run off to?" Clay and

Bob were conspicuously missing. "Clay? Bob?" He walked to the back of the trailer and checked in both the small bedrooms and the bathroom. Empty.

He and Harry grabbed shotguns and peeked out the front door. They couldn't see the satellite dish – as it was on the side of the trailer.

"See anything?" Harry whispered.

"Nope. Lemme run look out my bedroom window and see if there's anything out there." Chett's bedroom window afforded a wonderful view of the dish.

Harry heard him curse and watched curiously as he stormed out of the bedroom, muttering. "What the hell do they think they're doing?"

"What?"

"Clay and that bedsheet-wearing bimbo are out there messing with it."

"Maybe they're already trying to fix it," Harry countered.

"You're kiddin', right? They're the ones that screwed it up. And I'm the one that gets to go out there and drag their dumb asses back in here."

"Good luck," snorted Harry.

"Bitch, grab your gun. You're going with me."

Harry sighed and stood up, shaking his head.

Outside, Chett and Harry noticed the absence of live zombies. One of the dead ones lay slumped against the trailer, though it was still twitching. The headless zombie in the driveway, also still twitching, was at least twitching on its side and not going anywhere.

"I think we got all of 'em," Harry said.

"Hhmph," Chett snorted. He was listening closely to any sound he could hear. The breeze rustled a little, carrying a bit of Clay's and Bob's murmuring. Both he and Harry, being fairly in tune with nature, noticed the eerie silence. No birds, no dogs, nothing.

Chett crept up to the pair and stood less than a foot from Clay. He whispered loudly. "What the hell's wrong with you? You got a death wish?" he whispered. "If one of them things don't kill you, then I will for screwin' up my TV." Chett looked at the satellite and moaned. Mounted on the horn was Chett's microwave, duct-taped more than usual. From it were hanging wires of varying sizes and colors. Some made their way into a box that had one single wire coming out of it. Chett traced it to a laptop sitting on the ground.

Still open-mouthed, he looked at Clay.

"Sorry about your microwave," whispered Clay. "I know it's the only way you get any nutrition. And sorry about your satellite, but Bob needed it."

Chett was still speechless, so Harry spoke for him. "What the hell for?"

This time, Bob spoke. "E.T. phone home."

Clay laughed. "I taught her that." He could tell they weren't amused. He stopped smiling. "Seriously. She's trying to call home. Sorta." Clay looked up into the sky. "The only problem is, well, it'll only take fifty-thousand years or so for the message to get there. She's kinda hoping that there'll be someone a little closer who'll get the message."

There was someone closer. They did get the message.

Smoke drifted slowly upward toward the only light in the dark gray room. It cast a dim and stark pallor on the two creatures whose heads rested on the table below it. They were sitting across from one another. One of them was blowing bubbles with his saliva, and the other one was flailing his arm, hitting his head repeatedly in an unsuccessful attempt to hit a large flashing red button on the table.

A female's voice broke the silence.

"Gentlemen?" it inquired.

No response.

"Earl? Roscoe?"

Neither one responded. Earl was still flapping his hand around trying to find the button.

"Oh, good grief," bitched the computer. "Here." The rest of the lights came on and forced Earl to squint, covering his head with the arm that wasn't flailing around still trying to find the blinking button seemingly on its own accord. Roscoe still blew bubbles.

A yellowish smoke entered the chamber from the vents in the wall. Roscoe and Earl sat up immediately.

Roscoe looked alert, aware, and confused. "Did I win?"

Earl, just as confused, looked around. "No, it was me. I think."

Both of them looked down to notice the red button still flashing on the table. Both of them, still sitting across from each other, looked from the button to each other and back again. And both of them, as if on cue, scrambled to hit the button while at the same time stop the other from doing so. They were wrestling on the table, each trying to push the other away while pushing himself closer, when the computer spoke again.

"I mean, look at you two."

They paused temporarily, looking around, then started scrambling again.

"The game's over, nitwits," it said again. "Really, now. Look at yourselves."

They were still wrestling.

"Oh, if that's the way you're going to be." The button stopped blinking and receded into the table.

"Whad'cha go and do that for?" Earl whined.

"Yeah," Roscoe complained, "Why'd you go ruining our fun?"

"Fun?" the female voice retorted. "Next time you want to go play cards, how about I just don't save you? Huh? It would sure be a lot saner around here."

"Oh, we weren't that bad off," said Roscoe.

The computer snickered.

"Are you done with the satellite?" Earl asked, changing the subject.

"Well, if you two weren't that bad off, then you'd know that we didn't need to borrow a satellite after all. I docked with it and started the adjustments, when we got a message."

"Oh?" Roscoe still had Earl in a headlock.

"Came in over microwave. Very outdated. In fact, I wouldn't have picked it up at all except that I was trying to listen to what was already coming over the satellite. Couldn't make any of it out. All gibberish, I suppose. I could decode it, but what's the bother?"

"Get to the point," Roscoe barked.

"Oh, very well. If that's the way you're going to be. Well, like I said, everything was just gibberish, until..." She hesitated.

"Well?" Earl urged.

The computer hesitated again. "Apologize," it said.

"For what?"

"Your tone," it answered.

"Yeah, this has got to change." Roscoe stormed out of the room and deep into the ship.

By the time Earl caught up with him, he had mounted a rather large weapon on his chest and around his left arm and was cussing the lift.

"She won't let me on," he moaned. Roscoe's weapon was part plasma-gun, part bionic add-on. The gun was so heavy and Roscoe's race of aliens so skinny that an additional support system had to be built. While by itself it looked threatening, against Roscoe's tall and slender frame it had the unintended side-effect of appearing very cartoonish. It was almost as big as he was.

Earl looked at the weapon and understood why the computer was being stubborn. "She's not dumb, you know. She's a computer."

"We'll have to take the stairs."

"Give it a rest, Roscoe. Do you know how many flights that is? Just apologize."

Roscoe ignored him and stormed off down the gray corridor, stopping at the door to the stairs. He jostled the handle.

"Bitch locked *it* too." He looked at Earl, then down the corridor. "Back up."

"Oh, no," Earl said. "You are not about to shoot that thing..."

But he didn't have time to finish his imperative, because, indeed –

Roscoe had shot the thing. Bits of flaming door lay strewn about the floor. A few more shots took out the rest of the thick metal door, and Roscoe popped his head into the dark stairwell.

"Lights!" he barked.

Nothing happened.

"LIGHTS!" he yelled again.

Nothing happened again.

"You think what? She's not going to open the doors but she'll turn the lights on for you? I don't see why she doesn't turn all the lights off..."

"Good idea," said the female voice. All the lights went off.

"When I get done with her," Roscoe grumbled, "you're next."

Chapter 40   At Clay's Mom's House

Detective Moses banged on the door and listened closely in the silence.

"Hello? Mrs. Hensworth? Anyone home?"

Wally watched from a few feet away, wiping sweat from his brow as the sun overheated their dark uniforms. He thought he saw a finger appear between the venetian blinds in one of the bedrooms.

"Someone's home," he whispered to Moses.

"Huh?"

Wally pointed to the window where the offending finger appeared. "Think I saw someone."

Moses pounded again. "Mrs. Hensworth? Open up. It's the police."

No response.

Wally tried this time. "Mrs. Hensworth? We have news about your car."

A few more moments of silence followed. Wally and Moses gave up and turned to walk to their car when they heard the front door creak and a frail voice calling.

"Hello?"

Wally peered into the darkness and made out the light-blue silhouette of a woman in a mumu holding an icepack to her head. "Mrs. Hensworth?"

The reply came in a frail, shaky voice. "Yes?"

Detective Moses spoke. "Do you drive an older brown Buick Regal?"

She looked them over. "Who are you?"

"We're Sheriff's Deputies, ma'am."

She held the icepack loosely to her head and continued speaking to them from behind the darkness of her partially-opened front door. "What do you want? I already told you Clay's not here."

"Your car, ma'am," answered Detective Moses. "We received information that your car was involved in a hit-and-run accident, and we'd like to ask you some questions. What kind of car do you drive?"

She continued appraising them distrustfully. "It should be obvious the kind of car I drive."

Detective Moses hiked his pants around his large belly. "Why would that be?"

"It's sitting right over there, look for yourself." She pointed around the house to an empty driveway.

Detective Moses and Wally both craned their necks, looking for a car they already knew wasn't there. "Ma'am, there's no car there."

Wally could tell that Detective Moses was growing tired of Mrs. Hensworth's long pauses. Nevertheless, she paused a little more before answering.

"What do you mean? The car's right over there." She gingerly nodded her ice-pack laden head to where the officers had just looked.

Wally craned his neck to look again, but Detective Moses kept watching the lady still partially hiding behind the door.

"Mrs. Hensworth," the heavy man sighed, "there is no car parked in the driveway."

She stuck her head out the door and looked to the empty driveway and seemed to hesitate for another moment before shuffling slowly out the front door. Wally was reminded of a penguin (one wearing a light blue mumu and pink bunny slippers) as they followed her to the driveway.

She stood studying the spot for a few moments before turning to look down the road, as if the car would be parked somewhere else.

"Where is it?" she asked them.

"We were hoping you could tell us," answered Moses.

She continued staring at them, bewildered.

Wally decided to try to learn the make of her car again. "Ma'am, what kind of car do you drive?"

She turned to face him. "You already know, don't you? A Buick. You said you had news about it? Where is it? Did someone steal it?"

Wally was amazed at the sheriff's intuition. He had somehow known that the boy he had been looking for and the car were linked. His car, the Civic, must have broken down so he borrowed his mother's.

"Is there any chance your son may have it?" he asked.

"Clay? Why would he have it? He's got a car." She shifted the ice pack to her other hand.

Detective Moses went to speak, but Wally shook his head. He registered a brief flicker of annoyance on Moses' face and guessed it was his frustration at being overridden by a rookie.

Nevertheless, Wally carried on. "We can file a report for you, but I'm sure you'd like the chance to call your son and see if he borrowed it without telling you?"

She paused another moment, still looking them over, and said, "Yeah, I suppose he's borrowed it. Don't see why, though. I'll go call him."

She shuffled slowly away. Moses grunted. Wally had a minute to spare (given how long it took her to shuffle back to the house), so he tried another question. "Would anyone be with your son, ma'am?"

At this, she stopped shuffling and seemed to sway a little. She reached out with her free arm and Wally could tell she had a sudden dizzy spell. He took her arm and waited until she was steady to try again.

She started shuffling forward again.

"Your son? Would anyone be with him?"

She stopped and got dizzy again.

"Are you okay? Do we need to call an ambulance?"

A moment or two passed as she again steadied herself and waved them off.

"No, no..." she responded feebly. "I'm okay, but I do need to sit down for a few." A few seconds later, still shuffling forward, she asked, "This doesn't have anything to do with them two boys, does it?"

Wally and Moses glanced at each other, eyebrows raised. Wally responded.

"Two boys?"

"Oh, you know. Whats-his-names. Harry. Chett and Harry. Them two boys."

Detective Moses couldn't think of a reason they would be involved, so he asked for clarification. "Why would it have anything to do with them?"

"Oh, I don't know," she waved the thought away. "But usually if something's up, they're involved, aren't they?"

Moses grunted and followed her inside.

The kitchen was still dark with the curtains drawn, so she turned on the light and ambled over to the phone.

"Oh, look here. There is a note. 'Mom, my friend and I had some car trouble so we had to borrow yours. We'll have it back later tonight. Call me if you need it sooner, but try not to as we've got some errands to run. Sorry about earlier. Hope you're feeling better. Love, Clay.'

"Well, there you go." She turned to the officers. "He's got the car. No need to report it missing." She stopped to consider something for a moment. "But why are you interested in it? Did you say it was in an accident?"

Moses spoke up quickly. "Ma'am, we don't know for sure if it was your car or not. All we know is that an older-model brown Buick Regal left the scene of an accident earlier."

Still holding the icepack to her head, she questioned them nervously. "Was anyone hurt?"

Wally looked to Moses, who continued answering. "Luckily, no. But we're just trying to get information. Could you call him for us?"

She looked down at the note. "It says not to call..." She trailed off.

"I understand," Moses replied, "but we really need to speak to him."

"Oh, okay, I'll call him." She picked up the phone and dialed. After a few seconds, she covered the mouthpiece and whispered to the officers. "No answer. Leave a message?"

Moses whispered back. "Get him to call you as soon as possible."

She relayed the message to Clay's voicemail and hung up. Moses handed her a business card and told her to call his cell phone as soon as he calls her back and to try to get him to come home.

They turned to leave, and Wally remembered the note saying he was with a friend. "Can you describe who he was with?"

She looked faint again and sat down in one of the cheap barstools facing the Formica counter in the kitchen. The icepack slipped a little. She winced. "Oh, Lord."

Both Moses and Wally looked at each other, unsure of how to proceed.

Finally, she spoke, looking down at the table. "Yeah, he might be with someone. He was with someone this morning." She winced, as if saying it hurt. "A girl."

Wally questioned her softly. "Do you know her name?"

Mrs. Hensworth shook her head slowly, rattling the ice in the pack.

"Can you give us a description?"

She winced again.

They waited for a response.

"She was wearing bedsheets."

"You mean, like a toga?"

"No. Like one of them Muslims."

"Like a burqa?" Wally asked.

Detective Moses looked at him incredulously.

"What? I'm fresh outta college, remember?"

Moses rolled his eyes and looked back at the pitiful Mrs. Hensworth. "What color bedsheets, ma'am?"

"Black."

Moses summed up the situation to Wally as though Wally didn't understand. "So we're looking for her son and a Muslim accomplice in a brown Buick Regal." He turned to Mrs. Hensworth. "Thank you for your time, ma'am. And I hope you get to feeling better. Remember, if you hear from them, please let us know immediately. Have a nice day."

And with that, they turned and left the house.

Once they were outside, Wally turned to Detective Moses. "Just because she's wearing a burqa doesn't mean she's Muslim."

Detective Moses heaved his heavy frame into the car, shaking it violently in the process. He lit a cigarette and rolled the window down as he backed out of the driveway. "What the hell else would she be, rookie?"

Wally had to concede that he had a point. He got lost in thought about the last few days and was shaken out of his concentration by the detective's suddenly erratic driving.

Moses had already pulled the car to a stop on the shoulder of the road and jumped out before Wally could ask what was going on. He put his hand on his gun as he exited the car and saw Moses staring into the sky.

He spoke without looking down. "What, in the name of the Almighty, was that?"

Wally tried to follow his gaze and saw nothing. "What?"

"Jesus. You didn't see that?"

Wally tried to remember if indeed anything had caught his eye while he had been thinking. "No."

Moses shot Wally a look he was getting used to. "How could you not? It fell right over us."

Wally was exasperated. He had seen nothing. "What did?"

"That big-assed shadow."

Now that he mentioned it, Wally did remember a brief flicker of darkness. He had thought they had just driven under a bridge, but on second consideration he remembered that this road didn't have any bridges for miles.

Wally glanced at Moses, who was again staring at the sky. "Did you see what it was?"

"No, but whatever it was is big or flying low, and heading that way." He pointed to Nine Mile Cutoff.

"Do we call for backup?" Wally asked.

"No. Hell no. If it's something we need to hear about, we'll hear about it. We're not going chasing trouble. I'm going to call the sheriff and let him know that Clay's the kid in the car. That's who we try to find."

Wally was starting to wonder if he'd made the right career choice.

Chapter 41 At Chett's and Harry's Trailer

"Can I have my microwave back? I'd like to cook something up. Not to mention I'd like to have my bedroom back, please."

Chett followed the wires leading from Clay's laptop on his bed to the window, where they snaked outside to the dish in the yard. They had moved the operation inside after hearing some unsettling rustling coming from the woods.

Clay was absorbed in his computer and replied without looking up. "No, I already told you. We need to run it for at least a full twenty-four hours. We really need to let it go for a week or so. Bob and I figured out where the areas of highest extraterrestrial population densities are, and we've got to try to hit most of them. A good twenty-four hour spin will at least blanket the area with the signal, though it is pretty weak. Kind of a shotgun approach. Then we'll try – notice I emphasized *try* – to focus the signal to pinpoint a few of the more populated clusters. There's no one anywhere close to us – I mean, the soonest anyone'll get the signal's at least forty or fifty years, but you never know..."

"Holy shit," Harry laughed, "I think he's going to cream his rocketpants underwear."

Clay continued typing with one hand and flipped Harry off with the other.

"What's the message say?"

"I don't know," Clay said. "I don't speak whatever Bob speaks."

"But she speaks us. I mean, she speaks English now, right? Couldn't you ask her?"

Clay stopped to look up. "You need an interpreter to ask her something in English? How did you graduate high school?"

Harry looked to where Bob lay on the bed on her stomach, next to Clay. "Bob, what does the message say?"

She lifted her head and looked through the veil at Harry. "Help," she said.

"See?" Clay said. "She's just sending out an SOS."

Harry had an uneasy feeling. "How do we know it's an SOS? I mean, think about it. She's an alien. What's she doing here?"

"She crash-landed, I already told you," Clay sighed.

"Where's her ship, then?"

"I reckon it's out there in the woods somewhere where you picked her up." Clay paused to think for a moment. "And now that I think of it, we actually need to get back there sometime soon. It may help her. She's looking for something, and I think it's near the crash site."

"So let me get this straight." Harry folded his arms as Chett leaned against the door frame, listening to the weird conversation. "We've got a hot alien babe here in the house, all alone, wearing black bedsheets, and you seem to think there's no danger in this?"

Clay looked dumbfounded. "Well, not really."

Harry shifted his weight to another foot. "And you don't find it a little strange that when our friend here showed up," he pointed to Bob, "so did they?" He pointed to the window with his thumb, and Clay understood that he was talking about the zombies.

"Well, yeah, I think it's strange. But I trust her."

"I don't know if I do."

"Trust?" Bob asked.

Clay turned to her and spoke softly. "I trust you, Bob."

"You just trust her because she's the first girl that's paid you any attention."

Clay turned to Harry, anger in his eyes. "What has she done to deserve your distrust?"

Chett finally spoke up. "Well, for one, she stole my RV and wrecked my truck."

"I'm sure she had a reason. And she did you a favor; you should be thankful. When's the last time that nasty-assed thing ran?"

Harry jumped back in. "Well, it's just not right. It's not normal. None of this is."

Chett took his weight off the door frame and shrugged. "We probably wouldn't be fussing so much, but you had to go take away our NASCAR."

"Go pop in a movie or something. You'll get your precious NASCAR back, I promise." Clay took a deep breath and spoke with more determination, surprising himself. "But right now, we're helping Bob, and that's that. I seem to remember helping you guys out of a few tight spots in the last day or so, even tearing my car up in the process. We missed class, I'm probably fired from my job, the cops are looking for me, we got chased by who-knows-what in a big-assed truck that looks like it could tear yours to shreds..." Clay trailed off and looked over at Bob, whose warmth he could feel radiating into his leg as she laid beside him, "...and I've got a hot space chick next to me. I'm helping her. You're helping me. End of discussion."

Chett and Harry were stunned.

"Now, as for the Dodge of Death, I didn't get too good a look at it, but something about it is familiar. You two said it came out of the ground, which doesn't make any sense, but seeing as how you guys were sober when I picked you up I have no reason not to believe you. I've put two and two together and I'm guessing that whoever was in that truck has something in common with our friends outside." He pointed through the window. "But why would they come out of a lake bed? And what's bringing them back to life?"

"Um..." Harry stuttered.

"It was a rhetorical question. I don't expect you to know. But something is. And as we've already seen, it's bringing more of them back to life. But I can't do anything about that. All I can do is help Bob here get whatever she needs."

"Hmph," Harry snorted and walked out of the room.

"There's one more thing," Clay called after him. Chett was still listening. "As far as I can tell, this hasn't hit the news or the internet yet. So I'm going to guess that hopefully, and I do mean *hopefully*, whatever's happening is isolated to here."

Harry yelled from the living room. "You sure?"

"Pretty sure," Clay yelled back.

Harry's voice echoed through the trailer. "Good. Pack up and get ready to move. We're getting our asses out of here."

Clay slid the laptop off of his lap and rested it softly on the bed before storming into the room with Harry. "You've got to be kidding. What about Bob? This is going to take at least a few days."

"Forget it, bucko. Let me remind you again of the situation, okay? There's dead things out there wanting to get us! And somehow, some of those dead things got a truck, and they're out there somewhere trying to get us too. You got a woman who doesn't speak English, who wears bedsheets but strips 'em off at the drop of a hat, and who can fix a hopeless piece-of-shit RV without blinking. Now I don't trust her, but I trust her more than the things outside, and I am *not* going to put my ass on the line for her."

Clay was speechless.

Harry picked up where he left off. "You said those things aren't anywhere else? Then that's where I want to be – anywhere else. You with me, Chett?"

Chett looked at them from where he stood in the doorway and scratched his head. "He does have a point."

Clay's voice lost the bravado it had just recently gained. "What? We have to wait! We're safe here. Just wait a day or so, then we'll go."

Harry was already in the back of the trailer near his bedroom, loading a duffel bag. He yelled to be heard. "Thirty minutes, we're leaving. I suggest you get packing."

Clay looked down the hall at Harry, then to Chett, then to Bob. He sat back down on the bed, defeated. Bob snuggled up to his leg, spreading warmth.

Chett shrugged and went to his closet to grab some clothes as Clay watched him angrily.

Finally, Clay spoke. "I'm not going?" It came out sounding much more like a question than the declaration of fortitude he had hoped for.

"What?" Chett almost chuckled. "Don't be that way. Sure you are. It's safer for everyone."

"Just because I said it hasn't been on the news or anything doesn't mean it's not happening elsewhere."

Chett, his hand resting on a thick camo shirt, turned to Clay and smirked. "Come on, you bet it'd be all over the place."

"Well," Clay tried to think, "They could be covering it up or something."

"There's only one way to find out. I suggest you start wrapping things up there." He motioned to the wires leading out of the laptop through the window.

"Fine. But could we at least go back to the woods and see if we can find anything? Bob's looking for a computer of sorts, I think."

Chett thought it over, remembering the arc of the truck as it jumped out of the lake bed. "I don't know, Clay. I don't think the woods are too terribly safe right now. Why don't we swing out of here for a while, wait for things to blow over, then come back and look?"

Clay knew his was a lost cause. "What about my mother? We left her passed out on the bed. We can't leave her in this mess."

"Why don't you call her and tell her to pack up and skedaddle, too?" asked Harry from down the hall.

"Are we going to take her?" yelled Clay. "Because her car's still sitting back at camp with a zombie underneath it, last I checked."

"Either we'll have some people riding in the back of the truck or we have to take the RV. Not sure which is safer." Chett thought about it for a few. The truck could handle much that the RV couldn't, but the people riding in the back posed challenges. If the truck got in a sticky situation, could everyone hold on? He made up his mind. "We're taking the RV too. I'll drive my truck, Harry'll take the RV. Bob can ride with me, seeing as how she can apparently handle a shotgun, and you and your mother can ride with Harry."

"No. I'm riding with Bob."

"That's just not going to work, Clay. Someone's gotta be able to ride gunner in both vehicles."

"Then we take the truck."

"Where is your mother going to ride?"

"She can have the cab with you and Harry."

"What, and you and Bob ride in the back?"

"We can hold on."

Harry yelled from the other room. "I can strap 'em in pretty good. Might work better, anyway. Better angles, less chance to get split up. We'll keep the guns in the front and give one to Bob here."

Clay tried the last tactic he could think of. He spun his computer around and pointed to a line of yellow and red dots moving across the screen. "I think we should stay here. There's a serious squall line headed our way."

Chett just shook his head and hunched his shoulders. Harry yelled from the other room again. "Then we better get to bustin' some serious ass to beat that thing east."

Since Clay had nothing to pack, he continued sending signals to the great colony of space babes he hoped was in the sky.

Chapter 42   On Highway 80

The soft clack-clacks of the expansion lines in the old highway rolled rhythmically under the substitute cruiser. Wally thought he and Detective Moses had just had a productive meeting with Mrs. Hensworth, but his head was still swimming with the enormity of the situation.

After his stint in the National Guard while going to college, he had gone into law enforcement as what he felt was a natural progression in his career. And sure, he'd had his fair share of fun under the good 'ole boy system and gotten away with it, just like he'd let others get away with stuff. But that was part of the game of trading in respect. Give some, take some. He knew the value of keeping his mouth quiet, and while he had heard rumors that the Sheriff's Department was corrupt, he figured it for the typical stuff – looking the other way or taking a little off the top of back-room gambling deals, officers being a little reckless with their personal lives but not being brought to task for it – that kind of stuff. It was, he told himself, for the greater good. You got the killers and rapists off the streets in exchange for a little leeway. After all, it's a dangerous job. There needs to be perks. Wally could understand that.

But he was unsure of how he felt with the news that it got as bad as the sheriff himself having someone (or someones) buried in their truck in a lake bed. While undoubtedly there were reasons for wanting someone removed, how is it that they ended up there?

He couldn't just go asking questions, either. So he found himself stuck in the awkward no-man's-land of corruption. Not enough information to justify wanting out, but not enough to justify actively participating. Luckily, though, his train of thought was interrupted by a cursing Detective Moses.

"Damn. Damn damn damn. More nationwide coverage my ass." He threw the cell phone down onto the console in the middle and turned to Wally. "Lemme see yours."

Wally handed his over, and fought to catch it when Moses flung it back at him. "Shit. Yours is out too." He sighed. "I gotta use the radio."

"SO-Nineteen to SO-One."

A few moments of silence passed and Moses tried again.

"SO-Nineteen to SO-One."

A few more moments of silence passed before a crackly, upset reply came. "SO-One. What the hell is your twenty, Nineteen?"

Moses turned to Wally. "He wants to know where we are."

"I know that. I was in the military, remember."

Moses spoke back into the radio. "Nineteen to One – we're on Highway 80."

"Goddamnit, Nineteen, I been trying to call your cell for an hour. Get to a landline and call Parker."

"He's gone fishing, hasn't he sir?" Moses asked. Wally understood it was a veiled reference to the lake house.

"I reckon so. You need to make getting in touch with him your number one priority. One out."

Moses turned pale, which is tough for a large black man to do. "This ain't good, Rookie. Sheriff sounds like he's in a little hot water, and for him to lose his cool over the radio, you know something's going down. Hang on. There's a little mom-and-pop down here."

Wally felt the force of the accelerating car push him back into the seat. A few minutes later Moses eased off the gas and pulled into the empty half-gravel, half-paved parking lot boasting a lone gas pump and weeds growing through the concrete.

Moses lifted his heavy frame out of the car. "Stay put. I'll be right back." The car shook with its suddenly lighter load.

Wally was fiddling with the radio when he saw a very flustered and upset-looking Detective Moses storming out of the store.

The car sank as as it shifted to accommodate his weight. He threw it in reverse and started backing up before he even closed the door. "We got trouble. Oh, we got trouble. We gotta get to the lake house, and now."

"What's wrong?" Wally asked.

"Shit." Moses slammed on the brakes, thrust the car into park, and popped open the trunk. He jumped out, ran around to the back of the car, and came back with an armload of various heavy weapons – shotguns, rifles, and a semiautomatic or two. "Here, take as many as you can and throw the rest in the back."

Wally found the order a tough one to obey as the car was jerking back and forth with Moses' quick and erratic driving. The fact that the weapons were loaded and flailing about as he tried not to point them at anything important – like himself or Moses – made it more difficult.

Moses never answered his question, but smoked cigarettes silently as they sped to a situation which, given the recent turn of events, Wally knew would be sticky at best.

Chapter 43   On Highway 80

The houses dotting the highway blurred by as Chett's truck sped over the rolling hills. The warm wind rolled over the cab and into the bed of the truck, where Clay and Bob sat side-by-side against the cab and watched for anything undead, though truth be told, Clay's mind was more on the soft warmth he felt radiating into his legs and arms from beneath the burqa next to him.

Never mind that there were zombies on the loose, that he was on his way to pick up his mother (whose car he had wrecked), that the sky was turning an ominous gray, and that the cops were after him... As long as Bob was next to him, the world was okay. And after all, hadn't the short trip down Highway 80 been uneventful? Sure, Chett and Harry had to kill a few zombies as they exited the driveway, but since then for Clay it had been a peaceful summer day like the ones he used to have as a kid where he would sit on his front porch swing and listen to the calm breeze and the thunder in the distance before wasting a few more hours doing nothing more than listening to the peaceful rain. Yep, a peaceful summer day. If he forgot that everyone was holding large-caliber shotguns and running from an assortment of ne'er-do-wells.

So engrossed in his day was he that he really didn't register the police car whipping past them, headed the opposite direction. Not until he heard Harry yell from the front – cursing and telling them to get down in the bed of the truck.

Clay's heart stopped. Had the cops seen him? Surely not. They were, after all, headed very quickly away from them. There was hope, he told himself. There was hope.

****

"They were hauling ass," Wally said as he craned his neck to look back at the truck.

"They can keep hauling ass, for all I care," muttered Moses.

"Say, that kid – the one who blew up his dad's shed – what does he look like?"

Moses spoke succinctly, focused on the road. "Black hair, glasses, skinny kid."

"And didn't his mom say he was traveling with a friend?"

"Guess so. You got a point?"

"Well, I think they were in the back of the truck that just went by.

Coulda been any skinny kid with black hair and glasses and a black-bedsheet wearing person next to him, I don't know..."

Moses took his eyes off the road and glared at Wally. "What?"

"I said, I think that was the kid we're looking for. In the truck. Just went passed us." Wally was still craning his neck around, watching the truck disappear in the distance over the rolling hills.

"Shit. You sure?"

"Like I said, could be anyone, but there was someone wearing bedsheets next to him."

Detective Moses fumbled around for his cellphone before picking it up. "Damn it! Still no signal!"

Wally followed suit and checked his phone. "Same here."

"Well, shit. Gotta use the radio again. Sheriff's gonna be pissed. No choice, though.

Wally neglected to mention that the occupants of the pickup were packing some serious heat.

****

Clay was shivering with the first splats of fat raindrops that made it into the back of the truck. It had started raining. He yelled from the bottom of the cab into the sliding glass window on the back of the cab. "Do you think they saw us?"

Harry turned around to look and half smiled, yelling through the wind. "Nah. They haven't turned around, and they didn't slow down. It's all right. You're okay. But stay down."

Clay yelled back. "Well, if it's all the same, I say we take the back roads, okay?"

Chett joined in the yelling. "I'll take the first turnoff. It's just a few miles up the road."

They would never make it.

Instead, what would happen would be this: Thirty seconds of peace would pass. Clay would spend it enjoying the wind in his hair, the feeling of a warm girl sitting next to him, the humid fragrance of summer.

Then he would hit his head quite violently on the roll bar to which he and Bob were strapped as Chett slammed on the brakes and performed his signature bootlegger's turn. This maneuver would allow Clay to see the reason they were now all speeding in the opposite direction: a massive roadblock with at least six or seven cruisers. And it was a roadblock of the complete-stop variety. Every square inch of road ahead was covered by cop cars. There was no way through. The only way out was back the way they came.

Clay's heart would race as he ducked down into the bed of the truck, but he knew it was too late. They had seen him, and they knew where he was. He prayed and pleaded with every deity he had ever believed in that the roadblock was for someone else. Half of his analyzing brain went to work rationalizing that there was no way there would be a roadblock with six or seven cop cars and all those flashing lights just for him, but it did no good. The other half of his brain was working just as hard to convince him that yes, indeed, those lights were for him.

And just as quickly as his brain reached those decisions, it told him in no uncertain terms to duck down and hide in the bed of the truck, overlooking both the points that it was a bit like trying to close the proverbial barn doors once the horse was already loose and also that he was, thanks to Harry's former Boy Scout knot skills, strapped immovably erect to the side of the roll bars.

So, Clay could only watch hopelessly as the deputies began climbing over one another, racing to their cars. He was detachedly intrigued by their resemblance to a pile of ants that had just been disturbed by an errant foot – complete stillness followed by a confusing explosion of movement as the little critters rushed to the attack.

In the cab, Chett and Harry were already thinking the same thing. Better haul ass and try a shortcut. But Harry was already doing the math in his head. The nearest turn off was three miles away. The cops would be all over them in no time, and they knew the back roads as well as Chett and Harry. Their only hope was that the officers now already pulling out of the roadblock would not know the trails in the woods as well as them.

And Chett was already praying that somewhere, there would be the holy grail of a deep rut that only their truck could pass, stopping the chase at least temporarily.

Clay could only listen with a sick queasy feeling in his stomach to the thunderous engine giving everything it had to carry its occupants down the bumpy road. His head banged against the cold hard bed of the truck with each clack of the oversized tires on the highway.

Then the sirens started. Clay wouldn't be able to see what was going on, but he would be able to listen with increasing nausea as the sirens grew louder and closer, until they were right behind them and he could make out the flashes of red and blue on the back of the cab.

He also wouldn't be able to see the cop behind him aiming his shotgun at the back tire of the Scottsdale. He wouldn't understand why Chett had suddenly slammed on the brakes, but he would hear the screeching tires of the patrol cars behind them as they tried to avoid a pileup. And he would look up to see Harry yelling back at them, "Oh, shit! Hang on!"

And he would also feel even more nauseated by the sudden pitching of the truck down the forty degree embankment to the side of the road.

But the last thing he would feel is the crunch of his head against the truck's cab as the truck hit a tree and came to a quick stop. After that, everything was a little fuzzy.

****

Sheriff Barrack spat into the dust by the side of the road as he climbed out of the cruiser. "Sonofabitch, boys. We got 'im. Sic the dogs on them two boys and lets us get to the lake house and clear the goddamned mess up."

One of the policemen walked up to the sheriff. "Sir? What about the girl?"

"What about her? The dogs'll find her too. Git that boy first. He rides back with me."

In the confusion, no one would notice the sheriff's cruiser door open and close, seemingly by itself. And Clay would still be too unconscious to notice a strange indentation on the seat next to him.

Chapter 44   In the Woods

Negotiating a course of action is extremely difficult when the person with whom you are negotiating is running full blast with an armload of guns. And it is further complicated when the ground is slippery from rain.

Chett ran breathlessly, trying fruitlessly to keep his armload of guns from clanking against each other. "Where...to...?" he called to Harry.

"Camp!"

Chett stumbled as he partially tripped on a log. "Shit." Then, "That's gotta be ... five miles away ... or more ... Dogs'll get us ..."

Harry replied simply two words, "Silver Creek."

Chett understood his desire to hit the shallow creek to lose the dogs. It may work, he thought. But if they were going to hit the creek, why not head the other direction down the creek back to their trailer and pick up the RV? They needed transportation. The creek would put them out within a mile of it. So, he muttered, "Nope ... Head other way ... to trailer ... get RV."

"Hope we don't ... get guns wet," Harry panted. "... Would really ... suck."

Here the topography of their little town of Bovina came in to save them. Millions of years of wind blowing across the Midwestern plains had deposited rich, thick dirt just east of the Mississippi River. These Loess Bluffs, as they were called, created a really hilly geographical oddity rising out of the otherwise flat Mississippi and Louisiana deltas.

It was the untamed and eroded Loess Bluffs that allowed Chett and Harry to set foot in water almost immediately. Both of them knew how easy it was for a hunter to lose a deer in them, and they only hoped it would be as easy to lose themselves.

Like the saying "All roads lead to Rome," they knew that any drainage basin where they could walk in water would lead either to the Creek or to the Big Black. And like the saying "Beggars can't be choosers," they didn't give a shit where it took them as long as it was away from the mean people with the badges and guns. And dogs.

Too bad they had to leave Clay and Bob, but they had no time to unstrap them. The cops would have caught everyone, including Chett and Harry. No sense in that, they thought.

And, indeed, little trickles of rain had already begun weaving their way down little ditches worn by erosion from storms past. And those little ditches with little trickles of water wound their way down hills and ravines to create larger trickles at the bottom.

It wasn't long before Chett and Harry were ankle deep in water and sloshing along the miles to their trailer. Every time they felt like they were losing their wind, a distant bark would break from between the trees to remind them that there was a greater good they were running for. Namely, their asses.

A thought struck Harry as he ran. He called out to Chett without looking at him, breathlessly. "Bob?"

Chett had also noticed that she had managed to get away almost immediately, but that she hadn't joined them. But now wasn't the time to think of that. Now was the time to think of running.

Chapter 45   On Highway 80

Pain was the first sensation Clay got back, primarily because the knot on his head where he slammed into the truck cab was now bumping rhythmically on the window of the cruiser and his hands were going numb from where they were handcuffed behind him. Had he had more presence of mind, he wouldn't have groaned and would have let the sheriff keep on thinking he was unconscious.

The sheriff heard the groan and looked in the rear-view mirror, smiling with his eyebrow cocked. "Boy, you got *any* damned idea how much trouble you caused me?"

He was pleased by the wide-eyed and terrified reaction he got from Clay.

"Let's just say that I ain't had this bigga pain in my ass for a long while."

Clay stared on, eyes bugging.

"I got a mess to clean up. Big ole' mess. Shit everywhere. One them 'parents went away for the weekend and sonny threw a party but his friends destroyed the house and he's left trying to figure out how he's gonna tell mommy and daddy how it wasn't him that did this' kind of messes. Get me?"

Clay tried to answer but could only croak. He cleared his throat and tried again, timidly. "Not really?"

"Well, let's just say you're the kid left holding the bag." He paused for effect. "Now, you got some questions to answer, kid. Think of it as kind of a test. You know those kinds of tests where they tell you there's no right or wrong answers?"

Clay nodded.

"Well, it's kinda like that. At least there ain't no right answers."

Clay's face went white.

"Let's start with the truck. Who's that truck belong to? How are them boys Chett and Harry involved? And don't be lying to me, boy, because you sure ain't gonna like the consequences. You just need to assume I know the truth to begin with, and I'm seeing how much or how little pain you're going to be in later."

Clay's response came quickly. He told the story from beginning to end. "Shit, shit shit, I swear I don't know. I swear I don't. All I know is I was asleep one night, and they called me to pick them up and they were being chased by this big-assed truck and they were really scared and we managed to get away from them and I don't know why they were being chased – they never told me – and we've been running from these ... things ... ever since and just trying to get out of town for a little while and I don't know why I'm in trouble and I don't know what I did and whatever I did I'm sorry and I'll fix it I swear. If it's about the cell-phone company thing I'm sorry, I only did it to find Chett and Harry and help them and I'll never do it again so please don't hurt me. I don't know what I did, what did I do? I didn't mean to do anything and I didn't do anything. I wrecked my mom's car and she's gonna kill me and I killed my car too and oh, gosh, I don't know what's going on."

He closed his eyes and tried to rest his head on the window again until he remembered how much the knot on his head hurt.

The sheriff laughed. "Well, boy, it sure don't pay to be you right now."

"Why? Why? What did I do?"

"You? Oh, you didn't *do* nothing. You were just in the wrong place at the wrong time."

"So I'm off the hook? I'm not under arrest?"

"Oh, no, no. You're not under arrest." The sheriff flashed a cold smile in the mirror.

"Really? Oh, God," Clay sighed with relief.

"Speaking of God," the sheriff continued, "You ever read the Bible?"

"Bits and pieces..." Clay answered.

"Well, back in the old days – back in the Old Testament, you know, they couldn't just pray for forgiveness. It wasn't that easy. They had to get an animal to put their sins on, and then kill that animal."

"Really?" Clay was still relieved not to be under arrest.

"Oh, yeah." The sheriff kept talking, but kept his eyes on the road. It was raining hard and fast, and the wipers swished back and forth as fast as they could. "They liked to use goats. Put the sins on the goat, kill the goat, walk away clean and blameless."

"Goats? Why?"

"Don't know and don't care. Guess they had a lot of 'em to get rid of."

"Huh." Clay was silent. He didn't know what the sheriff was getting at, and the sheriff sensed that.

"It's where we get the word 'scapegoat'."

"Oh." Clay had a sinking feeling, but self-preservation kept his mind from going down that path.

The sheriff looked Clay in the eyes and smiled. "Baaaa."

Clay groaned again and laid his head back on the headrest and tried not to cry or pass out.

He rode that way, silently, and stared out the window as the dark gray sky brought night early.

Chapter 46   Close to the Trailer

The sky had gotten so dark that Chett and Harry could barely see by the time they hit the small ravine they knew from their days and nights spent hunting close to home. They climbed and stumbled up and down the steep hills, keeping one hand on the ground and one on their guns.

And, for perhaps the first time in their lives, Chett and Harry were scared shitless. Sure, there had been plenty of times when they could have been killed in their shenanigans. They had rolled more than one truck. They had had more than their fair share of industrial "accidents". Their lives had been threatened by angry husbands, jealous girlfriends, and various and assorted vermin.

But this was different. Visibility was at a minimum. It was raining. They were well armed, but they were also well aware that based on very recent events it was completely possible for a member of the undead to just pop around from behind a tree.

Even though they were well accustomed to listening for sounds in the woods as they were hunting, doing so now was painfully complicated by the rain hitting the trees. Every creaking branch and every snapping twig just flat out scared the shit out of them. Every fat drop of rain breaking through the thick canopy above and landing with a splat on a dried leaf scared the shit out of them.

Everything scared the shit out of them.

And rightfully so.

They were less than a hundred yards from the tree line demarcating their property. They could almost make out the lights of their trailer another hundred yards beyond that. Two hundred yards to go.

Then things got a little hairy.

The ground was wiggling. Writhing.

Chett felt something slide under his foot and recoiled from the smell of rotting meat.

Harry had apparently experienced the same and was already freshly into his batch of cursing. Neither one of them could find a foothold on solid ground.

"Man, really?" Chett asked exasperatedly as he hopped from foot to foot, trying not to fall. "What now?"

"Um, yeah..." Harry sounded less concerned all of a sudden. "Don't think it's anything but the remnants of our trash coming back to life."

Chett looked around in the fading light and made out all the signs of their detritus – bits of plastic and paper. "Really? You mean this is leftovers trying to get at me?"

"Yeah. I think so."

Still hopping from foot to foot, Chett began yelling. "Really? Trash? What the hell, Harry, I thought you were taking everything to the dump."

"Are you that dense? I'd only be gone what, fifteen, maybe thirty minutes."

Chett was about to respond with some derogatory remark, but noticed the faint outline of another person standing somewhere close to the tree line. Someone standing still. Maybe. Looked like someone. And it's probably damned smart to be safer than sorry.

He ordered Harry to quit cursing and hopping.

"But this damned lump of rotting nasty-assed hamburger meat is trying to climb up my leg. Shit, shit shit!" Harry kept kicking his leg, trying to free the offending gray goo.

"Seriously. Shut up." Chett whispered loudly. "There's someone up there. I'm taking aim. Just in case. Don't know who it is. Don't know if it's friend or foe. I hold a bead, you go investigate."

"Oh, hell no," Harry whispered loudly back. "We've been through this. God gave me good aim. I hold a bead, *you* go."

Still whispering. "Nope. Not gonna do it. It's *your* turn. I dealt with the nasties last time."

Harry didn't respond, but tried to sight the silhouetted form in his scope. "Can't make anything out. Too dark. But it's kinda jerking and twitching. And unless it's Uncle Crank, I don't think it's friendly."

Chett's view was partially obstructed by a tree. "Fine." He whispered without taking his eyes off what he could see of the thing. "We do it together. We both keep a bead."

Harry, also whispering without looking away. "No, damnit, *you* go. I'll keep a bead. You take in the big picture for more of 'em."

"Bastard. All right. If he moves, you bust him in the leg or something. Just in case it is friendly."

"It ain't friendly, Chett, but all right."

The two began moving slowly through the wiggling field of forgotten trash.

"Shit, Chett. It's tougher than hell to keep him sighted."

"If..." Chett paused. "When... when we make it out of this mess, remind me to kick your ass for making this dump and after I'm done kicking your ass, remind me to make you clean it up."

They walked on a little ways. Chett spoke again. "Where the hell are these things coming from? Seriously."

"*Now* you wonder that? I've been asking myself the same question since this morning when we had to blast our way out of our trailer. And I think I have an idea. But it's still not the time to talk about it."

They crept closer through the woods. Both of them noticed with building unease that the sounds of cracking and popping things were increasing.

And then, as was most often the case, all hell broke loose.

Harry was trained too intently on the bogey in the distance to notice what Chett both said "Shit!" at and suddenly shot at. But that's all it took for the thing in Harry's sights to jerk stiff and look their way and start running. No more argument needed, thought Harry. Sayonara, zombie mofo. His head exploded just an immeasurable fraction of a second after Harry pulled the trigger.

Harry had barely thrown the thirty-ought-six over his shoulder and swung the twelve-gauge around before Chett was cursing and shooting again. The forest roared with the thundering report of the shotguns.

Forgoing whispering for out-and-out yelling as the preferred method of communication (probably due in part more because of excitement caused by the flock of zombies which had just chosen to present itself around them than the deafening dialog of the twelve-gages), Chett yelled "Run!!!"

Harry yelled back. "No! Fight our way out!" A ragged, tattered, rotting zombie leapt from behind a tree just a few feet away from him. The first shot tore a hole through the left part of its chest, causing it to lean, top heavy, in that direction. The next shot, quickly reloaded, tore the rest of its torso off. Harry yelled again. "Shouldn't be too many more of them."

The two of them walked slowly toward the tree line, each firing in a semicircle around him as the zombies approached.

Chett was the first to notice that Harry was wrong about the number of zombies. "You're wrong!" he yelled.

The zombies were definitely ganging up on them, some in greater states of decay than others. And it was taking too long for Chett and Harry to reload. Each pause gave the forming circle of zombies another few feet.

And since they were both picking off the few undead that were closest to them, they succeeded in merely better forming the circle that was slowly approaching. They were worried when it was one or two. They were scared when there were five or six. They were sure they were dead when there were more than twenty. They'd have to stop and pop open a case of shells soon. Their pockets were empty. Both of them knew they wouldn't have the time. By the time they ran out of shells, it would be too late.

Chapter 47   Over the Trailer

"This is good. What is this? Is this what they have for television? What are those things?"

"I guess they're animals of some sort."

"So it's some kind of nature program?"

"No, dipshit. It's what's going on right outside."

"Hunh." Earl scratched his slightly bulbous head as they sat in the darkened room, watching the huge screen. "You don't reckon that's who we're looking for?"

"Nope. They don't look anything like the people we saw earlier."

They sat and watched the action.

Too bad they tore out the vocal circuits, those idiots, the ship's computer thought. *Serves them right. That's what they get. No vocal circuits mean there's no one to tell them that I've been accessing all sorts of data since we got here. These things got wide-open hot spots all over the place. No one to tell them that what they saw earlier was a bunch of stupid – albeit cute – penguins, and certainly no one to tell them that penguins are certainly not in charge of the planet. Those idiots think penguins are people and that those two people out there – who actually are people – are animals. And they're about to die, and they probably are the people Roscoe and Earl are waiting for. And they're going to let them die. Because they're waiting for the penguins to come home. Idiots.*

Chapter 48   Close to the Trailer

Chett and Harry were back-to-back, spinning in a slow circle and taking out as many zombies as they could. They were shooting as fast as possible, one firing while the other reloaded, each shot only seconds apart.

"That's it for me, buddy," Harry yelled over his shoulder. "I'm out. I gotta break open a box. Toss me one, will you?"

"Then we got a problem," Chett yelled between blasts. "Because you got the box."

Harry only had to say one thing. "Shit."

Chett dug in his pocket and handed Harry three shells. "Here you go. We got three more each. Use 'em well."

Harry knew it was no use. "You keep 'em." He swung his gun around like a baseball bat, hands on the barrel. "Let's play ball, bitches!"

Chett squeezed the trigger. Five shells left. The zombies got closer.

Chett squeezed the trigger again. Four left. The zombies got closer.

They spun slowly around so Chett could knock off one just a few feet away. Three left. Many, many more zombies than shells.

Chett fired the last three rapidly, his shoulder aching from the retort of the gun. He swung his gun around like Harry and yelled over his shoulder. "It's been good, Buddy."

The zombies closed in on them and they started swinging with everything they had left in them.

******

From nowhere, suddenly, light. Bright, white, 'holy shit my retinas are forever seared, I'm gonna get a lifetime suntan in fifteen seconds', light.

Even blinded by the zebra stripes of trees silhouetted in the foreground, Chett and Harry kept swinging as hands began grabbing and tearing at their clothes.

They didn't notice as the zombies on the perimeter of the mob silently vaporized. They didn't notice the smell of charred wood as the silent, powerful lasers cut through the thick trees at the speed of light and picked them off one at a time, killing five or ten a second. All they would hear is the sudden snap of wood charring as a laser cut through it. But even that was muffled by the moaning zombies. All they knew is that suddenly, there were no hands on them. Scraped, cut, torn, blinded and bleeding, they were alive. It ended as silently as it began with just the shotgun-deafness muffled sounds of rain falling through the trees overhead.

They were still shielding their eyes against the flood of lights coming from the direction of their trailer when everything went dark. Dark, dark. Darker than 'I could see my room in the dark until I turned on the bathroom light to pee and now my irises are closed' dark. Because they had just seen the brightest lights they had ever seen or would see. Had they been in a less scared shitless frame of mind, they would have amazed themselves with the possibilities of spotlighting deer with lights like those.

But, as it was, neither one had any idea what was going on. They didn't know that everything undead was once again dead. They didn't know that they were safe.

All they knew was that there were zombies and there were hands tearing at them, lights, then nothing. Just blindness. They kept swinging blindly at the empty air in front of them, waiting to connect with something. After a few minutes, the swinging slowed down. The blindness was still there, but no zombies.

Neither one of them could tell what direction they were facing. They had no option but to stand poised to fight and wait until they could see again. And they were very, very unhappy with the recent turn of events. The mind, they discovered, when challenged, settles upon the inevitability of death. Adrenaline kicks in and helps escort the body and mind, without panic, into the next life – if there is any. In this state, the mind and body are ready not to be anymore. There is no fear, there is only the white numbness of one's body giving every last drop of power it has to the task at hand. Either surviving or not. And it is not prepared to survive unscathed. The mind expects injuries. It expects blood loss. It expects, if it survives, to do so with a lot of damage.

So when all of a sudden, impending death never arrives – nor does any damage – the mind can only reel. The leftover adrenaline has nowhere to go. The danger is gone in an instant. The mind doesn't know how to cope.

It would, one would suppose, begin by piecing together its immediate surroundings. But Chett and Harry had been robbed of the sense of sight. The only course of action either of their minds could put together was to stand, as they were, back-to-back in the forest and wait. For something. For anything.

And they continued standing this way for a few more minutes until they slumped down, still back-to-back, and sat in the mud, guns in their hands and knees up to their chins.

Neither one spoke. They just waited.

Until both Chett and Harry simultaneously experienced the sensation of their guns being wrenched quickly from their hands.

Then total sensory blindness. Something knocked them out cold.

Chapter 49   At the Lake House

Clayton Hensworth had definitely seen better days. True, he told himself, he had never felt more alive. But he also never felt more dead. He was sure of it. He was going to die. And there were so many things he had never done. So many things he had done that were the wrong things. What accomplishment was hacking the Cray at the Waterways Experiment Station when he had never lost himself in the warmth that only a woman can provide? What accomplishment was having "free" internet service for life and every single movie and CD and mp3 and mp4 and Div-X movie ever made since the beginning of humanity without leaving some sort of the mark on the world?

The mind considers such things when it knows the end is near, especially as a device to remove itself from the predicament at hand. Pondering such things allowed it to forget about what was really going on. Namely, that a very beaten and bleeding Clayton Hensworth was hog-tied and handcuffed to a chair in a dank, dark, wood-paneled basement. He had been beaten by the sheriff's ruthless thugs to within an inch of consciousness and had been left there to consider spilling any vital information he might be holding back.

He drifted between a state of unconsciousness and sleep for what might have been hours. His only clue that any time had passed had been the changing of the two goons on opposite sides of the room that had been guarding him.

It might have been four hours. It might have been eight. His watch did him no good, seeing as his wrist was strapped behind him to the chair.

He remained in this state until the excitement started. All he knew was that he was deep into his second set of guards when some other deputies shuffled brusquely into the room and whispered to the other officers. He remembered that the officers seemed to really perk up and look rather concerned. There was a lot of gesturing and pointing to the floor, some of which he understood must have been a command to watch the hostage, no matter what. You stay here, those motions said, come hell or high water.

They both came.

It would be a few minutes more. Clay heard it first in the distance – that deep unholy rumbling sound he had first heard a few days ago. As the sound got louder, the officers seemed a lot more agitated. From where he sat, the sound seemed to come from different directions at different times. It was circling the house. Almost taunting him.

Clayton reacted the only way instinct would let him. He had never been a fighter. He had always chosen a self-deprecating humor to diffuse tense or aggressive situations. But his humor couldn't save him this time. No, this time he fought. He fought against everything he could – the handcuffs, the chair, the ropes – everything. Of course, his every effort was completely futile. But at least the thoughtless action of struggling freed him from regarding further what was, for sure, his very near death.

As the sounds circled the house, he noticed with a fear already so immense that it seemed unable to grow any more, that it – the truck – he knew it had to be the truck – was getting closer. Coming for him.

So it was a race now. Which was going to kill him first? The cops or the truck-driving zombies from hell?

Clay could begin making out other sounds coming from outside. Pops, booms. Short bursts of something cracking. Fireworks? No, Clay thought. That makes no sense. Gunfire. Somebody was shooting at something. The truck? Were they shooting at the truck? Clay could only hope.

The sheriff burst in, red faced, soaking wet, and panting. Clay noticed he was really, really wet. Dripping wet. Clay stopped struggling long enough to try to make out the conversation. He could tell that the sheriff was in even more of a horrible mood than the deputies. The cool veneer of emotionless evil was gone, replaced by sheer panic.

Were the cops scared of this thing too? Clay didn't know whether to find comfort or joy. If the cops were scared, then maybe they'd forget about their most recent pastime – namely, intermittently beating the shit out of Clay for sport.

The sheriff favored short bursts of high-decibel utterings to the quiet whispering of his subordinates. He stripped off his shirt revealing a broad, red, meaty body with a semi-transparent undershirt stuck to him. He ranted as he stripped off his shirt, he ranted as he stormed out of the room and down a hall, and he ranted as he came back with a towel and dried himself off.

"What the everlasting fuck is that thing? How much fuckin' ammo we gotta pump into that thing to put a dent in it? Fuck, boys, we are in ever-deepening shit. That damned truck is bulletproof. And it's fucking with me." He wiped his face off, spat on the floor, and kicked his sticky wet trousers to the floor. He eyed the beady-eyed lanky redheaded officer that Clay understood to be his greasy yes-man/henchman hybrid. "Parker, get me a dry uniform. Now, boy! Move it!" He threw the wet uniform in the deputy's face.

"Somebody find Moses and tell him to get his fat ass to the station and then stick it in dispatch. We're surrounded by acres and acres of woods and lake, but you can rest assured that some Clairol Blue-Hair is gonna be dialing nine-one-one soon. 'Cause things are about to get loud. Get the heavy shit. And tell Moses to come up with some cover story for the calls and make damned sure that people I don't want knowing what's going on don't wind up knowing. Understand?"

A thinner guard, the only one who Clay noted hadn't had a turn beating on him, asked "What about Clayton?"

"Fuck, Wally, you stay with him. He ain't going nowhere anyway."

"Sure thing, boss."

The sheriff turned angrily back toward the deputies. "Moses and Parker, you're riding with me. Heavy shit. Load everything up."

"Everything?" Parker asked skeptically.

"Especially everything. We're going to send that goddamned truck back to whatever fiery pit of hell it came from. I guaran-damn-tee that that truck won't exist in ten minutes. My truck's in the garage. Load it up. When that thing gets around the opposite side of the house again, we'll put just enough distance between it and us to get a good lock on it, then Boom! Sayonara, boys! Teach them fucks a good lesson."

The sheriff and a gaggle of deputies left the room through various doors as the roaring of the truck announced its aggravation in the distance. Clay wasn't sure, but he had spent enough time playing video games to understand what strafing and taunting was. Hell, forget *understanding* it. He was the king of it. Yes, that's it! That truck *wants* them to come out and play.

Clay had already seen the kind of firepower the sheriff and his cronies were packing. Especially the kinds of firepower that came in long, rectangular, eight-foot gunmetal graygreen boxes. Just the size of a real, no bullshit, military-grade rocket launcher. Not to mention the several deputies struggling two to a box behind them carrying what could only be rockets.

Still, Clay had no idea who the fight would go to. That truck might be able to withstand bullets, but a rocket launcher? There was no way. But what was clear was this: there would be no tie. Someone was going to be the unequivocal winner. Either the things in the truck underestimated the sheriff, or vice versa.

In a matter of minutes, everyone had evacuated the room except for Clay and the deputy the sheriff had called Wally, and Wally was keeping his distance, sitting in a black metal folding chair against the far wall.

Clay could hear footsteps on the floor overhead, hurried shuffling and dragging sounds – probably as they started loading up. Clay couldn't tell what room or rooms he sat beneath. But he assumed that his room must be below the main hallway, because most of the foot traffic he heard came in what seemed to be a straight line overhead.

Somewhere behind him, the four-by-four of death roared in the distance. Somewhere up and to the right, Clay heard a truck start. He assumed it was the sheriff's. Simultaneously, he heard the muffled rattling of a garage door opening, then a short bark of squealing tires, then yelling and rapid semiautomatic gunfire.

Clay looked up at the ceiling toward the direction of the sounds. Wally did the same. Strangely, Clay noted to himself that neither the truck nor the sounds of gunfire were getting any farther away.

There was a battle taking place right inside or outside the garage.

And, Clay noted with growing queasiness, the battle didn't involve the truck. Because the truck was still somewhere behind the lake house, but by the sound of it – it was moving in for the kill.

And Clay was still stuck, hogtied to the chair.

He hadn't noticed Wally stand up and uncross his arms, but the motion in his periphery of someone drawing nearer caused him to look up.

Wally started talking from about halfway across the room. "Clay, we need to get out of here. Don't know where to. But I'm going to untie you. I'm really sor..."

And Wally collapsed silently but violently to the floor.

Clay strained to see what had taken him out, and for lack of a better explanation figured it was a rogue bullet that had done the job. Must have been. There was nothing else in the room. Never mind the fact that they were underground and there wasn't a window in sight and the walls down here were thickly reinforced concrete.

Must have been a bullet.

Clay did the only thing he could. He started jerking wildly in the chair, because if logic reigned then it meant there was no stray bullet and that there was indeed something in the room, and jerking wildly to try to free himself seemed a better course of action than sitting there peacefully awaiting his fate yet again.

The sudden appearance of a wavering, semi-transparent, black shadow above Wally reinforced in Clay's mind that his plan of action – namely wiggling until something miraculous happened – was the correct one.

And that the shadow was becoming less transparent and moving closer to him accelerated his urgent need for his restraints to give. He finally rocked forward enough to balance on his feet, each of which was tied to a post of the chair. Still, by rocking his weight back and forth, he found he could shuffle a foot or so at a time away from the thing.

He turned to the nearest hallway and tried to turn his body and the chair attached as far as he could with each step to waddle awkwardly, but quickly, away.

Then it got him. He felt his chair jerk back and plant itself firmly on the ground.

Clay had given up on wiggling out of the ties, so reflexively he did the only thing he could. With every ounce of strength and anger and rage and testosterone and pent-up terror at being bullied all his life and going out this way – he yelled. He screamed. He stuck his head as far out as he could at whatever it was, tried to look it in the face (which was still a forming blackness), opened his eyes and from his gut aimed at it the culmination of everything he had ever felt or ever would feel and let it go. It was a thoughtless scream, full of manly anger and challenge.

Clay was still screaming, fully ready to bite the damned thing to death (thank goodness they hadn't gagged him, he thought), when it finally took form as part of the shadow peeled back and revealed beautiful blue eyes and raven-black hair.

Clay was so shocked and full of adrenaline that even though his mind registered the lack of any threat, his body kept fighting and screaming.

It took a minute of Bob kneeling down and placing her hands on his legs for him to calm down. She untied him deftly, stepped over to Wally and took his gun. She smiled. "Let's go!"

Clay was still sitting in the chair, panting.

Outside, the pauses between rounds of gunfire were getting longer, and the sounds seemed to be coming from all around the lake house now. Clay hoped for one of two outcomes: that the cops were winning and that there was less to shoot at; or that the cops had managed to run away and get free. Because the alternative did not bode well for him and Bob.

Chapter 50   Over the Trailer

The first thing to come back was taste. Both Chett and Harry had the taste of copper or pennies in their mouths. Most everything came back quickly afterward except for sight. Their retinas were still seared from earlier.

Both of them were lying on their backs, strapped at every juncture to tables. Neither knew how close or how far they were from the other.

Chett turned his head to the left. He was the first to speak. "Harry? You here?"

From somewhere to his right, Harry answered. "Where the hell are we?"

Chett turned his head in the direction of Harry's voice. "Are we dead?"

"Don't think so." Harry grunted. "But we are held pretty tight." He struggled against the restraints.

Someone or something in the room made funny noises. Neither Chett nor Harry could tell if the noises were animal or human, but the more Harry thought about it, he had heard something similar before. Star Trek? Maybe. No, that's not it. But he was headed in the right direction. It had been on TV. Where on TV had he heard those sounds? That's it! National Geographic. It had been a few years, but he remembered seeing part of a special on the Bushmen of Africa on the staticy public broadcasting channel he got when his coat hanger antenna was pointed just right.

So they were trapped by ... Africans? Must be. Why not? All bets were off. Harry's mind raced back over the litany of recent improbable and insane events. Being knocked out and bound by Africans. It fit if for no other reason that it doesn't make a lick of sense.

As Harry was deep in thought, Chett was already talking. "Hello? Who's there?"

More clicking, screeching and muttering.

Chett waited for something intelligible. After a few moments, he spoke again into the relative darkness. "What do you want with us? Hello? Who are you?"

Still more clicking, screeching and muttering.

Chett's inquisitions continued unfruitfully for a few minutes.

******

Roscoe looked from the two captives to Earl. "What the hell are they doing?"

The captive on the left was making funny sounds.

Earl stroked his goatee. "I think they're trying to talk."

"Why'd you go and save 'em?" Roscoe asked, looking back to the captives.

"You mean it wasn't you?"

"Nope. Thought it was you."

They both looked at each other with sudden insight. Earl was the first to voice it. "The ship. That bitch."

"Why'd she go and do that?"

"Don't know. But they do look a little more like us than those things we saw earlier."

"Where?" Roscoe asked.

"When we landed the first time. On the ice island."

"Oh." Roscoe paused. "You don't reckon that *these* are the intelligent life on this little planet?"

"Why not? We're intelligent, aren't we? And they look a little like us, don't they? I mean, sure, they're all weird and gross looking, but they could be. Seems they're trying to talk to us, don't it?"

"Well, what do you think they're trying to say?"

"Beats me," Earl replied. "But you had to go and basically destroy the ship's communication center, so she can't really translate for us, can she?"

"Well, it's probably not important anyway." Roscoe turned and walked out into the hallway. Earl followed.

"Might be worth checking out, Roscoe. After all, we did pick up a signal coming from their satellite. If we figure out what they're saying, they may be able to tell us how to find what we're looking for."

"Fair enough. But we're not involving *her*." Roscoe pointed at the ceiling. "Get your greenbox and let's get see what we can dig up." Roscoe removed a small handheld device from a pocket that looked a little like a hybrid between a PDA and a cellphone and started speaking into it.

Chett and Harry listened to their weird voices echoing farther and farther down the hallway until they dissolved into silence.

Chapter 51 At the Lake House

Clay and Bob waited until the sounds of warfare died out to sneak stealthily upstairs. The silence was more than eerie - it bore down on Clay with a deep sense of foreboding doom. He fumbled with the heavy Maglight he had purloined from the unconscious Wally and debated turning it on. But turning it on would mean the possibility of alerting any possible foes that might be waiting upstairs. Leaving it off, however, meant that he had to feel his way silently along the slatted wood paneled walls and hope that any sound created by the rubbing of his fingers on the shallow wood served less of a warning to anyone upstairs than the flashlight would.

Each step lasted a hundred years. After the small squeak and rustle of the following Bob, Clay would wait for his heartbeat to subside enough to listen for any sounds.

Several random and indistinguishable bumps in the night later, and Clay reached around to take the gun from Bob. He decided to do it like he had seen all the cops on TV - Maglight on, pointed forward, in one hand with the gun in the other.

It wasn't as easy as the officers made it seem. He tried a few different combinations unsuccessfully: first the light in one hand, then in the other, then back in the other hand with the gun pressed against it - which served to do little more than make him drop the light with a loud crash.

He watched with terror as his flashlight bounced down the stairs, illuminating the stairway with flashes and arcs of light, taking with it his hopes of being aware of anything that could be lurking in the darkness ahead - anything that could now be lurking in the very tangible darkness only inches away from his face.

He let out a feeble whimper.

His already paranoia-heightened sense of hearing picked up the minute sounds of possible shuffling upstairs.

Was it real, or was he just hearing things?

After everything else that had happened today, why wouldn't it be real?

He had no choice but to jump down the stairs after it, hoping that he wouldn't break his neck on the way. The flashlight spun to a stop at the bottom, casting its beam on the gray concrete floor of the basement.

Clay bent down to grab the light and felt something behind him. He spun around quickly hoping to brain the unknown offender behind him before he realized it was Bob. He tried to pull his swing, but it was too late.

She had already caught his arm, almost breaking it in the process.

She released it and touched him gingerly on the nose.

"Damn it, woman," he whispered. "Scaring the hell outta me. Really now." He paused. "I could have really hurt you." But somehow, he doubted that.

Clay took a moment to configure his gun and flashlight into a holdable pair. He and Bob turned around and began the slow creep back upstairs.

An agonizing five minutes later, they made it to the top. Clay strained to hear any sound he could, but in the complete silence he only zeroed in on the sound of blood rushing through his ears and his beating heart.

He had no idea how to proceed, so he figured if the cop movies could teach him how to hold a gun and a flashlight at the same time, they could teach him how to canvas a room.

The staircase emptied into a hallway going left and right. Straight ahead was a small bathroom. He could tell easily that the bathroom was empty, so he swung his gun and flashlight quickly to the left and right again making sure the hall was clear.

Going left meant that he'd leave Bob to the darkness and whatever might be behind him to the right. Going right meant that he'd leave Bob to the darkness to the left.

So he stood there for a minute, swinging his flashlight back and forth, trying to make up his mind. Bob finally nudged him to the left, and he reluctantly stepped down the hall, still focusing his concentration on his ears. If something were to attempt to sneak up behind them, hopefully he'd hear it. Or them. No, no reason to think it would be a *them*. It would be an *it*, he assured himself. No, if he were going to lie to himself, he might as well go all the way and tell himself that nothing was going to sneak up on them.

They came to a doorway leading into what they assumed was the living room. Clay swung his gun/light combo into the room at the same time as he stepped in, quickly turning his back to the wall. He pointed his light directly in front of him, illuminating an ugly tweed couch. He swung his flashlight around in short arcs, stopping every second or so to examine whatever fell in its path. Picture, pillow, table, another pillow, a painting, then back to the ugly couch, an ugly recliner, the wall behind the recliner, the wall behind the ugly couch, the old Zenith television set on the rickety brass stand. He repeated the search a few more times until he was sufficiently convinced that there was nothing lying in wait for them. There was really no place to hide in the room.

A faint blue misty light had begun to pour in from the approaching morning outside. Not enough to resolve the shadows in the room, but enough to let him know that the door leading outside – the door on the same wall he had his back to – was open.

He turned off his flashlight and crept across the room, almost tripping over the old television. He peeked out the window above the couch.

"Shit." He was very unhappy with the scene outside. It was the high body count that made him that way. And the morning light still did little to allow him to discern between zombie and cop. They were all just unidentifiable bodies at this point.

He felt Bob shuffle up beside him. Even though he was continuously aware of her position in the room, it still made him jump.

The two of them stood like that for a few minutes. Clay really couldn't wrap his head around it. He crept to a position parallel to the door and looked outside. Nothing but the empty garage. The window on the other side of the room reaffirmed the body count.

But no truck. No cop cars. So apparently, Clay thought, the cops had gotten away.

So Clay thought. *Do I run, or stay here and wait for someone? What would they do in the movies? Stay? They'd get eaten by zombies. Run? Yep. Still zombie food. Let's face it. I'm really not any safer in this house than I am out there. But I can hide in the house. Zombies are too stupid to go looking in broom closets. Aren't they?*

But Clay already knew the answer. *No. The damned things can drive trucks.*

So his only hope rested on the slim chance that the cops had managed to put some distance between themselves and the lake house with the zombies in pursuit.

But there had been a trap, hadn't there?

So with great trepidation, Clay walked silently to the door and gently pushed it open.

They stood in the garage, looking out at the swampy morning. Clay again strained to hear anything, but came up empty. Not even birds chirping. Just silence.

From the edge of the garage, Clay could piece together a scene of chaos and carnage. Muddy circular ruts in the yard spoke of trucks being driven without purpose, their only attempts at escape nearly cut off at the pass. Or it could have been that the driver was trying to position the people in the back with the heavy ammo.

To the left lay the torn up gravel driveway and the way back to the main road. To the right lay the lake and the back yard. No way to go but left. But there were an awful lot of bodies lying in their way.

Some were still smoking.

Clay looked back in the garage for something to poke the bodies with. Having found a broomstick, he snapped it in two close to the end to create a spear of sorts and the two of them set off, following two distinct sets of tire tracks.

That answered that question. The cops made it away. At least from the house. With the zombies in pursuit. But Clay really didn't feel any better. Until Bob pinched his ass and said "Beep!"

That made him feel a little better.

Chapter 52   Over the Trailer

The two skinny weird bald guys looked at each other and said something in that African language again. This time, noted Harry, they were holding little green boxes in their hands. They nodded to each other and the one on the right spoke first. After he finished, the little green box talked. In English!

"Praise Jesus!" it said.

Chett and Harry involuntarily whipped their heads around to look at each other confusedly.

The one on the right, the taller one, spoke again. "Praise Jesus!" the box said.

The shorter one on the left said something to the taller one then spoke at the box. It said "Breaker Breaker One-Nine, what's your twenty?"

Chett and Harry were now looking very perplexed, but not at each other. The extremely strange people sputtering nonsense from little green boxes had taken all their attention.

"What?" Harry said.

The one on the left spoke. His box translated. "Roger that. We've got a smokey ahead."

"What?" Harry said again.

This time the one on the right spoke. From his box, in a very deep bass radio personality kind of voice, "I'm Roscoe, and this is Earl, and you're listening to the smooth sexy sounds of Jazz ninety-seven nine. Just lay back and relax, daddy's going to take you all the way tonight."

"What?" Harry said again.

The one on the right, Roscoe, fiddled with a button again and talked into the translating box. "You have been saved! Praise Jesus! You have been called up into the heavens as God's children! You have forsaken your earthly world and moved closer to the light!"

This time Chett spoke. "Is this some kind of cult? What's going on here? Who are you?"

The one called Roscoe continued to speak. "I am Roscoe, and this is Earl. We are all children of God."

The one on the left, Earl, pushed a button and this time his green box took on the deep, slow radio voice. "Just relax, you're in good hands. We're gonna make you feel so bad it feels good."

Chett turned to Harry. "Dude, what the fuck is going on? Seriously. Can you see yet? What do they look like?"

"No luck, Chett. But I think they're trying to talk to us. And you really don't want to know who I think they are. Because we have moved beyond the point of 'What the fuck is going on' into 'I give up' territory."

"What do you mean?" Chett asked.

"Because at this point, I'm just waiting for Santa Clause and the Easter Bunny to show up."

Roscoe's green box sputtered to life. "Just believe and you'll be saved. Just believe! Confess your sins to us and you'll be with God's children!"

"What?" Harry asked. "Look, brothers, if I started confessin' everything I done wrong, we'd never make it out of here."

The one on the left, Earl, muttered to Roscoe and turned back to his box. From it in the radio voice: "We want to hear from you. The phone lines are open and daddy wants you to talk to him."

Harry whispered to Chett, "I think they're wanting us to talk to them."

Chett whispered back. "About what?"

"Don't have a clue. But it's worth a shot." He spoke up, talking to Earl and Roscoe. "Um, hi. I'm Harry."

"And, um, I'm Chett."

"And we'd like to know what is going on."

The boxes chirped and clicked and spoke in what Harry assumed was their native tongue. Roscoe talked back into his box. "Welcome, Harry and Chett. We are children of God. You are saved. The kingdom of heaven is yours."

Chett whispered to Harry again. "Are we dead? What does he mean? Are we in heaven?"

Harry whispered back. "Look, I actually have an idea, but for right now, play along. And no, we're not dead." Then, back to Roscoe and Earl. "Thank you. Can you let us go?"

Earl spoke into his box: "We're gonna love you so many ways, you're bound to like one of them."

Roscoe spoke into his box: "You must confess your sins to us. You must repent against the whore of Babylon!"

Chett looked back in Harry's direction. "Did we get caught by a bunch of televangelists?"

"Not quite."

"Good, because that would make sense, wouldn't it? We were fighting zombies and then woke up in a televangelist/jazz R&B DJ convention. I mean, why not?"

"Because I'm afraid the truth is a little stranger," Harry sighed. Then, back to the strange duo holding them captive, "What do you mean? Repent and confess? Confess what? You really need to rethink how you're trying to talk to us, because it's just not making a lot of sense."

Then, from Earl and his box, "We know what it's like for all you looking for love. So many fish in the sea, and you want to have a little nibble from every one of them. But maybe there's one little tasty piece who's got *you* caught – hook, line, and sinker. This one goes out to all you guys out there who know what I'm talking about."

From Roscoe's box: "Repent against the whore of Babylon!"

Harry answered them. "Look, it's obvious we're all having a wonderful time trying to communicate and failing miserably. So let's try this. Lemme talk real slow for you: We ... have ... no ... idea ... what ... you ... are ... talking ... about."

"Repent! Repent!"

"Fine! I repent! I wash my hands clean of her!" Harry said exasperatedly. "Can we go now?"

From Earl's box, deep and rich: "We're looking for love."

Immediately afterwards, from Roscoe's box: "Whore of Babylon!"

Harry was even more confused. "You want a hooker? Fine. Let us go. We'll get one for you. Hell, let us go and we'll even send up some beer and pizza with her."

Roscoe hit another button on his box and spoke into it. "What's her twenty, partner?"

Harry blinked in the darkness again. "What? What's her twenty? You mean, where is she? She's in the yellow pages under 'escort' I suppose. You got a phone book up here? No, reckon not."

The two spoke to each other hurriedly in their weird native language. Then, from Roscoe's, again in the twang of a trucker, "Roger that, pardner. What's the twenty on that phone book?"

"Um, in my trailer I suppose. I haven't seen it for a while. Have to look for it."

Chett cut in, parroting the trucker twang, "Look, pardners, you let us go, we'll send up a hooker with beer and pizza, *and* you can keep the phone book."

Earl and Roscoe muttered quickly to each other, then Earl spoke into his box. From it, in the DJ voice: "Don't touch that dial, we'll be right back taking you through another set of favorites sure to get you in the mood."

Then they left the room.

Chett and Harry listened to the sound of the door swishing closed behind them.

Chett leaned back over in Harry's direction. "Dude. What is going on?"

Being still mostly blinded, Chett couldn't see Harry smile and shake his head in disbelief. "We done got ourselves abducted, friend."

"What!?"

"Abducted. As in, Beam me up, Scotty. 'Cept they ain't Scotty."

"You're kidding."

"You got a better explanation?"

Chett was silent for a minute. "Not really?"

"Thought so."

Chett was silent for another minute, thinking. His voice sounded uneasy. "Do we have to get probed?"

Harry didn't answer.

"I think I'd rather take the zombies."

Harry sighed.

They sat like that, clamped to the tables, blinking at the red and green dots that were slowly beginning to fade away. Shapes in the room resolved themselves into tables, panels, computers. The room sported warmly lit gray walls with deep brown floors. The tables to which they were strapped were two out of maybe ten, all of the others empty. Sporadically on the walls were large black rectangles, apparently displays of some kind, since two were lit up with what Chett and Harry presumed to be their vitals.

The door whooshed open. Chett and Harry turned to look at an empty hallway.

"What was that?" Chett asked.

"Doors opened," Harry answered.

"Got that much." Chett replied. "But there's no one there."

"You get surrounded by zombies, talked to by televangelist aliens, and you're gonna be confused by doors that open automatically? We have that at the Winn-Dixie in town. Ever seen them automatic doors? They just have a mind of their own sometimes."

But as soon as Harry had finished replying, the bands around their wrists, stomach, and ankles folded back into the table.

Both of them sat up immediately, rubbing their wrists and flexing their ankles.

"Are we free to go?" Chett asked Harry.

"I'm not going to stick around for permission. You're more than welcome to," said Harry as he stood up.

"Nope. That's quite all right. This is all the invitation to leave that I need."

They walked to the door.

"One question, though," whispered Chett. "Which way?"

From down the hall to the left came the sound of an opening door.

"I say that way," Harry answered and pointed to the right.

"Good. Let's go. And quick."

The two of them dashed off down the dimly lit passageway.

After a few minutes, Chett spoke. "Um, Harry?"

"Yeah?"

"I noticed that, well, every time we come to a junction, we go right."

"Yeah?"

"Shouldn't we be taking some lefts here and there?"

"Why?"

"Well, just figured, is all. Wouldn't all rights mean we're going in a circle?"

"Nope. Saw it on some TV show. You get in one of those corn mazes or hedge maze – you can't get lost. Just keep your right hand on a wall at all times. You'll eventually get out."

"You ever been to a big city, Harry?"

"Plenty of times. Why?"

"You get lost downtown, you put your right hand on a building and keep it there, you end up making the block."

"So what's your point?"

"I think we're making the block, Harry."

"Fine. Let's go left."

From down the hallway came the sound of an opening door.

"Next time." Harry said. "We go left."

After a few minutes' walk, they came to a junction and took a left. And thus, after ten minutes of coming to junctions and turning away from any sounds they heard, they made it to an elevator. They stepped in. The doors closed behind them.

Chett considered the buttons. "Harry, can you make any of this out?"

"Nope. Just hit the one on the bottom."

Chett did so. The doors opened. "Shit. No. Close, close, close," he muttered, pushing the buttons repeatedly.

Harry leaped to pull Chett's hand away from the button. "Then quit hitting the button, dumbass," he hissed.

The doors slid closed. Chett hit the second lowest button. His stomach turned as the lift dropped them quickly then stopped.

The doors opened into darkness. They both stepped out with trepidation. Soft inset lights glowed on, revealing a cargo bay filled with metal boxes. They crouched down in the door and dashed behind a box.

No one came. They made their way to the end of the huge room. Ahead of them was what they correctly assumed to be cargo doors. As they approached, the doors began sliding open.

"Whoa." Chett was astonished.

"What?" Harry whispered.

"Sorry," Chett whispered. "But I think we're over our trailer."

"What makes you think that?"

"I'd say you'd be hard pressed to find anyone else with a microwave strapped to their satellite dish."

"Hmm," Harry noted. "Good point. How do we get down?"

Chett walked over to the other side of the large landing as it lowered. "Depends on how low this goes. Maybe we can just walk off."

"Onto our trailer?"

"Why not?" Chett replied.

The landing stopped ten or fifteen feet short of their roof.

"Damn," Chett spat. "Plan B."

"Plan B?" Harry asked.

Chett walked back over to the other side of the landing and knelt down to look below it. "Yep." He swung around and lowered himself over the side. "Don't want to risk crashing through the roof or sliding off and thumping the ground. Not an argument I think I can win." He eased himself down till only his chest showed over the landing. "I suggest you get close behind me."

"What are you doing?" Harry whispered loudly.

"Grabbing my antenna," Chett whispered loudly back. "It's just a few feet under this landing. See ya on the ground!" And with that, Chett lowered himself till only his fingertips showed. One hand disappeared, then the other.

Then came the loud sound of metal rattling and a few choice curses. Then from below the ship, "Hurry your ass up, dude. You should already be down here."

The elevator doors slid closed. Harry needed no further encouragement.

Chapter 53   On the Side of Highway 61

Clay found walking on the side of the road extremely difficult. Rather, he found walking near the tree line next to the road extremely difficult. His ankles were hurting from the uneven ground. The way he saw it was this: they had three options. One, they could walk on the slim shoulder of the road, but seeing as how the road was on a four- or five-foot incline from the tree line, it meant having to jump down the hill and hide every time they heard a car or truck in the distance, then having to climb back up once it was gone. Two, they could walk behind the tree line, but the ground was already soggy and wet, and that would make walking entirely too slow. Not to mention that there just might be the walking undead hanging around in the woods somewhere. Or three, they could walk where the slope met the tree line, which meant easier hiding than walking on the road and easier walking than going behind the tree line. The only problem was that the incline created by the rise of the road was still sloping downward when it met the tree line.

Hence his aching ankles.

Bob seemed to be holding up well, he thought.

Clay figured they had made a few miles of the trip. Wonderful. Because he figured they were probably twenty miles away from civilization. Such a shame, he thought, to have this beautiful morning in front of them with the ultra-hot Bob but having to spend it walking clumsily to somewhere unspecific.

His plan? He didn't really have one. Part of him thought about walking to the nearest house and asking for help. But really, who would want to help a bruised and tattered nerdy-looking guy with a tall burqa-wearing person at his side? Who would even answer the door?

But being twenty miles from town (and another five or so after that from his house), it would take them – at two or three miles an hour – the better part of the whole day to get there.

But then again, what better use of his time did he have right now? He couldn't really think about going back to RadioWorld. He was fired for sure. And if he did show up, his boss would have the damn cops there in a heartbeat. Especially in his current condition. Besides, was he even on the schedule today? What day was it? By his reckoning, it was Sunday. Early Sunday morning.

He didn't know how right he would turn out to be. It was definitely Sunday morning. It was very, very Sunday morning.

Clay and Bob walked on. He noticed that the cars were few and far between – maybe one every ten minutes. Not too bad. It was enough to make him constantly reconsider the pros and cons of his chosen walking option. Maybe the shoulder of the road wouldn't be so bad. Walk on it for a few, then switch.

Each mile brought a little more feeling of uneasiness to Clay, who tried to chalk it up to his asskicking finally setting in.

He tried talking about it.

"Bob, I don't feel so good?" It sounded like a question.

"No good?"

"No. No good at all. Something isn't right."

"No right?"

"That's right."

"Is right?"

"No, *that's* right."

"Good is right?"

"No. What you said is right."

"Is right."

"No. Forget it. What I'm trying to say is that I don't have a good feeling."

"No feeling?"

"No, I have a feeling. But it's not a good one."

"No good right."

"Um, yeah." Well, hell. Might not be the best conversationalist, but she was hotter than hell.

Clay was so worried and so dejected and so much in pain that he felt like giving up. Had he not been allergic to chiggers or afraid of getting his pants wet by sitting on the soggy ground, he would have plopped down by the side of the road and just sat there and waited for whatever to happen.

Because he sure wasn't feeling too good. And the unidentifiable something that was gnawing at the back of his mind was getting worse.

They would walk another mile or so before he remembered. And it would hit him when he saw it: A church.

It was Sunday morning. There was a church. He and Bob found themselves at the end of a long gray gravel driveway. At the end stood a small white wooden church, the kind for which the delta is famous, complete with little white steeple, bell, green doors, and a horde of zombies.

Not that the delta churches are famous for zombies. But this one had at least twenty or so, easily identifiable by their pallet of greens and browns – both in skin tone and rotted clothing.

Clay judged by the scene that either the churchgoers inside were unaware of the guests outside, or that they had been aware but no longer were. Because they were zombie food.

So, naturally, Clay's first good instinct was to run away quickly and silently. He did so. Finally, after a hundred or so yards, he noticed the absence of footfalls behind him. Bob!

He slowed to a stop and turned around. The blacktop highway was empty. Shit. He listened. Silence. He had no choice. He had to go back for her.

Already out of breath, he turned around to sprint the football field back to the church's driveway.

He made it halfway before he heard them – several loud bangs, followed by several more loud bangs. He ran with everything he had inside him, almost tripping over his feet. His legs ached and his lungs ached even more.

He made it to the driveway as a car was hauling ass out of it. He dove off the blacktop and rolled down the hill as the car squealed to a stop. The passenger door flew open.

"Hi!"

It was Bob! He climbed up the incline on all fours and jumped into the car as she sped away.

"Holy shit. That was you?" Already, he knew the story. Bob had marched herself down the driveway, killed some zombies, and made off with a nice, shiny, 1980's Lincoln Town Car with red leather interior.

"Nice car!" he said, still out of breath.

"Beep!" she tweaked his nose.

"Can I ask, where are we going? Do you want me to drive?"

"Vroom, vroom!" she said and mashed the accelerator. "We go fast. Find Balls." She smiled.

"Balls? What balls?"

"I crash. Lost my balls."

Clays heart sank, until he realized surely she wouldn't have testicles to lose, and that if she did she surely wouldn't be up and around as good as she was. "Where did you lose them?"

"Boom! I crash."

"You lost them when you crashed?"

"Yeppers."

"Where did you crash?"

She tried to find the words to describe what happened. "Trees."

"That doesn't really narrow it down. There are trees everywhere." He motioned outside the window.

"Okay. Trees. Vroom vroom. Boom! I shoot. Crash! Oh no! Mom's car!"

"Oh! You mean out by the hunting camp!"

"Yes! Hunting Camp! I crash hunting camp!"

"I get it."

"Yes! I need balls!"

"Great. Let's go get your balls. And let's work on the art of using prepositions on the way."

"And computer. I need computer."

"It's at Clay and Bob's trailer, still hooked to the satellite."

"No. Crash! I need computer."

"You mean *your* computer."

"Yes! Your computer."

"No, *your* computer."

"Yes! Your computer."

"Okay. I get what you mean. Prepositions, then adjectives. We'll get you there."

"Beep!" She tweaked his nose again.

Clay was hopelessly in love.

Chapter 54 At Chett's and Harry's Trailer

"Plan?" Harry asked as he slid down the antenna.

Chett blinked and looked around him. It had stopped raining. Everything was still fuzzy, but at least his sight was coming back. Somewhat. He looked up and saw the oddly camouflaged ship hovering above his trailer. Behind it, and through it – sort of – he could make out the blues and pinks of the early morning sky. Obviously, the ship had some sort of invisibility or cloaking device. Except it was shorting out. Most of the time, it was semi-transparent. But every once in a while, it would flicker completely off, revealing the massive bulk of the suspended monstrosity.

He turned to Harry. "Um... Well, we got the guns. They're wet. You hop inside real quick and grab some towels and my cleaning kit. Then we hop in my RV and put as much distance between us and all this weird shit as possible."

"Done deal." Harry opened the door ever so slowly and crept inside.

Chett sneaked over to the RV, all the time keeping his eyes on the flickering behemoth above him. Afraid he would alert anyone – or anything – that might be searching for them this very minute, he made every effort to be as absolutely quiet as possible.

Except that the one thing Bob had neglected to fix in her crazy-ass RV fixing mood was the door. It was stuck. Or at least it was stuck and rusted so that pulling it open meant making a most unquiet noise. Chett circled the RV, creeping to hide behind it. Same stroke of bad luck with the passenger door.

Damn her. What would it have troubled her to squirt some damned WD-40 on the hinges? Seriously. Why go through all the trouble of getting it to run again if you weren't going to oil the doors?

All Chett had wanted to do was put the guns in and get in position to crank up and drive off. But now he'd have to wait till Harry came back with the supplies, which seemed to take forever.

Chett had just about made up his mind to go see what the trouble was when he was startled by the sound of his trailer screen door slamming.

He turned around quickly and saw Harry, arms full of towels and the cleaning kit.

"What the hell were you thinking?" he whispered loudly.

"Shit. Sorry. Forgot."

"What took you so long?"

"Couldn't find the damned cleaning kit."

"Well, come on. We're going to have to make a racket getting in anyway. Damned Bob didn't oil the hinges."

"Very rude of her," Harry whispered back.

"Come on. One, two, three!"

The hinges complained loudly as they jumped in.

"Here," Chett said, throwing the guns at Harry. "Drop your stuff in the back and hold the guns. You clean 'em while I get us the hell outta here."

Chett cranked the RV and was surprised when it turned over the first time. "Damn, this thing's purring like a kitten. Who the hell is that lady?"

"Don't know. Don't care. Find the gas pedal and push it. I'm pretty sure whatever's up there," he pointed to the sky, "is going to be following us anyway, so if you're gonna go, there's no better time than right now."

Chett needed no further encouragement. With the contraction of a few leg muscles, the RV roared off down the gravel driveway, swerving to miss recently decapitated rotting zombies.

"Harry?"

"Yeah?" He was already drying the guns.

"Why do you think they're going to be following us?"

"Only thing that makes sense." Harry was wiping the twelve-gauge.

"Why you reckon?"

"Well, they just kinda let us go, right?"

"I thought we snuck out."

"Did you sneak out of your shackles?" Harry was talking to Chett but still focusing intently on the guns.

"Well, no, not really. But we snuck out of the ship. I mean, they didn't exactly escort us out, did they?"

"Why would they have just unshackled us?"

Chett thought about it. "We said we were going to get them hookers and beer. Who can turn down good hookers and beer?"

"I don't know, Chett." Harry had a cleaning rod in his mouth and the twelve-gauge across his lap and was using his free hands to tear strips out of a towel to wrap around the cleaning rod. "But that's one of four possibilities."

"Oh?" Chett was dividing his attention between trying to stay on the road and craning his neck out the window to make sure the ship wasn't following them.

"Yep. Way I see it is this: One, you're right and they let us go to get beer and hookers. So they're watching us and just noticed us hauling ass away from them. They come after us. Two, you're right and we snuck out. They notice us missing and come after us. Three, they let us go because they want to follow us somewhere. Or four, they just let us go out of the niceness of their hearts."

Harry let it sink in as he cleaned furiously. "Out of all the possibilities, I think we can rule out number four. Number one's a maybe. Me? My vote's for number three. Any way you cut it, there's at least a seventy-five percent chance that they're going to come after us."

"Look who's been paying attention in math class." Chett punched Harry slightly on the shoulder.

"Ouch. I wouldn't do that. And now's not a time to joke. We're not scott-free, Chett. And judging by the fact that what we just climbed out of is just hanging there in the sky ever so gently, it's probably got a few more horses under the hood than this here RV, no matter how much like a kitten it's purring. Get my drift?"

Chett let it sink in as he navigated onto the blacktop.

"And see, we got little things like roads and trees to bother with. Not them."

Chett let that sink in too.

"So, again, what's the plan?"

"Well, the back roads will let us hide better under the cover of trees. But the highways and interstate'll let us put more distance between us and them. And shit if I know. You seem to be the expert right now, so you tell me. What's the plan?"

Harry thought about it. True, they could surely use the benefit of the trees. But his logic went like this: If that thing's just floating up there, and if it had some sort of camouflage device, then it's an alien ship. Wait a sec...

Harry turned to Chett. "Didn't Clay say something about Bob?"

Chett shot him a look. "Clay said a lot of things about Bob. Which one you want? Kid's pussy whipped. He wants in her panties so bad it's hurting *me*."

"No, seriously. We were in the trailer, talking, and he just burst in yelling some nonsense."

"Yeah. So?"

Harry racked his brain. "He said she was an alien!"

"Okay, and...?"

"That thing, it's an alien ship!"

"Just now figured that out?"

"Shut up. Seriously, Clay said Bob was an alien, remember? And we just blew him off. I'll bet she knows what's going on."

"Good for her."

"We've gotta go get her."

"Oh, hell no. You can forget about that, buddy."

Harry fell quiet and got to thinking again.

"You're thinking, aren't you?" asked Chett.

"Yeah, why?"

"Because you sure as hell ain't cleaning them guns."

Harry reached down and grabbed the thirty-aught-six and cleaned as he thought. He turned to Chett after a second or two. "Nope."

"Nope what?" Chett was still looking back and forth from the road to the sky.

"We gotta go get her."

"Read my lips," he turned his head to Harry while still keeping his eyes on the road and pursed his lips. "Hell fuckin' no."

"Listen. If they are alien, then one: they could easily catch up to the RV as we haul down the highway, if they hadn't already implanted us with some homing devices. Or two: they could track us just as easily with their alien technology if we take the backroads. Therefore: we're screwed either way."

"Mmkay," Chett said, "Let's say you're right..."

"I am."

"We'll, let's just say you are. You got any idea where the hell she is right now? Last I remembered, she was with us in the truck when we wrecked. Then she wasn't. And I really haven't been keeping time since then, but I'm pretty damn sure it's been over eight hours since then. And we've been up there in that ship and God knows where else and we've got less than a snowball's chance in hell that we're gonna find her."

Well, shit. Chett had a point. But wait, there was something else. Hadn't he heard something? Right after his head hit the window when they wrecked the truck. It had been off in the distance, but he had heard the sheriff yelling to the boys.

"He said something about the lake house."

"Harry?"

"Yeah?"

"What the hell are you talking about? Who said something about the lake house? Are you okay? You ain't got PTSD do you?"

"No, I'm fine. The sheriff. The sheriff said something about the lake house."

"Oh, did he now? Good for him. You just go back to cleaning guns and quit talking crazy. You're kinda sounding like Uncle Crank, and that ain't a compliment."

"No, jackass. When we wrecked, I heard the sheriff say something about taking Clay to the lake house. I bet you that's where Clay is. And if

Clay's there, maybe Bob'll be too."

"That the best you got?"

"You got any better?"

"A bunch of maybe's?"

"Again, you got any better? I thought I've done a pretty good job explaining to you that we're screwed no matter what we do. Getting Clay and Bob's the only thing that might make this make sense. Clay's all into this Star-Trek shit. I'm telling you, he's our best hope."

"If a skinny greasy little computer nerd and his Muslim alien wierdo RV-fixin' friend are our only hope, we're up shit creek."

"Might as well try."

Chett sighed. "Well, shit." He banged the steering wheel. "Damn shit fuck."

He slowed down, cursing. "We gotta double back. Shortest route's that way." He pointed behind him. He talked to Harry as he performed a delicate three-point turn on the narrow road. "Do you even know where the lake house is?"

"I'm pretty sure it's up north at Eagle Lake."

"Well, that's good, I guess. It's about thirty minutes out of town. But we'll have to make it over to Highway 61 to get there. But how are we going to find it?"

"We got thirty minutes of putting distance between us and that thing." Harry pointed at the sky again. "We'll figure it out. For now, go."

They both craned their necks out the windows to see what was or was not following them.

Chapter 55   At the Lake House

Wally opened his eyes and noticed no change between their open and closed states. The room was pitch-black, and if there were such a thing as pitch-quiet, he'd have thought the room was that, too.

His head hurt like a bitch. It throbbed with every heartbeat. He sat up and noticed with distinct displeasure that, although seemingly impossible, this action had the effect of ratcheting up the pain even more.

He swung his feet around, rose to his knees, and grabbed for his flashlight and gun. Which, fittingly, given the current state of affairs, were missing. He cursed silently and patted the ground around him, hoping in vain that they were lying nearby.

No luck. At least not in the immediate three-foot area around him.

Unsure of what exactly had happened, his military and police training kicked in and he assumed he was in hostile territory. He began to try to reconstruct the layout of the room and determine his position all the while keeping absolutely silent in case he wasn't the only one there.

He felt his uniform to make sure his radio was still attached. It was. He noticed the amber light indicating it was on. He turned it off so that it wouldn't squelch and give away his location.

Sure, he had seen combat – though most of it "light", if there were such a thing. He had been stationed in Iraq during the Gulf War, but managed to avoid by sheer luck most of the gunfights. The roughest action he had seen had been during boot camp.

And nothing could really prepare him for waking up from being cold cocked in a completely dark room. It wasn't much like waking up from your bed in the middle of the night either. He had no idea which way he was facing, to begin with. He couldn't even tell if he was even in the same room he had been knocked out in. People with a notion to knock someone out sometimes have a further notion of dragging them somewhere to do something with later.

He forced himself to concentrate through the throbbing pain. He felt the back of his head and went right to the knot he knew would be there. It smarted.

The room, if he recalled correctly, had two staircases leading up out of it, a restroom, a door leading to a staircase that would take him into a "wine cellar" (which actually was a wine cellar complete with a full selection of wines, except that it had a classic hidden-door configuration leading to a room storing heavy arms and artillery), and another hallway leading to a storage space and workroom.

Wally finished standing up and began walking slowly forward, holding his arms in front of him. He picked up each foot and swept it only centimeters off the floor to retain his balance in case he ran into something. He finally made it to a wall and began feeling his way around. He found the first door and walked in slowly, kicking something hard almost directly in front of him. His arms had hit nothing, so whatever he had kicked must be shorter than where his arms reached. He stopped and felt around.

A sink. He had made it to the bathroom. Good. At least he knew where he was. The very next door to the right once he exited would take him to the staircase leading up.

He felt his way slowly up the stairs, careful to step lightly without making noise. The house was dead silent.

At the top of the stairs, he noticed light beginning to leak through from outside. It was turning into morning.

He had been out for an hour or so.

That was a hard hit, and it was probably going to need stitches.

The complete silence of the house unnerved him. He crept outside and was just as shocked as Clay had been at the carnage outside.

The first thing he noticed was the lump of a body at the end of the garage.

Here's what Wally thought:

Holy shit.

Wally instinctively reached for his firearm again and was doubly disappointed at its still glaring absence. There were bodies everywhere. Wally realized that the perpetrators behind this mess might still be at large.

Here's what Wally thought now:

Holy shit.

He backed into a corner of the garage, keeping his periphery open, and reached into his pocket to retrieve his cell. He dialed the sheriff's number from memory and waited for it to ring.

It clicked and emitted a noise like it was trying to connect. But it never rang. Instead, a few moments of silence went by and his phone made a very distinct beep telling him cheerily that his call was dropped.

"Dropped, my ass," he whispered to the phone. "You never fuckin' rang. Best nationwide coverage my ass." He consoled himself with the thought that somewhere out there, millions of other frustrated people chanted the same chorus in unison.

He tried again.

More beeps.

He tried again.

More beeps.

He tried again.

More beeps.

What was the problem? He had a signal...

He waited thirty seconds and tried again.

More beeps.

He fought to temper his rage and control his urge to chuck the phone soundly into the nearest wall. He shook the phone instead and banged it against his hand.

He dialed again.

Silence... Silence... Then – more beeps.

"Fuckin' shit." He fumbled in his pocket to find a pen.

Having located it, he found the little pinhole that would allow him to reset his phone.

The pen wouldn't fit.

The phone he didn't chuck. The pen, he did. It hit the wall and burst into two or three pieces and afforded him some satisfaction of at least breaking something. But he noted with some sadness that the pen didn't have the explosive finish he hoped the phone would have.

He took the battery off the phone and waited a few seconds.

He put it back on and powered it up.

He tried again.

More beeps.

He scrolled through the menu to find Detective Moses' number.

He dialed it.

More beeps.

He shook his head and cursed as he pocketed the phone. "Fuckin' a."

Wally was stranded, unarmed, in a pile of bodies with no weapon or ammunition, no ride, and no one to ask what in the holy blue fuck was going on.

He still had his radio. He could key up and call the sheriff over it and direct him to a land line. Sounded like a good idea.

He switched his radio on and keyed in.

"SO-Forty-one to SO-One."

Silence.

He waited.

Still more silence.

He tried again. "SO-Forty-one to SO-One."

Still more silence.

He tried Detective Moses. "SO-Forty-one to SO-Nineteen."

Nothing.

He cursed and keyed in again.

"Anyone there? This is unit forty-one trying to reach unit one or nineteen. Repeat, can anyone read me?

Nothing again, until finally the radio finally broke the silence with a very garbled and broken someone saying something. It had the cadence and timbre of one of the ladies in dispatch, so it must have been someone at the Sheriff's Department radioing back. But the signal was terrible.

He tried again. "Hello? Unit forty-one here, my twenty is Eagle Lake. I didn't copy you. Please repeat. Over."

A few more seconds of silence, then the lady's garbled voice again.

Well, fuck and damn it all. This is getting me nowhere, he thought. *Isn't this radio system supposed to have repeaters out here so we can get a signal?*

As Wally could see it, he had one course of action. He only hoped that someone, in this god-awful bloodbath, had not wrecked what would be his best shot at getting out of here alive, if the ones responsible were still on the loose.

He turned off his radio and crept back into the house. He had a plan, but he needed a flashlight, so he weighed the thoughts of *where would the best place be to hide a flashlight* against *what are my odds that there's someone still in this house who can harm me whom I might stumble upon in my willy-nilly search for a flashlight?*.

Bedrooms. Upstairs in the nightstand.

Not gonna happen. Didn't want to go exploring another floor.

Kitchen. Pantry.

That's a start, he thought. Worth a try, even if he did doubt it.

He crept back through the living room, exploring it for a possible light source. No luck.

He crept back down the hallway leading past the staircase down to the basement.

The door to the kitchen was open, so after making sure the room was empty of anyone, he entered and began opening and closing all the drawers and cabinets.

He murmured to himself as he searched.

"Of course there wouldn't be a flashlight. Why would there be? It's a fucking flashlight in a house out in the middle of fucking nowhere and you know damned well the power's gotta go out almost every week so there's a damned flashlight on this floor and I'm gonna have to tear the house down to find it. But why would I find one even if it was in the house? My luck the fuckin' batteries would be dead."

He made it around the counter to the pantry.

Fuck. There was a pool of blood leaking from under the door.

He walked as silently as possible to the door and listened for anyone inside who might be shuffling. No one was.

Well, of course they wouldn't, he thought. *They just heard me slamming every damned door and drawer in here.*

He put his ear to the door and listened.

He heard heavy, broken breathing.

I'm unarmed and I'm not going to deal with what's behind door number three right now. Someone might be legitimately hurt, or someone might be in there with them waiting in ambush.

Another hallway led out of the kitchen into a den.

Here, he found luck. There were no flashlights, but on the wall were mounted two antique-looking kerosene lanterns. With kerosene. And he had a lighter in his pocket.

Wait, he *had* a lighter in his pocket.

He fumbled around and found it. Good. He did have a lighter.

He was in business.

He took one out of its mount, lit it, and headed back down the hall to the basement.

Chapter 56 On the Highway to the Lake House

"Is it after us?" Chett was sticking his head out of the window to see if they were being followed.

"I wish you'd pay more attention to the road and let me keep lookout. You're scaring the shit out of me." Harry stood up to walk to the back of the RV and peer out of the back window. "Clear so far."

"Look, Harry?" he yelled over the open window and engine noise.

"Yeah?" Harry yelled back.

"I know Bob fixed this RV and all, but I'd be a little more comfortable back in my pickup. Let's go get it."

"No doing. It'll take too much time, and there's no guarantee it'll run anyway after the lick it took with that tree."

"Well, call it a hunch, but there's probably going to be some sticky situations coming up, and I'd like something with a little more get-up-and-go if you know what I mean.

"Yeah, I've been thinking about that too. A few more miles and we'll hit Uncle Cranks'. He's always tinkering on something. Maybe he'll have something that'll have more get-up-and-go."

Chett turned his head to face Harry. "Are you serious? Uncle Crank? What'll he have? A '92 Geo Metro? A Gold Pinto? You serious? We'll be damned lucky if the thing don't catch on fire by the time we make it to the end of his driveway."

"Will you please, for God's sake, keep your eyes on the road?" Harry yelled back.

Chett looked back in time to catch the curve in the road. The RV felt close to tipping over as Chett wheeled it back on course.

"See what I mean?" yelled Chett.

"I didn't say I disagree with you. But you got a better idea right now? Wouldn't hurt to go see him."

"I guess so."

Five minutes later they found themselves at the turnoff to Uncle Crank's trailer.

Chett was the first to notice the ruts and deep tire marks.

"Looks like Uncle Crank's been up to something," he yelled.

"Why's that?" Harry made his way back up to the front of the cab.

"Look at all these tire tracks. I don't know if I can make it down his driveway."

Harry saw exactly how torn up the road was. Going down the side of the driveway wouldn't work because the entrance was guarded by a thick line of trees wrapped heavily and haphazardly with barbed wire. Only the first fifty feet of the driveway would pose a challenge, because after that they could just drive through the yard, which was a big-assed dirt pit anyway.

"Do you think we can make it?" Harry asked.

"Don't want to risk bottoming out. That mud's still pretty fresh from the rain the other night, and it'd be our luck to get stuck." He motioned to the back of the RV where they had kept their hunting boots for years. "Grab your boots. Let's walk."

Harry came back with two shotguns and two pistols and handed one of each to Chett.

"How we doing for ammo?" Chett asked.

"Well, it depends. If we were just heading out for a day hunting in the woods, I'd say we'd have enough to live on for a few years." He eyed the pallets and boxes of ammo. "So normally, we'd have enough to start a small militia. But seeing as how we're fighting an army of the undead, we might only have enough for a few hours. Who knows?"

Chett didn't respond. He pulled the RV to a stop on the side of the road and took a look at the ammo for himself.

He shook his head and left the RV, gun in hand. "Come on. Let's hurry. Last thing I want to see is that ship with its shorted camouflage blinking in and out overhead."

Harry didn't need to be told twice.

"What the hell? They're all over the place!"

Roscoe and Earl had been chasing the little red dots all over the place. Each time they reached another junction or corridor, they checked the display monitors to see which way they needed to go.

"Well, no worry," Earl chirped as he checked the display. "They're in the lift, headed up instead of down. There's no place for them to go."

"Computer," Roscoe barked.

Nothing.

"Computer!" Roscoe barked again.

"You ripped out her voicebox, remember?"

"Shit. Well, she can still hear me." He paused. "Computer, stop the lift and bring it back down to this floor. Keep the doors closed until we get there."

No response.

Roscoe looked at Earl. "I know she doesn't have a voicebox, but couldn't she just chime or beep or something so that we know she heard us?"

Earl was still studying the display. "Well, the lift is headed back this way."

"Good."

They headed to the nearest lift to wait for the computer to deliver their captives.

They waited. And waited.

Earl was still looking at the display. "The lift sure is taking a long time. It's moving, but very slowly."

Finally, just as the doors opened to an empty lift, an alarm sounded.

Roscoe stared at the empty lift. "What? Where are they? What's that damned alarm?"

"The cargo hatch just opened."

"What? How do you know?"

Earl pointed to the display where in big red alien letters the message "WARNING: Cargo bay doors opening" was flashing.

"Who's opening the doors? Where's the two things we picked up down there? Why aren't they on this lift?"

"I don't know, Roscoe. Shut up for a second." He looked up at the ceiling. "Computer," Earl ordered, "Close the cargo doors. If those things are trying to escape, do not let them."

No response.

"Damn this thing." Roscoe said. "See? We made the right decision in not paying for it. Come on, get in the lift. Computer, take us to the cargo bay. And if them things are loose somewhere else in the ship, stop them and trap them wherever they are."

A minute later, Earl was the first to speak. "Roscoe?"

"What?" he grumped.

"Shouldn't we be there by now?"

Roscoe banged the sides of the lift and yelled. "Come on, you stupid thing. Move faster!" He turned to Earl. "Are we moving at all?"

He pointed to the blank display on the wall. "Why are you asking me? You can see as easily as I can that there's nothing on here. Must be broken. My guess is that we are moving a little – I mean, look at those little lights that are sliding by. They're moving awfully slow, but they're moving. Don't they normally move a lot faster?" He motioned to the three or four little slats in the wall where he guessed the floor markers were. It was moving at a crawl.

"I don't know," Roscoe responded. "I don't really pay attention. Computer!" He barked again. "If you can hear me, go faster!"

The lift shook and dropped so quickly that both Roscoe and Earl were temporarily weightless. It stopped so abruptly that they both collapsed on the floor with the wind knocked out of them.

"If ever I had half a mind to get a refund on something I stole," Roscoe wheezed, "this piece of shit ship would be the one." He picked himself up and felt the knot on his head. "When all this is over and we've made the shipment and we've gotten paid..."

"Oh, who are you kidding?" Earl whined as he picked himself up. "We're already dead. I guarantee you there's already a search party for us on both ends of the deal."

"That's bullshit, Earl. Sure, there'll be a few pissed off people, but we're going to finish this job and everyone's going to get their end of the bargain. We'll serve a few months doing grunt work, but nothing big." He turned to the doors. "Open!"

Nothing.

"Am I going to have to do this myself? Open!"

Nothing.

"Damn. Help me with this, Earl."

The two of them grunted as they pried open the lift doors.

Roscoe and Earl saw the open cargo doors as soon as the lift opened. They ran to the edge of the ramp.

Roscoe was bewildered. "Did they get free? How did they get free? Are they still on the ship? They're still on the ship. Computer! Are they still on the ship?"

"Psst. No voicebox, dumbass," Earl reminded.

"Whose great idea was that?" Roscoe snapped. "I thought they were on the ship. Weren't we following the little red dots in the display? I thought they were in the lift. Computer!"

Earl shook his head and walked back to the back of the cargo bay and opened a door to the stairwell.

"Where are you going?" Roscoe called after Earl.

"To run a manual scan of the ship. Seeing as how you hijacked it before it was fully fixed and the lifts are screwed and you ripped out the computer's voicebox..." he trailed off.

"Could you blame me? She was an annoying bitch."

"Yeah?" Earl took his hand off the door and walked down the bay to whisper to Roscoe. "Yeah? Which one of us chose the personality? You're the one that stuck our wife in the personality booth and told the computer to copy her exactly. What were you expecting? You got what you wanted. I'm leaving now, and I'm going to run a scan. And I'd highly suggest you getting in here and closing that hatch. Something tells me that while those things down there don't have our nifty-difty little blastin' lasers and gadgets, they do have firesticks nonetheless. And I've come to the conclusion that those little black and white critters we saw back there on that ice island don't run the planet, and that critters like the two we captured earlier do. I mean, they look a little like us. You notice that? Plus, they have a language and everything – and they've figured out how to broadcast over the airwaves with radio and moving pictures. You seen them old-assed satellites they got floatin' around? Sure, that's the latest technology for them. That's how back-galaxy these critters are. Ain't very evolved – but evolved enough to be dangerous with their firesticks. And now the two of 'em we need if we even have a prayer at coming out of this alive are missing, either in this ship or down on that little planet of theirs, probably runnin' scared and bringing more of 'em with their firesticks after us. So if you'll politely excuse me, I'm going to walk away from the open hatch where we're hanging like dumbasses in the middle of their sky drawing all sorts of attention to ourselves."

"We've got the cloak on," Roscoe said sulkily.

"Do you pay attention to jack shit?" Earl motioned to the part of the ship they could see from the bottom of the ramp where they were standing. "This thing's flickering like a damned strobe light."

Roscoe studied the ship and knocked on its flickering underside. "It's not that bad."

"It's bad enough," Earl retaliated. "Now you don't see it... Now you don't see it, Now you do! Kinda! Oh, there it goes! Cloak's all the way off now! Now it's back on... It's busted, just like everything else in this jalopy of a ship."

Earl stomped the floor in frustration. "Ow." The cargo bay rang with metallic reverb. "Now, like I said, I'm going to run a manual scan. And if that turns up empty, I'll search for the homing beacon I put in them. Your help would be much appreciated, though if you stay here with your thumbs up your voiding orifice it'll just mean you won't get in my way." Earl paused for a second. "Yep. Never mind. On second thought, stand here. I'll do this myself."

Earl turned and walked off.

"I'm coming," Roscoe called with defeat.

"Whatever."

Chapter 58 At the Lake House

Wally had made several trips from the cellar's hidden weapon room to the four-wheeler parked under the second story deck, but still treated each trip like it was his first - taking his time to listen and watch for anything harmful. At least for now, he felt sufficiently better armed. While the room irritatingly lacked a single handgun, it did have its share of AK-47's, M-16's and semiautos. Not to mention not one, but two (two!) rocket launchers, mortars, and other heavy weaponry. He had carried several of the AK-47's and one of the rocket launchers up in previous trips, but had not yet brought up any ammo.

Wally was very uncomfortable holding the flaming kerosene lantern directly over boxes of live, army-grade ammo, but he had no choice. He found clips for the AK and the smaller semi and loaded both the guns and his pockets with as much ammo as he could carry, but he needed something larger to carry all the bullets he would need in one trip. The wooden boxes they were currently in were too heavy and would take several people to move.

He remembered seeing a cooler in the kitchen and climbed upstairs.

He also felt sufficiently armed enough to handle whatever might be lurking behind the pantry door.

The puddle of blood still looked fresh. Not a good sign. He realized he still did not have a flashlight, so opening the door quickly and having the element of surprise was gone. He thought that opening the door and jutting the lantern in to squint into the darkness might not have the effect he wanted of frightening whomever might be behind the door.

So he did the next best thing. He crept to the side and opened the door into the kitchen, hoping that if indeed anyone was lying in wait they would make the mistake of jumping into the room, at which point Wally could put himself back in control.

Nevertheless, after he flung the door open, nothing happened.

The breathing he had heard only moments before stopped. He wanted to announce his presence in a very authoritative voice, but at the same time did not want to give his position away to the world – the world being anything inside our outside the house that was hostile.

So he talked very calmly, but as forcibly as he could muster, to whomever was in the pantry.

"This is the police. Put your hands in front of you and walk to the door. I want to see your hands first."

Finally, a broken voice emerged from the pantry. "Hello?" More raspy breathing. "Who's there? The police? Thank God." Whoever it was stopped to catch his breath. "I'm Detective Moses, and I need emergency medical attention."

Wally burst around the door and lowered the lantern to the floor, where Detective Moses lay.

"Moses? Where are you hurt? What happened?" Wally surveyed the bloody gashes in his uniform, all on the arms, legs, and neck where his bulletproof armor didn't cover.

Moses was having a hard time breathing. "It's a fucking nightmare. I mean it." He coughed, and Wally could tell that talking hurt him. "Went all fucking Elm Street."

What? What was Elm Street? Somewhere downtown where drug deals and gang turf wars went on?

"Elm Street?" Wally asked.

"Oh, fuck, boy. Eddie Kruger or whatever his name was."

"Freddie Kruger?"

"Unh."

Wally had no idea what Moses was talking about. But he was about to explain that they needed to get out of the house as quickly as possible when he heard a thud from the stairwell. It sounded like the sound had bounced up the staircase from the bottom, so assuming it was a person – either they were coming up where they were now, or were going down where he needed to go to get the rest of the ammo.

He leaned down to Moses and whispered. "We need to be quiet. But can you move?"

Detective Moses shook his head slowly. "Look at my fuckin' legs, son." Wally aimed the lantern down to take an even better look than before, and was nauseated by the sight. There were bones sticking out of his pantslegs.

"Jesus. Does that hurt?"

"It did," he answered slowly and sleepily. He sounded drugged. "But I downed a handful of painkillers," he patted his pocket and Wally heard the rattling of pills in a case, "and I think my nerves are shot and I'm in shock. I need help."

Wally thought for a moment. Detective Moses was big. More than three-hundred pounds big. Moving him would be a major undertaking.

"We gotta move you," Wally said.

Moses spoke slowly with great pain. "Get an ambulance. I ain't moving."

There was another dull thud from downstairs.

"Then I'm dragging you."

Moses sighed.

"There's a four-wheeler outside. I need to go downstairs and get some more ammo. As soon as I come back, I crank it up, come get you, and we're out of here."

"Look, I ain't gonna make it. I don't know how long I've been in this closet, but I know that I ain't got too much longer in this world." He paused to take a staccato breath.

Wally cut him off before he could continue. "Don't talk that way, Moses. You're a little banged up, but you're gonna be fine. I'll get an ambulance to meet us. I'll be right back."

"Wait!" Moses yelled. "Get back here, dumbass." He paused for another breath. "You got any idea of what's going on around here?"

"Not really," Wally admitted.

"Didn't think so. So shut up, goddamnit, and listen. You sure as hell don't need me kicking off in the middle of a sentence, do you?"

"No."

"Okay. So shut up and listen. Sheriff Barrack is dirty."

"I kinda figured that one out."

"Seriously, boy. Shut the fuck up. I mean he's probably the biggest criminal in the state. He's got all sorts of dirt on all sorts of people. Everyone – you, me, fucking senators and even the damned Governor. And you want to know who controls most of the drug traffic between Dallas and Atlanta? The sheriff. That's how he gets away with it – dirt on people."

"Okay, Moses. I understand. But look, we really gotta get moving. I can get you to help."

Moses cut his eyes at Wally and whispered raspily. "You're a damned idiot, you know that? What did I say? Shut up, boy, and let me talk."

"Sorry."

"So here's the facts. Quick and easy, because I really don't feel too good. One, he's dirty. Two, he's connected. Three, he's got more weapons and ammo stashed in different places than the National Guard base down the road. Four, and this is the big one, one of his little problems that he had has come back in a motherfucking big way."

"Okay, I'm listening."

"You remember Billy Ray and Dale?"

"Who?"

Moses paused sleepily to think. "Never mind. Was before your time here. They were Sheriff's Deputies. Billy Ray was the undersheriff, Dale was a narcotics officer. Make a long story short, they found out about the sheriff and confronted him, threatened to get the FBI in here and everything. Big mistake. Sheriff tortured them poor boys and buried them in the pond a few years back. Back when you were probably still in high school or in diapers." Moses paused again. Breathing was becoming more difficult. "Anyway, so here's the part that don't make no sense, but it is what it is. I don't know how, I don't care how. All I know is Billy Ray and Dale came back. The last time before now I saw them was when they were screaming for mercy as the crane lowered them, in Billy Ray's truck, into the pond."

"Why didn't they just swim out?"

"They were chained in. Tied in and chained in. No getting out of that. Sheriff doesn't want to hear from you again, he doesn't hear from you again."

"Right. Got it."

"Until now." Moses reached up and grabbed Wally's shirt collar, dragging him close to his face. "They came back. You hear me boy? They came back from the dead, in their truck. I wouldn't have believed it if I hadn't a seen it with my own two eyes." Moses stared at Wally for emphasis. "And they got a whole damned army of them things with them."

"Army of what?"

"Zombies, boy."

"Come on, Moses, you're in shock. Let's get you out of here."

"Goddamnit, boy! You listen to me!" Moses was still holding Wally's collar. He shook him. "I ain't making it out of here alive. You got a chance, but not if you stay around here. You need to get the hell out of here – out of this county – and call in the big boys. FBI, CIA, Army, National Guard, I don't care. Because them things can't be stopped." He paused for another pained breath. "There's so many of them, and you can't kill 'em." His voice grew panicked. "You just keep shootin' 'em and shootin' em, and they keep coming. And if they get your hands on you," Moses leaned his head to look at his legs and arms and sobbed, "Oh, God, it's horrible."

"What about the sheriff?"

"He's gone?"

"Oh, God. He didn't make it?"

"No, no," Moses coughed, "He left with some of the others. Fucking bastard left me and some of the others here to die." He coughed again and pulled Wally close to his mouth to whisper. "You see that son of a bitch again; kick him in the nuts for me. Okay?"

"Okay, Moses. Okay. Hang tight. I'll be right back, and we're getting out of here. We'll get help. Just hang tight."

Moses let go of Wally and seemed to pass out. Wally checked to make sure he was still breathing. After confirming that he was, Wally looked to see if Moses had a flashlight and sidearm. He did, but the flashlight was covered in blood and other lumpy unidentifiable body matter. Wally fought to keep from getting sick. He took the pistol and tucked it in his holster, grabbed the kerosene lantern and his Uzi that he had found earlier, and eased his way back to the hall.

Shit, he thought. *The cooler.* He backed into the kitchen and tried to figure out how to carry it, the lantern, and the Uzi without dropping any of the three while still being able to defend himself should the need arise.

He didn't necessarily believe Moses' story, but it creeped him out nonetheless. He held the lantern in one hand, the Uzi in the other, set the cooler on the floor and tried fruitlessly to peer into the dark staircase ahead of the weak orange light.

Remembering the thumps he heard earlier, he was ready for anything that might be waiting for him at the bottom of the stairs. Again, he wanted to announce his presence in a strong voice but had Moses' story ringing in the back of his head. He called out softly instead.

"This is the police. Identify yourself."

Silence.

"I repeat: this is the police. You must identify yourself or I will consider you hostile. I am authorized to use deadly force to neutralize any threat." He thought that sounded pretty good.

Still more silence.

He decided to hold the cooler in the same hand as his Uzi, so he grabbed the handle and jerked it upwards. The weight of the cooler made it twist in an awkward way so that he had to wrap his fourth finger and pinky around the handle so he could keep his thumb and middle fingers wrapped around the Uzi with his index finger on the trigger.

It was a very uncomfortable configuration.

Not to mention difficult to keep the cooler from banging on the narrow walls of the staircase.

So he had to extend his arms to hold the cooler in front of him.

Which was very heavy.

This is not a good situation, he thought as he navigated the stairs to the bottom.

Wally waited for his eyes to adjust to the light and peered into the small area of the basement he could see from his position in the staircase and could barely make out the wall on the opposite side of the room. He cursed Moses for getting bits of his body all over his flashlight, thereby ruining Wally's chances of using it instead of the feeble light provided by the glass kerosene lantern.

Well, here goes, Wally thought. *If there's someone in there, I might as well surprise them.*

He burst into the basement, putting his back against the wall and turning quickly to analyze anything posing a threat in the room. He caught a shadow out of the corner of his right eye and spun quickly to open fire.

There was nothing there.

He thought he heard something move behind him, so he spun left to open fire.

Nothing again.

Damn shadows dancing all over the place. I'm seeing things and hearing things. This is a stupid idea. I have no backup and am walking into a really dangerous situation.

He strained to hear anything other than his own heartbeat and heard only silence. The room appeared clear. There were other hallways leading out of the room, and the lantern provided too little light to peer down them. Rather than checking the entire lower floor to clear it, he decided to take a chance and bolted across the room, stopping to put his back against the wall opposite of him. The room was still clear from this angle, so he just had to navigate the short hallway to the "wine cellar."

He stuck his lantern in the opening and peered inside. It and the small area of the cellar he could see from his position appeared clear.

He inched quietly down the hallway, straining to be aware of anything that made a sound. He knew something was down on the bottom floor; he just didn't know where. Odds were that it was down another unexplored hallway. But still, better to be careful.

His heart was racing. Had that something been in the basement the whole time he had been down there? It was a scary thought.

Treating the wine cellar the same way he did the other rooms, he edged in and made a quick survey. The lantern light twinkled off the wine bottles. The door to the ammo room was still open, so he eased over to see if it was clear, but not before checking the hallway behind him to the main basement room.

Something moved.

He froze to gaze into the darkness.

He waited.

The flame flickered.

Nothing happened.

He waited some more.

Nothing happened.

Finally, he turned to go into the wine cellar.

It was empty too.

This is the last trip I make, he thought. *I am really, really creeped out now.*

He looked up to the ceiling and found a single light bulb with a pull switch. He pulled it. Nothing happened.

Of course. Power's out. If it were that easy I'd have just flipped the light switches all over this house instead of fighting with a kerosene lantern.

He searched several boxes until he found the ammo for all the weapons he had taken earlier. If he put the lantern on the ground, the box was too dark to see into. If he held it up, he only had one hand. The glass lantern had a thin metal rod, which he tied to the pull switch of the non-working light bulb overhead.

The lantern swung softly, causing every shadow in the room to dance hypnotically.

Wally set the cooler down and rubbed his aching fingers where the handle had twisted them and rubbed against them.

It then dawned on him that the cooler would be much, much heavier once loaded with ammunition.

He looked around for something more portable. Just shelves and shelves of heavy wooden boxes.

It was no use thinking about it now, because his mind was certainly starting to play tricks on him. He was hearing things. He needed to load up and get out of there *now.*

He grabbed boxes of ammo and placed them in the cooler as quickly and gently as possible. He also grabbed a few grenades and spying the 50-caliber gun on the top shelf, paused to debate whether or not to make just one more trip for it.

He decided to make that decision once he was back outside, but he knew that he wouldn't really come down those stairs again. Too creepy, 50-caliber or not.

He put the grenades in with the last box of ammo and went to close the lid when it happened.

Someone or something was coming up the short hallway to the wine cellar.

If he ran to close the trap door, he didn't know where the secret trigger was in this room to open it. He'd be trapped.

Which, given the current situation, might not be so bad.

But whatever he decided, he needed to do it quickly.

Because it was ambling up the hallway.

And it did not look alive.

He stumbled backward in an attempt to put distance between the thing and himself and succeeded in tripping and falling backwards in the process. He watched in slow-motion horror as he flung his hands to balance himself, causing the tip of his gun to whack the hanging lantern.

It swung wildly and hit one of the shelves, but the glass didn't crack.

Wally hit the ground as he realized one side of the paperclip-thin metal handle he had tied to the string slid ever-so-peacefully out of the little tab where it had been hanging. The lantern leaned heavily to one side, giving the other side of the handle more room to maneuver its way out of its tab.

Wally jumped up to catch the falling lantern.

He dared not let the Uzi go – after all, the thing was still ambling up the hall and he needed to take care of it.

So, he cupped his hands and leaned to catch the falling lantern, Uzi in one hand, nothing in the other.

And watched in terror as the lantern landed, and then slid slowly off his fingertips.

He was still seeing everything in slow motion.

He fumbled to catch it and succeeded only in bouncing it around even more and throwing it harder against an open box of ammo.

Where the glass finally broke.

Well, fuck.

Wally lost sight of the thing in the hallway as the lantern landed in the box.

By the time the fire spread to the leaking kerosene, he'd be dead from the explosions. He'd have to fire into the darkness in the hope he'd kill whatever was there.

He screamed (he found it helped him not overthink situations) and opened fire. Pitted between the undead in the hall and the rockets and grenades soon to be exploding around and underneath him, he figured the zombie to be the lesser of his troubles.

He pointed the Uzi in the direction of the zombie and let her rip. He wished he'd have grabbed the AK-47 instead.

He emptied the clip and listened for a sound, but the fire was already crackling in the wooden box.

Well, fuck again.

He grabbed another clip and loaded it. He noticed the fire was a bit brighter now and decided his only option was to grab the cooler and run for it, firing the whole way and spraying whatever and whomever with bullets.

He ran full-force into the hallway and ended up body-checking the zombie, sending both of them to the ground and his cooler spilling loose ammo.

He was still screaming.

He could feel the zombie clawing over him. He fought to free himself.

It felt a bit like wrestling with a large buffalo chicken wing, he noted. There were bones. There was meat. Only it didn't smell anything like chicken wings and would probably be the single event that set him off them for life.

For now, though, he was trying desperately to find its neck through the slimy and meaty parts.

Because it was trying to eat him.

He was on top of it and guessed that he had landed with his head somewhere around the zombie's chest.

Sure enough, he reached his arms and found its neck as it squirmed and snarled to get a bite in somewhere.

The fact that this thing was dead made itself readily apparent. As such, Wally didn't have to worry too much about crushing its esophagus. He jumped off it and grabbed its arm in an attempt to force it to roll over on its stomach in a submission move.

Except it didn't work.

The arm came off in his hand.

Which really kind of disorientated Wally. First the arm was offering resistance, then when it came off, his hand jerked up with the sudden lack of weight behind it. The arm was still wiggling.

The zombie was trying to stand up, so Wally tossed the offending arm behind him into the room which was now burning and making ominous popping sounds.

He tried the other arm and was still surprised when it popped off, too. He threw it into the room with the other one.

At least now it couldn't claw at him, though it had managed to scratch him in a few places on his face.

Wally decided that since it was lying on the floor now without any arms, he could probably get away from it.

He stood up to run and yelped when it bit him on the ankle.

He pulled his ankle away, tearing his pants and some skin in the process, and hobbled quickly to the cooler and scooped what ammo he could into it. He ran, dragging the cooler behind him, to the hallway he knew was on the other side of the basement. He found the staircase and paused at the base to change clips one more time before climbing it.

His ankle smarted with each step, and he let the cooler bang on each step on the way up.

Behind him, he heard the very deadly sounds of gunshots coming from the hidden room as the first of the ammunition heated enough to fire.

He made only cursory checks of each room as he ran outside with the cooler to the four-wheeler and strapped it on.

Detective Moses was still inside. He'd be dead for sure if the house went up. If he wasn't already. He needed to get the four-wheeler as close to the kitchen as possible to get him.

Wally paused to curse himself for the one thing he had forgotten.

The keys.

He searched the engine quickly for the kick start rod he knew wouldn't be there. It was too new and too nice of a four-wheeler.

He doubted he had enough time to hotwire it.

He jumped off and skipped inside, keeping as much weight off his injured ankle as possible, running over to where Moses lay. Maybe he'd know where the sheriff kept the keys.

"Detective Moses?" he asked as he shook the heavy-set black detective.

"Moses? Come on, we gotta go."

Nothing.

"Moses!"

Nothing.

Wally felt for a pulse.

Moses was dead.

Wally felt like throwing up.

Should he try to drag his body out of the house? He didn't know if he would have enough time. He decided to try anyway.

Moses was heavy, and dragging him with an Uzi in one hand and an injured ankle was slow moving. Wally had only made it a few feet when he heard something clambering up the stairs.

He renewed his awkward pulls on Moses' uniform in an effort to scoot him a few more feet to the door outside.

He looked up and saw a key hanger on the wall.

There were keys on it.

Quite a few of them, in fact.

He grabbed them all and stuffed them in his pockets as the armless zombie came around the corner, followed by the sound of gunfire.

It would be any second before the heavy stuff started going off.

He reached down and gave Moses' body another pull, dragging him maybe two feet.

The zombie ambled closer.

There would be no way he would make it away from the thing. But he couldn't just leave Moses, either.

He gave Moses one more pull and managed to pull him halfway out the door before the zombie came within a few feet of them.

Wally screamed at it and opened fire with his Uzi, only managing to knock bits and pieces of stray meat and bone here and there.

It kept coming.

He aimed for the head and pulled the trigger. He kept pulling the trigger until he heard the clicking of an empty clip.

The head exploded bit by bit in a spray of dark brown, black, and gray matter over parts of the wall and kitchen.

It stopped coming. It teetered on its legs and seemed to look around.

Wally could see the wall and window through the gaping crevice in its head where presumably its brain had recently been.

And finally, it died. Again. The dead thing died. Redied?

Wally didn't have time to consider zombie syntax and semantics or the verbal challenges posed by reanimation.

The house began to shake with the rumblings of the explosion in the basement.

He'd never pull Moses to the four-wheeler, which was still forty yards away. His only hope was to find the key that would start it out of the batch of thirty or so he had. Why would the sheriff need so many keys?

He sprinted to the four-wheeler, still skipping on his wounded ankle. As soon as he sat down he thumped the gas tank to make sure it had gas in it (it did) and began fumbling for the keys.

The commotion underground was really starting to make itself obvious, and a light haze of smoke was beginning to seep out of the windows in little wisps. Wally prayed as he began trying one key after another.

He was on his seventh or eighth key when the first major explosion roared from the house. The heavy stuff was starting to go off. He had no idea how many grenades or rockets there might be underground. He had no intention of sticking around to figure it out.

He was maybe halfway through when two more explosions went off, shaking the house and creating a fine layer of excited dust over the ground around it.

And he had a new problem.

All the racket had brought some attention.

Another zombie appeared in the doorway above Detective Moses and gazed at Wally before leaning down to snack on the detective's innards. Only he couldn't because the Detective was wearing his bulletproof vest, so the zombie settled for his head instead.

Wally tore his eyes off the gruesome feast to try more keys.

Another zombie peered at him from a second story window.

Please tell me that one of these damned keys works, Wally prayed.

Something in his periphery caught his attention. Three or four zombies had appeared at the edge of the woods next to the house and were walking quickly, though somewhat jerkily, toward him.

He figured them to be maybe a hundred and fifty yards from him.

Far enough away for him to try the last few keys.

Smoke from the house was beginning to pour out of the windows now. Somewhere inside a dangerous fire was growing.

Wally noticed with a sudden sense of dread that the four-wheeler on which he was currently sitting was maybe fifteen feet away from the tank of natural gas that fed the house. He looked up to notice with even more dread that a few zombies had appeared from around the other side of the house.

These would be upon him in seconds.

He grabbed the Uzi and opened fire, wasting a clip shooting several in the chest. It did nothing to them except to spray apparently non-essential body matter into the air behind them.

He cursed and reloaded, this time aiming for their heads. He dropped the first zombie in seconds. Then, realizing the trick, he made short work of the second and third zombies. If the five or six from the woods got close enough to pose a threat, he'd have no problem getting rid of them.

Then the house really caught on fire. Wally could feel the oppressing heat from where he sat, merely thirty feet away under the deck. The wooden deck. Which would shortly be on fire too and falling down on him if he didn't find the key.

He was down to ten keys left, and he was trying key number nine when something crashed overhead.

He jumped and dropped the keys in the grass.

The first tendrils of fire began making their way up the side of the wooden home, headed for the deck.

He leaned down and grabbed the keys, fighting to remember which ones he had tried. He refused to accept that he had to start all over again.

He tried a few more, and finally – luck. The four-wheeler started. He kicked it in gear and sped toward the driveway as the deck above where he had just been burst into flames. A zombie that had unbeknownst to Wally just been on top of the deck caught on fire, spun around, and fell off the deck.

Wally tore around the corner of the house, trying to dodge the bodies lying in the driveway from the bloodbath earlier.

He drove away as the house roared with more explosions. He could hear the thunderous booms and tinkling glass as he drove away. He guessed correctly that there were more stashes of weapons and ammunition upstairs.

He had driven a few miles when he heard the last explosion. It was loud enough and powerful enough that he felt the ground shake under the whining four-wheeler. He had no way of knowing for sure, but he had a feeling that there would be nothing of the house left.

A few miles down the road he turned to look. The plume of smoke and small cloud rising from the house affirmed his suspicions.

He was keen on taking Detective Moses' advice. He needed to get out of town and alert the ... who?

The Army? The FBI? The CIA? Which one of those had training on zombie warfare?

He didn't know. But he did know that he needed a car.

There would be a church up the road where he could commandeer one.

Chapter 59 At Uncle Crank's

Chett spoke slowly and drew out the curse as he surveyed the scene. "Hooolllyy shit. What happened here?"

Harry looked around at the scene lying before them. The trailer had been tipped over; deep ruts cut through the yard; the barn was demolished and still smoking from whatever did the demolishing.

Harry cleared his throat and got Chett's attention. He nodded to the junk car lot. "I don't know, but weren't most all of those cars at least right-side up when we were here last?"

Chett saw the dozens of overturned cars, most of them resting on top of other crushed vehicles. Like the barn, some were still smoking.

He scratched his head and jogged to the tipped over trailer, shotgun held at the ready. "Uncle Crank?" he called. "Hello? Anyone here?"

No response.

He kicked the rubble of what had previously been the trailer's supporting cinder blocks out of the way and grabbed part of the frame to climb onto.

The door was facing skyward, and he had to climb up to get in to check on Uncle Crank. Harry rushed to join him.

"Is he in there?" Harry asked, grabbing an axle to climb.

Chett didn't even look at him to reply. "Since when have I had X-ray vision, Harry?"

"Sorry. You don't need to be a jackass. Just didn't know if you could hear him or something."

"You're three feet away, Harry. If I hear something, you'd hear something too."

"Okay, okay," he mumbled. "Jackass."

Chett set his shotgun on the side of the trailer that was now facing up and pushed himself onto it. Harry followed suit.

The pair walked over to the open door and peered inside.

"Uncle Crank?" They called in unison. "Uncle Crank?"

Still no response.

It was dark inside, primarily because most of the small windows that would have let in light were now giving a beautiful view of pitch-black dirt.

"Well, I guess it's a good thing that the door is open." Harry said.

"Why's that?"

"I reckon if it was closed, that'd mean that he was in it when it tumped over and still in it. At least with it open like this, it means he might not've been in it when it happened, or if he was then he's made it out."

"Good point," Chett conceded. "Uncle Crank?" He waited to hear something. After a minute of waiting, he looked up at Harry. "Okay. Cover me as best you can. I'm going in."

Everything was lying on the new bottom of the trailer. The easy chair, the newspapers, the tv, everything was in an even bigger mess than before.

He walked over to the door and lowered himself in, dropping the four feet to the other side, landing on the side of the coffee table and the side of the recliner, tripping in the process.

He recovered and looked around. No sign of Uncle Crank. He unclipped a flashlight from his belt and turned it on and began to dig around in the rubble. Still no sign of Uncle Crank.

The last place to search in the stiflingly small trailer was the bedroom, whose door – because of the recent ninety-degree remodel of the home – was now three feet tall and completely blocked by debris.

Chett tried to dig down and move the stacks of stuff in the way – the other end of the coffee table, the TV, the chair, the plates, the magazines – and finally got to where he could see the door. He leaned down to take a look and noticed that the mattresses in the bedroom had tumbled down and were blocking his view.

He banged on the wall and yelled for Uncle Crank. "Hello?" He banged some more. "Are you in there?" He put his ear to the wall and heard a faint noise.

"Uncle Crank! It's Chett and Harry! Can you hear me? Are you okay? Do you need us to get help?"

No response. Just a faint noise. Chett knocked harder on the wall. "Uncle Crank! I'm going to try to get in!"

But the mattresses were too heavy. Uncle Crank must be laying on them, he thought. He turned to look at the door/skylight. "Harry! Need some help here. I think he's in the bedroom!"

Harry's head poked in. "You sure?"

"Think so. But there's too much crap in here. Mattresses are stuck."

Harry's head disappeared from the doorway and was replaced by his feet as he lowered himself to the floor/side of the trailer.

Chett made an effort to warn him of the tricky landing angles posed by the chair and coffee table, but it was too late. Harry landed first on his feet, then hard on his ass.

Chett ducked just in time to avoid the shotgun blast that knocked a head-sized hole in the wall.

"Harry! Shit! You just damn near blew my fuckin' head off!"

"Sorry! Shit! I'm sorry! You could've warned me. Shit!" Harry looked at his gun as though it was its fault, and not his, that he had nearly shot off Chett's head.

"That was too close to be cool, man! You gotta watch out!" Chett's ears were still ringing. He stuck a finger in an ear to wiggle some sound back into it. "And you might have killed Uncle Crank!"

Harry stumble-walked through the mess over to the new hole in the bedroom wall and craned his neck to get a good look inside.

The room was dimly lit from the little dirty window on the side/roof and gave little definition to anything inside.

Until a zombie stuck his rotting, grimy, grinning head up to meet Harry's at the hole.

Harry yelped reflexively and jumped backwards, falling over the easy chair and taking Chett with him.

"Shit, Harry, watch out!"

"Zombie!" He pointed to the snarling face peering out of the hole in the wall. It looked a bit like a rabid dog.

"I see! I see! But it won't do either one of us any good if you keep trying to kill me!"

Harry leaned up, took aim, and before Chett could plug his ears he made short work of the zombie head.

"Damn, Harry! I know that was necessary and all, but for the love of God, I'm going to be deaf by next week if you keep this up!"

"What? Seriously?" He turned to look at the now slightly larger hole in the wall and motioned to it with his free hand. "Zombie!"

"Yeah, but it was kind of behind the wall and not posing too big a threat, huh?"

"Look, man, enough arguing," Harry yelled over the ringing in his ears. "I'm damn near deaf too, okay?"

"But I haven't tried to kill you today."

"Give it a rest."

"Give it a rest? You damn near blew my head off! I'm not giving it a rest!"

Harry sighed. "This isn't doing us any good. If Uncle Crank was in there, he'd have been gone by the time we got here, and I for one don't feel like going and sticking my head in there again to find out. Let's climb out and get back to the RV."

"Wait a sec," Chett paused. "Didn't he say something about a dune buggy last time we were here?"

"Yeah. But what do you want a dune buggy for?"

"Gives us a few more terrain options in a sticky situation, doesn't it?"

"Would be nice. But there's a problem," Harry said.

"What's that?"

"Did you see the barn?"

"Oh, yeah." He paused. "Maybe they're under the rubble."

"You really want to stick around and waste time digging them out?"

"Shit. Good point. Let's go."

And with that, they climbed out of the door/skylight and landed in the dusty, rubble-strewn yard.

Chett was dusting himself off when he heard Harry mumble something.

"What?"

"I said," Harry answered in a loud whisper, "do you hear anything?"

Chett stood up and listened closely. The sounds of wildlife had already faded away over the last couple of days for whatever reason. Crickets, birds – all silent. Just the breeze. But... there was something else too. A faint humming and crackling. And it was getting closer. Fast.

Chapter 60   On Highway 61

"Hey! Hey! Wait!" Clay whipped his head around as the car passed a rusted yellow-beige-brown RV parked on the side of the road. "That's Chett's and Harry's RV! Pull over!"

Bob turned her burqa-covered head to Clay and cocked it at a slight angle to convey her lack of understanding.

Clay motioned with his hands like he was turning a steering wheel. "Stop the car. Pull over." He turned around in the seat to see the RV behind them and pointed to it. "Go back. Chett and Harry!"

"Oh!" came the disarmingly cute reply from behind the sheet.

Clay was thrown for a loop as the car slowed down a little – but not enough to stop – and whipped around to face the other way in less than a split second.

He picked himself up from where he had been flung between the door and car seat and looked unbelievingly at Bob.

"Chett and Harry! Vroom Vroom!" she answered without being asked.

"Great. What other habits have you picked up?" he muttered.

She made the motion of opening a can of something and said, "Chh! Glug glug glug! Ahhh!"

"It was a rhetorical question. But that's great too. Beer and bad driving."

The Lincoln Town Car pulled up to the dusty gravel driveway.

Clay opened the door and surveyed the scene. "Oh, God. I know this place. This is Uncle Crank's. I hope he's not cooking dinner." He turned to look at Bob, who was also exiting the car. "Because if he is, don't eat it."

Clay walked over to the RV and knocked on the passenger door. "Chett? Harry? Hello!" He tried it and found it unlocked. He was about to step in when he heard yelling in the distance.

He couldn't make out what they were saying, but he could see Chett and Harry running quickly down the driveway towards him and Bob.

"What?" Clay yelled back at them. They were perhaps sixty or seventy yards away.

"RUN! We said RUN!"

"Run where? We have cars!" Clay yelled back. He noticed that while they were running, they were taking turns looking back over their shoulders and into the sky.

"Get in the RV!" Harry shouted. "Both of you."

"What's going on?" Clay yelled back. "Need us to help you?"

"Yes!" Chett yelled. "By getting in the RV. Now! Crank it up!"

Clay climbed back into the RV and eyed the steering column. "No keys!"

"None needed!" Chett yelled. "Bitch hotwired it!"

Clay looked at Bob and sighed. "Come on, Bob, get in. You're not a bitch."

Bob had one hand on the passenger seat and was sliding in when a very large shadow fell over them.

Clay hadn't noticed before in all the excitement, but there had been a loud humming and popping noise that with the appearance of the shadow seemed to get much quieter – almost like the way a car falls quiet when you're not gunning the engine.

Clay looked up through the windshield and saw the sky. For a second. Then for a second he didn't, because something was in the way. But then it wasn't again, for a little while. But then it was again.

"What the hell is going on now?" Clay asked.

Bob was standing half-in the RV, looking up.

And she started yelling.

Clay couldn't make out the language, but he knew pissed-off female when he heard it.

She had stepped back out of the RV to jump and shout at the aberration in the sky when Chett and Harry finally got close enough to shove her in.

"Gun it! Go! Go! Go!" Harry said breathlessly as he and Chett tackled Bob as they dove through the still open door. They lay in a jumbled mess on the floor as Harry looked up to yell again. "Now! Go!"

Clay remembered the dire urgency of the last time the two of them had jumped in his car and commanded him to go, so he wasted no time arguing.

But while Bob had undoubtedly done a superior job fixing the RV, she hadn't managed to get around to turbo-charging it in her fixing frenzy. The RV lurched slowly backwards into the road.

"Shit! Faster! Go faster!" Chett ordered.

"I've got the pedal to the floor, Chett! If it's speed you're after, let's bail and get the Lincoln."

Harry had managed to scoot out of the tumble of bodies into the back and stand up. Chett was still on top of Bob, tangled in her burqa. The two of them managed to roll into the back, Bob cursing and spitting in her native tongue.

The side door swung closed as Clay pulled the RV onto the

highway and accelerated southward.

Clay watched in terror as the flickering outline of the shadow moved with them.

"Um, guys, I don't want to interrupt your little love-fest back there, but whatever it is that you're running from this time is following us." He pointed up. "And I'm scared to ask, but are these the same things that were chasing you before?"

Harry sat breathlessly in the passenger's seat. "Shit. Actually, no, Clay. At least, I don't think so. I don't really know what they are, but I think it's safe to say that they're not our best friends just wanting to hang out."

In an unprompted act of confirmation, a bright flash of light temporarily blinded them. Clay regained his vision in time to jerk the RV back into the correct lane. He was about to ask anyone with more knowledge what in the hell just happened, but the sight of a singed and smoking tree a little in front of them answered it for him.

"Anyone got any ideas? They got fancy laser-blaster thingies!" Clay was hysterical. "Anyone? Anyone?" He paused. "Hello? Fancy laser-blaster thingies and they're shooting at us?"

"Chill out, Clay." Chett had freed himself from the tangles of Bob's burqa and had grabbed a shotgun. Bob was standing next to him and steadying herself. Still cursing.

"Chill out? Seriously? When I'm about to be vaporized thanks to you? You know what? Forget this." Clay hit the brakes. "Bob and I will take the Lincoln. If it's you they're after, if we're in the Lincoln and they manage to get you, we won't get got again in the process."

"What?" Harry asked.

"We won't get caught again. Or killed – because no one's brought out the blasters against us yet."

"If you stop, we're dead ducks," Chett answered calmly, though a little out of breath. "All of us."

Harry chimed in. "Look, their aim is shit. They hit a tree."

"Could have been firing a warning shot, you know?" Clay said, letting off the brakes but still not hitting the gas either. "Like 'Stop now, before we blaster you.'"

"He's actually got a point, Chett," Harry said. "That looked a little like a warning shot."

In another perfect fit of timing, a bright flash blinded them.

Another tree was smoking. This time a little closer.

Harry felt like he had butterflies in his stomach. "You know, Chett, I'm kinda at a loss here. I'm not one for just giving up, but they do have blaster-thingies and they are shooting at us."

Chett was grimacing, seemingly in pain. "Look, we were lucky to get away the first time. We may not be so lucky again.

"Are you all right?" Harry asked. "You don't look so good."

"I'm not feeling so good," Chett answered. "But I'm feeling fine enough to put a bullet in anything outside the RV that doesn't look friendly."

"Yeah, that's all good and stuff, but do I need to keep driving or what?!"

But he never had a chance to answer.

Something massive exploded. Somewhere very near the RV.

Then something massive exploded again.

Little bits of red glowing fiery things floated down the windshield like little pissed-off pixies.

In the distance, a few more trees disappeared in flashes of bright lights.

"You know," grunted Chett, "I'd be one happy mofo if I never saw shit on fire coming from the sky. Ever again." He moaned again. "I'm sorry guys, but I gotta go." Holding his stomach, he stood up and bolted for the little bathroom behind him.

"There's no bottom to the tank! It's just gonna hit the road!" Harry yelled.

"That's the least of my worries right now!" he yelled back, slamming the door.

"Actually, I'm not feeling too grand myself," Harry moaned.

"Well, I'm sorry about that, but in case you've forgotten, WE'RE BEING SHOT AT!" Chett barked through the door.

The RV had slowed down considerably and coasted to a stop. Ahead and all around, bright flashes of light were taking out trees with a vengeance.

"What the hell are they doing?" yelled Clay as he surveyed the sky. "Are they just screwing with us? Because that just ain't cool."

Harry was doubled over in pain and spoke through gritted teeth. "I'm going to venture a guess that they're not doing that on purpose." He turned around to face the bathroom. "Hurry up, Chett!"

A muffled response: "I'm not in here to waste time, jackass."

Harry stood up to work his way to the bathroom when the side door of the RV flung open. He swung his shotgun and prepared to pull the trigger when someone called, "Wait! Don't shoot!"

He held his gun at the ready and called out, "Who's there? Identify yourselves or prepare to eat buckshot."

Someone from the road called, "It's just one person – Detective Wally with the Warren County Sheriff's Department."

Clay nearly fell apart in the front seat. "Great! They've finally found me! I'm dead, I'm dead, I'm dead. Mom's going to kill me. I'm going to get fired and I'm going to go to jail. And I'm being shot at." He ended by sighing heavily and pounding his head on the steering wheel.

Chett, having finished his business, opened the bathroom door but stayed inside. "What do you want?" he called to the detective who was wisely hiding out of sight.

"A ride, if that's okay. I'd really rather not stay out here with all this craziness going on."

"You work for the Sheriff's Department? What are you doing out here?" Harry chimed in.

"Look, I'm heavily armed, riding a four-wheeler, and right now I think all of us would welcome the extra hands and firepower. I just wasted my only two rockets I had on that thing, and that's why we're not all dead right now."

"You shot that thing?" Chett asked.

"Twice. Shot the gun that those laser beams are coming out of. Hit it twice and didn't destroy it, but I did apparently manage to hurt its ability to aim. And again, I'd like to load up and get out of here before it gets lucky."

Chett thought it over for a second, white flashes still popping around them like a heavy lightening storm. "I don't think so, thank you. We're pretty well armed ourselves. Good luck."

"Look," the detective called out, "I didn't have to save you. I could have just hidden in the woods. I don't mean to arrest any of you. I give you my word that you are the very least of my worries right now."

"Fine," said Harry. "Chett, help him load up. Bob, keep an eye on him. I gotta go."

Harry leapt into the bathroom. Chett and Detective Wally unhooked the cooler of ammo from the four-wheeler while each kept one eye on the flickering monstrosity in the sky.

Clay was still sitting with his head on the steering wheel when they finished loading.

"We need to get out of town," Wally said as he stood by the back door.

"We'll never make it," Harry said from the bathroom. "Holy shit, I'm in pain," he said out loud.

"No," Clay said, determination in his voice, "We need to go back. Back to the woods. Back to where Bob has been trying to get us to go since this whole thing started. She lost some computer or something. That's what she's been looking for. And I think it can help us. She crashed close to where you guys said you found her, so that's where we're going."

"Absolutely not," Wally said. "We're getting out of town and calling the feds. All of them. And I'm not talking about stopping with the FBI. I'm talking Army, Navy, Air Force, Marines."

"Call them on your phone," Clay said. "Because we're going to look for whatever Bob needs."

Bob walked over to Clay and knelt down, taking off her veil. She smiled and kissed his cheek. Clay rubbed his cheek and felt warmth and confidence radiate through his body. Bob sat down in the passenger seat, holding a shotgun.

Clay mashed the accelerator and the RV chugged to life. The flashes of light beamed all around as the ship overhead started following them.

"There is no signal," Wally said as he walked up to the front. "Not on the phones, not on the radios, nowhere. I order you to turn around."

Clay was about to tell him where to shove it when Chett spoke up. "Whoa, hold on there, Detective. No offense, but you don't know the shit we've been through. And Harry's right. We'll never make it with that thing following us. Now, I'm glad you're along for the ride, but if you're riding with us, you're going where we go." Chett walked up to the space between the driver's and passenger's seats. "And we're going where Clay here says we need to go. And that means we're going to Rocky Bayou. We'll take care of you after that."

Clay looked at the speedometer and smiled as it registered sixty. A muffed groan escaped from the bathroom. "Look, that's fine. But as soon as we get this taken care of, I really, *really*, want to go get my mom."

Wally and Chett were silent.

"Okay?" Clay asked.

Chett looked at Wally, who shook his head.

"What?"

Wally shifted his position again. Sitting on the counter was uncomfortable. "We'll discuss it when we get done doing whatever you need to do."

"What does that mean? 'We'll discuss it'," he repeated. "I just want to go get my mom."

Wally shot Chett another look. "Okay, fine," he said.

But Clay was uncomfortable. That look meant something. "You're thinking she's already in trouble, aren't you?"

"I didn't say that," Wally responded.

Clay looked at him in the rear view mirror. "But you're not denying it, either."

Wally shifted again. "Let's just handle one thing at a time."

Clay looked at him for a few more seconds before turning his attention back to the road.

Chett walked back and knocked on the door. "You okay?"

"Hell no. I didn't eat none of that damned zombie chicken, did I?"

Chett laughed. "Not that I can recall, no."

"Then I'd sure as hell love to know what is going on in my guts right now."

"Feels like you ate something really hot?"

There was a pause as Harry considered it. "Yeah, kinda. Why?"

"Well, I didn't want to go freaking anyone out, but you just need to not be surprised at whatever comes out."

"What? What?! What the hell are you talking about? Am I about to give birth to some freaky alien child? Aw, man, that's not cool! I'm not ready to be a daddy to some freaky alien butt baby! Oh, good lord, it hurts!"

Chett was doubled over in laughter. "Calm down, calm down. Nothing like that's gonna happen. Just hang tight. You'll see."

The RV chugged into the canopy provided by the old oaks, pecans, and sweet gum trees, still under the menacing shadow of the huge ship overhead.

A loud cry escaped from the bathroom just as the RV hit sixty.

Chapter 61   At the River

"Damn these damned things!" shouted the bloody, angry sheriff.

His crew had been all but decimated, and there was no way he was going to come out of this clean. Absolutely no way.

His only option now was his backup plan – a plan he had crafted years ago but never actually expected to carry out.

He had to leave the country. And never come back.

It was either that, or prison. Sure, the most they'd do in this good ole' boy state was slap him with a few years in the federal golf course penitentiary. But he'd lose everything – his "investments" so to speak.

Which is why he found himself at a little hidden dock on the Big Black River. Sheriff Barrack knew that taking the Big Black River would put him quite a few miles south of the connecting Yazoo diversion canal. But that was with the mindset that he'd never really have to take this route.

And getting here was beyond a nightmare. The BoGro gas station had been deserted. Totally silent. All the lights were on, but it looked like the place had been ransacked. He and the four officers that actually managed to get away from the lake house by jumping in his car were all of his posse that he had communication with.

Everything in the entire county was down - 911 service, cell phones, radio, everything. An eerie silence had descended over the acres and acres of woods and wild country. The back country drive here had been uneventful - save for the truck driving zombies hell-bent on destroying the sheriff and his crew.

He had left the lake house with four cruisers worth of officers behind him, comprising everyone on his "personal payroll." One by one, the four-by-four of death had picked off each cruiser until his was the only left.

And it did so with something that could only be described as evil intent. Each car it forced off the road would spiral out of control before slamming into a tree or flipping in a ditch. The three road-bound cruisers had all stopped for the first car down, the officers exiting with weapons drawn and firing.

Nothing could stop that truck. It was the pickup's version of the unholy undead. The sheriff wracked his brain to comprehend the very idea of zombies as it was, but that the truck itself seemed to be alive was more than he could fathom. Maybe it wasn't, maybe it was - but somehow what he had once made good and damned sure was buried at the bottom of a lake in the middle of nowhere was now back to get him.

When they stopped for the first car, they fired most all of the heavy stuff they had while still being sure not to kill the other officers. They were a hundred yards away. The drivers of the truck drove it like it was its own beast - what you would imagine a royally pissed-off, steroid-fed, two-ton bulldog to act like. It would lunge forward and feign left and right at the wrecked car as if to taunt it, stop and back up, rev its engine, and repeat. To the sheriff, it seemed that if it could have barked, it would have.

The firing officers drew its attention and it soon turned to face them, revving its engine in its unholy booming scream.

They understood the unwritten language of what was about to occur and scrambled into their cars.

The sheriff and the cruiser behind him sped off, but the third one never made it. The truck raced behind it and in a move normally reserved for police officers, performed a "pit" maneuver where it forcefully rammed the bumper of the cruiser and made it lose control, racing off the highway and into some trees.

The two remaining cruisers never stopped and could only watch the truck's bootlegger turn as it raced back to the fleeing officers.

Sheriff Barrack thought they were safe.

Until a few miles had passed. And they were pegging the tachometer.

The second car never saw it coming. They approached a small intersection where the highway bisected a wooded gravel country road so small that the highway didn't even have a stop sign. The sheriff tore through the intersection and flinched as something black caught his eye, but it was too late. The truck pounced from the road and broadsided the following cruiser, taking it across the highway and onto the other side of the gravel road, disappearing behind the trees.

It was hunting him.

And he was a sitting duck on the highway.

He knew then where he had to go: the Big Black River. His old 'escape the country' plan, now being put into place just to escape with his life.

At this point in his confusion, the sheriff didn't know if the total lack of people was a good thing or a bad thing.

All the better for the sheriff, he thought. Less people to complicate his escape. All he had to do was go down the Big Black, safe from zombies in the middle of the river, past the Rocky Bayou hunting camp, connect with the Mississippi River and head north, then take the Yazoo river all the way up to Eagle Lake. Simple as that. And all the recent rainfall should have made the water level rise - making the hidden streams leading to the lake more navigable. His private plane would be waiting there in the hangar by the lake house. He had enough fuel to get to Mexico. After that his contacts would help work him into the obscurity provided by the billions and billions of people populating the various continents all over the planet. And he had enough money to live like a king anywhere he went.

The four officers loaded their shallow bass boat with all the weapons and ammo they could. Most of it had been lost with the other three cruisers, but they still had enough to weigh the boat down considerably.

The sheriff turned to Officer Parker, his now second-in-command, and barked the order to load the gas tanks and fire up the seventy-five horsepower outboard. It would take most of the gas they had onboard to get all of them to the lake, but it was this or nothing.

And so, to ominous, oppressing, eerie silence, they shoved off from the old bridge and made their way downstream, the sheriff still training his ears intently for any sound of the four-by-four of death looming in the distance.

It was just them and the random ripples and bubbles of the underwater wildlife floating down the river.

But he still couldn't shake the feeling that the truck was somewhere close, waiting for the perfect moment to strike.

Chapter 62 - On the Way to Rocky Bayou

The loud grunt coming from the bathroom startled everyone on board. The entire crew had fallen silent after Bob and Chett stood up to Wally. Clay piloted the boxy RV down the road, constantly aware of the huge shadow above them matching their direction and speed.

Until Harry groaned.

"Oh, dear God," Harry said through the bathroom wall. "That was unholy."

"Told ya'," smiled Chett. "Feel better?"

"What the hell was that? Did you have one too?"

"Long metal thing? Blinking red lights? Little antennas?"

"Yeah," answered Harry.

"Nope. Didn't have one."

"Ass."

Chett laughed again.

All of a sudden, the shadow trailing the RV lifted, leaving the occupants blinking in the bright daylight. The ship was so large and flying so low that its departure had the same effect as leaving a long, dark tunnel.

Harry exited the bathroom as the shadow lifted. "Where is it going?" he asked.

Clay was snickering. "My guess is that you and Chett got probed!"

"What?" Harry asked, incredulously.

"Probed?" Chett echoed.

"You don't mean..." Harry stuttered and paused.

"Yep," Clay smiled, "You got probed and got a homing beacon."

"What's that mean?" Chett asked.

Wally spoke up. "It means just what it sounds like." He pointed upward. "Whoever's driving that thing up there wanted to keep tabs on you, so you got a little stainless steel suppository. And you just got rid of the device that was helping them tail you. I think. But it doesn't make sense that they stopped like that. Wouldn't they still be following us?"

Harry's face lit up. "Nope! There's no tank! Just open road below." He sat down on the mattress in the back.

Clay was disgusted. "That's gross. You just went on the road?"

"I couldn't help it. And it just saved our asses, thank you very much."

Wally had a thought. "Look, if it's all the same, I highly suggest you get off this road at the next available turn. We need to go another way to wherever you want to go."

"Why?" asked Clay.

"Because whoever's driving that thing's gonna notice that the two of them aren't with their beacons. And they're going to come looking. First place they're going to look is on this road. Hence my suggestion to turn off of it."

Chett was sitting on the little couch in the RV, across from where Wally was sitting on what constituted the kitchen counter. "Okay, Detective. We've got a few miles to cover. Why were you driving a four-wheeler and carrying a rocket launcher? And save the bullshit. We have a good idea that there is some really downright weird stuff going on."

"Well, that's a load off," Wally sighed. "But I've got some questions first."

"Go ahead," Chett said.

"You know the sheriff's been after you boys for quite some time."

"Us?" asked Harry. "I thought he was after Clay."

Everyone leaned as the RV slowed down and took a turn on to a back road.

"Well, Clay's his main target, sure." Wally turned away from them and looked at Clay, rubbing his head. "By the way, Clay, glad to see you're alive. I was coming to untie you when something hit the back of my head and punched my clock."

"Yeah, likely story," Harry said.

"No, really," Wally argued. "I was coming to untie him. Listen, I know the sheriff's as dirty as they come, and you'll see that he's probably dirtier than you think in a minute. But I'm new to the force. I got mixed up in it before I knew what was going on."

"I asked you to drop the bullshit, Detective," Chett warned.

"No bullshit," Wally answered. "We caught Clay and took him to the lake house, tied him up and interrogated him."

Harry turned to Clay. "Is that why you're so beat up? I've been meaning to ask you, but with us being shot at by aliens and all..."

"Yep," said Clay. "They kicked my ass."

"You son of a bitch," Chett spat. "What the hell did he do to you? He's half your size."

Wally threw his hands up. "I didn't touch him."

"Is that true?" Chett asked Clay.

"Actually, yeah. He stayed back."

"Doesn't mean he's clean," Chett replied.

"Look," Wally said, "I'm not here to hurt anyone. I'm not here to bust your asses. As far as I'm concerned, whatever the sheriff wants with you is his business. Get it? Because if you don't, take a freakin' look outside! That's what I'm worried about, because you – you're not out to kill me or eat me for breakfast or shove God-awful probes up my backside. Hence, we're all on the same team, okay?"

"Fair enough," Chett said. "That being the case, then why was the sheriff after us in the first place?"

"Well, he wasn't really after the two of you any more than he usually was." Wally was talking to Chett and Harry.

"What's that supposed to mean? We've generally stayed pretty clear of the law," Chett responded indignantly.

"Disturbing the peace, disorderly conduct." Wally eyed Chett. "That whole indecent exposure incident."

"Those little things? I didn't think the sheriff would pay attention to stuff like that."

"Are you kidding? Sheriff Barrack? How the hell do you think he's been sheriff so long? He pays attention to *every* little thing."

"Okay, fine. So he wasn't after us," Chett continued, "So who was he after?"

"He was after Mr. Clayton Hensworth."

"Clay?" Chett was surprised. "He was after Clay?"

Harry chimed in. "All Clay ever did was blow up his Daddy's shed."

Clay groaned from the driver's seat.

"Apparently," said Wally, "Clay's car was the best link to this damned awful pickup truck that's been tearing around."

"The Dodge of Death," Clay said.

"What?" Chett called back.

"It's what I call it. The Dodge of Death."

Chett's eyes grew wide as he looked at Wally. "You know about that thing?"

"Oh, quite a bit, I'm afraid."

Harry cut in. "That thing jumped, literally *jumped*, out of the ground at us back there at Rocky Bayou."

Chett picked back up. "What do you know about it?"

Wally scratched his head and shifted his weight on the counter. "Well, you mean aside from the fact that it's been terrorizing the entire Sheriff's Department, and has managed to actually take a few of us out..."

"What else?" Chett asked.

"I don't know if I should be telling you guys this."

"Really?" Chett peeked through the small flat of venetian blinds covering the window behind his head. "With all that's going on right now? You're worried about giving us information which actually might help to keep us from getting eaten by zombies or run over by the Dodge of Death?"

"Okay. Good point." Wally was considering the ramifications. If he told, he spilled some serious secrets. But then he got real with himself: *there were fucking zombies everywhere*. Chances are life as he knew it was going to be anything but normal from this point foreward. What could he possibly lose?

"Here goes. Let's just say that if I understand correctly, that truck has a very personal vendetta against the sheriff."

"What's that?" Chett asked.

"He had it buried."

"What?" Harry said. "The truck?"

"And its occupants," Wally added.

"At the same time?" Harry asked.

"And in the same place," Wally finished.

"It couldn't have been too terribly long ago," Harry mused, "because it's not that old of a truck."

Chett tried to stay on track. "So the truck's after the sheriff because it wants revenge. Simple enough. Who's in the truck?"

"That truck has a very unique paint job, correct?"

"Wouldn't know," Chett said. "We've only seen it at night."

"And we didn't feel like sticking around to scope out the details," Harry added quickly.

"Well," Wally carried on, "It does. It's this big black truck with orange and red flame stenciling on the front and side. Turns out, some people that supposedly left town under mysterious circumstances drove a truck exactly like that, down to the KC lights and roll bars and guard on the front and stenciling on the side." He let it sink in.

"So you think it's the same truck," Chett said.

"It *is* the same truck," Wally corrected. "Complete with two occupants."

"So," Chett was growing impatient, "Who's in the truck?"

"Two guys named Billy Ray and Dale." Wally waited for it to sink it. He had never met them personally, but he bet Chett and Harry had. Most everyone had.

"Billy Ray?" asked Harry. "No... You mean William Rayburn?"

"One and the same," Wally sighed.

"Billy Ray and Dale?" Harry asked. "The undersheriff and detective?"

"Well, actually, Dale was a narcotics officer, but yes."

Chett sat up straight. "I thought they went up north somewhere. Took a better job."

"That was the story, all right," Wally said. "After the sheriff and his crew did away with them, he told everyone they moved up to Alaska to work for the government. He even hired a moving crew to pack up their houses and everything. Sure, there were a lot of people wondering why they didn't give any notice, but of course Sheriff Barrack managed to produce letters of resignation going back a month before they disappeared. His story was that they left without telling anyone because they didn't want anyone making a big deal about it. I mean, there were a bunch of little reasons like that, none of which anyone believed. From what I gather, pretty much everyone figured that there had been some sort of little disagreement about the sheriff's 'freelance' dealings, if you will, but that they had been merely run out of town. Not killed."

"But most everyone that knew them liked them," Harry said. "They didn't seem like bad cops. Why'd he go and bury them?"

"You said it," Wally answered. "They weren't bad cops. The sheriff figured he could get them on his side. But he never could. Finally, he found out they were about to go to the feds. He had to do what he felt like he had to do."

"So that Dodge of Death," Chett added, "Is really Billy Ray and Dale, back from the dead, trying to get revenge?"

"Seems to me that's the case." Wally said.

"I'll be damned," Chett said.

"Makes two of us," Wally commiserated.

"Makes three of us," Harry said.

"Four," added a voice from the driver's seat.

"Five!" came a sweet voice from the passenger's seat. "Counting! One two three four five!"

Everyone, including Clay (who had to take his eyes off the road to do so) turned slowly to stare at Bob. She giggled.

Finally, Chett turned back to Wally. "So they're out to get revenge on the sheriff. Good. As long as they leave us alone."

"I don't really know what their motives are," said Wally. "But I'm with you. Let 'em snack on dirty cop brains, just as long as they don't start wanting to snack on me."

"Do they really do that?" asked Harry.

"Do what?" asked Wally.

"Snack on brains."

"Oh, you better believe it. I've seen it with my own two eyes." Wally seemed to grow pale with the memory. "They got Detective Moses at the lake house. Cracked his head like a coconut and went right for 'em."

Chett looked to Harry. "Why brains?"

"How would I know? I don't remember taking zombie psychology back at Harvard on the Hill," he responded sarcastically.

"Probably because you slept through it," Chett snapped back.

Bob turned around to talk to them through her veil. She spoke slowly, reaching for the words. "It... makes...scratches...go away!" She sounded excited to be in the conversation.

"What?" Chett asked.

"Zombie benzocaine?" Harry added.

"Who... *is* she?" Wally asked.

"Long story," Chett replied.

"We got another few minutes till we get to the camp," Wally said.

"Hot space babe from another planet," Chett answered.

"Oh." Wally paused. "Sorry I asked."

"No, he's serious," Harry said.

Wally stared at Harry for a moment, blinking. Then he looked up.

"She's on our side," said Chett.

Wally looked at him and arched a single eyebrow in question.

"She's saved our asses a couple of times," Harry vouched again.

Wally arched both his eyebrows in reserved acquiescence.

"No!" Bob ordered her way back into the conversation. She shook her arms in frustration as she continued searching for the right words, flapping her burqa. "It...makes...them...all better!"

Everyone turned to face her again.

Harry leaned forward. "What do you mean, it makes them all better?"

"Oooh..." She made a frustrated sound. "Need computer!"

"We're going to get it, sweetie," Clay said.

She tried again. "I zombie, okay?"

The three in the back stared at her.

"I zombie, okay?"

They stared at her some more.

"Not real zombie..."

"Oh," they sighed in relief.

"But I zombie, okay. I have...hole...in my arm. I eat you, hole goes away."

Harry caught on. "It heals them?"

"Yes!" Bob said delightedly.

"But you also mmm mmm good to zombie." She smacked her lips for effect.

"So they get better if they eat people?" Wally asked.

"Yes. But must keep eating...people...because... holes come back." Bob was beaming underneath her burqa.

"They eat people to heal themselves, and because they taste good, and because if they stop eating people, they start to rot again?"

Bob nodded yes.

They were all silent for a while.

Harry spoke back up. "So where did the zombies come from?"

"Um, the ground?" Chett answered sarcastically.

"Jackass. No, I mean what brought them back to life?"

"Balls!" Bob beamed again.

"What?" they asked in unison.

"Need...computer!" she barked. She shook her head and tried again. "Little balls. Many balls. In ship..." She pointed overhead. "Bad balls in ship. Boom! Boom!" She made her hand fly like the ship and hit it with a finger from the other hand. She made the sound of an explosion. "Pchew!" Then she dropped her voice an octave and said, "Drop balls. Drop balls on Earth!" She raised her voice again. "Balls hit Earth. Some break. Make...zombies? Make...dead...come back."

Realization struck Clay. "That's what you tried to draw in the dirt back at the trailer? You weren't drawing zeros, you were drawing little balls!"

"Yes! Balls! Need to find balls..."

"And you said your computer would help you find balls..."

"Yes!" She was clapping. "Ship..." she pointed upward "...has...water?...make zombies... go away."

Clay was putting it together, and getting a bad feeling. "Were you on that ship?"

"Yes," she said.

"And you crash landed?"

"Yes."

"Wait a minute!" Chett cut in. "They were looking for you!" He pointed at Bob. "They were! She's the whore of Babylon!"

Clay mashed the brakes, sending them lunging forward. He and Wally both said "What?" in unison.

"I think," Harry said, "that what Chett means is that while we were up there, these two ... things – I guess they're not exactly people, huh? – tried to talk to us. We couldn't really see them, but it looked like they had little boxes or something that they would talk into and whatever the boxes were would translate for them."

"Except they sounded like crazy televangelist trucker jazz DJ's," Chett added.

"What?" asked Clay.

"When they talked to us. They took turns sounding like a televangelist, then one would sound like a trucker, then the other would sound like a late-night DJ," Harry said.

"And they asked for the 'whore of Babylon,' and they kept talking about looking for a girl to love. We thought they wanted us to get them a hooker, and I think they were after her."

Clay thought for a few seconds. "It makes sense. Bob is looking for a little box – a computer of sorts – which she says can help us out. I think it can help her translate. And that's probably what happened with the people who caught you. These things are pretty advanced – they've got technology we don't. I'm sure it's possible that they tuned in to some radio stations and CB channels and had their computer box thingy analyze what the people were saying. Hell, I could probably get my computer to do something like that myself..." Clay was already thinking of the possibilities and how he could program it.

"So they're looking for you," Harry said to Bob, "and we got probed so they could find you. Thanks."

"How'd they find us?"

Clay knew. "The satellite! They picked up her signal. She was trying to call 'home'."

"Right, she was," Chett said patronizingly. "She was calling her buddies to come get her."

"That's not true," Clay said.

"Can you prove it?" Chett asked.

Clay really couldn't. He just had a hunch she was on his side.

"Well, yeah, she's helped us out a little so far. I give you that. But I still don't trust her," Chett said. He looked back at Bob. "So why *are* they looking for you?"

Bob shook her head. "Don't know words to talk. Need computer. Will talk computer."

"Fine. But for the record," he addressed everyone. "I don't have a good feeling about this."

Wally had been listening silently to the talk of jazz aliens and whores of Babylon. He had only one thing to say.

"What?"

Chapter 63   On Highway 61

"What do you mean, you lost them?" Roscoe was livid.

"Well," Earl replied, squinting his beady black eyes, "They were in that ground ship and then they weren't."

"Where did they go?" Roscoe surveyed the empty road ahead.

"Huh..." Earl made a quizzical sound and walked over to the side of a road to pick up a stick.

"What are you doing? Answer me. Where did they go?"

Earl walked a few feet on the side of the road and poked something that Roscoe couldn't see.

"What's that?"

"You gave them the ass probe, didn't you?" Earl asked.

Roscoe walked over to see what Earl was poking. It was a red metal object, about the size of a small pine cone. It was blinking red. "Why not?" Roscoe snapped. "You got a better idea?"

"Out of everything you could have used," Earl sighed, "The under-the-skin beacons, the in-the-ear beacons, the in-their-shoes beacons. You gave them an ass beacon. The biggest and clumsiest one."

"Yeah. So?"

"The one that comes out eventually." Earl looked up at Roscoe disapprovingly.

"Then why do we even have them?"

"Because it's not our ship. It's 'borrowed', remember?"

Roscoe and Earl had 'borrowed' it from its previous owner ages ago, leaving the poor sap stranded on a planet – not far from here, actually – to fend for himself. In their minds, it had been justified. Last time they zoomed by the dusty red planet, they had laughed at the guy's poor attempts at catching someone's attention. If he thought that any of the stupid little inhabitants of the little blue planet next to him had the technology to see the big face he made in the sand and dirt, much less to come and rescue him, then he was in for a laugh. Actually, some people had seen the face and gone all ape-shit over it, but nobody had sent him any rescue crew. All anyone had sent were just a few dumbassed, six-wheeled, extremely slow buggies that did him no good. He wrecked the first one he tried taking for a spin.

"So what's your point?" Roscoe asked.

"My point is that you lost them."

"Temporarily..." Roscoe said sheepishly.

"Let's get back in the ship and follow this road. We'll catch up to them. I hope," Earl said.

Chapter 64   Almost to Nine Mile Cutoff

They had been cruising down Highway 61 when they were passed by two people on a motorcycle.

"They're not wearing helmets!" Clay cried. "They're going to get themselves killed."

"There are zombies everywhere and you're worried about motorcyclists without helmets? You need a priority check," Harry said.

"Wait," Wally said. He bolted to the narrow opening between the cabin and back of the RV.

The bike's driver looked back to check his clearance before he cut back in front of them.

Wally stared at him. Something was familiar in his long brown hair and haunted eyes. A large patch of skin was missing from his cheek, revealing bone and tissue underneath, but still..."I know him. I know that face. There's a country-wide APB out on him. I think. If it's the guy that I think it is. We need to stop them."

"What?" Chett and Harry said in unison.

"I think *you're* the one who needs a priority check." Chett said. "We have much, much bigger problems than you playing cops and robbers right now."

"No," Wally paused, thinking. "It makes sense. There wasn't a lot of information available, but he's supposed to be armed and very dangerous. But there was something else..." Wally struggled to recall the details. His eyes lit up. "No, no... We weren't supposed to stop him! We were supposed to call the Feds and the CDC."

"The CDC?" Clay asked. "As in the Center for Disease Control? Why the CDC?"

"Don't know. But they said he's supposed to be a biological terrorist and that something he has may be contagious. We were supposed to stay very, very far away from him and call in a hazmat team." Wally tried to key up his radio and contact dispatch. No reply came.

"Speed up," Wally said. "Honk your horn to get his attention."

"No way," Clay said. "You've got to be kidding. Especially since he's supposed to be contagious."

Wally bent down to honk the horn when Chett and Harry grabbed him and threw him against the counter in the back. Chett held his lapels in a threatening manner and put his face close to the officer's. Harry stood directly beside him, pinning Wally's hands to the counter.

"Look," Chett said sternly and quietly, staring Wally directly in the eyes. "We are in control here. You pull something like that again, I don't care if you're a cop or not, I don't care if you're the President, but we will throw you off this RV."

Wally tried to whip himself free, but Chett and Harry responded only by tightening their grips.

Chett continued speaking, unfazed. "And we will not stop the RV to do so, understand?"

"Fine."

"That motorcycle is none of our business. And if you're riding with us, it's none of your business. When we part ways, you can do your thing. From this point out, with everything going on, I will ask you politely to forget about the law and just focus on not getting us killed, okay?"

"Fine."

Chett and Harry relaxed their grip, letting Wally jerk free.

The rest of ride was an uneventful one. Almost no one spoke as the RV gently rocked and swayed and swerved every once in a while to avoid the occasional zombie.

The closer they got to Nine Mile Cutoff, the more zombies they saw. Clay managed to miss most of them, regardless of several mentions from Chett to go ahead and take them out while he had the chance. He cringed every time he accidentally hit one.

But then they got to Nine Mile Cutoff.

The RV turned off the blacktop and coasted to a stop.

"Holy... shit..." Wally said as he stood up to peer at the sight through the windshield.

Clay made a groaning sigh and rested his head on the steering wheel.

"Son of a bitch," Chett added as he stood up. "We really got to get this computer she's looking for? Because suddenly, my heart's not really in it."

Because on the road in front of them, in no particular rank or formation, were thirty or forty zombies ambling around. They stopped in unison to eye the boxy RV a hundred yards in front of them.

Clay's mind raced. He believed Bob. He believed that the answers to a lot of their problems lay back at the crash site. He needed to get her there. All that stood in his way were the thirty or so zombies in front of him.

He raced the engine.

"Clay!" Chett snapped. "What the hell are you doing? Turn around! Let's get out of here."

Clay ignored them and put one foot on the accelerator and the other on the brake. He raced the engine and spun rocks behind him.

"Seriously. Now."

Clay raced the engine again.

Chett jumped forward and attempted to put the transmission in park. Clay fought off his attempts with one arm while he let off the brakes and the RV shot forward – comparatively speaking for an RV.

"No!" Chett yelled as he attempted to wrestle control of the RV away.

But something threw Chett into Wally and Harry, knocking them all on their backs in a pile on the floor. A tall, dark, burqa-clad woman stood between them and Clay.

She shook her head. "Un-unh."

The trio in the back scrambled to stand up. Chett, being on top, was the first to accomplish it, followed by Wally and Harry. But, all of them having stood up, a sudden decrease in the RV's speed pitched them all forward – Chett leaning face-first into Bob's soft bosom as she braced against the walls to act as a barricade between them and Clay.

Clay had hit a dozen or so zombies. The RV struggled miserably to keep its momentum as the bodies piled up in a haphazard impromptu zombie barricade in front of it.

"Crap," Chett sighed loudly. "Get the guns." He turned to Clay. "You got an ass-kicking coming for this one."

Clay heard the clicking and latching of clips being loaded into guns, shells into others. "Hand me one," he said.

"Might as well. Can't really miss from this range," Chett said without looking at him.

The sound of scraping rang loudly in their ears as the horde outside began trying to claw their way in.

"Aim for the head," Wally said. "It'll drop them in their tracks."

"Yeah, we've actually figured that one out already," Chett said. "But thanks all the same."

"How are we going to do this?" Harry asked.

The zombies were already starting to edge up to the windows.

Bob acted quickly by rolling down the passenger window. Chett followed her lead and stuck the barrel of his shotgun out of the opening crack and began blasting away, deafening everyone in the RV. She lunged to the driver's window and began rolling it down, ducking under Harry as he took a position opposite of Chett and aimed his shotgun.

Four shots fired. Four zombies down.

The little metal door directly behind the driver's cabin began rattling.

"Ah, hell," Wally sighed as he shouldered two AK-47s, one on each arm. "Here goes."

He kicked the door open hard enough to knock back the zombies outside, but it only opened two feet or so. Standing in the opening was the gruesome grin of the undead. The very undead. Not a fresh body. The hair was long and stringy – but only existed in rare patches and clumps. One eye was missing. So were several teeth, plainly visible through the large portion of missing flesh that should have been its lips. Wally took aim and pulled the trigger, trying not to blink as bits and pieces of its head disappeared in sync with the report of the bullets.

It staggered backwards and fell, replaced quickly by a slightly fresher zombie. Time seemed to dilate and stretch as each bullet found its mark and left an opening in one head after another. Two zombies down for Wally. The door swung open in slow motion a little farther, revealing two zombies at once. Sufficiently convinced that zombie number two posed no more threat, Wally swung both AK-47s around, pointing one at each body, and let them rip.

His technique was simple. He tried to judge the exact moment when a zombie gave up the ghost, so to speak, and would already be taking aim at the next ones before the last ones hit the ground. But still, the zombies advanced, pushed onward by the gathering group behind them. Wally found himself backing up as they reached the threshold of the RV.

He felt something slide across his feet and almost recoiled in terror until he noticed it was Bob, laying prone with another shotgun. She took out two or three zombies – enough to push them back a little, before sliding away and standing shoulder-to-shoulder with Wally, both aiming through the narrow door which had just swung completely open. Wally took out another two zombies, and Bob took careful aim with her shotgun.

Wally noticed in surprise as each blast took out not just one or two – but three or four zombies at once. He was surprised by how good she was – lining each shot up for maximum impact.

Clay ran to the back and picked a rifle up off the mattress. The small rectangular window above the mattress in the bedroom opened outward by a small hand-crank. As Clay rotated the small handle, two gray, slimy, bony fingers slid through the opening. Clay shrieked and swiped at them with the barrel of the rifle, knocking one of the fingers off.

Still, the hand continued reaching through the window. Clay stood up on the mattress to get a good view, but the angle and the size of the window afforded a view of only a few square feet outside. Which, as it were, was more than enough to let Clay see the rotting body trying to claw its way inside. He stuck the barrel out, pointed at its head, and pulled the trigger.

Click.
Click.

No ammo.

The zombie grabbed the barrel of the gun and started jerking. Clay fought him off while searching the bed for bullets. He grabbed a handful and started trying to load.

No luck. Wrong type.

He tried some more. The zombie jerked harder. Clay could feel himself losing the grip on the rifle.

Finally, success. He found a shell that fit, loaded it, and pulled the trigger. A small hole opened up in the zombie's head, but not as big as the other guns were making. And not big enough to put the zombie out of business.

He reloaded and fired again. Another hole appeared and the zombie stopped jerking as hard, but it was still alive. For a zombie.

Clay cursed, grabbed a few shells, and reloaded. Three more bullets finished the job.

Another hand appeared at the window.

Clay reloaded and called out to everyone in the RV. "My gun's not as good as yours!"

"What?" Wally was the one who responded. No one could hear anything through the earsplitting explosions and resulting tinnitus.

Clay repeated his yell, as loud as he could, motioning to his rifle and shaking his head. "My gun's not as good as yours!"

Wally looked back at the growing group of zombies in front of him and tried to yell back. "You've got a .22. Get a bigger gun!"

Clay understood and searched for a bigger gun, finding an Uzi. It looked like a toy gun, but it would probably do the job, he thought. He found a clip, loaded it, and stuck it out the window, pulling the trigger. It worked. The quick spray of bullets made quick work of the zombies' heads, and due to his position, they really posed no threat to him.

And while the partially-open windows in the front cabin were covered with gore, ooze, and the hands of clawing zombies, Chett and Harry could keep them at bay thanks to the natural barricade of the windows, which the zombies didn't seem to think about breaking.

But to Wally and Bob, it was a different story. They just weren't able to kill them as fast as they approached. There really wasn't enough room for a third gunman at the door, so they couldn't get help from anyone else.

Wally, still firing, noticed that Bob had stopped for some reason. He looked over at her and she patted the tops of his arms, pushing them down.

Why would she be trying to tell me to stop? He thought.

She continued pushing down, and reluctantly Wally let off the triggers.

As soon as he did so she took one quick step and dove out the door, jumping over some of their heads but ultimately landing somewhere in the fray.

Wally was hesitant to resume shooting, because if Bob were to stand up at the wrong time or in the wrong place, well, the bullets don't really care if you're a zombie or a space babe.

But the zombies were getting closer. Wally had to do something. And quickly.

He dropped down to a sitting position, lowered the AK-47's as low to the floor as he could, pointed them upwards, and started shooting from the hip. His hope was to keep taking out zombies while decreasing his chances of hitting the woman who idiotically just jumped in the middle of them. He figured that by assuming a low angle and shooting upwards, he would minimize any chances of hitting her.

To his relief, he heard the thunderous boom of her twelve-gauge coming from outside the RV towards the back. Somehow, she had escaped them and managed to put a few yards distance between herself and the zombies. And she was taking them out, two or three at a time.

She was also attracting their attention. Some of the mob at the door turned to walk towards her, relieving the pressure of their forward momentum and allowing Wally to push them back.

Wally guessed that everyone together had taken out maybe half of the zombies, meaning they were winning the battle. He noticed that the frequency of blasts from the front cabin had also died down considerably.

He heard a muffled scream from outside as he took out the last two or three of them out from the doorway.

Chett and Harry joined him as he cleared the immediate vicinity outside before stepping out of the RV and into the harsh glare of an early Sunday afternoon.

They had misjudged the number by twenty or so.

"Where did they come from?" Chett asked irritatedly.

Wally and Harry made a quick study of the scene. Bob was struggling underneath a mob of ten or fifteen zombies. Having been attracted by the commotion, ten or fifteen more had appeared from the side of the road, lumbering toward them.

Bob let loose another cry, though Chett noted it didn't sound alarmed or hurt – it sounded frustrated.

Wally's military training took over and he began barking orders. He motioned to Harry. "You pick 'em off. You," he nodded to Chett, "Come with me." They ran to Bob's pile-up.

But they didn't get there in time.

Because bodies started flying.

One hit the RV and bounced off. Wally sprayed him with his AK-47. Another flew right into Chett, knocking him back. Chett yelped in surprise as he lost his balance and fell, using his gun to beat back the clawing body on top of him.

Harry made a quick grab for the zombie's arm. Had Wally been thinking more clearly, he would have warned him that physical manipulation was an ineffective method of moving a zombie. And very gross to boot.

Its arm came off, throwing Harry off balance with the sudden lack of weight.

He reached to grab the zombie's other arm, this time prepared for possible detachment.

But then a flying zombie whacked him pretty hard and knocked him to the ground.

Bob let loose a low, powerful growl that crescendoed into a mighty scream.

Zombie parts went everywhere. Heads, hands, arms, unidentifiable bits flew from the center of the melee with astounding speed and force. The RV rang with the sound of body parts hitting the siding.

Lying flat on his back, Harry took aim at the putrid face floating above his and blew it to bits, then rolled over to get a good angle on Chett's zombie and repeated the process.

Clay had finished shooting the last zombie he could see from his vantage point. Hearing that the noise had moved outside, he rushed to join the others in their fight. The first thing he noticed was Bob, fighting off a dozen zombies with ferocious abandon.

He ran to help but a hand held him back.

"Don't." Wally said. "You'll only be in her way. She's got it under control."

As if to exaggerate the point, they ducked under a flying zombie head.

Clay watched in a weird mixture of admiration and terror as Bob performed moves out of every kung-fu and karate movie he had ever seen. She was an artist – manipulating her leverage and body weight to deliver deadly chops and kicks, twisting her body in tandem with several zombies to pop their heads off. She was dismantling the entire mob all at once. Bare-handed.

Meanwhile, Chett, Harry and Wally were picking the rest off with good old-fashioned gunfire.

When the dust from the crunchy gravel road settled, bodies were everywhere.

Clay ran to Bob, praying she was unharmed.

She stood there, breathing heavily, her black burqa covered in gunk.

Clay ran to her and threw his arms around her, zombie guts squishing between them.

She hugged him back.

Clay could have stood there for hours in the hot sun – flies gathering, corpses rotting – just held in that embrace.

But then Chett had to go and ruin it by putting his hand on Clay's shoulder and turning him around forcefully.

"Now," he said, "About that ass-kicking."

Clay was caught off guard. He stood there stammering, trying to think of what to say. He *had* kinda gotten them into this. But he had to. Bob needed him to.

He was about to make a defense when Harry spoke up. "Cut him some slack, Chett. You can kick his ass later. We need to get to the woods and get this damned computer of hers and we need to do it quick."

Chett stared at Clay for a moment longer, then smiled, releasing his grip.

Clay sighed with relief.

"Still want to know where all these zombies around here came from," Harry shouted over the ringing in his ears.

Wally took out his earplugs. "What?"

"Where did you get those?" yelled Harry, pointing at them.

"My pocket."

"You got any more?"

"Nope. Only pair."

"How come we never thought of that?" yelled Chett.

Wally rolled his eyes.

Chett turned to Clay. "Where do we need to start looking?"

"I don't know. Where did you find her?"

He looked up the road, scratching the stubble that had been growing unshorn for days. "Couldn'ta been more than two or three miles from here."

"A mile makes a big difference when we're basically gonna have to search the woods on foot," Harry reminded him.

"Were there any landmarks you can remember?" asked Clay.

"You kidding?" laughed Chett. "Only thing there is on this road is gravel and trees and dirt. That's it. Everything looks the same from one mile to the next.

"Well, then," Wally said as he walked back to the RV, "I say we hit the road and see about jogging your memory. No sense standing around talking about it. Let's just drive real slow until we figure something out."

Chett was scratching his beard. "No, really, I figure it had to be a few miles from here, because that Hank Williams song..."

"Family Tradition?" Harry offered.

"That's the one. It had just come on, right when we turned onto the road here. We were three minutes into the song, going forty or forty-five when we hit that snake – I remember looking at the speedometer right after hitting it, before I hit the brakes..." He tailed off to do the math.

Clay spoke up for him as they all climbed into the RV. "Well, forty-five is three-fourths of sixty, and if you'd have been going sixty you'd have gone three miles. We're right here at the start of Nine-Mile cutoff, so if you're right, you'd have gone three-fourths of three miles." Clay did the math quickly in his head. "You went two and a quarter miles! Reset the odometer and let's go!"

"Damn, Clay," Harry joked, "Look at you putting your head to good use."

"Anything to get us out of here quicker," he grumbled.

Harry took the driver's seat and they set off. Chett and Wally kept their eyes on the road, straining to see any potential threats. Three minutes later they slowed to a crawl.

Wally was the first to speak up. "Damn. Everything on this road really does look the same."

"Told ya," Chett said.

"Well," Harry said, "At least we're in the ballpark. Let's get out and hit the woods. Everyone load up."

"Wait!" Chett said. "What's that?" He pointed to something shiny up the road a few hundred feet.

Harry saw it too. "I don't know," he said. "But we can find out."

He let off the brake, letting the RV creep forward. He stopped and put the RV in park when they got close enough to step out and look at it.

Chett hopped out and leaned over to examine it more closely. "Well, I'll be damned," he laughed. "Missed one." He chucked the very hot, very unopened and beat-up beer can to Harry.

He turned to Clay. "This is it. This is your spot." He motioned with his arm to the woods behind him.

Clay looked at Bob. "Bob? This is it. Let's hurry and go get it. Do you know where you crashed?"

Bob looked at him, grabbed a shotgun and jumped out the door, walking hurriedly to the tree line beside the road. Clay followed closely behind, trailed even closer by Chett, Harry and Wally – all of them armed to the teeth with anything and everything they could grab. Wally had his two AK-47's; Chett had a twelve-gauge and pockets bulging with ammunition. Harry had the thirty-aught-six and more pockets with bulging shells. Clay swung his twelve-gauge from side to side, sweeping a healthy paranoia of getting shot in its wake.

"That thing's unloaded, right?" Wally whispered to Chett as they walked.

"Yep. Still gives you the creeping willies, though, right?"

"Yep. Every time it points at me."

Bob stopped to scan some trees and walked a line thirty or so feet long, apparently eyeballing the trees from behind her veil. Then she stopped in her tracks, walked close to examine one in particular, and stepped in the woods.

Clay paused a second to see what she saw, but couldn't do it. Just a broken branch.

Every ten feet or so, Bob would stop and examine the trees around her.

Then Clay got it.

So did Harry. "Smart girl," he said.

She had stopped every ten or fifteen feet after the crash to break a branch. They walked almost a mile into the woods. It gave Clay enough time to piece something together.

"You knew you'd need to get back to the crash site, right?"

"Yep!" Bob said as she walked on.

"And you knew you needed your computer. Why didn't you bring it with you?"

"You'll see!" she sang back.

Several minutes later, they ended up under a dark shadow. Clay looked up to notice the shade was created by a gigantic parachute.

Below the dark canopy rested a large, white, round object nearly thirty feet long, tipped over on its side.

Clay stated the obvious. "It looks like an egg!"

Chett stated the obvious. "I'd hate to see the chicken..."

On the bottom, Clay could make out a very small opening. Upon closer investigation, it appeared that this must have been the opening through which Bob escaped. The thing had landed on its side, partially burying the hatch in the soft ground. Through the hatch on the ground had spilled hundreds of little ball bearings.

Bob had apparently been able to force the hatch open enough to crawl through. Clay leaned in to examine it and could see deep footprints in the ground around it, where once she freed herself she must have tried to force the pod upright.

She walked up to it, put her hands on it, and motioned for them to join her. Clay seriously doubted the five of them could actually move it, but that didn't stop him from being the first to rush up and join her.

Slowly, the egg started moving. Rather than standing upright, it spun awkwardly on its side, propelled not just by sheer manpower but by the spring-loaded hatchway door as well. It rolled over enough to let Bob in.

"Light!" Bob barked.

The group looked at each other, questioningly.

Bob held out her hand and looked at Clay. "Click, click, light!"

"Oh," Clay said. "Flashlight."

"Flashlight."

Clay reached to his belt, where he had tucked the large Maglight he took from Wally back at the lake house and handed it to her.

Once she shone the light inside, Clay could see why she couldn't have just squeezed herself back in to begin with. There were hundreds of canisters of those ball bearings everywhere, making reentry impossible without rolling the egg off its hatch.

"What are all these things?" Wally asked, kneeling down to pick some up.

He looked up at the sound of Bob screaming from inside the egg just in time to see her body-check him into the mud.

"No!" She barked. "No touch!"

Wally looked up at her, incredulously, still holding the balls.

She saw that he still held onto them even after being knocked over, so she slapped them out of his hand.

"I don't think she wants you playing with her balls," Chett joked.

Clay shot him a look.

Bob ran back into the egg as Wally stood up, wiping the larger chunks of mud off of his uniform.

"Seriously. I think those are the things that bring the dead back to life. The balls she was talking about," Harry added. "I don't think they're anything you want to be touching. Unless you die. Then maybe you'll want some."

Bob trudged back to the egg and crawled in the hatch. Clay went to join her.

"No," she barked from inside, "You stay outside. Safe outside."

Clay still kneeled down to peer inside. He could see the flashlight's conical beam waving around, bouncing off the thousands of gleaming orbs littering the ground. He could hear Bob scratching around.

"Clay!" Chett yelled.

Clay looked up to see him pointing at the egg.

"What are all these things?"

Clay stood up and walked to see what Chett was pointing towards.

On the side of the egg were black and blue markings that started at the tip of the egg and continued down to its bottom.

"It's obviously some sort of alien writing," Clay said. "Maybe when Bob gets out she can translate it for us."

Wally walked up to join them. "That's good and all, but I gotta ask: What's our plan after this?" He pointed to Clay. "We still gonna try and get his mom, or are we gonna do the smart thing and get the hell outta dodge?"

"You think somewhere else is safer?" Clay asked, angrily.

"Weren't you the one who said there weren't any reports of this shit going on anywhere else?" Chett asked.

"Things might have changed," said Clay.

"Or they might not have," said Wally. "And frankly, I think that's our best chance. There's a National Guard armory down on our way out of town. If something's going on, they'll know. And I don't know about you, but if this stuff is going on everywhere else, I'm going to feel safest in a fortified base with easy access to high-powered weapons. So there's our plan."

"Might I make one more suggestion?" Harry said, also walking up to the group.

"What's that?" Wally sighed.

"The armory is south of here, right?"

"Right," Wally admitted, hesitantly.

"And who knows what we'll meet on the road, right?"

"Right," Wally admitted, even more hesitantly.

"Then I suggest we take to the water."

"You're kidding," Wally said.

"Why not?" Harry answered. "Less chance of zombies in the river. It'll take us due south and put us out a few miles from the base."

Wally didn't answer. He paused to consider the ramifications.

Something dawned on Clay. Why would there be zombies anywhere else? Here's where they all came from! "These things," he pointed around at the little metal globes littering the ground, "These things made the zombies, right? This thing crash landed here. There wouldn't be zombies anywhere else."

"Kid's got a point," Chett said, rubbing his chin.

"So, we go get my mom and get out of town. Problem solved."

Wally was just about to concede when they heard a loud crash from inside the egg, followed immediately by an exclamation by Bob.

The group dashed over to the opening, getting there just as Bob stumbled through the mess out of the egg.

"Ha!" she said. In her hand was a shiny green box, about the size of an iPod. She typed in a few strange characters in the small keypad below the screen and started talking in the clicking, chirping, sing-song language that must have been her native tongue.

The box chirped back at her.

She didn't look pleased.

She repeated the command.

The box repeated the chirp.

She looked even less pleased.

She said something else, and the box started making the sound of an old analog radio tuner, trying to hone in on different frequencies.

After a minute of unsuccessfully trying to find something, she gave up and barked something else to her little device.

She looked at Clay, Chett, Harry and Wally and pointed the box at them, uttering a single word. "Talk!"

"Um, okay..." Chett said. He looked at Clay like maybe he'd be able to explain what she wanted. "What?"

"It seems pretty easy to me," he said, speaking very clearly, "She wants us to talk to each other. And I would suggest doing so as clearly as possible. Use proper grammar."

"What?" Chett was growing impatient.

Harry's eyes grew wide. "I know what she wants," he said. "Do you remember how, on the ship, those two guys were holding something in their hands?"

"Yes," Chett said.

"And do you remember how they would say something into them, and then the box would translate?"

"Yes," Chett said, still waiting to see where this was going.

"Well," said Harry, "I bet she wants us to keep talking because that thing is trying to figure out how we talk."

"Exactly!" said Clay. "That box has to have some sort of basis to translate. Right now, it's probably trying to understand everything from vocabulary to inflection and sentence structure. The longer it listens to us, the more accurately it can translate from her language to ours and back and forth!"

"That's all good and well," Wally said, "but if that's what she's looking for, can't we have our little English lesson as we're going away?"

"I don't see any reason why not," said Chett. "So let's go get Clay's mom, if for no other reason than to keep him from whining the whole time, and then we can put the pedal to the metal and hit the road."

"Deal," said Wally.

"Thanks," said Clay.

"Don't mention it," said Chett.

"Nope," Bob jumped in, pointing at the box again. "Need call home."

"Are you serious?" Chett popped his hand against his forehead and rolled his head to the sky.

"Need call home again," Bob said. "Call more Bob."

"More Bob?" the four chimed in unison.

"More Bob help," she answered.

Chett turned to Clay. "What does she mean, more Bob? Is she part of some weird Amazonian outer-space tribe of clones or something?"

"I don't know," Clay shrugged. "But I'm supposing she doesn't have the language capacity yet to say the word 'backup'."

"Fair enough," said Chett, "but going back to my trailer's not an option. Bob's not the only outer-space freak we're having trouble with. If we go back to our trailer, we're headed for certain trouble. I say let's hit the river, head south, get to the armory and she can call collect from there as far as I'm concerned."

"No way. Absolutely not." Clay stopped walking, forcing the rest of the group to do the same. "The last thing we want is to go walking up to some military base while zombies are everywhere and say 'Hi, meet Bob, a hot babe from outer space. Can she borrow your satellites?' There's no way they'd let her go messing with international communication equipment."

Harry cut in. "And that's assuming they don't cut her up to run all sorts of tests on her."

Clay's face turned white.

"Thanks, jackass," Chett whispered.

"Look," Chett said, beginning to show signs of extreme fatigue and aggravation, "We've already agreed to go get your mom. You managed to drag us out in the middle of the woods with all these zombies everywhere. I think we've repaid our debt to you for saving our asses earlier. We can't just keep putting ourselves in harm's way. We got her computer; we're going to get your mom. But I draw the line there."

"Fine," said Clay.

"What does that mean?" asked Chett.

"Drop me off at my mom's house. We'll find our own way out of town. *After* she calls home."

"What's that mean?" Chett asked.

"It means," said Clay, "that however I need to get her to a satellite dish, I'm going to do it. If I have to drive us back to your trailer, just the two of us, then so be it."

"Don't be stupid, Clay." Chett started walking again, followed by the rest of the crew. "You're dead without us. You need our guns."

"And I'm pretty damned sure," Clay said with as much force as he could muster, "that this town needs whatever backup she can bring."

"We'll see when we get your mom," Chett said. "That's the best I can do for right now."

Bob jumped in again. "Balls leak. If it hits water, big bad."

"What's that mean?" Wally asked.

"I think it means that whatever's in those things is leaking, and if it gets wet, there's going to be trouble," Clay explained.

"How you reckon?" Wally asked again.

"How, Bob?" Clay said.

"Mmm..." Bob paused to think of the right words. "Stuff in ball, it leaks, it hits water, it makes more stuff. But water has to have..." she paused again, struggling.

Wally was growing frustrated. "Has to have what?"

Bob was still searching for the words.

"Has to have what!?" Wally barked.

"Back off," Clay said. "If she doesn't know the word, she doesn't know it."

Bob tried again. "Has to have stuff make tasty."

"What?" This time, it was Chett.

"Eat," Bob said, motioning with her hands. She made a sad voice. "Not tasty." Then, in a happier voice, "Put stuff on, now tasty!"

"I have no clue what you're talking about," said Wally. "Nor do I feel like hunting down a metal detector and searching out every one of these things that could be spread across the county."

"Well," Clay said, "if she says we need to find them, we need to find them."

"One thing at a time," said Chett. "Let's get to your mom's first."

"Big bad," reminded Bob.

"Yeah, yeah," said Chett. "We got that too."

"No, you not get me. I like Wally," she pointed to him.

"Well," Chett chuckled, "Sorry, Clay. Seems you've been replaced."

"No," Bob said. "I *like* Wally." She buffed herself up and spoke in a false deep voice. "I here to serve and protect." She raised her voice again. "I like Wally. Am trying to stop big bad."

"Okay," Clay sighed. "We get it. You like men in uniform. And you're trying to keep something bad from happening. We gotta teach you how to let a guy down gently."

Bob sighed. "No, you see." She pointed to the green box. "When it understands and has words, you see."

They trudged off back towards the RV, eyes peeled for a random zombie.

Chapter 65　On the Big Black River

The sheriff and his rag-tag crew had floated briskly down the Big Black river thanks to the recent downpour. No one spoke. In fact, no one made a sound save for the occasional shuffling of Officer Parker as he repositioned his bottom to take the pain off his hemorrhoids or the occasional click of a lighter as one of his officers lit a cigarette.

Sunlight swept silently across them in small golden patches from the canopy of tall mossy oak trees as they navigated the narrow river closer to the mouth.

The sheriff checked his GPS unit and was about to announce that they were just a few miles from the Mississippi River when they heard it.

The rumbling.

It was in the distance, sure. But there was no mistaking it.

The truck had found them.

It roared once in the distance, then fell silent again.

The sheriff broke the silence with a drawn-out whisper. "Fuck...me..."

Officer Parker leaned close to the sheriff, also whispering. "It's okay, boss. They can't get us in the water."

The sheriff didn't respond. He kept looking into the dense forest to the north where the sound had come from.

Twenty miles. Twenty miles upriver to the Yazoo. Then another ten or fifteen to Eagle Lake and his airplane.

Chapter 66   On the Way to Clay's Mom's House

"For the record," Harry noted, "I really don't like this at all."

Harry and Wally were sitting in the ripped Naugahyde seats in the cabin. Harry was driving, Wally was riding shotgun – literally. He was well armed.

"Me neither." Wally noticed what Harry had noticed – the complete and utter stillness. There were abandoned cars on the side of the road – some of them crashed in the trees, some of them apparently pulled over on purpose. But all of them were empty.

They passed back by the empty BoGro gas station. As they pulled into town, they saw more and more empty cars and broken shop windows.

They pulled up next to Clay's house. Wally turned to look at the group. "Listen up. We're going to do this the right way – the military way. We're going to treat this like an extraction, got it?"

"What's that mean?" asked Clay.

"It means," answered Wally, "that Chett, Harry and I are going to cover each other. Bob's going to stay here as the driver if we have to come out fast."

"I'm coming too..." Clay said.

"No, you're staying here."

"Why?" he asked. "She's *my* mom."

"Exactly," said Wally.

"What?" he asked again.

Harry understood what he was saying. If Clay's mother was a zombie, there would be all sorts of trouble from Clay. Trouble that could get them killed. He wouldn't be able to act in his own interest, meaning he wouldn't be able to kill the zombie because she was his mother.

"What Wally's saying," said Harry, "is that you need to stay here to cover Bob." He grabbed a twelve-gauge and tossed it to Clay. "Here. Use it only if you need to, understand?"

"Okay," Clay said, placated.

"Good one," Chett whispered.

"All right," Wally said, "I don't want us yelling to each other to communicate. Here are the signs we'll use." He instructed them on common military signs for "look" and "clear" and a few others.

He turned to Clay. "Got a key?"

"Sure." Clay fumbled in his pockets and handed it to him.

Chett, Harry and Wally hopped out of the RV and fanned out to cover the front and sides of the house. Each made the sign for clear and regathered at the front steps. Wally unlocked the front door and they burst in, each fanning to cover all angles.

Clay watched them as they disappeared into the darkness of the house and strained to hear anything over the loping of the RV's engine.

Several long, excruciatingly slow minutes passed before he saw movement again.

He squinted, trying to see his mother, but only saw the three of them coming back outside, walking to the RV.

The RV shook as the door squeaked open and Wally stepped in. "No luck. She's gone."

"What?!"

Harry was close behind. "No, she's not *gone*, Clay. She's just not there."

"What do you mean?"

Chett was the last to climb in. "It means she's somewhere else right now, Clay. I'm sure she's okay. We couldn't see any signs of struggle."

"We've got to find her."

"Absolutely not," said Chett. "For all you know, she may have already gotten out of town. There's no way we could know. Let's hit the river and get out of here."

"In case you guys have forgotten," Clay said, "the town cemetery is just a few miles from the waterfront. You really want to go closer to that big of a zombie farm?"

"We don't have a choice, Clay," Wally said. "We'll evaluate the situation when we get there."

Bob gave the driver's seat to Chett and sat in the back with Clay, who was sitting slumped over on the mattress with his head in his hands.

She put her hand on his back and lifted her veil, smiling a deeply beautiful smile that seemed to wash away all sense of time and worry.

He felt himself getting lost in her eyes, falling so deeply in love that there was no turning back. There were no zombies outside, they weren't in an old RV – there were only the two of them in infinite black space, ready for the deep, life-affirming embrace that would lead to heaven.

He leaned forward to make his move and snapped out of his trance when he saw her eyes flick to the small side window. His eyes followed her gaze. How long had they been driving? They were almost past the radio station, which was just a few miles from the river.

"Wait!" he yelled. "Stop the RV!"

Chett decelerated and yelled back to the small bedroom. "What's up?"

"Stop! Just stop it for a second!"

Chett brought the RV to a stop in the middle of the deserted road.

The radio station was a few blocks north of them.

"The radio station! They've definitely got satellites. If they don't have one that transmits, I can rig one up in no time."

Chett, Harry and Wally all turned to survey the street. Several zombies had gathered in front of the radio station, clawing at the windows.

"I don't think so," said Chett. "We don't need another zombie fight. I want to go away from them, not dive headfirst into a group of them."

Clay was dumbfounded. "It's just a few of them..."

"That we see," finished Wally.

"Sorry," said Harry, "but I'm with them."

"Ugh. Fine." Clay slammed the small bedroom door shut.

Chett put the RV back in gear and started the slow chugging acceleration that the RV could manage.

No one would notice how quickly Clay acted. In a matter of seconds, he grabbed two boxes of ammo, a shotgun and a rifle, and was out the top escape hatch with Bob before Chett hit twenty.

They waited until he stopped at an intersection and jumped off the ladder on the back.

Chapter 67   On the Street to the Radio Station

"All right, Bob," Clay said, tossing her the rifle. "You're the good shot. I'll knock them off if they get too close."

"Okay," said Bob.

Clay made a quick survey of the scene. Downtown really only consisted of a square of maybe five or six blocks. The radio station was a few hundred yards away. Everything was silent, which would have been normal for a Sunday afternoon, except that everything was a little too silent. There were no sounds of cars in the distance, no sounds of people talking or milling about. The only things Clay could hear were the whistle of a breeze through the streets, the flapping of a flag in the wind, and the clanging of a metal fastener as it banged periodically against the flagpole.

So, all they needed to do was take out the four or five zombies milling about in front of the radio station, break in, and there you go.

It dawned on Clay that they might be in bigger trouble than he realized.

Bob could dispatch the zombies quickly, sure. But as Clay recalled, zombies seemed to be attracted to the sound of gunfire.

Meaning, if there were more of the undead around, the gunshots would act as an open invitation to a zombie party.

Damn.

And what if there were zombies in the radio station? What then?

Damn again.

"Okay, Bob, so I may have not thought this through." He and Bob stood with their backs to a building around the corner from the zombies. "We're going to try to sneak in. Come on."

Several of the buildings had small alleyways between them; places where Clay assumed the business owners would take out the trash and whatnot.

Sure enough, while each alley was not a straight-shot to the next block, it provided them with enough cover to give Clay a small sense of security.

They paused at every intersection to make sure the roads were clear. Luckily, each was.

Clay was the first to arrive at the door of the radio station, which was very appropriately locked.

The satellites would be on the roof, and there was a good chance that there was also a roof entry hatch up there with them. Maybe it would be unlocked.

He and Bob wasted a few minutes standing on each other's shoulders to reach the ladder to get to the roof only to find out that it was indeed locked. From the inside.

Damn.

They climbed back down and Clay did the only thing he could think of. He shot the lock off. He figured once they were inside, they could barricade the door, and it'd be a few minutes before the brainless zombies figured out where the noise came from.

They entered and faced a long hall, several open doors on each side. Daylight from the plate glass windows in the lobby filtered down the hall, casting ominous shadows of shuffling zombies.

Clay and Bob made a quick sweep of each room. The break room was clear, as was the bathroom. Each room proceeded that way: sweep, clear, next room.

All were empty. Except until they got to the DJ booth.

There sat a brainless zombie, wearing headphones and pawing at the audio board. Clay could hear a tinny Garth Brooks in the headphones. Clay pumped his shotgun, and the zombie whipped around at the sound. Clay pulled the trigger without hesitation, spewing brown and red and gray across the poster-lined walls of Faith Hill, Tim McGraw, and Rascal Flatts.

If they had planned on going unnoticed, it was too late now.

The zombies outside looked to the large plate-glass window looking into the DJ booth and started ambling towards it.

"Whatever we need to do, we need to do quickly, Bob, because I don't know how long these windows will hold." Clay scrambled out into the hall, searching for the server and satellite closet he knew must exist.

The small group of zombies they had seen on the street was now beginning to bang and claw at the window. The pounding echoed down the hall as Clay and Bob started searching every room and closet for signs of the satellite feed.

"Bingo," whispered Clay. They had made their way back to the break room, which had a small storage room full of radio knick-knacks and cheap giveaways. The storage room led to a smaller closet with rack-mounted computers and equipment.

From down the hall came the sound of someone violently trying to shake the front doors open.

"Hurry," Bob whispered.

"I am, sweetheart," he whispered back to her. "Here's the main terminal. Seems like we're in luck – they have a transmitting satellite. From the looks of the programming, I don't think it's been used in a while. I don't have my laptop with the star chart, so we'll have to guess at the direction we'll need to aim it."

"Wires?" Bob whispered. "Plug box into computer?" She pointed at the little shiny green box she had rescued from the egg.

"I don't think you've got plain old USB capability on that thing," he said.

He thought for a moment, and an idea struck. "But... maybe... if that thing of yours understands radio..." Clay searched for the little box he hoped would be sitting on top of the rack. The closet was dark, and the rack was taller than he, so he had to fumble around until he felt the little stubby antenna he had wanted to find.

"Great!" He turned to Bob and pointed at her box. "If I'm right, they're not too bright – most people aren't about WiFi – and they've left the door wide open."

He turned back to the mainframe and switched on the old monitor resting on one of the shelfs. Less than sixty seconds later he turned to Bob. "Okay. All done. All you need to do is point that thing to 2.437 gigahertz and let it do its magic. Let's hope for our sakes that your little box there is capable of the kinds of things I hope it's capable of."

Bob looked at him through her veil, not moving.

From down the hall the sounds of the doors shaking were growing more violent, as was the pounding on the window.

"What?" he asked. "What's wrong?"

Bob whispered "two poin fur tree sven giggle-hurts? Don't understand."

"Oh!" Clay said. "They're numbers. Watch my fingers." He repeated the frequencies as he held up the appropriate number of fingers. He paused when he got to gigahertz. Would she even know what a hertz was?

He concentrated on the best way to explain it to her, but she was already busy at work, typing in keys and chirping and whistling at it.

Clay noticed the mainframe's hard drive light flash on, signifying activity in the computer right as the little green box dinged.

Clay assumed she had established contact and managed to take over the computer. He really had to get one of those things.

She whistled and chirped at it, and Clay imagined it was translating her commands into the programming language of the mainframe. He heard the satellite actuator click on, meaning she was repositioning it to make her interspace phone call.

Clay was feeling very good. Until the sound of shattering glass rang down the hall from the lobby.

"Shit," he said. "Please make it quick." He never looked back as he dashed out of the small closet, through the storage room and into the hall.

Bob heard the pump of his shotgun, followed by an angry yell, and finally the booms that had become all too commonplace during the last few days as Clay emptied shell after shell into the zombies.

Being in the closet, trying to call home, she would have no way of knowing that the small group of zombies had grown to a small mob of twenty or so.

Chapter 68   Somewhere above Highway 61

"Well, hello there," Roscoe drawled as he looked at the massive computer display. Displayed on it was a large aerial map of the town. A series of red circles appeared on screen, one within the other, and centered on the radio station.

"Luck be a lady tonight..." Earl sang.

"What the hell does that mean?"

"I dunno. Heard it on one of their radio stations."

"Well, it's stupid."

"Of course it is," Earl shot back.

"We've got another incoming signal."

"So what? We've had lots of them. These things make a lot of noise with their talk-shows and top-forty countdowns."

"Well, this one is in a language a little closer to home."

"Oh?"

"Yep," Roscoe answered. "Seems like she missed us. Let's go pick her up."

Chapter 69   At the River

"Oh, what the hell?" Chett was beyond pissed. He slammed the thin sliding bedroom door closed again.

"We're not going back for them," Wally called from outside the RV.

"Look, Wally, let's get something straight," Chett said as he stormed out. "In case you forgot, *we* brought *you* along for the ride. My RV, my gas, my decision. And I haven't decided if I'm going back for that little jackass or not. But if I decide to, I'm going. And Harry's coming with me. And if you don't want to, fine. But that decision is mine, do you understand? You've got a badge, and you've got your guns, but that don't mean you're in charge right here and right now."

"Look, buddy, my job is protect and serve. And right now, I'm putting the greater good against the wants of one or two people. We need to get out and get help. And if I have to do it alone, then I will. But we stand a much better chance of getting out of here alive if we all stick together. Your little friend made his own decision when he jumped ship, got it? It was reckless and irresponsible, and if we go hunting for him, it'll put all of us in danger."

"How you figure?" asked Harry.

"How do I figure?" Wally responded, angrily. "Have you taken a look around? Where the fuck are all the city residents? Huh? The only people we've seen around are dead ones. There used to be a lot more live ones. And either they're alive or they're not. And if they're not, then they're definitely not going to be on our side. Are you following me?"

Neither Chett nor Harry said anything.

"Each and every one of those houses and buildings is potentially housing a wasp's nest of zombies," Wally explained. "Every time we make ourselves visible by driving down the road, we make ourselves a little more vulnerable. We've seen little mobs of them here and there already. Ten here, twenty there. There are several thousand people unaccounted for. And theoretically, most of them would live right in this area."

Chett and Harry were still listening, arms crossed.

"Do I need to finish spelling this out for you? I don't remember getting any evacuation notice. If there are people around, either they're holed up with shotguns ready to blast the first thing that moves – like us – or they're dead, ready to eat the first thing that moves – like us. So we're kind of in the middle of a powderkeg. I don't have a good feeling about this, and generally my instincts are pretty good. So let me repeat. We need to go search those piers for a good boat with plenty of gas. And then we need to head south and get to the military base. While your skinny friend doesn't seem too much like the one to know what to do, your Muslim girl does."

"She's not Muslim," Chett said.

"I know, she's from space," sighed Wally. "Muslim, or girl from outer space. It's all the same to me." Wally stopped long enough to notice Chett and Harry staring intently over his shoulder.

Chett broke into a whisper. "It's time to start shootin', Wally. We'll finish this discussion soon as we make it out of here alive."

Wally hadn't seen Chett so shaken. When he turned around, he understood why.

He had been more right than he realized. More than a hundred stumbling corpses had begun ambling down to the waterfront.

Right toward them.

Harry tossed Wally a rifle and all three took aim.

"Can these things swim?" Wally asked.

"Why would I know?" Chett shot back.

"Because I'm hoping they can't. One of us needs to go get a boat started."

Chett looked down the waterfront. The zombies were maybe a hundred yards away and approaching.

The pier was thirty yards away. Thirty yards directly toward the zombies.

"Are you kidding?" he asked.

Harry answered. "I don't think he's kidding. Chett, you go. We'll cover you."

"Me? Why me?"

"Damnit, Chett, how many times are we going to go over this? You don't shoot worth a shit. I do. I'm sure Wally does too. Your lack of talent means you better start hauling ass to that pier. We'll cover you. Now go!"

Wally and Harry put their backs to the RV and took aim.

Chett opened his mouth to argue but couldn't make himself heard over the blasts as Wally and Harry began firing.

Terrorized, he ran to the pier, keeping his eyes on the slowly approaching mob of zombies. Each time a shot rang out, he'd see a head tilt instantly backwards, spraying the gruesome people behind it with whatever used to be in its head. Each bang meant one zombie went down.

None of the ones who had been sprayed flinched. Several tripped over the bodies in front of them.

Chett made it to the first boat when he turned around to see Harry and Wally, who were obviously not watching behind them.

Because where there had been only a hundred or so of the undead in front of them, there were at least two hundred slowly approaching from behind them and beside them.

Chett screamed to get their attention.

No luck over the gunfire.

He screamed and jumped and waved his hands. He saw Harry look away from the mob long enough for Chett to point behind them.

Harry ran around the RV to get a better look at the unbelievable mass of approaching corpses and dashed back to get Wally, who stopped shooting.

"Run!" Chett yelled. "Over here! Screw the gas, we'll float! Come on!"

Wally and Harry needed no further convincing.

Chapter 70   Back at the Radio Station

"Change the channel. We've already seen this show." Roscoe paced impatiently around the bridge. The ship had been acting a little strange since they ripped out its vocal circuits. Earl had suggested swapping out the personality entirely, but that would have taken days. Precious days they didn't have. All Roscoe wanted was to pick up the shipment and make the delivery. He was counting on his very unstable mixture of cunning, guile, and sweet talking to keep them from getting killed once they made the delivery.

"Black," as it was called, was very, very, *very* toxic. And even more addictive. It was, by far, the most illegal substance in the galaxy. Which of course made it very profitable to transport.

It was also heavily, heavily controlled, because it had the nasty habit of replicating upon contact with a sodium chloride/dihydrogen monoxide solution. Salt water.

So why would anyone need to buy it? What good was a highly toxic, highly addictive chemical if anyone could keep a small solution on hand and mix it with salt water to get more?

For one, it meant that only a highly organized intergalactic crime syndicate could manage it. Any user of the drug could only do so in the presence of the crime family, thereby assuring none was kept by the user to replicate.

And managing an intergalactic crime family was no easy job, either. Because even a small loss of loyalty carried the potential of someone else getting their hands on it to start their own little syndicate. As a result, the Family went to the most extreme of measures to show its members that breaches of loyalty, even minute ones, would not be tolerated.

Which is why Roscoe was much more nervous than he let on.

Black. The intoxicating bacterioviral drug that brings the dead back to life. Of course, that was an unintended side effect. But the active ingredient – the very mutated, very alien bacteriovirus that infected the brain, muscles, and other organs to intoxicate the user – would take over the user in the absence of white blood cells (which were pretty universal, as it turns out) and render them zombies. So, normal users would fight off the infection, as it were, in a few days time and return to normal. The dead, however, having no blood cells at all, provided a very fertile feeding ground for the drug.

As long as there was water around to keep the muscles moist. The bacteriovirus had trouble reanimating the dead if it was, pardon the expression, bone dry.

Toss some fresh water – say, rain water – into the mix and you've got trouble.

Toss some salt water – say, the ocean – into the mix and you've got a clusterfuck.

The drug's easy replication and nasty habit of bringing the dead back to life were the prime reasons it was so heavily controlled.

And even more heavily policed.

And now, here he was, several days past deadline. Missing, as far as the Family was concerned, with more than enough of a shipment to start his own syndicate.

It didn't matter if he was innocent or not. An infraction was an infraction.

Roscoe's brain had been working overtime to come up with the impossible rationalizations that he used to tell himself that anything but a sure and painful death was awaiting him at the end of his trials.

All the noise from the large monitor was distracting him from feeling sorry for himself. He turned to Earl. "I said, change the channel, we've already seen this show."

Earl was sitting in the control console, munching on something brown and wiggly. "It ain't a show. You remember when we were trying to figure out who sent them signals the first time? We thought it was a show, but then we went out there and it was real."

"Coincidence," Roscoe said. "We were watching them two aliens shoot up all them other dead aliens. When we got out there, yeah, those two people were out there, but the dead ones weren't. If we weren't watching a show, where'd all them dead aliens they were fighting go?"

Earl stroked his thin goatee. "I been thinking about that. And I think I got an answer. It wasn't a show, Roscoe, and we might not be the brightest members of the Family, but even you're not dumb enough to think it was coincidence that the two people we saw on the monitor on what you *thought* was a show were the exact same two people we brought on the ship. Now, something happened to kill all them zombies, and I don't think it was them. Think about it. We were watching them, then the screen went blank. I had the idea to pop our heads out and see what was going on. There they were. They didn't kill them dead aliens. Because with their little firesticks, there'd still be bodies laying around. Something had to have vaporized them. I don't remember giving the order to vaporize any dead aliens.

"Then," Earl continued as he stood up to walk to Roscoe, "we brought them on the ship. But somehow, they got loose and got off the ship. We didn't set 'em loose, Roscoe. Then the computer said that they were on the lift, but they weren't. Then we got on the lift and got stuck."

Earl let it all sink in.

Roscoe walked over to the monitor, where the action had ceased. The group of zombies had disappeared into the radio station on the monitor.

"Okay," Roscoe said, "Um... what's your point?" It wasn't sinking in.

Earl joined him, looking at the large monitor. "My point is that something funny is going on, and I don't have a good feeling about it. And my second point is," Earl pointed at the monitor, "that what we're watching ain't a show. Our little girl there got our attention again, and I'm guessing that we have royally fucked up. Those aliens we just saw on the screen, those twenty or so aliens, they don't look too good. Just like the ones we saw earlier. And when I say 'they don't look too good,' I mean they look dead. Because they are dead. Which means that, Roscoe, by proxy we are dead too. Because our shipment, which you so hastily dumped, has crash landed somewhere close and not so icy and gotten to a water supply. And I don't know if these aliens like fresh water or salt water, but either way, it spells trouble."

Roscoe stammered. "I... um... I... thought I aimed... for the ice patch..."

"You did. But after we had already got ourselves shot up in that little skirmish. Computer was a little busted, remember? Coordinates might have *looked* right. Doesn't mean they were."

"And what's more," Earl said in a reprimanding tone, tapping a display on a panel in front of him, "you picked up the ship before they refueled it."

Roscoe didn't say anything.

"Didn't think to check, didya?"

Roscoe didn't say anything.

"And we would have had enough energy to get away..." Earl trailed off and touched a few more buttons on his screen. "Just what I thought. Our fuel level depleted when all those people we were watching vaporized. Meaning it was our ship that killed them. But we didn't give the order."

Roscoe continued staring at the empty street, eyes wide. It was finally sinking in. "So... that's actually going on outside? But I don't remember you calling it up on the monitor. So who did?"

"Exactly," Earl said.

"So our girl's inside there?" Roscoe pointed to the radio station on the screen. "About to get eaten by those dead aliens that our busted shipment is bringing back to life?"

"Not exactly," came the reply in their native tongue. But it wasn't Earl's voice; it was in a cute, smiling voice they had heard before.

But before Earl and Roscoe could turn around, they felt the cold metal of alien firesticks on the back of their heads.

"Hi!" Bob squealed, in English.

Finally, the ship's computer thought.

Chapter 71   ... And Then, Hell Breaks Loose. All of It.

Chett, Harry and Wally were standing on the pier surrounded by seven bobbing boats when they heard it – a series of faraway sounds like those that would come from unmuffled four-wheeler engines. At first, they panicked, because each of them had borne witness to the terrorizing exhaust of the roaring four-by-four of death.

But this sound was something else entirely – higher pitched, whining. Still, they had to take it as a threat. The mob of zombies had now closed in from three sides, leaving the group of three with their backs to the river.

Chett had already ruled out two of the boats by the time the others joined him. "No Gas!" he yelled as he pointed to the ones he had tried.

Wally and Harry were still firing away, dropping zombie after zombie, but ultimately making no dent in the sheer wall of corpses closing in.

Wally eyed another boat as the faraway sounds got closer. "Fine!" He motioned to one of them. "Get in! Now! We'll paddle with our damned hands if we need too! They can't hurt us in the water. There's a few hundred gallons of gas in some tanks downriver by the oil company. We'll float down and borrow some."

The crew turned to dash down the pier when another sound stopped them in their tracks. There were three distinct sounds now – one of the four-wheelers drawing ever closer from the west, one of a boat maybe a mile or two to the south high-tailing it upriver, and there was something else. It was the third that worried them – a low, unholy rumbling seeming to come from right under them.

Boards starting shaking loose as the pier began to rattle with the tremors that seemed to come from somewhere below them – somewhere in the river.

Harry noticed ripples in the water as whatever it was approached the pier.

"What the fuck is that?" Wally asked.

The wake was several yards wide. Whatever it was seemed about to crest. And it was moving quickly.

The three stood in awe, their brains too overtaxed to see a logical way out of the situation.

Finally, as the wake approached the pier and seemed poised not to slow down, Chett figured out the key to surviving.

"Jump!"

He pushed Harry and Wally into the water as the four-by-four of death charged from the river bed, tearing the pier to shreds and hurling wet lumber everywhere. The flame stenciling passed inches in front of Chett's head as he kicked back into the river and grabbed the nearest boat. Harry and Wally also grabbed on and pulled themselves in.

The truck landed in the middle of the semicircle of zombies and pulled a perfect one hundred eighty-degree bootlegger.

"Nice," Chett commented.

Wally quickly untied the rope from one of the remaining pillars and shoved off.

The truck rocked and its engine roared, which looked and sounded a little too alive, too *animal,* to the three to stick around for another show.

They began paddling as the doors swung open and the two occupants stepped out, dripping.

"How the hell can they drive underwater?" Harry asked, breathlessly.

"You see a couple hundred zombies and you're worrying about them driving under water?" Chett shot back.

He stood up to try the gas tanks. "We got gas!" He ran to the console. "But no keys. I'll have to hotwire it. Gimme a minute."

"Oh, take your time," Wally said sarcastically as he tried futilely to paddle with both arms in the muddy brown water.

The only movement their boat had made had been to coast a few feet back, caused much more by the wake of the truck than by their paddling.

Something on the shore caught Chett's attention before he could kneel down and begin the process of hotwiring.

"Chett!" Harry yelled. "How's about not standing there like an idiot and getting this thing running?"

Chett didn't respond.

Wally looked up from his two-handed paddle to reinforce Harry's question. "Chett!" He was going to say something forceful, but then he saw what Chett saw.

A cable.

Coming from the winch on the front of the dripping, muddy zombie truck. The two occupants, standing outside, laughed a loud, deep, ragged, terrifying laugh.

Wally followed the cable into the water. The angle of the cable didn't seem to be pointing at the boat they were in, but he knew appearances could be deceiving. The cable could be coiled underwater and could be very well connected to their boat.

Chett had already made that assumption and was considering the options.

Harry noticed that the other two had stopped doing anything and looked up to see what they were staring at.

Chett yelled to them without taking his eyes off the cable. "If you feel the boat even jerk, hit the water!"

"No way!" said Wally. "Apparently, water don't stop them things!" He shook his dripping rifle. "And I gotta field clean this thing before I can get another shot. Harry, I suggest you do the same."

As if on cue, a grimy hand thrust out of the water and latched on to the side of the boat near Harry.

Wally attacked it with the butt of his rifle and the hand slid off.

"Well, I don't know about you," said Wally, "but I'm pretty sure I'm done paddling for the day." He kicked off another offending hand that had appeared out of the water and attached itself to the boat. "You guys got any other ideas?" He sat down, stripped off his shirt and began tearing it to use as a rag to dry his rifle. "Because, and I'm not trying to be negative here, as I see it, we're pretty close to screwed. Anybody got something I can use for a rod? I'd really like to be pumping some lead into these things right now, and I can't do it until this thing's dry."

Chett and Harry fumbled around the boat, looking for something to use all the while kicking off the occasional zombie hand.

Chett noted, with some resignation, that the number of appearing zombie hands was increasing. It was beginning to be a full-time job just to keep them off the boat.

Finally, Harry reached into a side compartment on the boat and found a rod and reel. "Got it!" he yelled. He tossed it to Wally.

Wally wrapped the torn strips of shirt around the rod as the sounds of the boat downriver and the four-wheelers in the close distance grew louder and closer.

The crew watched as the other boat tore around a bend in the river and sped closer. Wally was the first to recognize the sheriff and his officers. He turned to get a look at the truck and was dumbfounded by the scene. The two zombies who had been driving the truck had climbed onto the bed, while the hundreds of zombies surrounding them had barricaded themselves in front of and around the truck. They seemed to be bracing it.

Wally whipped his head around to get a better view of the sheriff just in time to see him and his crew aim their weapons at the rotting mob on shore.

"Get down!" Wally yelled as he dove to the bottom of the boat, followed by Chett and Harry.

Shots began ringing out from the sheriff's boat as it charged closer.

The truck-driving zombies roared with the laughter of the dead, followed by moans and screams from their rotting army.

Wally made the connection as the boat closed in. He swung his scope and quickly eyed an empty barge parked on the other side of the river. There, mounted to a steel casting on the side a few feet above the water, was the tell-tale gleam of a cable hook.

Wally didn't have to look to know what the newest sound was: a winch.

He saw the thin, snaking waves created by the cable pulling tight and watched it wind its way across the river. He didn't even have time to alert the sheriff as the cable rose high enough out of the water to catch all five people on the boat directly in the chest, where they hung momentary as the cable took the force of their impact.

The zombie truck's tires barked once as they hopped on the pavement.

The zombies themselves roared loudly at their catch.

Wally couldn't tell who had been killed or who had been spared, but judging by the speed of the boat, any one of them would be lucky to be alive. Or, not so lucky as the case may be.

All of a sudden, the water began boiling with activity. Zombies popped to the surface and began swimming to the sheriff and his crew. Well, most of the zombies did, anyway. The rest started grabbing the boat that Wally, Chett and Harry were currently occupying. Chett and Harry were fighting them off with the butts of their soggy shotguns as best as they could, but it was no use. The boat was rocking enough that one or two had managed to pull themselves up to the side.

"How much longer, Wally?" Chett yelled as he kicked the rotting jaw off of sneering corpse.

"Less than sixty seconds!" He yelled back.

"Don't know that we got that long!"

"It's the best I can do!" Wally was also kicking anything dead and moving while trying to dry out his rifle.

"Ga!"

"What?" Wally said.

"Gumph..gurgle..." It was Harry. Wally swung around just in time to see a zombie grab Harry and try to take a bite. Harry headbutted it, knocking it and himself off balance and over the bow of the boat into the thrashing arms of the zombies below.

"Shit!" Chett said and dived in.

"Damn," Wally cursed as he loaded some shells. "Hope it's dry. This'll have to do." He raced over to the side, propped his leg up, and took aim.

He waited until he saw Chett and Harry within feet of each other before he started shooting. There were enough zombies in the water to make each shot find a good target. The scene resembled a bed of water moccasins thrashing around. Each bullet Wally fired created a split-second spray of muddy water and zombie matter.

Neither Chett nor Harry could see what they were doing, but they felt hands and legs dragging them down. Each one fought to reach the surface and take a breath. Fighting zombies underwater was quite difficult, they were learning.

Their strategy, which formed out of the natural argument that it was the only thing that seemed to work, was to reach down and snap off whatever was grabbing them. And then, if they had enough air and could find the zombie's necks, they'd take off a head or two.

They also fought to stay in the same place, because they could hear the plink and small whiz of bullets hitting the water.

Chett's leg ached suddenly with a searing pain. Either he had been shot or a zombie had managed to take a nice chunk out of his calf. Either way, it hurt like hell and he let out a yelp underwater. Something grabbed his other leg and he swung around furiously to dislodge it.

It was, apparently, one of the fresher zombies. Its head was disinclined to come off easily.

And, he noted with one of his stronger feelings of panic, he was running out of air.

The only thing he had on his side was the sheer will to live, but the overwhelming number of zombies wrestling him farther and farther underwater was just too overpowering.

He thought of everything he never was or would become. About how his entire life had been the story of doing just enough to coast by. About how in the next few minutes, his expiration would prove correct anyone who ever said he would die without amounting to anything.

And the zombies were pretty hungry. He could feel pain in all his extremities now as he supposed they were munching away on their soggy snack.

A wave of calmness passed through Chett as everything went black.

Above water, Wally had picked enough zombies off to temporarily free Harry, who coughed and sputtered as he tread water.

"Chett?" he asked. He searched the water.

Wally shook his head.

Harry turned to survey the water.

Wally saw what Harry planned to do and called out, "Wait!" but it was too late. The water rippled and splashed with Harry's disappearance as he dove to find his friend.

"Well, shit," he sighed. He knew there were probably too many zombies still down there and that Harry had just assigned himself the same fate his friend had probably already met. But if it were one of his military buddies, he reminded himself, he'd have done the same thing.

Nonetheless, the situation looked grim. As far as Chett and Harry were concerned, he really could not do anything. He needed to hotwire the boat while the zombies were otherwise occupied. He was about to lay down and slide underneath the console when he saw a commotion in the group of zombies on the shore.

The whining of the distant small engines had finally reached a crescendo, signaling that they weren't so distant anymore. What was more, Wally could tell that the sounds weren't just coming from one direction.

They seemed to surround the floodwall behind the zombies and their apparent truck-driving leader.

And whatever it was, it was attracting more than just Wally's attention. He saw that all the zombies had turned towards the direction of the sounds as they neared.

Then, in a fiery blur of motion, several things happened: Three blue buggies of some sort shot from the openings in the floodwall and quickly surrounded the zombies. And just as quickly, they turned around to face *away* from the zombies, so that their huge, unbelievably oversized chrome tailpipes now pointed directly at the mob.

Wally looked to the bigger of the buggies as the driver – a wiry, shirtless man wearing camo shorts and a trucker's cap – stood up and yelled "Let 'er rip!"

In unison, the three buggies revved their engines and let loose from their tailpipes what to Wally looked like a little bit of bottled hell. Rolling orange flames shot out and coated the mob with a solid wall of fire.

The leader, the wiry man, let out a jubilant yell.

The mob began breaking up; flaming zombies were waving their arms and stumbling around blindly. Wally winced at their torn screams. He doubted the undead could feel pain, but they had definitely quickly become a very unhappy lot.

And then, for a split second, someone turned the sun off. It came back on, then blinked off again.

Wally and the buggy drivers looked up into the sky, which was apparently deciding whether or not to be occupied by a very large spaceship, but having a very hard time making up its mind as one second the ship was there, then the next it vanished.

Below, the zombies' leaders had stolen the opportunity to jump back in their truck, and it roared straight toward one of the buggies as it rolled over the straggling flaming zombies.

Its occupants jumped out of the way and scrambled as it crunched under the truck's massive tires.

From behind the south entrance to the floodwall another mob of people appeared. Wally groaned at the thought of even more zombies coming for backup, but instead, these weren't zombies. They were people – the rest of the townsfolk, Wally assumed – and they were packing serious heat. It looked like a slightly updated medieval town mob, complete with torches and pitchforks, but also (and more importantly) with shotguns and pistols.

And while the fiery antics of the crazy dune-buggy driving people had dispersed and dispatched forty or fifty of the several-hundred strong mob of zombies, reinforcements for the undead were arriving from the north gate. Wally guessed that these were the batch from the town cemetery – the zombie farm, as Clay had called it – from up the road.

Wally looked up as a hatch in the ship overhead opened and two skinny, bald, pale-gray skinned goatee-clad very funny looking people stepped out onto a ramp, immediately followed by Clay and Bob, who were apparently holding the other ... people? ... hostage.

Clay looked different. Bigger. Wally squinted to see what was different. He was wearing some sort of prosthetic device on his chest and arm. Bob was holding an old-fashioned shotgun on the duo as Clay aimed whatever he was wearing at the mob of zombies and started firing away. Bolts of blue plasma screamed across the waterfront and exploded in the group, sending zombies flying.

Both the assembling townspeople and the encroaching zombies took this as a war cry and gave charge, people shouting and shooting and yelling and waving their arms, zombies just moaning and stumbling and waving their arms.

The townspeople, of which there were a few hundred, were severely outnumbered by the thousands of corpses which had sprung from the cemetery, fresh from being revived by the recent rain and following floodwater tainted with the (un?)deadly black drug.

Bob spied Wally floating in the boat and dashed back in the ship, which lowered and moved closer to Wally, coming close enough to allow him to take hold of the ramp and pull himself up.

Clay, without taking his eyes off his targets, yelled out to Wally. "Where are Chett and Harry?"

Wally stood up on the ramp, still dripping slightly from the earlier unintended foray into the river. He shook his head and pointed to the water, yelling back over the screaming plasma and roaring of the truck.

"They went down. Chett got dragged by a couple of zombies, Harry went after him. I've heard Harry surface a few times, but that's all I know."

One of the dune buggies broke free of the mob and bolted over to the ship. The wiry man called up. "Did I hear sompin' 'bout Chett and Harry?"

"Uncle Crank!" yelled Clay. "They're underwater! Wally said he saw them..." He trailed off because Uncle Crank was already gone, pulling on scuba tank and mask and grabbing a harpoon as the buggy took to the river and drove straight in, submerging itself.

"Can that thing go underwater?" Wally asked.

"Seems like it just did," Clay said, still firing away.

"No, I mean can it *go* underwater?"

"Who knows?" answered Clay. "It's Uncle Crank."

Finally, the ship's failing cloaking device gave out, much to the relief of Clay and Wally, who found standing on intermittent nothingness a little unsettling.

Then, with all the commotion below still continuing, several more shadows blinked onto the shoreline. Along with the shadows came several more ships. Slightly smaller than the current one, but built with the same architecture nonetheless. They were surrounded.

A voice boomed out over the ground, deep and alien. It also repeated through the speakers of the ship Clay and Bob were currently in control of. Clay was about to ask what was going on when Bob's little green box went ahead and did the honor of automatically translating.

"Roscoe and Earl, you ran off with our shipment. Turn it over now."

Roscoe and Earl hung their heads. Roscoe chirped something to Earl. The little green box translated again. "You think we can bargain?"

The alien voice, whether aware or unaware of Roscoe's comment boomed out again, this time a longer sentence. From the green box again, "Go ahead and turn it over. We're still going to kill you, you know. But the quicker you turn it over, the less painful your death would be. Just thought you should know that. You know, in case it influences your decision."

Below them, pandemonium had taken reign. The mob of townspeople had met the mob of zombies and Clay was having a tough time telling who was who. It looked quite a bit like the battle scenes from his favorite movies where armies from the dark ages would meet each other on the warground and charge in, slashing and cutting away. But there were no distinct colors or flying of flags. The only things different now were the signs of modernity – guns and roads and floodwalls, and of course the new offending alien ships demanding the return of their shipment.

"Fine, then," came the tinny translation of the last alien broadcast. "Have it your way."

The ship rocked with the first jolt of the energy blast one of the ships had just fired.

Bob dropped the green box at Clay's feet and bolted inside. She pointed to the two skinny aliens. "You watch them!" she called out to Clay.

"Okay," he shouted back.

"Seriously," came another tinny translation from Bob's green box, "Hand it over. We don't want to come over there."

Another jolt rocked the ship.

Bob came back, breathless. "Not enough energy for shield."

Clay looked at her. "Why don't you just tell them where the stuff is?"

"Can't," she said from beneath her burqa.

"Why not?" he asked. "Wouldn't that save us a lot of trouble?" The ship rolled heavily this time. "Like not getting us killed?"

"Trust me, okay?" she said.

She didn't have to say anything else. Clay trusted her.

Wally walked up to Clay. "Look, if it's all the same, I was feeling a little safer down there on the water, and if it's okay with everybody here, I'm just gonna ease myself down on to the boat there."

He walked over to the edge and lowered himself down.

A bolt of energy crackled the air beneath his feet and vaporized the boat.

"Okay, maybe not," he said and pulled himself back up. "It's a much better view from up here anyway."

Clay saw something in the mob that caught his attention. There, in the midst of the battle, was the light blue mumu of a thin older woman giving the battle her all.

"Mom!" Clay called out.

She looked skyward toward the voice she thought she recognized. The distraction provided enough of an opportunity for one of the zombies to grab her and take her to the ground.

"Mom!" Clay called out again. He took a running leap towards the shore and dove off the ramp directly into the water, only giving thought to the waterproofedness of the bionic plasma weapon he was wearing after his feet had already left the ramp and as he was headed for the river below. Not only that, but it was heavy. He'd have to swim with it. If it didn't explode.

Still, his mom was in trouble and he did what he thought he needed to do. He took a deep breath as he felt the heat of the energy beam probably meant for him shoot over his head and he plunged into the water, sinking quickly as expected.

But, not as expected, his feet hit not the muddy river bottom but something soft, and moving.

He held to the leather seat of the blue underwater dune buggy as it shot out of the river, now holding four occupants: Uncle Crank, Clay, and Chett and Harry, the last two both very unconscious or dead.

"My mom!" Clay yelled to Uncle Crank. "I've got to get my mom! She's in the blue mumu!"

Uncle Crank stopped the buggy, hopped into the back seat, sandwiched his legs between the two bodies lying there to get a foot hold, opened the obviously watertight trunk and pulled out a shotgun, fished a ziplock baggy out of his shirtpocket, shook it open, pulled a Virginia Slim out of a pack of cigarettes, lit it, took aim, and said, "You drive. I shoot."

They made it to the spot where Clay had seen his mom go down. He dove into the thick of it, swinging his bionic weapon around and knocking back zombies. In doing so he accidentally knocked one of the townspeople, a familiar preppy guy with a mop of blond hair, into the waiting arms of a small mob of zombies. They moaned with pleasure and folded their arms around him, completely encompassing him in the middle of the rotting circle of corpses they formed. Clay winced as he screamed, then winced again as his scream suddenly fell to silence.

He found his mother unconscious on the ground, but thankfully unharmed by hungry zombies. They were apparently too busy fighting over their most recent snack a few feet away.

Uncle Crank was picking off the surrounding zombies as quickly as possible. Wally, who had found his way to the remaining unoccupied dune buggy, raced over and jumped out to help Clay put his mother in the second buggy. Clay looked in the back seat and saw the sheriff.

"Why do you have him?" Clay asked. "Is he alive?"

"I think so," Wally answered. "But he's hurt pretty bad. I know he's dirty. But I couldn't just leave him."

"Uncle Crank?" Clay yelled out over the crackling of energy beams and booms of shotguns and pistols, "Didn't I hear Harry say these things can go pretty fast?"

"Yep. Yep." Uncle Crank said, shooting away. "Pretty fast, these doom buggies."

"Then let's get Bob, the lady wearing all black bedsheets, and haul ass."

"Sounds like a plan to me," Wally shouted in agreement.

Uncle Crank hopped into the driver's seat of his buggy and reversed it away from the crowd. Clay followed suit as Wally sat in the passenger seat, taking aim and still firing.

A loud explosion rocked the ground. What had just recently been the alien ship with the bad cloak was now a smoky fireball splashing in the river.

"Bob!" Clay yelled. His heart raced and he shot forward to the riverfront.

A hooded head bobbed to the surface, followed by the two drug running aliens as they paddled to shore.

"Thank God! Hop in!" he yelled to her. She came up out of the water, threw Roscoe into the back seat, saw that the sheriff was there and threw Earl into the small trunk, and dove in the back seat on top of Roscoe and the sheriff as one of the ships fired on the spot where they had just been.

Clay needed no further encouragement to see exactly how fast those buggies could indeed go.

He tore through the crowd, knocking over both zombie and human and made for the exit in the floodwall that would take him hopefully away from the madness.

Uncle Crank followed closely behind.

Somewhere in the back of Clay's head, he knew the hopelessness of the situation. True, he was in a buggy that could haul ass. And yes, he had the nifty little bionic plasma weapon. But there his advantage stopped. His pursuers had ships. And computer-guided aim. It would be a matter of seconds before all of them would become little more than puffs of smoke.

The alien voice boomed out. Clay strained to hear the translation from Bob's green box in the back seat. "Where is the shipment? We beamed over to your ship, Roscoe. It wasn't there. It said you dumped it. We really don't want to have to go looking for it."

So that's why they haven't killed us yet, Clay thought. *They need Roscoe and Earl. As long as they're alive, we're okay.*

They hit the road that would take them to the interstate, trailed all the way by a small fleet of alien ships. Clay strained to formulate a plan. They'd never be able to outrun the alien ships. Their best option was to hit the woods and hide, covered by the foliage of the trees above. But Chett and Harry, if they were still alive (which Clay doubted) would need serious medical attention.

So Clay opted to hit the woods, until he could think of a solution.

But two things would happen to prevent him from doing that.

First, all of them had been too busy with the sudden appearance of the alien ships to notice that the four-by-four of death had quietly disappeared. It would very shortly reintroduce itself.

Second, several new curvy, sleek-looking alien ships would tear through the sky, leaving a pink blaze in their trails.

It was the first of these occurrences that caused Clay and Wally to curse in unison.

"Shit!"

The truck jumped from behind a building and nearly rammed them directly in the side. Were it not for the fact that they were currently topping eighty or ninety miles an hour, throwing huge plumes of fire and smoke behind them, the truck might have more accurately gauged their speed and been able to make a successful hit.

As it was, the truck's tires screeched in protest as it corrected itself and gave chase.

Good, thought Clay. *We can definitely outrun at least* that *thing*.

Which, for what it's worth, was a correct thought to have. Except that in the foray with the townspeople, the truck-driving zombies had managed to get themselves some guns. So that now they were shotgun-wielding, truck-driving leaders of the undead.

And they started shooting.

Wally turned to look at the passenger of the truck as he leaned out of the window.

"Everybody stay down!" he ordered. He started firing away as they raced down the street.

Meanwhile, in the sky, the newer sleeker alien ships were also giving chase, also firing their own weapons.

But, as Clay noticed, they were not shooting at anyone on the ground. They were firing at the boxier ships currently giving chase. He heard an explosion and one of the boxy ships went down. The other ships broke away and began what he could only guess was one hell of a dog fight. He was concentrating too intently on the road to worry about what was going on above and could only listen to the earth-shattering explosions of the battle in the atmosphere.

"Yay!" shouted Bob. She clapped her hands and squealed. "Help!"

"Are those your people?" Clay called to the back seat.

"Yep!"

"And they're here to help?"

"Yep!" She called back. "That's what we do! Here!" She handed the green box to Clay and started talking in her native tongue. It translated. "I'm what you call a police officer, like Wally."

"Oh," Clay sighed. "You *are* like Wally. You don't *like* Wally. I get it."

The box continued translating. "I told you. I have been trailing these two for years to stop their drug smuggling. I was ambushed in a shootout and got taken hostage. They were going to use me for slave labor."

A blast of a shotgun cut her off as the passenger of the four-by-four of death tried to take aim through the thick black smoke of Uncle Crank's buggy exhaust. Thankfully it had been acting as a great smoke shield.

Bob continued. "But they had me in the same cargo hold as the shipment, so I managed to reprogram the computer from one of their terminals. Nothing much, just enough to think of me as friendly. When I saw they were going to dump the shipment, I hid myself in the pod and made my escape. I called for backup. Now they are here. As soon as they are finished, they will come for me."

"Oh," Clay sighed again.

His brief pity party was interrupted by another shotgun blast from the truck behind them.

The shot had found purchase in one of the tires, and the buggy began to spin out of control. Clay fought to maintain control and to keep it from flipping at ninety miles an hour. He managed to get the speed down to fifty when he finally felt the buggy begin to tip. He cursed and yelled "Jump!" as the occupants were already doing so, with the exception of the sheriff and Clay's mom, who were both still unconscious, and Earl, who was trapped in the trunk.

The four of them began the painful process of skidding down the concrete road at forty-five miles an hour while the buggy flipped wildly behind them.

Uncle Crank jerked his buggy to the shoulder and slowed down, not wanting to run over the people still skidding in the street.

Clay fought to right himself and managed to stop tumbling long enough to point his weapon at the truck, which had mysteriously slowed down with the tumbling buggy. He tried to fire a few shots at it, but was rewarded only with a jolt of terrible electric pain from his bionic weapon.

It began to emit some sort of alarm.

A few strange alien lights were flashing on its control panel on his forearm.

They were now only skidding at twenty miles an hour, though he had no way of knowing it. He tried to shoot again, and again was rewarded with a shooting pain, and now an even louder alarm.

He decided it was time to ditch the weapon, but whatever device it used to clamp around his other shoulder and chest would not unclamp itself.

It now began giving off an extremely high-pitched, earsplitting alarm. Along with the sound, it was shocking him. Clay quickly surmised that it had been badly damaged in the wreck.

He slowed to a stop, bloody and skinned to hell and back. Bob was also standing up, rushing over to him. Wally was alive but hurt, moaning in the street.

Bob looked at Wally and yelled. "Get down! Get down! Cover head, now! Get in ditch!" She pointed to the side of the road. She turned and yelled toward Uncle Crank, who was now speeding toward them. "You too! Go! Go away fast! Vroom vroom! Hurry! Go! Get him!" She pointed down the street towards Wally.

Uncle Crank understood and drove to Wally, grabbing him by the shoulder and yanking him into the seat. He sped off.

Clay looked at the weapon. When it began giving off random sparks, he was worried. When it began giving off little jets of fire, he was scared. When it really began damn near electrocuting him and leaking little random bits of plasma (taking out trees and leaving small craters in the road), he was beyond terrified.

All the while the alarm grew louder and louder and louder.

And through the pain and noise, Clay knew what was going to happen. He hoped he could make it count for something.

He screamed and began running toward the truck, now parked a hundred yards away near the overturned buggy, its occupants busy trying to right it and extract the sheriff. They paid Clay no mind.

Bob screamed to get Clay's attention.

He paid her none and only picked up the pace, running all-out to the truck.

Bob yelled something into her green box, but Clay couldn't hear it either. He had one thing to accomplish, and there was no stopping him.

Except that finally, the screeching and shocking stopped. The strange white characters on the forearm control panel were blinking at a lightening pace. Clay stopped at the halfway point to the truck to consider trying to pull a shot off.

"No!" Bob screamed again as she reached toward him.

Then a blue-white blast of light filled the air, leaving a smoking crater where Clay had just been standing.

Uncle Crank was already a few miles away, speeding to the nearest out-of-town hospital he could think of.

Chapter 72   The End.

Harry blinked back to consciousness slowly. The pain medication kept him confused. Faces swam around him, resolving and dissolving ten different times before he could convince his eyes to focus.

He sat up in his hospital bed, surrounded by concerned doctors and nurses.

"Where am I?"

"Jackson Regional Medical Center," came a reply from an older doctor. "Do you know who you are?"

"Of course. Harry Bernard."

"What is today's date?" the older doctor asked.

"Seriously? Oh, hell, I don't know. I never know. How long have I been out?"

"A little over three weeks, at best," he replied. "We have a few things to go over if you feel like talking. We have some serious questions to ask you."

"Can't it wait? Where's Chett? Did he make it?"

The doctors and nurses exchanged glances.

"You have a card, Harry," one of them said, nodding to the table beside the hospital bed.

He blinked it into focus, and indeed, there a card sat, in front of a vase of flowers.

"Who are they from?" he asked.

No one answered. Finally, a doctor coughed and said "Maybe you should read it."

Harry opened the card.

Get Well Soon, read the printed type on the front. The message, written in neat handwriting inside, read: *For reasons best left unsaid, we wish you a speedy recovery. We certainly care dearly about your health, and as we assume you do, too, we advise you that returning to the county at any point in your future would only serve to jeopardize any gains you may make in your hospital recovery. Sincerely yours, Sheriff William Rayburn and Undersheriff Dale Evans.*

Harry blinked some more, trying to clear the obvious hallucination from his eyes. "Billy Ray?" Harry asked, incredulously.

"That's him."

"That can't be," Harry said.

"He came back from up north," the doctor responded.

Harry rubbed his head. "How did he get elected sheriff?"

"It's a long story, but the people elected him sheriff. The old one went missing, and Billy Ray and Dale turned up. Guess the people missed him and wanted him sheriff. But he says you can't come back."

"Right. I got that. That's what the card said."

"Well, he said you might be a little dense."

Harry rubbed his head again.

"You didn't answer me earlier. Where's Chett?"

No one answered.

"Is he alive?"

One doctor coughed. "Maybe you should come with us."

They transferred him to a wheelchair and headed towards the elevator.

Harry noted with a growing sense of panic that they had hit the button for the basement.

"Where are we going?"

"The morgue, Harry," one doctor responded. "But I need you to be prepared for what you're about to see."

They made their way to the double steel doors that signified the entrance to the morgue. Harry's stomach sank with the thought of what he was about to witness.

The kind, older doctor parked Harry's wheelchair next to one of the drawers and knelt down to talk to him, face-to-face.

"I really need you to be prepared for this. We brought you in with your friend, Chett. He passed away last night."

Harry's heart skipped a beat. "No!"

"I'm afraid so," came the doctors reply. There was an edge to it.

"So why have you brought me down here?" Harry asked. "You need me to identify the body?"

The doctor stood and placed his hand on the drawer. "Not really. We need you to explain something."

He pulled the drawer open and unzipped the body bag.

A very pale, very gray Chett lay inside. It looked like he was sleeping.

Harry looked away.

"Harry, is that you?"

He looked back in amazement. Chett was looking at him.

"Would you please tell them that I'm not dead?"

Harry looked at the doctor, speechless.

The doctor looked back at Harry and said, rather stiffly, "I'm afraid he is dead. But he doesn't seem to know it. No heartbeat. He's got brain and muscle activity, sure. But no pulse and no temperature."

"Man, I could sure go for a good rare steak right now," Chett said.

"Or a cow. Just gimme a cow. Man, I am starving."

"Chett?" Harry said, worriedly.

"Or some brains. Never sounded good before. But I could sure go for some brains."

Everyone stared at him in horror.

"Oh, not yours, of course. That's just nasty. But how about a squirrel? Mmm, mmm..." He smacked his gray lips. "Harry, could you go get me a squirrel? Don't cook him or anything. Just catch one and bring him here."

****

Back in the Warren County Sheriff's Office, Sheriff Billy Ray ran his hand over his crisp uniform and checked himself out in the mirror in his office. He smiled a handsome smile and ran his fingers through his light brown hair. He really did look pretty good, he thought. Better than before, actually.

He was hungry. It was snacktime. Maybe Dale was hungry too. He called the undersheriff and invited him to the basement of the jail for a little meal before they made their rounds.

The duo walked through the dark dungeon in a part of the jail laying underground, unused and forgotten for most of the latter part of the century, rattling their nightsticks on the jail bars.

"What do you feel like eating today?" Billy Ray asked. "Something good and juicy? Or something leaner?"

They stopped at the cell holding the terrified remainders of former Sheriff Barrack's dirty crew.

"I don't know," said Dale, drawing every word out. "Which one of them sons-a-bitches was it that shot me in my foot before they ripped off my fingernails?"

"Why, I believe that would be Officer Parker, Dale," Billy Ray said.

"Oh, yeah," he said, smiling. "That's right!"

Officer Parker struggled against his bonds and yelled into his gag.

"Oh, now, don't fight it," said Dale. He laughed. "Or, better yet, you just go ahead and fight all you can. Saves us the trouble of tenderizing the meat."

Officer Parker screamed a muffled scream that no one would ever hear in the old forgotten basement.

Later, as they sat in the cell, snacking, Billy Ray turned to Dale. "Pass me a thigh, would you?"

Dale obliged and said through a mouthful "How are we going to stay, um... healthy... when we run out of officers?"

"We'll cross that bridge when we come to it," he said. They finished their greasy meal in silence.

****

The townspeople would grow to love their new sheriff, who was kind and fair and just. Okay, so the occasional hardened criminal disappeared, there was that.

But if those criminals couldn't keep themselves out of trouble, well, then, it was their fault, wasn't it?

EPILOGUE *Another Country, Another Year*

The tall, dark, muscular man crossed the tarmac, walked silently up the stairs and stepped onto the airplane.

No one was expecting him, as anyone who would normally be approaching the plane would have had their appearance announced by the tedious security checkpoints they would have to go through to get there.

Having all the security measures upfront, the plane was sitting unguarded on the runway, getting ready for takeoff.

So everyone was a little surprised when the tall stranger just walked right on up into the plane and coughed.

Of the ten or so people on board, nine were wearing suits. They drew their pistols and immediately took aim at the stranger.

Only one passenger was wearing civilian clothes. His head was shaved, and he looked leaner and tougher and more tanned than he had in the past. He hadn't drawn his pistol, but did look up from the laptop where he had been working.

The unannounced stranger threw his arms up and smiled. "Harry Bernard," he said to the man with the laptop. "Long time no see, friend."

Harry blinked for a few seconds, trying to match the face. It too was tougher and meaner than the last time he had seen it. And much, much, *much* more muscular. The face he recognized. The bodybuilder's body he didn't.

"Clayton? Clayton Hensworth?"

Clay smiled.

The suits kept their weapons aimed.

"It's okay," Harry said, "he's with me."

The suits looked around apprehensively.

"It's okay, guys. He's with me. Put your guns down."

They did so, slowly.

"Government?" Clay asked. "Didn't think you could ever get a government gig with your history."

Harry laughed. "You're right. Definitely not government. Meet my bodyguards."

"This your plane?" Clay asked, looking around.

"Yep."

"Nice."

Harry motioned toward Clay's chest. "How'd you get like that?"

"Long story, Harry, but staying a few years on a planet with gravity a few times stronger than ours and living with a colony of hot, sex-crazed space babes will do it to you."

He blinked, his jaw hanging open. "We thought you and Bob were dead."

"Nope. It's a long story. I'll have to tell you some time. But here, look at these." Clay tossed him a packet of photos.

"Whose are these?" Harry asked, looking at the pictures. "Cute kids." He paused and looked up at Clay as it dawned on him. "No... really?"

"Yep. Bob's back on her planet right now. We're expecting another."

"But there are six or seven kids on here. You've only been gone a few years."

"Gestation period's only three months," said Clay. "So tell me about what happened around Bovina."

"Well, Chett and I aren't allowed back in, but you should be the one telling me. All I heard was that these really smooth curvy alien ships went around zapping all the zombies and generally cleaned everything up – except for Billy Ray and Dale, who managed to stay under the radar, so to speak, until they left. Why don't you fill me in? I haven't heard reports of any zombies anywhere else, and I know Bob was hell-bent on getting whatever that stuff was quarantined."

"You pretty much have it right," Clay answered. "They have ways of cleaning it up – sort of an intergalactic haz-mat. They managed to beam me and my mom up right before that weapon exploded. And I mean *right* before. Think milliseconds. After they got us, Bob took them to the botched drop-off site and they got to work. But I didn't know about Billy Ray and Dale. They still have the pickup?"

"It's the only thing they'll drive, and it's still scary as shit," Harry chuckled. "I swear the damned thing's alive and has a mind of its own." He paused. "How's your mom?"

"She pretty much stays unconscious."

"Oh?" He looked concerned.

"She's plenty healthy," Clay assured him, "but every time she comes to, there's another nekkid space babe parading around and she's out like a light."

Harry laughed.

Clay looked around the cabin. "Where's Chett?"

"He's in the field."

"Field?" Clay asked.

"Well, when you're a zombie you can't really be killed, unless you get your head shot off. So all you need is a good steel and Kevlar face mask and helmet and voila! You have one damned good mercenary. We specialize in hostage extraction. We get the call, we get the money, we go in and drop him on the ground. He gets in, gets shot up a little, gets the hostage out, and gets back and munches on some squirrel. They're his favorite. A little bit of brains and he heals right up, ready for the next mission."

"Well, that's all well and good," said Clay, "but we kinda need you for a little assignment we have."

"We?" said Harry.

"Bob's whole race of aliens is basically the equivalent of badassed Amazon space cops. But we need a little inside help for a job. You up for it?"

"What's it pay?"

"Gold. A lot of it."

"Is there going to be any trouble?"

"Oh, it may put the planet in a little jeopardy, but nothing you can't handle," Clay said.

"Count me in."

Author's Note:

Astute readers will no doubt notice a few liberties I may have taken with the topography of Vicksburg and Bovina. Certain buildings and roads may have moved a little, but the general sense is still there.

Also, it goes without saying, this book is purely a work of fiction. Names, places, and incidents are products of the author's imagination, or are used fictitiously and should not be construed as real. Any and all references to any people, living or dead, is purely coincidental.